DR. QUINN
Medicine Woman

The phenomenally successful *Dr. Quinn, Medicine Woman* series has quickly become a part of the lives of millions of television viewers. Its sensitive portrayal of a young woman who sets out for untamed Colorado Springs to pursue her dreams of becoming a doctor underscores the important role women played in the development of a burgeoning nation.

Now, for the first time in print, comes the story behind the story—the tale of the daughter of a Boston doctor who defied convention to become a respected healer in America's Wild West . . .

DON'T MISS THE NEXT ORIGINAL
DR. QUINN, MEDICINE WOMAN NOVEL,
COMING IN JUNE 1997

DR. QUINN
Medicine Woman

Teresa Warfield

BOULEVARD BOOKS, NEW YORK

DR. QUINN, MEDICINE WOMAN

A Boulevard Book / published by arrangement with
CBS Enterprises, a Division of CBS Inc.

PRINTING HISTORY
Boulevard edition / December 1996

The Putnam Berkley World Wide Web site address is
http://www.berkley.com/berkley

ISBN: 1-57297-036-7

BOULEVARD
Boulevard Books are published by The Berkley Publishing Group,
200 Madison Avenue, New York, New York 10016.
BOULEVARD and its logo are trademarks
belonging to Berkley Publishing Corporation.

PRINTED IN THE UNITED STATES OF AMERICA

10 9 8 7 6 5 4 3 2 1

ACKNOWLEDGMENTS

Writing this book would have been difficult without the support and assistance of certain individuals and institutions:

Beth Sullivan, executive producer of the television series *Dr. Quinn, Medicine Woman* . . . thanks for taking time out of your busy schedule to share your thoughts (and your excitement!). My gratitude also must be extended to Julie Henderson, research coordinator of the series, for sharing valuable research material and information regarding historical contacts.

The Archives and Special Collections on Women in Medicine, courtesy of the Medical College of Pennsylvania and Hahnemann University, formerly the Female Medical College of Pennsylvania, is a gold mine for any historian. Occasionally an author is fortunate enough to luck onto librarians who go out of their way to be helpful. Suzanne Williams-Meliams and Sue-Ann Paschucci never once balked at helping with the research for this book. Both ladies gladly investigated, made copies and phone calls, and mailed invaluable materials to me. Constructing certain parts of this novel may have been impossible without their assistance. Suzanne, thanks for the information about the medical lectures in Boston!

Pat Maurer, librarian at the Bostonian Society, was an invaluable source of information regarding the abolitionists' rescue of Shadrach and the attempted rescue of Thomas Simms. Ms. Maurer also provided information about the early railroads that ran through Boston.

Finally, big thanks must be extended to Judith Stern Palais and any editorial person who had a hand in deciding to ask for my involvement in this project. I enjoyed creating Mike's early life.

To all fans of Michaela Quinn.
May you enjoy this account of her life leading up
to Colorado Springs.

DR. QUINN
Medicine Woman

PART ONE:

Early Years

From the beginning, she was an unusual child . . .
— JOSEPH QUINN, M.D.

1

Frozen nearly to the bone, Joseph Quinn reined his horse and buggy to a stop inside the carriage house and with a brief nod of his head, greeted the waiting stable boy. He brushed snow from the shoulders of his greatcoat and ice from his beard, then he snatched up his medical bag and scrambled down from the buggy, having been out much later this evening than he had planned to be. With his wife's confinement only a month away, he hated being away from home at all. But when the sick called, the physician answered.

He entered his family's Mount Vernon Street town house through a back entrance, and shook his head upon hearing the chords of a violin drifting from up the hall. It was odd, the fondness Elizabeth had had for music since this pregnancy began. This was not the first time Joseph had come home at such a late hour to hear a tune filling their home. Grinning, he approached the drawing room as the violin stopped and the pianoforte began, a lively piece this time.

He arrived in the drawing room doorway in time to catch sight of his wife, her middle swollen with child, twirling nine-year-old Marjorie, the youngest of their four daughters. Rebecca, the oldest at fifteen, played the tune while Claudette

3

held her violin and Maureen giggled and clapped her hands as the girls watched their energetic mother. Martha, Elizabeth's Swedish personal maid, stood near the fireplace twisting her hands, looking nearly distraught, her eyes round and wide, her skin as white as the fresh snow. And with good reason. Her mistress had gone mad. Utterly mad.

"What the devil are you doing, Mrs. Quinn?" Joseph blasted, barreling forth, hoping to grab Elizabeth before she lost her balance and fell. "Dancing around so, and only a month away from giving birth!"

The music stopped. Rebecca twisted around on her seat. Maureen raced toward Joseph, who nearly plowed her over in his haste to get to his wife. Marjorie screeched, "Papa! Finally, you're home!" just as he reached Elizabeth and took her by the shoulders. Color rode high on her cheeks and sparkles lit her eyes. She wrinkled her brow and smiled up at him.

"Yes, dancing, Joseph. Celebrating your birthday. A trivial matter you seem to have forgotten. Don't fret so. The baby is fine. Kicking and turning somersaults, as always," Elizabeth said, placing her hands on either side of her womb. "I had to do something to compete with him."

Joseph almost chuckled. Almost. No woman in her condition should experience such physical excitement— surely it was bad for both her and the child.

"*Him?*" Joseph said, snatching up the word. Elizabeth had referred to the unborn child as a male. She was hoping—as he was hoping.

Martha skittered forward. "I told her not to, sir. I pleaded. She insisted on continuing. She does not seem to realize the damage she could do!"

Elizabeth's smile broadened. "Hush, Martha. I am stubborn that way."

"Mama dreamed it was a boy!" Maureen said, skipping around, her bronze curls shimmering in the firelight.

"And that you named him Joseph Quinn, after you, Papa," Claudette broke in, hanging back, always the rather quiet, reserved child.

"You've wanted a boy, Papa," Rebecca said, smiling from

4

the pianoforte. "None of us mind, us girls. We know you love us. Besides, you need a son to carry on the tradition. If not, who would you pass your bag on to?"

That was true. The very medical bag he held had been his father's, though it surely was more worn now and carried some instruments and elixirs that were different from what his father had carried during the years he had practiced as a doctor.

"Yes," Elizabeth said softly. "Who would you pass your bag on to?"

He loved her beyond reason. When that had happened, he could not remember. It had not always been so, though he had certainly felt an immediate fondness for the girl he had met so long ago on a frozen pond in Beacon Hill. They had been skating, him whizzing along with his daring friends, her turning graceful circles and making figure eights with her cousin. After the death of her parents she had been taken in by her aunt and uncle, who, as her parents had, lived in the Back Bay area. The match she and Joseph made was a good one—he knew it, she knew it, their families knew it, and since both Joseph and Elizabeth had had the sense to realize that a good match was more enduring than a passionate one, they had eased into an engagement and marriage. But somewhere along the way, in the years immediately following the necessary ceremony, Joseph had fallen in love with his wife. Somewhere along the way the match had become more than a logical one; it had become a passionate one as well.

"You've no guarantee that the baby is a boy, Mrs. Quinn," he cautioned, his voice low. "Besides, we spoke of names, and if it does happen to be a boy we agreed to call him Michael, not Joseph. He'll be his own person, not a duplicate of his father. If he chooses to take up my profession, then so be it. But we'll not force him into anything." He tipped his head and narrowed one eye. "It could be a girl, and I would cherish her the same."

"I dreamed it, Joseph," she countered, "and the dream was real. It's a boy."

"Elizabeth."

"Joseph."

"Why must there be a baby?" Marjorie said, withdrawing from her mother and folding her arms. "*I'm* the baby. Why do you need another one?"

Elizabeth and Joseph exchanged apprehensive glances. She kneeled in front of their youngest child, though how she did without losing her balance, Joseph could not imagine. He listened to her soft voice, relishing the sound of it as he gathered Maureen and Claudette close, jabbing them in the ribs and scolding them for not dragging their mother up to bed.

"Marjorie, I've told you," Elizabeth said, "you're nine years old now, plenty old enough to help with a baby, but too old to continue being a baby."

Marjorie pouted more at that, stomping over to a settee that had been moved back to clear space for dancing.

"The child was not planned, Marjorie. He was given by God," Elizabeth continued, though her words did not erase her youngest child's pout.

Slower than Marjorie because of her condition, Elizabeth placed an open hand on the floor to push herself up. Joseph hurried over to help, but just as he bent to loop his arm beneath hers, she gasped and her face contorted with pain. Martha rushed from her place near the hearth, ready to aide her mistress.

"What is it?" Joseph asked Elizabeth, stooping close. She held her breath, unable to answer. Bedlam followed.

"Mother?" Rebecca cried, coming off her stool.

"Is it time, is it time?" Maureen had to know as she tried pushing her way between her parents and the maid.

"Hush yourself, now, and get back right this minute," Claudette advised her eager sister.

Marjorie, still pouting, made certain she was heard. "That baby can just stay there forever! I don't want him coming out. Everyone'll be fussing over him, like they fuss over the Beckers' baby. I—"

"Don't be indelicate," Claudette warned, red-faced.

"It's only us here!" Marjorie retorted.

"I don't care."

"Quiet! Girls, move back and out of the way," their father boomed. "Your mother is going up to bed."

"It was nothing, Joseph, really," Elizabeth said, finally catching her breath. "I simply moved the wrong way. I shouldn't have bent like that. Sometimes it feels as though his head is in my ribs and—"

"It is."

She stared at him. "Joseph, what are you saying?"

He hadn't wanted to alarm her. He hadn't wanted her to spend the rest of the pregnancy worrying, fretting that the child might die. Far too many breech births resulted in the death of the infant—and the death of the mother herself, though the day he discovered the abnormal presentation, Joseph had placed the matter in the hands of the Almighty, refusing to believe that his precious wife would be taken from him. This child aside, they had four others to finish raising yet, and the Father was merciful and good, compassionate enough that he would not allow Elizabeth Quinn to be taken so soon.

"Exactly what I said," Joseph said quietly. "I've known for several months now, Elizabeth."

She continued staring. "How could you not tell me?"

"I'll take you up to bed now," he said, helping her rise.

She looked pale suddenly, and she placed a hand on the small of her back as she straightened. "Not yet. Surely not yet," she murmured. "Yes, help me up to bed. You know how I hate being an invalid. But I honestly don't know that I could make it up alone. Girls! Off to bed with all of you, too. Your naughty mother kept you up far too late. Close up the piano, Rebecca. Put away the violin, Claudette—you play beautifully. Upstairs with you, Maureen and Marjorie."

"I don't want a baby in this house," Marjorie said, stomping her foot.

Elizabeth gave her a stern look. "Whether you do or not is irrelevant. It will arrive and when it does, I shall expect better behavior of you."

Marjorie stood in a huff and stomped all the way to the drawing room door. Joseph walked at Elizabeth's pace, and the other girls followed, quietly and obediently.

• • •

Not wanting to disturb his wife, Joseph slept the night in a chair beside their bed and woke with the thought that the pain Elizabeth had experienced in the drawing room had had nothing to do with premature labor. She'd slept all night as far as he knew, and he thought that perhaps she was right—she had moved the wrong way and the child had objected. Being in a breech presentation, he had kicked a tender spot, gripping his mother with pain.

Joseph grimaced. Even he now referred to the baby as a boy.

He sat staring sleepily at the heavy draperies on the windows, for a moment entertaining the notion of actually having a son, perhaps someone with whom to share his profession . . . a male heir to pass his medical bag on to. He stiffened when a soft moan escaped Elizabeth.

She had rolled over onto her side, turning her back to him, exactly as she had the other times he had attended her during labor. During the hours before birth, Elizabeth always preferred to be left alone, and if possible she would have managed alone during each birthing process, too. She was a strong woman, Elizabeth Quinn, full of pride and stubbornness.

"How long now?" he asked, almost certain her confinement had begun. Early, but it had begun.

"All night," she said, her voice strained. "Hard . . . only this . . . past hour. Oh, Joseph."

"Good God, Elizabeth. You should have awakened me."

She groaned and rolled onto her back. Perspiration covered her pale face. "Early. It's so early. I'm sorry. The dancing . . . We danced all evening."

"Hush," he ordered.

"Your son . . . Check, Joseph. Make sure he's well. The labor . . . it's advanced. I want to push!" She arched her back, straining, holding her breath.

At a washstand in one corner of the bedroom, Joseph rolled up his shirt sleeves past his elbows, poured water from the pitcher into the basin, and washed his hands and arms. He had always been one for cleanliness, never going

8

from one bed to the next, or from one surgery to the next, with soiled hands and clothes, as did many of his colleagues at Massachusetts General Hospital and other institutions.

Back at the bedside Joseph pulled the coverlet down and pushed Elizabeth's night rail up over her thighs and hips. Blood marked the sheets, a normal amount. No fluid yet, which meant the membranes were still intact. Normally modest, Elizabeth had gone beyond caring; she spread her legs wide, anticipating the examination, the birth. Joseph eased his fingers into the birth canal, and she panted and strained . . . let loose a scream that jolted the entire house.

He found the os uteri nearing complete dilation—as he had suspected. Through the intact membrane he felt a foot, so tiny and fragile, and he grimaced. No breech birth was pleasant, and the quicker the better for the mother and child. In his practice, he had seen far too many feet emerge first, followed by a blue body and head, a dead infant.

This might very well be the most difficult birth he ever would attend. He knew what needed to be done—and he knew he must steel himself against the fact that Elizabeth was his wife. There was no time to send for another physician. Or even for a priest.

Slowly he introduced his entire hand into the birth passage, trying hard to ignore Elizabeth's gasps and then her cries. A pounding on the bedroom door and then Martha's voice, high and frantic, demanding to know what was going on, unnerved him. "Hush the whining, girl!" Joseph ordered. "Get more water, and bring cloths. What the devil do you think is happening in here?"

Though Elizabeth strained and writhed against him, Joseph closed his eyes, trying to forget who she was for the moment. He found the foot again, felt it kick, then he ruptured the membrane between the nails of his forefinger and thumb. Elizabeth screeched as fluid gushed down around his arm and the child's foot and leg slid down into the vagina. He felt around . . . found the other foot and leg and brought them down. He felt the cord, found its pulsation growing weak. He opened his eyes.

"Look at me, Elizabeth," he said. She writhed more, held

9

her breath, gasped. *"Look at me, Elizabeth. Look at me and help me or the child will die!"*

She calmed, staring at him as she panted, her eyes glazed with pain.

"With the next pains, push hard. *Hard.* A quick birth might save the child."

She nodded, jerking her head. Joseph felt around more, found the arms and brought them down, again ignoring Elizabeth's cries. He felt the uterus tighten once more. "Now!" he cried.

But Elizabeth needed no urging. She pushed hard enough that the child's feet emerged from the vagina along with more blood and fluid, and his abdomen descended into the canal. Joseph pushed up more and felt the head, then eased a finger into the baby's mouth, depressing the chin. Elizabeth shrieked as the head came down. But Joseph's shouts of *"Help me. Push!"* again jolted her and she bore down with every ounce of her strength. The child's head soon shot through the pelvis and from the os externum onto the bloody sheets just as someone shoved open the bedroom door.

Thank God Martha did not freeze at the sight of her mistress and the bluish purple, unmoving infant on the bed. She issued a sharp cry of shock, but forced herself to rush toward them. Besides cloths and another pitcher of water, she also brought Joseph's medical bag.

"Scissors," he ordered, and she promptly placed the pitcher and cloths on the floor, then hurried over to him, the bag in hand.

"A girl," Elizabeth said, lifting her head to have a look at the child, clearly disappointed. Nothing about the infant not breathing or its poor color. She had had her mind set on a male, and her dismay was evident.

Joseph rubbed the baby's chest, then bent and blew into its mouth the way he had seen a colleague do two years ago and had since done himself when he felt it necessary.

The child stirred, sucking in a breath, lifting an arm.

Joseph blew again.

Another breath. More stirring. A weak cry.

10

Gasping, Elizabeth lifted her head again and glanced down at the child. "She's alive?"

Joseph nodded. "By the grace of God." He blew again. "Breathe, my baby girl. Breathe. Cry." He rubbed more, spoke more soft words . . . took the medical bag from Martha, dug inside, and found string and his surgical scissors. He soon had the cord tied off and cut, and all the while the infant stirred more and more, finally sucking in a quick deep breath, coughing, and heaving a vigorous squall along with mucus. Joseph worked at clearing her mouth.

"She is!" Elizabeth cried weakly. "She's alive! Give her to me. Oh, please, Joseph, give her to me."

She seemed to have overcome her shock and disappointment at giving birth to yet another girl. Martha brought clean cloths and Joseph wrapped the infant in them, then handed her to Elizabeth, who worked at lowering the neckline of her gown and putting the child to her exposed breast. Seconds later another mild pain gripped her and she delivered the afterbirth.

"She's precious!" Rebecca said, bubbling over the infant.

"It's not a boy," the serious Claudette remarked.

"Can I play with her sometimes, Mother?" Maureen asked, trying to tickle her new sister. The child began crying. Maureen stroked her cheek, trying to soothe her.

"I hate babies," Marjorie announced. Then she huffed off of her parent's bed and stomped from the room, having been angry for a solid week now.

"She'll grow accustomed to her," Joseph assured Elizabeth, who nodded weakly. But it was her he worried about most of all.

Though it appeared that Elizabeth had taken to the child within moments of its birth, she clearly was despondent still over not giving Joseph a son, and she took interest in the baby only when it was hungry. Other than that she left the child in Martha's care. Joseph brought her trays of food and tea. He reassured her that he did not want a son. He even tolerated her talk of having another baby again as soon as possible, though he gently asked, "What if it's another girl?"

11

When the child turned two weeks old, having gained even more strength and weight, and a loud disposition Joseph hoped would calm as she grew older, he tried to discuss a name with Elizabeth. They had discussed only one name previously—a boy's name—and she could think of none for a girl, or so she said, turning to stare out the window.

"She was supposed to be Michael," she murmured.

Joseph scowled at her. "Why should we treasure this daughter any less than we do our others?" he demanded, cradling the infant. "She did not ask to be born a girl."

The child coughed, then began crying. The cry soon progressed into a squall, and Joseph rocked the infant in his arms. He loved her as much as he loved his other daughters. She had been born into an exciting, ever-changing, some-times frightful world and country. The invention of steam was having a remarkable effect—a ship could now actually carry enough coal to travel across the ocean without sails—and the cotton gin had changed the entire course of industry in the southern section of the Union. And other things . . . This flourishing nation, doubled with Jefferson's Louisiana Purchase in 1803, was now being settled in the West. But along with that settlement came grumblings, worries, and questions: considering the vastness of the land, how could one man be president of the United States when it was eventually settled from Atlantic to Pacific? Righteous New England opposition to western territories gaining state-hood sickened Joseph. He was a Jeffersonian, a Unitarian, believing in his heart that even the plain uneducated man deserved a say in his world. The political poppycock irritated him, frustrated him, the ever-present New England sentiment that westerners were uneducated and ragged, therefore incapable of representing the people. New En-glanders certainly did not want this new breed of uncivilized people having a hand in making their laws. Meanwhile all around, the migration, the desire for a new beginning in a new land, gained momentum; huge lumbering wagons filled with all manner of belongings were becoming a common sight on the roads leading west. And Joseph understood the migration, the desires . . . he had listened countless times

12

to his father's accounts of his emigration from another country.

Slavery was becoming a common topic, sometimes heated, sometimes spilling over into social suppers and parties. Despite the fact that one free state was always admitted to the Union along with one slave state, the prevailing feeling among Bostonians was that abolitionists were radicals, that slaves were property and that property must be safeguarded. Property was the cornerstone of civic virtue, after all. The antislavery faction was gaining force, however. Only recently John Quincy Adams had presented an abolition petition to Congress from the Philadelphia Society of Friends. And in Boston itself, William Garrison's *Liberator,* an inflammatory, highly incitant newspaper with its engraved logo of a slave in chains, was being circulated.

Around the city and at Harvard University in nearby Cambridge, last year's debates and political arguments over Jackson's bid for presidential re-election still sparked comments from many. Some Whigs had taken to spitefully calling him "King Andrew." "How can we continue to allow this nation to be represented by such a wild man, an Indian fighter, a backwoods Tennessee scoundrel, a man redolent of coonskin and the frontier . . . indeed, an untamed creature?" they asked. "A man of the people, but one who is incapable of representing the New England states." Still, enough men had faith in Jackson to install him in the White House for a second term. But not again, most Bostonians swore. Surely not for a third term. This was intolerable.

Causes were championed, preached from pulpits. Marches were held. Temperance, prison reform, and the abolition of debtor's prisons were the topics of the day. Oliver Wendell Holmes's publication of *Old Ironsides* had recently fired the people and saved the Revolutionary frigate *Constitution* from certain congressional scrapping—". . . Oh, better that her shattered hulk should sink beneath the wave; Her thunders shook the mighty deep, and there should be her grave . . ." And into all of this Joseph's fifth daughter had been born, innocent, unaware, tiny but vigorous. Much lay ahead of her, ahead of all of them, and she had as much right to taste her world as did the next person. She would be given a strong start and a healthy life, despite that fact that her mother did not care for her.

"She cries so much, Joseph," Elizabeth said.

"Perhaps she knows you don't like her."

"It's not that. It's really not that." She turned her face back to him. "She's our child, Joseph. I love her. But I did so want a son for you. She was breech, and she was early, and I'm scared to death to have another child. I want to always be here for the ones we already have. You may never have a son now—do you realize that?"

"I shall have grandsons," he said, undaunted.

"I don't know what to name her," Elizabeth said. "I named the other four. I haven't another girl's name in my head."

He carried this new child to the window and gazed down at her in the soft morning sunlight. A shock of dark hair with strands of copper. Dark lashes. Dark blue eyes that could very well change color in the upcoming weeks. They stared up at him now, shimmering with tears as the baby's cries died down to sobs and she blinked and glanced around, exhibiting an alertness and curiosity not often seen in a newborn. Soft pink skin and lips that twisted, darkened, and parted to let out squalls whenever someone moved her in a way she did not like or changed her swaddling cloth, or whenever she was removed from the breast before she had had her fill.

Joseph chuckled. She seemed never to have her fill. Her right fist seemed to be in constant motion, either across her chest or at her mouth or pulling away when someone tried to hold it. She displayed a stubbornness even at her young age, a determination to do what she wanted to do.

Joseph had never observed such a quality in an infant, and during the following month, he caught himself spending a great deal of time in the nursery, studying the baby. He found Elizabeth rocking her, nursing her, and singing to her from time to time, obviously warming to her. The day the infant turned three months old, Joseph again held her before the window in their bedroom, observed her, and felt a rush of pride.

"We'll call her . . . Michaela," he said finally, and Elizabeth made no objection.

2

Before a gathering of family and friends, she was christened Michaela Anne Quinn in the Park Street Church. As always, Joseph regretted the fact that his father, Dr. Jeremy Quinn, the very man who had brought the Quinn name to the United States in 1791, was not in attendance. "Another Quinn to bury the root of the fam'ly ever deeper in American soil," he might have said, had he known of the birth and witnessed the christening. As it was, Joseph's father had contracted brain fever and died of the illness within a year of Rebecca's birth after attending the Irish in Boston's North End.

More binding than the Hippocratic oath had been the fact that a number of those ill-fated, poverty-ridden Irish were Jeremy Quinn's friends, and he'd given not a thought to turning away the sickly-looking girl who came tapping at his door and asking for help that March night. She was Peg O'Brien, the eldest daughter of Michael O'Brien, a man with whom Jeremy Quinn had planted crops and sheared sheep in the old country, a friend who was now broken down and feeding his family with butchers' scraps he yanked from the mouths of hungry dogs. Having prospered through numerous mercantile and real estate investments,

Jeremy had taken food to the family time and again and found Michael work over the years. But that night the man who had so exuberantly led their short-lived political band back in England sat huddled in a corner of a Boston shanty, a scrappy woolen blanket clutched around his shoulders, his other two daughters and his wife—all of them ill with the fever, too—gathered around him.

Jeremy attended Michael's family and at least four others that evening, not once stopping to summon Joseph to help him, though Joseph himself had been a physician for a number of years by then. Upon returning to Beacon Street, Jeremy had been wet and cold, and only a few days passed before he fell ill with the fever himself. By then Michael, his wife, and daughters were being buried, and Jeremy Quinn had said good-bye to his old friend from his own sickbed.

Anne Quinn, Joseph's mother, attended the christening, as always giving her own silent blessing to another grandchild. She and Jeremy's union had produced two sons, Joseph and Patrick, though Patrick had been killed in a dock accident some ten years ago. So Joseph was the only remaining Quinn male, his grandparents having expired of old age a few years back, and though he knew his mother was overjoyed to have another grandchild, he saw the sadness in her eyes as she held Michaela that afternoon, a sadness he knew stemmed from the fact that there was still no male to carry on the family name.

In the Quinn's parlor a little later, friends from all up and down Beacon Street and beyond gathered round to toast the new child—Lewises, Beckers, Coles, Hammonds, Lymans . . . Dr. James Jackson, the renowned professor of physics at Harvard, mentor to all, lecturer in Boston, and his family. The tiny Michaela in her snow white, embroidered christening gown was passed from one arm to another. She was patted, rocked, soothed, uncovered, covered, touched, and cuddled while a feast went on around her. Finally Rebecca took her off upstairs to put her down for a nap, and the festivities continued. The Quinns were congratulated over and over again for producing yet another child, and soon

17

Joseph found that he'd had enough of the hubbub and he went off upstairs to look in on Michaela himself.

In the doorway of the nursery he stood and observed four-year-old David Lewis and two-year-old Jimmie Becker, both dark-haired, wide-eyed boys, standing next to Michaela's cradle.

"Why do people like babies so much?" Jimmie asked, a precocious child already. He would prove to be much more so in upcoming years.

"I dunno," David answered, shrugging, intelligence shimmering in his eyes. A bright one, the youngest Lewis son, always full of questions, always seeking answers, always watching intently. "My father says too bad this one wasn't a boy so one of the Quinns could grow up to be a doctor, like Dr. Quinn."

"Why can't she grow up to be a doctor?" Jimmie queried innocently, glancing up with wide blue eyes at the older, taller boy.

"She's a girl," David said simply. "Girls grow up, get married and have babies, like Mrs. Quinn had her." Quite a conversation between these two young boys, Joseph thought, fighting a grin and losing. Little did they realize that he was no ordinary father, that if any one of his girls asked to do something that went against the grain of convention, he would do his best to provide her the opportunity. Within reason.

"Oh," Jimmie said just as Joseph heard Michaela sniff, then start crying. "What'd we do?" Jimmie asked.

"Nothin'. Don't worry," David said, stretching out his arm and putting his hand in the cradle. To soothe the baby, surely. He spoke to her: "I'm gonna be a doctor when I grow up. I'm gonna learn from your father since my father says he's the best doctor in all of Massachusetts."

That information seemed to comfort Michaela; her cries quieted to sniffles, then a few seconds passed and Joseph heard no sound at all from the cradle.

"We'd best leave her alone," David advised.

"Yes," Jimmie said, turning away. He caught sight of Dr. Quinn standing in the doorway and he gasped, stopping in his tracks. "Didn't mean to bother her! Just wanted to look at her without so many people around."

Rapidly nodding his agreement, David planted his back against the cradle and peered up at Joseph.

"So you mean to become a doctor when you grow up, David Lewis?" Joseph asked, half smiling as he walked into the room.

"Yes, sir!" the boy responded just as Michaela began crying again. He turned back to the cradle, unable to help himself, and stroked the baby's cheek. "Do you think I can do it, Dr. Quinn?" David asked once Joseph stood beside him looking down at Michaela. Under David's gentle touch she once again quieted.

"I believe that with the right amount of determination you can do anything you want to do," Joseph told the boy.

David beamed. "Well, then, I wanna be a doctor like you, and I will be a doctor like you!"

Smiling, Joseph nodded, then bent and lifted the infant into his arms.

At times Joseph would come home after a late night and find Michaela awake in her crib, exploring her fingers and toes, and he would lift her, sit with her for a time, and talk to her. He took to taking her downstairs with him into his library and sitting with her before the fire, at first working hard to make up stories to tell her. He quickly gave that up, having little imagination, and began reading to her from the *New England Quarterly Journal of Medicine,* and from other publications that he needed to read anyway. It was an odd thing to do, but for some reason he wanted to share that love with this little creature who had come into his life, captivated him, and intrigued him so. When he considered her birth, the fact that she had been born a month early and practically dead, he marveled over and over that Michaela had survived. He held her, puffed on his pipe, read to her, cradled her, puffed on his pipe and read more. She quickly became his tiny companion, staring up at him with eyes that only in the last month had appeared to change color—indeed, each eye was a *different* color, one appearing brown, the other appearing green. How was that possible? he often wondered, and they would sit staring at each other, father and daughter, his medical mind turning, while she sucked her fingers.

Elizabeth wandered downstairs one night and found them sitting together just so, him reading to Michaela, and she stood in the doorway and laughed.

"When I read to her she doesn't cry," he explained, half grinning.

"It's the sound of your voice, certainly not the fact that you're reading to her from a medical journal. Joseph Quinn, you fawn over that child," she said, sighing. Then she sobered. "Careful. Maureen remarked to me only yesterday that you pay far more attention to the baby than to any of them. Marjorie has been jealous—you know that—but of late she throws tantrums and refuses to do her lessons, and she cries for you. I tell her she's too old to cry and she pouts more."

"Claudette?" he asked.

"Claudette says nothing. Things have a way of not bothering her overmuch."

"Rebecca?"

"Rebecca takes your place with the baby when you're not here," she said. Her voice softened even more. "And me? Would you like to know about me? I miss your company in our bed, Joseph." She colored a little at the admission, pulling her wrap more securely about her and glancing away for a moment. "You've hardly touched me since she was born. I go to sleep without you and wake without you. If you're not attending patients you're attending the baby."

"She's awake when I come home," he said, shifting, growing uncomfortable with the subject.

"I would wake if she cried. Or the nursemaid would tend her."

"She's meant to be here, Elizabeth."

Silence. Then, "Joseph, we're all meant to be here or we *wouldn't* be here."

"No. A moment more and she would have been dead. Her heart would have stopped. The heart stops soon after respiration ceases. Add to that the fact that she was born early and that hardly any child who is—"

"Don't ignore the others," Elizabeth snapped. "Look at you, reading to her from that journal! You need a son, Joseph. You need a son." She said the last succinctly, emphasizing her point. "I watched you at the wharf when Oliver Holmes sailed for France to study medicine there, and I could almost hear your thoughts, your envy—to have such a son!"

"Damn you, woman!" Joseph growled back, coming out of the chair. "Your twisted mind imagines things!" In their nearly seventeen-year marriage he had not often raised his voice to her. But he'd had enough of this nonsense about a son, and he had had enough of her cool treatment of their youngest daughter—all because she had been born a female.

The journal landed on the floor in a flutter of pages. Elizabeth stared at Joseph, unflinching. Michaela wrinkled her face and sniffled. "She's ours and she's a girl," Joseph blasted, "and I won't hear another word from you about a son. We have five healthy children and we should thank the Father for that."

Elizabeth tipped her head, then tossed it defiantly just as the baby broke into a wail. An instant later Elizabeth disappeared from the doorway.

It was the first of many heated arguments Joseph and his wife would have about Michaela over the years, though eventually the differences changed in nature.

Like Michaela, spring came early to Boston that year. The days began to warm near the end of March, to the great dismay of "coasters"—the people, mostly boys, who liked to sled in and around Beacon Hill. At first the ground was soggy from the melting snow and ice, then from the almost constant spring rains. Mount Vernon Street and all of Beacon Hill in general began to blossom with color. The grass and shrubbery in and around Louisburg Square, the Common, and the Public Garden turned various shades of green, buds began opening on trees, and here and there bulbs pushed up to greet warmer air and moisture. Carriages replaced sleds, and instead of sleigh races up and down the wide expanse of Beacon Street, some residents of the Hill now held rowdy horse races. All were involved in the horse racing, not just boys.

"'Tis scandalous the way they place bets, then nearly run people down!" Anne Quinn objected one evening while supping with Joseph and his family. Shortly after his father's death, he had urged her to move in to his family's town house. But she preferred to live in the house on Beacon Street in which Joseph had been born and raised. Every spring when the mad races began up and down the passage, she complained, and every spring Joseph said the same thing: "We've an open room upstairs should you change your mind about living here, Mother."

She always thanked him nicely but declined, and Joseph always worried. She had turned sixty-three in January, and she no longer stood straight and strong; she was a bent and feeble woman. He stopped by his boyhood home at least every other day to look in on her, and if he wasn't looking in on her Elizabeth or Rebecca were. Knowing that some family member was with her almost every day was a comfort to him. She had servants—a cook, a chambermaid, a housekeeper—but for some reason they didn't seem enough.

Vines crept up, around, over and under the wrought-iron railing that flanked the steps leading up to the front entrance of the town house. Ten Mount Vernon Street . . . the home Joseph had purchased shortly after he and Elizabeth married. The home they had filled with love and warmth and children. Red, white, and violet flowers bloomed in the front-window pots. People strolled up and down both sides of the street, children laughed and played. . . . The gray of early spring soon lifted and the entire city came to life, or so it always seemed to Joseph at this time of year. Festivals were held, parades sauntered by, rowing began on the river, cricket was played on the Harvard grounds.

But with the warm weather came outbreaks of cholera and fever, too, illnesses that frequently swept first through the scattered, ramshackle Irish settlements, South Boston, the South End, and nearby Charlestown. Pestilences almost always eventually trickled into the finer areas of the city, too, invading Beacon Hill and Back Bay. . . . Joseph had speculated for years that the filth that lined many streets and wharves bred the illnesses. But the city was overflowing with people, with a steady stream of immigrants, and though Joseph and others, colleagues from Massachusetts General Hospital, had complained about the filth, their voices were few among thousands.

So the illnesses came, as always, and Joseph began spreading himself thin as he frequently did this time of year. He divided his time between home, private patients, patients at the hospital, and those he was assigned to by the Boston Dispensary, through which he did charity work, going out on weekly assignments to the indigent. He had been doing the latter for the past year, after learning that there was hardly a physician in the city who would serve in District Eight—where the Irish were concentrated. A wealthy Irishman was an acceptable thing, it seemed; a poor Irishman was the scum of the earth. Or so many people believed. The potato famine in Ireland had brought thousands of Irish families to America, and Joseph was often irritated and shamed by the fact that much of Boston had developed a caste system toward them, considering them inferior.

"Why would you want that district?" a surprised Dr. Adams had asked when Joseph walked into the cramped dispensary office on Washington Street one afternoon and asked for the assignment. He had overhead a conversation between two fellow physicians in a corridor of Massachusetts General, and the hair on the back of his neck had prickled. He'd thought of reminding the doctors of the oath they had taken, that it was their responsibility to serve anyone in need of medical attention, that they should not pick and choose. Instead, he had clenched his jaw and come here.

"Because every individual, no matter his race or religion, has the right to live a long and full life," he had answered Adams, echoing his father's sentiments.

"Well, you're in luck this day," the physician had responded, giving him a hard stare and holding out a handful of tickets—requests for treatment. "The board of governors just doubled the pay for the area. Couldn't get anyone to go there otherwise."

Joseph had taken the tickets and shuffled through them. Broad Street . . . Fort Hill . . . Where the warehouses and waterfront businesses had been built and had flourished in Boston's early days. Where merchants had grown wealthy then moved on to other, fashionable areas. Now the warehouses were subdivided and subleased out to the Irish as they poured from the holds of ships, filthy, disheveled, ill, and growing more ill when they settled in the tiny rooms that had no windows, therefore very little light and air.

As always, stench rose from the alleyways that stemmed from Broad Street, from the rubbish and human waste and the remains of animals and sometimes even from people who simply had lain down and died. Joseph had found his way from one sickbed to another that day—as he did weekly now—walking past children who gnawed on bare bones like dogs, past drunkards who slurred the words of old songs, past gutters filled with more human waste, and through tiny rooms sometimes populated with as many as ten people who all slept on a few tattered blankets. He smelled boiled cabbage, dirty bodies, sweat . . . the odors of illness. In many cases he simply tried to make the sick as comfortable as possible since he felt certain that they would expire within hours or days.

A heavy sadness always gripped him during his assignments to Fort Hill. The doubled pay hardly mattered; what mattered more to Joseph was that he felt akin to these people, to these immigrants who had boarded a ship with hopes and dreams, and who, in many cases, had found instead poverty and sickness worse than any they had known. Broad Street was where Jeremy Quinn, Michael O'Brien, Kevin Geoghegan, and a handful of others had disembarked, exiles from their native land, men who truly believed and upheld the "utilitarian" teachings of Smith, Locke, and Bentham, philosophers and teachers who all opposed any system that threatened the freedom of the individual and prevented him from realizing his full human potential. Jeremy Quinn and friends had walked these streets and alleys. They had worked the docks and warehouses and in the homes in and around Fort Hill. And in later years, even after Jeremy Quinn had risen far above poverty himself through investments and other business dealings, he frequently mounted a horse and visited and tended his friends here, often bringing his own son along. Even before Joseph had begun making trips down to Broad Street himself as a physician, he had known many of these people, and he tended them carefully, as if they were his own flesh and blood.

By the time Michaela was six months old her hair had thickened and grown wavy, still appearing dark brown until she was observed in good lighting. Then one noticed the coppery strands. She had matured from an unhappy infant during her early months into a bubbly baby who had a smile for everyone and who easily won hearts, even her mother's finally. Whether Elizabeth simply grew fond of having her about, Joseph could not be sure since his wife said nothing about the way she had shunned the child during those early months. She began taking Michaela about Beacon Hill in the perambulator, or so a blossoming Rebecca reported to her father one hot August afternoon as they strolled through the Common.

"She really had her heart set on a boy, Papa. That's all," Rebecca told him. She had sensed the tension between her mother and father and she silently fretted over it sometimes, knowing it had begun the day Michaela was born. "She dreamed the baby was a boy and she believed her dream."

Joseph nodded. He never liked to discuss Elizabeth's resentment of Michaela, indeed he had been shocked by it, and he changed the subject now, though he was grateful for Rebecca's news. "You'll be sixteen soon," he remarked. She had recently finished her schooling, and while at this age most young men were thinking of college, most girls nearing Rebecca's age were beginning to think about marriage and having a family. It didn't seem possible that his oldest daughter was nearly grown and that she was even of marrying age yet, but she was.

She blushed. "That's four months away."

"Four months is a short time," he said. "We'll have a gathering to celebrate, perhaps dancing. I'll talk to your mother."

"Will you?" she asked, unable to hide her excitement. She was growing into a woman, his Rebecca, a proper and well-mannered lady, and though he felt proud, he also was beginning to feel old.

"I will."

"Oh, Papa," she said, and embraced him. Not a second later she withdrew, smoothed her sleeves, and smiled shyly as if embarrassed that she might have made a spectacle of herself in a public place.

Days later, he had just finished tending a patient with a throat ailment and was leaving the residence, preparing to mount his buggy and ride for home, when he heard distant shouts and screams, the clamoring of frantic voices, and he immediately sensed that trouble had exploded somewhere in the city. It had been threatening for weeks and months now. The rising abolitionists, the anti-Catholics . . . the issue could be any number of things. As it was he was shocked and horrified to see a mob dragging William Garrison through the streets, a rope around his neck. Joseph tried to intervene, was nearly trampled, and then his good friend James Jackson was pulling him back, shaking his head, telling him to consider his family, that the mob would surely kill anyone who interfered.

James was right, and that inflamed Joseph all the more. His shame grew, this time because he felt almost the coward, cherishing his family too much to risk his life—and theirs. Michael O'Brien had done exactly that with his political activities, and while Joseph had loved the Irishman like his own father, he had watched Michael and his entire family waste away, a result of Michael's rash behavior and radical thinking.

The mob tore up the street, and Joseph and James watched it go. James nodded at Joseph, who turned away finally.

That night he heard that Garrison had survived the ordeal. Joseph went to him and treated him secretly, washing his bruises and cuts, now knowing the terror the colonials must have felt during the mobs of the Revolution. The thought greatly disturbed him—that such an issue, slavery, could incite such behavior—and he had to wonder if the topic would not explode more in the upcoming years.

Cholera and the various fevers finally began loosening their hold on the city and Joseph took Elizabeth's earlier advice and devoted less time at his office, at Massachusetts General, and out and about with patients, and more time to outings, whether they be with the family as a whole or with one member at a time.

Michaela often charmed and brought smiles to serious Claudette's face, and as the baby's first summer burned into fall, Maureen began toting her about the town house and outdoors as if she were her very own child. Marjorie still threw tantrums and stomped about, and both Joseph and Elizabeth worried about whether she would ever give up being jealous and think about enjoying her new sister. Twice Joseph swore she pushed Michaela down when the baby was learning to pull herself up to tables and chairs. One second Michaela was reaching, pulling up, and the next— always during times when no one was looking—she began howling and Joseph would glance over to find her sitting on the floor crying. Marjorie was always nearby, and she always had a smug look on her face. The last time, when the family had gathered in the drawing room for music and reading, Joseph scolded her as he lifted a howling Michaela.

"Marjorie wouldn't do such a thing," Elizabeth objected. "Joseph, how could you accuse her of—"

"Elizabeth, she sat right there, smiling at Michaela as she cried. Why?" he asked Marjorie. "Why not pick her up and console her? Up to your room, Marjorie, and do not come down until tomorrow morning."

"That's harsh!" Elizabeth objected, rising. "It's not yet five o'clock and—"

"It's not harsh enough," he snapped. "What will it be next—pushing Michaela off a settee? What after that? Down a flight of stairs? Michaela cannot defend herself! Go, Marjorie, and do not stomp. Walk, or you will remain in your room for another day. Stay where you are, Elizabeth," Joseph ordered when she moved to follow Marjorie from the room.

She did, but angrily, settling back down on the opposite settee, her eyes seeming to shoot fire at him for an instant. She was sullen throughout the remainder of the evening—throughout supper, throughout kissing Rebecca, Claudette, and Maureen good night, throughout taking Michaela up to bed, and even when they settled into bed themselves. Joseph finally rolled over, propped his arms on the pillow just above her shoulders, and looked down at her.

"You do not agree with the punishment, but Marjorie's jealousy has persisted for nearly eight months and now I see it growing worse, not better, despite us both spending a great deal of time with her. I will not tolerate jealousy in our home, Elizabeth, no matter who displays it, no matter who it's aimed at. I will certainly not tolerate violence."

A moment passed. Her eyes softened. Her jaw loosened. Presently she reached up and touched his beard, then his cheek. Then she moved up to kiss him, exhibiting a boldness he rarely saw in his wife. Joseph responded almost immediately, kissing her back, reaching up to caress her breasts, which were still heavy with milk. She arched up to him and he became lost in the scent and softness of her.

3

Elizabeth had been ten years old when her mother and father decided to travel to England for a time. How could she have known, when she stood on the dock that day with her aunt and uncle, waving good-bye to her parents, that it was truly good-bye? Always and forever. Word arrived some four weeks later that they had perished when their ship broke up during a storm at sea.

Elizabeth had cried off and on for a solid year, or so it had seemed, ignoring her bubbly cousin Sarah, nearly drowning in her grief. She had wondered if she would ever stop missing her parents, and for a time she had even been angry at God. Though her parents had by no means been wealthy, they had managed to scrape and save and provide their only child with a fine education up until their deaths; Elizabeth had been raised thus far with a degree of religion and gentility, with a vast store of respect for all living things and for the Maker.

Her grief had been severe and consuming, and she hadn't broken free of it until she was nearly thirteen, when she looked into her mirror one day, really looked, really studied herself. She was changing, growing up. The childhood chubbiness was disappearing from her cheeks, and her breasts and hips were sprouting. It was spring outside—everything was lush and alive. Yet in her heart and soul she felt almost dead.

She had pushed her cousin away when many times Sarah would have taken her hand and laughed, told girlish secrets with her, and done many other things. But oh, how she'd wanted to feel alive again! As alive as spring looked and Sarah acted and obviously felt. So she'd forced herself not to forget her parents—she would never forget them—but to look toward the life ahead of her. It had taken a strange turn, what she had thought was a horrible turn. But perhaps there was a reason for that. Hadn't she read in her Bible somewhere that there was a reason for everything?

She exchanged her drab mourning clothes for prettier, livelier ones, smiling when Sarah asked if she was ill. "I've decided to live," Elizabeth answered. "That is, if you'll agree to show me how." After a long moment, Sarah took her hand and they tore off through the house, barging out the front entrance, racing down the street, finally running barefoot along walkways near the park.

They began attending parties and other social gatherings together. Elizabeth even began taking dance and music lessons with the cousin who soon became like a sister to her. They slept together, they ate together, they studied together . . . they did everything together. Their playground was Boston's Back Bay area, its ponds, its stately trees and broad walkways, its conservatory, dainty flower beds, shrubbery, and plants; the gravel paths that wound narrowly through the Public Garden where she and Joseph eventually spent a great deal of time during their courtship.

After a time Elizabeth and Sarah began looking toward the finer streets and homes of Beacon Hill with the glittering eyes of dreamy young women. They walked through the public parks there, through the Common; they frequented the shops and skated on the pond—after all, they had just as much right to roam this area of Boston as did anyone else—but they rarely dreamed aloud of ever actually living in the grand area.

Eventually it was through Sarah that Elizabeth met Joseph Quinn one crisp winter day.

Sarah had met him and a group of his friends while skating at the Beacon Hill pond the week before, while Elizabeth had been recovering from a stomach illness, and Sarah had come home that day bubbling over with talk of him and his friends. The twenty-eight-year-old Dr. Quinn was well on his way to becoming a respected Boston physician; he and a handful of colleagues, fellow Harvard Medical School graduates, were batting around the idea of starting a medical school of their own, one that would offer a tighter, broader medical education. He zoomed around on the ice, laughing and carrying on with his friends like a half-crazed man, Sarah said. When Elizabeth accompanied her to the pond days later, he and his friends were there again, and she found that to be true . . . a half-crazed man, one full of vigor and energy. Though Sarah found him intriguing, Elizabeth preferred a quieter type. So other than skating with him a few times, she paid him little mind, though she was well aware that he watched her from time to time.

Sarah wanted him for herself, but later she noted aloud, and without playful resentment, that he had eyes only for Elizabeth. "The two of you would make a much better pair," Elizabeth responded, half-interested. Sarah shrugged, and moments later the girls began reading a book together.

The next afternoon Joseph called on Elizabeth, taking tea with her in the parlor during what were the most awkward moments of her life, and after he left, Aunt Cordelia clapped her hands together excitedly and said, "Oh, your parents would be thrilled. Do you know who he is, Elizabeth? Why, that's Dr. Quinn's son—another Dr. Quinn! He's only twenty-eight years old but already he's on staff at the City Hospital and he's made a number of investments in and around Boston. Your uncle speaks of how brilliant he is—I've heard him! And he came to call on you, Elizabeth!"

Elizabeth had grown somewhat uncomfortable with the entire situation—with Sarah wanting him but willing to

31

hand him over to her, with the stars in her aunt's eyes. Aunt Cordelia had it in her head to make a match of them, Elizabeth just knew it. Lately she often commented that this or that young man would make a good husband. It didn't seem to matter who fetched a husband first—Elizabeth or Sarah—only that they both acquire one.

"I don't want him to call again. I don't ever want to marry. I don't ever want to leave you," Elizabeth told Sarah in their bed that night. "I don't want us to grow up and leave each other. I don't ever want to grow apart!" She was petrified with fear that she would soon be forced to marry and leave this home, therefore leave her very best friend in the world.

"I'll find a man soon and we'll marry on the same day and convince our husbands to purchase houses right next to each other," Sarah said, laughing a little and smoothing back Elizabeth's hair. "Doesn't Joseph make you feel anything? Don't you find him exciting? Dashing?"

Elizabeth huffed onto her back, folded her arms, and stared up at the tester. "I don't want a beau. I don't want to be courted. I don't want to marry. I won't, I tell you. I won't!"

"Stubborn girl," Sarah scolded gently. "Open your eyes. Mama will have the two of you married within the year."

But her eyes *were* open, and that was exactly why she was so frightened. Because she knew Sarah spoke the truth. "No, she won't!"

"Yes, she will."

"I won't marry him. Him or anyone else!"

"Think, Elizabeth," Sarah said. "Be sensible. Do you want to marry some poor boy you fall madly in love with? . . . Do you want to live in a shack and perhaps beg for food? . . . Or would you rather live on Beacon Hill and never ever have to worry?"

"It's not so bad as that. I wouldn't look twice at a pauper—you know that!"

"It could be. It's a wonderful match if you ask me. Encourage Joseph, marry him, then you won't just be skating on Beacon Hill and walking along the walkways.

You'll be living there! People will envy you in your fine house with your fine dresses and fine things. You love Beacon Hill. We both do."

"I don't care. I want always to live here, with you and Aunt Cordelia and Uncle Henry."

Sarah sighed. "Back Bay to Beacon Hill . . . I'd choose Beacon Hill. If you don't encourage him, perhaps I'll give serious thought to snatching your beau from under your nose."

That got Elizabeth's attention. "Sarah Kimball, you wouldn't!"

"Wouldn't I?" Sarah's blue eyes twinkled in the lamplight.

"You would!"

Sarah poked her. "Of course I would. I could, you know, I simply haven't wanted to."

Elizabeth poked her back and then both girls erupted into a fit of giggles.

But Sarah hardly had time to snatch Joseph Quinn from under Elizabeth's nose. Two weeks later she contracted influenza and died of the illness.

Another devastating event. Devastation.

Throughout the sickness, the death, and the subsequent burial, Elizabeth felt numb. Consumed again by a horrible sense of loss and grief, but in a different sort of way this time, a quiet, petrified sort of way. Her life had been Sarah's life, Sarah's had been hers, and now Sarah was gone. Elizabeth expected to cry again. She tried to cry again. Instead, memories of Sarah's laughter, her smiles, her gaiety danced in her head. She remembered how Sarah had helped bring her to life again, how she had encouraged a cold, desolate girl to laugh and be carefree. With Sarah she had grown into young womanhood. But now . . . now Elizabeth was nearly eighteen, and she could either lie down and die on the bed she and Sarah had shared for so many years, on the very bed on which Sarah had died, or she could go forward.

Sarah would want her to live. She knew that. Over and over Sarah's voice whispered that in Elizabeth's head—

while she slept, while she ate, while she did any task at all. *Live!* She saw Sarah dancing, glimpsed her smiles, heard her laughter, and somehow she knew that Sarah was with her still and always would be. *Live,* Sarah said. *Back Bay to Beacon Hill* . . .

Elizabeth no longer needed Aunt Cordelia's encouragement. Sarah died during the winter of 1815, and though her family was still in mourning, Elizabeth accepted Joseph Quinn's proposal of marriage the following spring. In many ways he was a kind, gentle man, devoted to his profession and to the people he loved—and he would take her from Back Bay to Beacon Hill. It was a sensible decision, one Elizabeth knew would make Sarah proud. Uncle Henry agreed to the engagement without pause, and Aunt Cordelia shed her mourning garb within just a few weeks, then began planning a party to announce the alliance.

Rebecca and Claudette had been born by the time Elizabeth realized that she loved Joseph. He had gone to call on a patient over in Charlestown one evening and the next afternoon he was still gone. He hadn't been home at all, or so Harrison, their butler, had informed her. Oftentimes, Joseph came home during the night, slept a few hours, rose early, and was gone again by daybreak. But he hadn't even been home to do that, or so a concerned Harrison reported. Elizabeth had sent messages to his colleagues, then to the hospital, then out to the patient Joseph had told her he was going to tend. The responses from his colleagues and the hospital were that he hadn't been seen at either place. The patient had seen him last evening, but that was all. Where had Joseph been since then?

Elizabeth had always worried to a degree; being the wife of a physician who was frequently called out into the city in the middle of the night and at other odd hours, she couldn't help but worry from time to time. She worried about him tending patients in the slum areas. She worried about him riding along deserted streets and alleys. She worried whether he received drinks and meals whenever he kept a lengthy vigil at a patient's bedside. She worried many times and about many things.

But this . . . this feeling was worse than worry. In the pit of her stomach she felt that something was horribly wrong, that Joseph's luck had finally run out, that if he had a guardian angel then she had glanced away for a few minutes and something had happened. And while she worried, while the day dragged on and Elizabeth sent out inquiry after inquiry, while she rocked Claudette and read to Rebecca, while she forced herself to do the simplest of tasks, she realized how much she would miss him if he were taken from her. How much she already missed him.

She realized that she would miss his gentle touches, the way he planted a light kiss on her cheek before he went out, the way he slid his fingers up into the hair at the nape of her neck and drew her to him whenever he wanted to kiss her full on the lips, the way he sometimes insisted on pouring her wine during their evening meals; the way he had looked at her, his eyes glowing with love and affection, for at least the last year and perhaps longer now. She realized that he had become far more than her marital companion. He was her friend and her lover, and she cherished him.

He was found in a Charlestown gutter, having been assaulted and robbed on the way back from tending his patient. For nearly a day he had lain in the rain and mud, and after he was found and brought to her, Elizabeth bathed him herself, tenderly washing his cuts and bruises. Pneumonia took hold of his lungs and she nursed him for a solid month, sleeping in a chair near their bed where he lay, stirring whenever he stirred, responding to his every need and desire. Most of his healing came from her loving ministrations, he told her later—and as he continued to tell her over the years whenever they spoke of that illness.

Knowing she loved him, she could now look back and see why everything in her life had happened so far—that her parent's deaths had led to her sisterly relationship with Sarah, that that relationship with Sarah had led to her relationship with and subsequent marriage to Joseph. . . . She had learned to be strong, to be optimistic instead of fearful, to face life with courage and dignity, and to stand straight and tall no matter what. Not to be afraid to love someone because she feared that person might be taken away.

She thought the latter might have been part of her reluctance in allowing Joseph close to her emotionally — why she had been so unfeeling about the marriage, why she initially had regarded it as nothing more than a "sensible" arrangement, one that was in her best interest; why she had not admitted to herself before now — why she had not even thought about it really — that she was in love with her husband. Almost everyone she had loved thus far — her parents, Sarah — had been taken from her. Yet Joseph hadn't. He had been spared. She still feared being vulnerable, but she also feared not loving at all. Life would be empty without Joseph, she knew that. She now had the opportunity to be his wife because she loved him, not because it was expected of her. She had the opportunity to show him that love, and she meant to do exactly that.

She was like a blossoming flower in the ensuing years, loving the warmth and the sunshine of her life, becoming vibrant in the glow of happiness. She devoted herself to Joseph. She had more of his children, each time hoping for a male. Uncle Henry had wanted a son. So had Elizabeth's father. So did every man she knew. Even Joseph. They had talked of having a son. And yet they had three more girls, and Michaela's birth was so frightening, with the baby being born early, feet first and not breathing for a time, that Elizabeth was not certain she should risk having another child. She considered it at times, but as Joseph had mentioned on several occasions now, it might also be a girl.

Elizabeth knew that although he fawned over Michaela, in his heart Joseph had wanted a son. She'd seen his eyes light up when she told him about dreaming that the baby was a boy, and surely he must give thought now and then to who his medical bag would pass to one day. After producing four girls, Elizabeth had wanted to give him a son, and she had failed.

It wasn't Michaela's fault that she was born a girl —

36

Elizabeth knew that, too. But depression had gripped her so thoroughly and with such force within hours of Michaela's birth that she simply hadn't been enthusiastic about caring for her new child. She was ashamed of that now, though Michaela had so many people around her—her sisters, the house staff, Elizabeth's aunt Cordelia and uncle Henry, Joseph's mother—that she hardly noticed her mother's neglect. But Elizabeth felt it was past time for her to act like the baby's mother, for her to give Michaela as much nurturing and love as she gave her other four children.

When Michaela's first birthday rolled around and their youngest daughter took her first steps, Elizabeth smiled and glowed, though not nearly as much as Joseph did, she felt certain. She would not venture to say that Michaela was his favorite because Joseph wasn't the sort of man to play favorites with his children. But she would say that, because of the nature of Michaela's birth and other circumstances surrounding her first year of existence, the child occupied a special place in Joseph's heart. Elizabeth knew almost from the beginning that their relationship would be more than the normal father-daughter relationship. She knew Joseph would have a difficult time saying no to Michaela when the child wanted anything. But even more than that, she knew Joseph had taken this child completely under his wing, that there was a special, heartwarming, though sometimes irritating, bond between Michaela and Joseph.

She also knew that when Joseph said he no longer thought about having a son, he meant it.

4

Though snow often covered the streets and walkways and removing it was a tedious affair, sometimes requiring days of labor by city workers, Beacon Hill was not a dull place during the cold season. At the beginning of every winter one person in the household—a woman, if there was one—sent out cards to numerous people, announcing at least one day of the month when the persons of that household would formally receive callers. And so, during the winter of '33 to '34, people converged on the Quinn's town house the second Tuesday of each month between two and six P.M.

Michaela was too young to count the number of people who called, but Claudette put a mark on her tablet for each person who showed up, and Rebecca kept a running total in her head. Maureen counted them aloud, stating a number for each person who entered the house, and Marjorie jabbed her with each count, saying she would outrage them all. The jabs inevitably caused a fight, and to Elizabeth's embarrassment, the nurse separated Maureen and Marjorie more than once, taking them upstairs to their room. Rebecca totaled thirty-eight callers in December, forty in January, and thirty-three in February. In March, however, the callers were so numerous that she lost count and finally was forced to accept Claudette's grand total of forty-four. It seemed there were more visitors, there was such a constant coming and going of people on that particular Tuesday, five of them being young bachelors Elizabeth had invited to call on Rebecca, the very thing that rattled the girl into losing count.

Thank goodness the nurse came along before any of the bachelors, who all arrived at different times and were shown into the parlor. Rebecca knew she would endure enough teasing from her sisters later without them sitting in the same room with her and her gentlemen callers, and she was grateful that the nurse took the confused-looking Claudette, Maureen, and Marjorie upstairs. Michaela was brought down during these Tuesday evenings only if a caller asked after her, so she was already upstairs playing in her cradle.

Rebecca knew her mother had picked the finest Boston bachelors, and so she made a determined effort to be polite and to remember the manners she had been taught over the years, although her callers were a surprise and not exactly to her liking. One was too tall for her taste, another too short; one was too clumsy, upsetting his cup and saucer and then the pot of tea when he tried to remedy the mess. Yet another, a Harvard upperclassman, was too certain of himself, holding his chin and nose in an upright, arrogant manner and speaking only of himself for over an hour, of his horsemanship, of his success at ninepins. . . . Rebecca found herself wanting to yawn, and even her mother looked bored. At least neither of them had to keep up the conversation. He *was* the conversation.

Rebecca's last caller, Marcus Bradford, seemed nice enough, and he was neither too tall, too short, too clumsy, nor too full of himself. His father was a merchant, had made the family fortune in business, in fact, and Marcus planned to follow in his footsteps. His eyes were brown and filled with gentleness, his chestnut hair waved to just above his shoulders, and when he asked if he could call on her the following week, Rebecca agreed. Elizabeth was certainly pleased; of all the young men she'd chosen to visit, she liked

Marcus the most—and his family was one of the more influential and well-to-do in Boston. She was already planning Rebecca's debutante ball, but until it took place the following spring, she had decided that Rebecca should have at least one suitor.

Rebecca lay in bed that night thinking of Marcus, of how polite and charming he was, of how he had kissed her hand ever so sweetly, of how her heart had skipped a beat. . . . She told herself she was being foolish, that she shouldn't lose her heart to the first man who took an interest in her. Why, she was just getting started with all of this, with suitors calling, inviting her for strolls and carriage rides and other outings. If she lost her heart to Marcus, she would surely miss a great deal of fun. For the last year she had watched Donna Meyer, her best friend who lived just up Beacon Street and who was a year older than she, be courted and taken here and there. She had listened to Donna's accounts of her many outings, her cheeks flushed and her eyes aglow as she told about them, and many times she had clapped her hands together and sighed and thought, *One day soon I'll have suitors and outings to tell about.*

Many times. But it wasn't jealousy, her wonderings whenever she listened to Donna talk. Well, not exactly. In a way, Rebecca guessed it was. . . . What else could feelings like *I wish it were me* be? It was jealousy, then, but a healthy sort of jealousy. She didn't want to take Donna's suitors and her outings, she just wanted some of her own. Instead of sitting and nodding her head and saying ooh and ah now and then when Donna danced around the room telling of her activities, Rebecca wanted to dance around with her and tell about a few of her own. She wanted to take part in the fun.

The Quinns always made numerous calls themselves, as they did every winter season, mostly on Sunday afternoons but frequently on Wednesdays or Thursdays, days their friends and acquaintances chose to open their homes. Children did not always go along, but Elizabeth picked two of her girls to go with her each time she went out on a call, two different girls. They had to be exposed to the social customs in order to learn them, or so she usually told Anne

40

Quinn, Joseph's mother, every year when she began going out and her mother-in-law objected.

Besides teas there were dinners, some held by the Quinns, others by their many friends and acquaintances, all with an array of dishes, a feast of seafood—oysters, shad, turtle, clams, perch, trout, lobster. . . . Soup was always served, a different kind with each dinner. Radishes, cucumbers, brussels sprouts, mushrooms, celery, lettuce and olives always livened the main dishes. Alongside the many seafoods, creamed chicken, filet of beef, and duck in a variety of sauces graced tables. Turkey salad, chartreuse of grouse, and lobster farci were served on shimmering silver platters. Ice creams, cakes, and tarts, and this year something new—oranges and lemons from Sicily—made mouths water and eyes widen. Delicious sauces and puddings were made from both fruits. The oranges were often served sliced, and the lemons used to make lemonade, a drink mixed from water, sugar, and juice from the fruit and said to be a marvelous refreshment during summertime. Lemon juice also was squeezed over fish and other seafoods, always a mouthwatering addition.

Claudette, Maureen and Marjorie enjoyed the outings, each being a different adventure, but Rebecca enjoyed them most of all, something that had not always been true. They had once bored her nearly out of her mind. Since her sixteenth birthday, her mother had had some of her dresses made to dip a little lower at the bosom, Rebecca now had gentlemen callers, and she was not always expected to sit quietly at the teas and suppers anymore—she could join in the conversations. She was beginning to feel altogether grown-up, and participating in the social events, actually taking part in them, made her feel even more grown-up.

She wasn't at all bored anymore, except during times when the men drifted into talking about politics over a meal, the most heated being the issue of South Carolina's act of rebellion in attempting to nullify a federal tariff law passed in 1828. In objection, the state had even threatened to secede from the Union, an issue that still had people in an uproar. The federal government had tried to compromise, enacting a new tariff last year. But a bill authorizing the president of the United States to enforce collections of tariffs by use of military force if necessary had gone hand in hand with the new tariff, and now South Carolina was in an uproar again, lately holding a state convention and passing an ordinance nullifying the bill. Conversations and debates about that convention and its action almost always began between the men during meals, and most of the women present usually tried to bring the talk to an end, either by cleverly leading the men on to other topics or by distracting them with feminine charm.

Invitations to Rebecca's debutante supper and ball were written, delivered, and answered. The cook began preparing food the day before the event, and the evening of June six-teenth forty-one women and fifty men assembled in the town house to honor Rebecca. This was truly her day, the day that she, now a young woman, would be officially presented to her elders, special friends, and to more young men, some of whom would surely become beaux. The children were put to bed, though Claudette and Maureen lay wide awake for hours listening to the festivities, and the Quinns and their guests danced cotillions and waltzes played by the three-piece ensemble that had been hired for the occasion.

In her new gown of shimmery blue satin, trimmed with lace and silk roses and tassels, Rebecca went from dance to dance, twirling, laughing, smiling, and talking. The elders commented on what a fine young woman she had grown into, many a married woman shared an account of her own coming out, and many a married man watched the young Rebecca as she savored her evening. After a few glasses of wine and champagne, flirting became easy, and Rebecca enjoyed herself immensely. She danced until two A.M., until her feet ached and felt as if they would drop off, then she drank more and ate of the enormous supper that was served. The food was astounding: twenty pounds of creamed oysters, a huge salad surrounded by lobster, two whole turkeys, several roast beefs, and so many roasted chickens she lost count as they arrived on the table whole, were taken away once eaten down to the bones, and were followed by another and another and another. . . . Rolls were served, too, and individual ices.

After three A.M. Rebecca, her mother, and father saw numerous guests to the door and bid them good-bye. Hours later, when the crowd had thinned considerably, a breakfast was served—eggs and bacon and hotcakes and sundry other foods. Rebecca was so full from the earlier feast she couldn't possibly eat more. But other people managed to, and an hour after that all the guests were gone and the town house was quiet once again.

Somehow the maids and the servants who had been hired especially for the evening had managed to clean up a little, so the mess wasn't too great. Rebecca reached for a glass containing a trickle of flat champagne, intent on taking it to the kitchen. But Martha, the Quinn's maid, was there, stopping her, urging her upstairs, where she helped Rebecca wash her face and change for bed.

Rebecca snuggled against her feather pillows just as the sun began rising and just as her sisters began spilling from their beds. But the nurse was there for them, thank goodness, because Rebecca had never felt more tired in her life, or more pleasantly exhausted.

When the summer of '34 breezed in, Michaela was toddling about and beginning to talk. Rebecca tried over and over to teach her how to say her name. "Mich-ae-la," she would say, telling Michaela to look at her mouth. Michaela always giggled and laughed, rocking to and fro on Rebecca's lap, and sometimes Rebecca would glance up to find their mother watching them, a warm smile on her face. She loved the baby, she really did. It was as she, Rebecca, had told Father: Mother had had her mind set on a boy and she had needed time to get used to having another girl instead.

Michaela finally managed to say "Mick," and after a month of that, Rebecca gave up trying to teach the baby to say her full first name; she converted Mick to Mike instead. Michaela could say that without a problem, and she ran around the house grabbing onto her sisters' and the servants'

43

legs, grinning up at them and calling herself Mike over and over. Joseph laughed whenever he heard her. Claudette always picked her up and hugged her tight. Maureen always tickled her to the floor and told her how cute she was. Marjorie always scowled and said, "Get. That's a boy's name. You can't call yourself by a boy's name. Mother! She can't call herself by a boy's name."

Elizabeth agreed that no daughter of hers should be called by a male name, and though she and the nursemaid tried, as Rebecca had tried, to teach the baby to call herself Michaela, the youngest Quinn child would have none of their efforts. She cried and twisted and shouted "No, no, no!" Joseph said ever so quietly one evening that Michaela was not hurting a thing, and after two more frustrating efforts the next afternoon, Elizabeth shook her head as she watched the baby waddle off.

"Mike, Mike, Mike . . ." Michaela said. She snatched up a small wooden animal from a drawing room settee and clasped it to her breast with both hands, then glared at her mother. "Mine. Mike!" she said, flashing her dark eyes.

Elizabeth shook her head, commenting that she'd never seen a more determined, stubborn child. Rebecca tried to hide her smile, loving her baby sister more each day, as Michaela heaved her way up onto the settee, settled on her tummy, and closed her eyes. It never took her long to do something once she decided to do it, and right now she had decided to take a nap. Minutes later she was asleep.

Almost from the time Michaela began walking she toddled around after her father at the town house. Joseph still read to her at least three times a week from his medical journals, and by the time she began putting words together into sentences, she had a medical vocabulary that exceeded that of most adults. As Joseph read to her, she often pointed to anatomical sketches and illustrations and blurted the words, not always correctly—but then what young child pronounced even the most commonly used words correctly?

Joseph grew fond of her nickname for herself and, at least in private, to avoid scolding looks from Elizabeth, he began calling her Mike. Her smiles were precious to him, her intelligence was exciting, her affection heartwarming. His love for Michaela was so profound that his heart nearly burst whenever she crawled up onto his lap many nights, snuggled against him, and urged him to read to her.

As she grew, she became more curious than the average young child, if possible—and in her case, as Joseph observed, such a thing was very possible. From the age of two she asked an inordinate amount of questions and demanded answers. Why this happened, why that happened . . . What made the rain? What made the gas lamps go *pop* whenever the parlormaid went around with her long-handled gadget and began turning on the keys and lighting the burners? Joseph took her with him one afternoon to see a demonstration of McCormick's new machine, which was drawn by horses and could reap a field in a third the time that such a task once took. An "ice box," a new creation, had recently appeared in the home of a family friend, Elizabeth and the girls had gone to have a look at it, and Mike had asked questions ever since, observing that the ice took a very long time to melt, but also asking why meat had to be kept cold to keep from "spoiling." She learned that a bathtub had been fastened to the upstairs floor in the same household—the Quinn daughters were still marched to the Tremont House, a popular hotel, once a week for tub baths—and she marveled over that for a time, telling everyone she encountered about it, punctuating her conversation with waves of her arms and with her animated facial expressions. People loved to converse with her—and she loved to converse.

She was a rebel, or so Joseph, and her entire family, had quickly realized, bucking any sort of restriction or constriction, wearing only what she wanted to wear, going only where she wanted to go, doing only what she wanted to do. The nursemaid and Elizabeth had many an experience with trying to force Michaela into an unwanted dress or trying to take her somewhere she did not wish to go. Michaela threw intense tantrums, screaming like no child had ever screamed, kicking her legs and flailing her arms, crying for either Rebecca or Joseph and many times, for both.

"I've never seen such an obstinate child," Elizabeth frequently remarked, exasperated. And she occasionally blamed Joseph and Rebecca since they often rescued Michaela from her mother's and the nursemaid's attentions, gathering her in their arms and taking her out for walks or off somewhere in the house where they could quiet her. Marjorie had taken to ignoring Mike most of the time, Maureen tried to distract her with various objects during the tantrums, and Claudette grimaced whenever Michaela's temper flared.

Joseph's mother seemed proud that Mike was so head-strong, "but she does need to exercise restraint," the woman commented one day, nearly halfway through Mike's fifth year. She had marched bold as brass into his study and made the announcement while Joseph was reading.

Doesn't everyone? he thought, as he finished reading the obituary of a man who had been a relic of the Revolution, rumored to have been involved in throwing cases of East India tea into Boston harbor. Need to practice restraint, that was. His young daughter's rebelliousness did not trouble him nearly as much as it did Elizabeth and his own mother. After all, she was never rebellious with *him.* The world, the Union, had more serious problems than one unconventional child who refused to be molded. Financially speaking, men had overinvested in such things as the steam locomotive, the reaper, the steel plough board, and the iron that was now being used to build ships. While Samuel Morse was said to be improving his telegraph machine, which had started with a range of forty feet and now extended for miles, and while even he now had backing, Joseph was still skeptical. The quick westward expansion and the unsoundness of banks had led to the worst financial panic in the history of the nation, and people were suddenly pulling back, spending less, becoming cautious. Jackson had gone out and Van Buren had come in, suddenly finding himself being blamed for the financial disaster. The papers on Joseph's desk and the city outside his windows were filled with people who were organizing, laboring, and speaking out more and more about women's rights, educational reform, and social welfare. Ralph Emerson, a frequent speaker in Boston, had recently delivered an impressive address to the Phi Beta Kappa Society at Harvard—the young Oliver Holmes, fully degreed now, back from studying abroad, and with a prized Boylston Award to his credit—had remarked that the address was an intellectual Declaration of Independence. Perhaps so, but a lot of people still had trouble digesting anything Emerson said. Holmes had also approached Joseph later the same evening about the possibility of starting a medical school in Boston, something he knew Joseph had wanted to do for years now. A number of brilliant minds had attended the presentation and the following festivities that evening. But as Joseph glanced up at his mother, his mind always turning matters over, always thinking and appreciating a fellow thinker . . . as he heard his exasperated mother mention Michaela's name, he smiled, wondering what the child was about now—and he couldn't help but feel that another intelligent mind was taking shape under this very roof, many times right here on his lap.

Anne Quinn went on: A shocked Elizabeth had recently discovered a certain box hidden in the room Mike shared with Maureen and Marjorie and had been about to burn it when Mike flew into one of her tantrums, screaming that the box was hers and that Mama would ruin her collection inside.

The incident and his mother's telling of it did finally arrest his full attention. He went off upstairs, hearing Mike's cries grow louder and louder. And when he reached the door of the room she shared with her sisters, he saw that there was no swaying Mike. The box obviously held something dear to her and she meant to keep it. She snatched it from her mother's hands and ran off with it, plowing headfirst into Joseph as he stood in the doorway.

"Joseph, she's not keeping it," Elizabeth said, spotting him.

He was baffled. "What is in the box?"

"It's filled with dead bugs. I wouldn't allow her to keep a live bug, I certainly won't allow her to keep that."

Michaela clung to her gray treasure box, hovering behind

Joseph's legs and peering around at her mother with wide, tear-filled eyes. "Mine. She wants to burn it. No!" she shot at Elizabeth.

"Why have you filled a box with dead bugs?" Joseph asked, soothing Mike by stroking the side of her chubby face.

"To see how they work, how many legs and arms and wings. Worms don't die, Papa. Only if I put them on stones in the sun." Behind Mike's tears, Joseph now glimpsed flashes of curiosity and bafflement. "Cut them, they don't die. Why? David fishes with worms and he says—"

"That will be enough," Elizabeth scolded. She had grown as pale as a freshly laundered sheet and had put a hand to her breast. "Joseph, listen to her!"

"An interesting point," he commented, absorbed in Michaela's curiosity. "They do not die. Earthworms . . . lumbricidae have the physiological ability to regenerate. They—"

"I won't have this!" Elizabeth objected. "You are ruining her mind, filling it with medical words and phrases, encouraging this type of outrageous behavior. Give me that box," she said, trying to wrestle it from Mike's hands. Michaela screeched and wriggled away, wrapping her arms around her precious box and pressing it against her chest.

"I would like to see what she has in the box," Joseph said quietly, with steady calmness, raising his chin the slightest bit and staring at Elizabeth.

"Then take a quick look and give it to me. It's going into the fire," she said, undaunted.

"No!" Mike screamed.

Joseph's jaw tensed. "It will not be going anywhere Michaela does not want it to go."

Elizabeth paused, staring back at him now, carefully controlled anger burning in her eyes. "You spoil her. You do worse—you ruin her. She knows no discipline, no limitations. You are filling her mind with medical nonsense."

Joseph tensed. "Medical *fact.*"

"If you would leave her to me . . . She's not a normal child."

"No, she is not. She is a brilliant child," Joseph said, and he scooped Mike up into his arms and took her off to his study to hear about each and every creature she had collected and stored in her box. He passed his mother along the way, "Grandmother Quinn," the children called her, and he did not miss her sneer, her complete look of disapproval. He closed the study door, closed himself and his precious daughter inside the room, separated them from her tormentors.

Mike sniffled again, pushed away the last of her tears, and opened her box. She pulled out an earthworm that was still very much alive. "It has rings," she said, placing the worm on the newspapers. "They stretch. That's how it crawls, Papa. See?"

"I do see."

"It was crawling up the brick wall in David's garden. How does it crawl up the brick wall? It has no legs."

"Oh, but it does, my curious Mike. You cannot see them because they are so tiny. But they are there, hundreds of them."

"Papa," she said skeptically.

"You do not believe me," he said, trying to appear wounded.

She giggled a little, his precious Michaela, and shook her head. "No."

Joseph thought for a moment. "Very well, then, tomorrow morning I shall take you to the hospital and show you."

"Hospital?" she queried, wide-eyed.

"Hospital. Now, let's see what other treasures you have in there."

She picked up the worm and started to put him back in the box. Joseph stopped her. "He will die in there, Mike. No food, no air. He'll die simply because he is caged. You must put him outside on the ground, back in the world he knows."

"But I won't have him," she objected.

"You only borrowed him."

She twisted her face, undecided about what she should do with the worm. Then she put him back on the newspapers.

"Very well," she huffed. "I like to watch him crawl. I don't want him to die."

"Splendid. Now for the other treasures."

She began pulling them out, crickets, butterflies, spiders, flies . . . there was even a small frog and a bird. Nine-year-old David and his mother had apparently called one afternoon when Mike's collection consisted of only the crickets and butterflies, and Michaela had shared her interest with him. Then David had added to it a little at a time, a day at a time. The frog and the bird were a bit much, being partly decomposed and emitting a stench that Elizabeth had surely noticed. In fact, her nose may have lead her straight to the box. At least one thing was for certain—the box couldn't be kept in the house.

Joseph and his youngest daughter compromised. He would preserve at the hospital any specimen she and David wished to collect. But no live specimens—and they were not to kill the animals in order to study them. If they found them dead, they could bring them to the laboratory. Mike seemed pleased with that, delighted in knowing that she and David could go to the hospital any time they wished when he was there and study their collections.

"Where is such monstrous encouragement supposed to get her?" Elizabeth snapped when she was told about the arrangement.

"You would do well to remember the child's sex," Joseph's mother cautioned him. "A girl should hardly hunt dead animals and run off to a hospital laboratory to study them. She should study other things."

He was weary of arguing with Elizabeth and his mother about Mike's temperament and what they considered her "odd habits." He refused to quarrel with either of them, saying firmly and only once, "Michaela is permitted to add to her collection and to visit the hospital with David."

No discussion was permitted on the matter, and thereafter David and Mike often appeared at Massachusetts General to study their findings and to discuss them with Joseph. Joseph never permitted the children in the dissection rooms, thinking the sight of mutilated human cadavers too much for their

50

young eyes, but he assisted in David's dissections with Mike looking on and always, always asking questions.

The Quinns had an occasion to celebrate that year. Rebecca had been engaged to Marcus Bradford for some time, but to Elizabeth's dismay—and Joseph's delight—she had put off the wedding until she was nearly twenty years old. Joseph was rather proud that Rebecca had not allowed her mother to bother her into an earlier wedding date. Although Rebecca was always respectful, she had a good strong will about her, as strong as her mother's but not quite as belligerent as Michaela's. She had wanted to be certain of her decision, and after nearly four years of seeing Marcus off and on, she was.

Joseph didn't especially care for the thought of giving his daughter away, no matter how much he liked Marcus Bradford; in fact, he refused to think of the marriage as him giving her away to anyone. Marcus could share her, but only if he promised to love, cherish, and protect her, which he did without hesitation to Joseph, Rebecca, the minister of the Park Street Church, and before the entire crowd that gathered one spring day.

Her gown was of the purest ivory satin, trimmed with dainty French lace and seed pearls. More pearls were woven in her dark hair and dangled from her earlobes. When Joseph walked her down the aisle, patting her hand, his eyes were so filled with tears he almost couldn't see the red carpet before him.

Marcus's family had given the newly married couple a town house over on Pinckney Street, but Marcus and Rebecca planned to head south for a time, to the nation's capital and then on to Virginia, where Marcus had other family.

Joseph and Holmes, along with two other physicians, opened their Tremont Street Medical School in 1839, when the coolness of autumn began reddening the maples leaves. Several afternoons a week, after they had been released from their studies, David and Mike made their way to the school to study and to ask questions. Joseph glowed while helping them along, Oliver seemed skeptical but witty (when was he ever without some amusement on the tip of his tongue?), and colleagues raised their disapproving brows.

"People have a way of talking," Holmes commented one day, when only he and Joseph remained in the dissection room. "Students . . . fellow physicians. They whisper about how you encourage your daughter's 'odd interests.' "

"They whisper?" Joseph queried. "Why whisper?"

"Because you're a greatly respected physician in this city. No one truly wishes to offend you. But this they find beyond comprehension."

"And you, Holmes," Joseph said, glancing up from a corpse, "What do you think?"

Oliver hesitated, then rubbed his whiskers and pulled himself up in his dignified way; when he did this, a person forgot that he stood only five feet and five inches tall. His stately presence was remarkable. "I think... that you love Michaela very much."

He had expected something witty from Holmes, something more thoughtful perhaps, something based on hours of analysis, which was what Oliver was best at doing. Reaching a conclusion after much study, Joseph knew that right now, Holmes was in the middle of collecting information on puerperal fever.

"Actually, Holmes, they are not new, the whispers," Joseph said, returning to his work. "I am well aware that they abound all around Boston, all over Beacon Hill, up and down Mount Vernon Street. I've become disgusted with the gossipers, with society's restrictions. Propriety threatens to limit Mike's potential, and I'll not have that."

Holmes was silent for a long moment. Then he placed his beaver hat atop his tilted head and gave a quick nod. "Well, given her rebellious spirit and your determined soul, I doubt that anyone or anything will ever truly limit Michaela. I'm off to Dartmouth."

Off to his part-time teaching position there, where he was professor of anatomy. Oliver took this all very lightly, the matter of Mike, considering Joseph nothing more than a doting father. This Joseph realized when Holmes turned to leave. A difficult thing to swallow, but even Oliver, as advanced as he was in much of his thinking, silently scoffed at encouraging Mike's scientific interests. Joseph shouldn't feel irritated, but he did. Holmes had become a very good friend. But then, even friends were entitled to differing opinions.

David, at least, faced little resistance from his family and friends about his newfound interest. He was rarely forbidden to visit the medical school, and his father, George Lewis, made only a small objection—to Joseph. The Lewises were a fine Beacon Hill family, often attending social events alongside the Quinns, and Joseph knew George well. A prominent Boston attorney, George had seemed humored when David had informed him that he meant to become a physician like Dr. Quinn. Now David's interest was intensifying, and George was somewhat nervous.

"He's still a child," George remarked to Joseph one day in early 1840, after a meeting of the Boston Philosophical Society. "He doesn't know what he wants."

"He dissects animal cadavers and asks questions as though he knows what he wants," Joseph said.

George studied him, considering that. "Well, the older two will make fine attorneys then," he said at last, and that was the end of the discussion.

How irritating that most fathers expected at least one son to follow in their footsteps. Thank goodness David was the youngest of George's three sons. Most fathers who had more than one son never took as much interest in the younger one. That was fortunate in this case, because David Lewis, with his quick, precise way with a scalpel, belonged in surgical rooms, not in courtrooms, and Joseph had been prepared to tell George exactly that.

Mike and David continued to appear at the Tremont Street school at least every third day, and would have been there more often if Joseph had not reminded them gently of their other studies. Long ago, Joseph had instructed his groom to take Mike and David to the medical school whenever they wished to go, especially on days when the weather was bitter cold. At the school, they peered into microscopes, drew diagrams, and discussed the anatomy and workings of animals with Joseph. Out of the childrens' acquaintance grew respect and a steadfast friendship. Joseph saw it, Holmes remarked on it.

David grasped the importance of keeping up with his other studies, but Michaela, with her stubborn, unbridled spirit, did not always. She often read from Joseph's medical journals instead of from her study books, and she occasionally sneaked off when she knew the teacher was coming to take her, Claudette, Maureen, and Marjorie up to the third-floor room Elizabeth had set aside as their schoolroom. Other neighborhood girls attended the classes, too, and their Beacon Hill parents shared the cost of the teacher.

Michaela became passionate about watching David do dissections, and she even began assisting him. She kept a notebook in which she made drawings of what she had seen, and she shared her findings with Joseph, who silently marveled at the knowledge his young daughter was collecting.

He wondered at himself sometimes, at the things people said, at Holmes's unspoken doubts that occasionally appeared in his eyes, wondered if encouraging this interest, this passion, of Michaela's was indeed such a wise thing. Elizabeth often asked him what he hoped to accomplish by encouraging her—a girl certainly couldn't grow up to become a doctor of medicine. No female doctors existed that Joseph knew of, that was certainly true. So he was careful never, ever to suggest that she should pursue the profession. Still, her learning should be unlimited. In that, he felt strongly. Sometimes, however, she studied the dissections and her drawings so often, Joseph worried that she was too intense for a child, that perhaps she should be dancing and making music with her sisters and mother instead of sitting with her tablet. If nothing else, he thought one day as he glanced at her, her scientific interests were quieting her, maturing her. She no longer threw such ghastly tantrums, and she listened intently instead of flying off, insisting on doing everything her way. She was becoming self-disciplined, whether or not she realized it, and he thought that a good thing.

He was relieved to hear that she had taken up fishing from the Charles River with David Lewis and Jimmie Becker, although Elizabeth disagreed with that interest also. She wished to mold Mike, and the stubborn Michaela refused to be molded by anyone or anything. Elizabeth failed to understand that, despite Joseph telling her that almost weekly, whenever Elizabeth launched into an account of what Mike had done *now*.

Elizabeth's frustration with Joseph, her exasperation with Michaela, and her lack of understanding about why Joseph encouraged Mike's interest in scientific matters did not improve with the passing of time. It worsened into cool disapproval, occasionally into icy disdain, and finally into complete silence for a number of years regarding the matter.

PART TWO:

Mike

A girl of indomitable spirit . . .
—Oliver Wendell Holmes, M.D.

Mind has no sex.
—Daniel O'Connor

5

Now and then David and Mike were distracted from their studies by Jimmie Becker, who had always been David's friend and playmate and who had recently become Mike's, too. They explored the shops of Beacon Hill—the fish markets, the summertime fruit stalls, the hardware stores. A certain bakery had a lunch counter where you could purchase a ham or chicken sandwich or a bowl of delicious steaming soup, and the trio frequented the place. They fished together—that was a weekly occurrence now.

Jimmie had never seen a girl so unsqueamish as Mike, who, in an abandoned building on the banks of the river Charles, would always change into a set of David's rolled-up trousers and shirtsleeves before fishing. Once the trio climbed into the rowboat they kept hidden inside a building that had once housed a dry goods store, Mike never hesitated to bait her own line, using crickets and worms and sometimes kernels of corn. She never hesitated to remove the fish she caught either, or to tote them home to her family's cook and help clean them.

That was because she helped David dissect things at the medical school, Jimmie felt certain. Normally he wouldn't have wanted to run around the Beacon Hill area with a girl since most girls wore frilly clothes, had their hair curled and pinned just so, and screeched at any sight they considered offensive. He'd put a mouse in the room with one of his sisters and her friends one time, and then he'd sat back and laughed at the commotion it caused, laughed so hard he thought he might soil his trousers. His mother had said, "Now, Jimmie," and his father had grinned and shaken his head, rarely scolding his only son for anything. Jimmie had felt certain that if Mike had been sitting in that room she would have . . . well, just sat there. A mouse didn't scare Mike. Few things did.

She had even stared in fascination one day when he set off the Volunteer Fire Engine Company's alarm and they hid behind some bushes and watched the firemen scramble. The horse-stall doors opened automatically and each of the four black horses went to its place at the engine or hose. Then the harnesses dropped into place and the firemen slid down their poles, lit the fire under their brass boiler, and went roaring off down the street. "To where?" Jimmie had asked, erupting into giggles. David and Mike had giggled, too. Mike laughed until Jimmie thought she would split her side. They had all laughed more when the firemen returned, looking baffled, finding no fire in Beacon Hill anywhere, and they had raced off before anyone could spot them.

"'Member that old house on Lynde Street?" Jimmie asked today, as he, David, and Mike sat on the grassy riverbank tossing their lines. Nothing was biting, and Jimmie was bored. He believed in patience while fishing, but they'd been sitting here for going on an hour and only David had received even a small tug on his line.

"I know it," Mike said.

David stared out across the sun-dappled water. "Sure."

"Let's go there. Mr. Hanley was tellin' how there's spirits in there." Warm excitement rose to Jimmie's face. He didn't care about fishing anymore today now that going to the Lynde Street house had occurred to him. He started bringing his line in.

60

"Let's do," Mike said, a slow smile crossing her face. Jimmie sometimes did this, thought of a new afternoon adventure for them, rescued them from boredom. David didn't always agree with the things Jimmie wanted to do, like when he had wanted to see if that mare of Mr. Oakes's had any more spunk than it seemed. The animal always clopped slowly up and down Charles Street every morning, Jimmie had said, and Mike and David both knew that was true because they had seen the animal time and again. They had all been caught behind the horse, buggy, and driver when the street was congested with conveyances.

Jimmie had "borrowed" the horse from Mr. Oakes's stable, and he, Mike, and David had taken the mare out for a ride. Mike had enjoyed it, too. She and David had been walking alongside Jimmie when the old mare slipped into a trot, then galloped away, her awkward legs tangling along and Jimmie on her back, laughing as Mike had never heard him laugh.

Mike and David had ridden the mare after that, then returned him to Mr. Oakes's stable, where a constable was browsing, occasionally tapping his walking stick on the ground.

The austere-looking man had escorted each of them home, one at a time, taking Mike first, and Mother had forbidden her to leave her room for the rest of the day. Mike had had no meal until Papa had come home that evening, learned what had happened, and had come up to visit her, bringing a tray of food to share between the two of them. He had not been happy, and he had told her so. Mike had vowed never to do such a thing again, but she certainly hadn't told that the mischief had been Jimmie's idea. She wouldn't tell such a thing. Jimmie and David were her true friends and she wouldn't betray them for the world. So she had told Papa that the idea had been hers.

Sitting up in her room all day, alone, had been enough punishment, he'd said, and then he had made her promise never to do such a thing again. Mike, David, and Jimmie had had no big adventures since, and that had been nearly four weeks ago, if she had the days and weeks straight in her head, and she thought she did.

The old Lynde Street house . . . Well, it was just sitting there as it had been sitting for a long time, for as long as Mike could remember, creaking and rattling anytime a breeze happened by and sometimes when there was no air to stir it. Its paint was cracked and peeling, and many of its shutters hung by one or two hinges. The house hadn't always been in such a state, Mike felt certain. She, Jimmie, and David sometimes walked by it and talked about it. People had surely lived there once upon a time ago—once upon a *long* time ago, Mike thought now, as the boat rocked gently beneath her. But then, they might still live there, in a different sort of form.

"What are we going to do at the Lynde Street house?" David asked skeptically. He often prevented Jimmie from doing really outrageous things, like the time Jimmie had talked about nailing down the shutters on the Jamisons' house while that family was away, then watching the servants try to open them when the family returned. David wouldn't stand for vandalism, and he had told Jimmie that outright. Jimmie had pouted a little, telling David he didn't think a few nails in each shutter would be considered vandalism. But David still would not tolerate talk of doing such a thing, and he had told Jimmie that if those shutters happened to become nailed shut, he meant to go straight to the Jamisons about who he thought had done the nailing.

"Watch and listen for spirits," Jimmie said, pulling the worm off his hook and tossing it out into the water.

Mike had never seen or heard a spirit, but she had certainly heard enough talk about them. Jimmie told stories about the things he saw from time to time. David always looked at him funny, as though he might not believe him, but Jimmie's stories never failed to make Mike tighten all over. She was frightened now, scared that they might go into that old house and actually find a spirit. Scared that it might not be one that preferred to leave people alone. She wouldn't let Jimmie or David know she was frightened. Instead, she began pulling her line in, too.

"All right," David said after a few minutes of thought during which he sat and watched his line. "But no taking anything," he said, glancing at Jimmie. "And no *breaking* anything. Someone must still own the house, or it would have been torn down by now."

"Will the spirits come out in the daytime?" Mike asked.

Jimmie went still, and looked at her. "She's right. They might not."

"We'll find out," David said.

"I'd rather wait until dark so we can be sure."

"We can't go after dark," David argued.

Jimmie squinted one eye. "Who says?"

"I do. Mike will be at home in bed. I'll be at home in bed. And you—"

"Will be at the house," Jimmie said saucily, "even if I have to go alone."

That worried Mike. She watched him, trying to see if he was serious. One never knew with Jimmie. He elected to rebait his line and toss it out again, and he sat there, just watching the water and just waiting. He had his mind set to visit the old Lynde Street house at some point. He had originally planned to do that this afternoon. Now his mind was set on visiting after dark.

"Don't go alone, Jimmie," Mike said. "I'll go with you."

"You will?" Jimmie asked, looking delighted. Light sparkled in his eyes suddenly. "Did you hear that, David? She's going with me."

David didn't like that. His hands tightened on his fishing pole. "Not alone."

"No," Jimmie said, "with me."

"Not alone with you."

"We mustn't let him go into the Lynde Street house by himself, David," Mike objected. "I'm going with him. You go, too."

"How do you think you'll be going?" he snapped at her, something he rarely did.

She sat back a little, her voice softer now. "I don't know yet. I'll wait till everyone's asleep and I'll leave through the kitchen door."

"I promised Dr. Quinn I would never let anything happen to you, either on the way to the medical school or at any other time."

"Nothing'll happen to me," she promised. Then she tilted her chin. "I'm going, David. Go with us?"

From an early age, David had had a difficult time resisting any sort of plea from Mike. At first he had adored her cuteness and her spirit, things that had been evident early in the infant he had watched grow into a toddler. Now her intelligence and her determination always warmed him (though they sometimes irritated him, too!), and his attachment to Dr. Quinn and to Mike herself had made him protective of her. He liked Jimmie. Jimmie was his best friend. But Jimmie had a wild spirit that often caused him trouble, that could cause all of them trouble, and David did not intend to let Jimmie's reckless ways cause Mike trouble.

"I'll go," David told her, only because he knew she was determined and because he wouldn't stand by and let Jimmie take her alone into that old house.

The trio did manage to salvage a few fish out of the quiet afternoon. David walked Mike home, as he always did, while Jimmie shuffled on up Mount Vernon Street to Charles Street.

Their plans were set then. At midnight, Mike would wait for David and Jimmie outside the kitchen door of her family's house. If she crept down the stairs quietly enough, not a difficult thing to do, no family member would hear her, and if she opened the kitchen door slowly, it wouldn't creak as it sometimes did. If she didn't appear at the door within ten minutes of their arrival, Jimmie and David would leave, assuming that something had prevented her from coming downstairs. "Don't fall asleep," Jimmie had told her before shuffling off. Mike had scowled at him. She would not fall asleep. She wasn't a baby.

She took her one fish to Mrs. Pitman, the cook, who

beamed at her, commented on the size of it, thanked her kindly, then commenced cleaning it. Mike went off upstairs to wash, knowing that if she encountered Mother in the hall, the woman would give her a disapproving look.

Later, after the family meal and after an evening of music and guests and gaiety, Mike slipped her night rail on over a rather plain gray dress, which was usually reserved for schooltime. She secured the night rail's ribbons beneath her chin, hoping to hide the dress well enough, then she climbed into bed and pulled the counterpane up tight. She and Maureen slept together—Mother had long ago stopped insisting that Marjorie share the bed with them because even with Marjorie now being seventeen, Mike and Marjorie fought and argued well into the night whenever they shared the same bed. Claudette had been married nearly a year now, and she lived with her husband in a house on Garden Street.

Marjorie's small bedstead stood directly across from Mike and Maureen's larger one, and from the look and sound of things on that side of the room when Mike heard the downstairs clock strike midnight, Marjorie was asleep. She always snored lightly, and Mike heard her snoring now, softly and evenly. She didn't have to worry about Maureen; even if Maureen woke when she climbed out of bed, she would say nothing to their parents since she remained steadfast in her loyalty to her sister. Marjorie was a different matter, however. She had always disliked Mike, Mike had come to dislike her, and Marjorie would tattle on Mike for anything. She would relish having something as huge to tattle about as Mike sneaking from the house in the middle of the night. Marjorie would tattle with delight dancing on her face, relishing the moments ahead when Mike would surely be punished.

Sneaking out of the room and downstairs was accomplished easily. The kitchen door creaked a little as Mike pulled it open. She froze in place, listening, moonlight shining through the sliver between the door and the frame. Then she closed her eyes and listened even harder for the sound of other portals being opened in the house, for the noise of footsteps on the staircase that wound upward just beyond the entryway. Her breath lodged in her throat.

Finally, when she heard nothing but the hammering of her heart, she pulled the door open enough to slip between it and the frame, and there was David, waiting just as he'd promised he would, and Jimmie crouched near a row of bushes.

David wore dark clothing, his head was dipped slightly, and his hair was so dark he might have blended with the night if not for the white of his eyes. Mike ran to him and slipped her hand in his. His was warm, as always, familiar and comforting, and he closed his fingers around her hand as they set off, traveling beyond the bushes and finally slipping off between the row houses, trying to be as inconspicuous as possible.

The Lynde Street house was large and dark and foreboding with its shutters creaking and snapping in the light breeze. The two turrets on the eastern side looked especially sinister, their peaks stabbing upward, the moonlight accentuating them, making them appear a dull gray, although Mike knew better. She knew the dirty white paint was cracked and peeled and that the turrets stood out more now than during any other time she had looked at the house. Maybe the moonlight caused that. She wasn't sure.

"Perhaps that's where they're living," Jimmie said over her shoulder, his voice a thick whisper.

Mike jumped a little, and David gave Jimmie a shove and a fierce look. "Stop. She's spooked enough as it is."

"I'm not spooked," she said, but her voice sounded tiny and shaky to her. She hoped David and Jimmie didn't notice the shakiness. She felt it more than anything, and not just in her voice. Inside, where all her parts seemed to bump around with fright suddenly. She didn't want to go into that house. She really didn't. But she wouldn't turn back now, face Jimmie's ridicule, and have David defend her to him.

David studied her, and Mike grew uncomfortable under his scrutiny.

66

A weathered wrought-iron fence surrounded the house, and when David unlatched the gate and pushed it open, it screeched sharply. Mike felt as she had when she had been trying to sneak out of the house to come here and the kitchen door had creaked; tense inside that someone might hear the screeching gate, see them, and report them to a constable. Other houses stood not far away, and she expected to hear shouts and footsteps coming this way. David waited, too, glancing at Jimmie, who shot him a dry grin.

Finally David went on and Mike followed, with Jimmie behind her. They stepped their way along the path that led up to the house. Tangled vines and overgrown bushes almost hid the walkway from view. The moon was especially bright tonight, thank goodness, because they had no other light. The street lamps had already been extinguished, even around the State House, which was located just up the street.

"What if it's locked?" Mike asked suddenly, referring to the house.

"We'll get in through a window," Jimmie replied, and Mike knew he shrugged. Jimmie always shrugged when faced with a difficulty.

The front door wasn't locked, but when Jimmie twisted the knob and pushed the portal open, Mike had to wonder if it would crumble. The wood smelled of earthy decay, of dampness and mold. Giving another satisfied grin, Jimmie stood aside the door, gave a graceful bow, and with a flourish of his arm, bid them to enter the residence.

David stepped inside the house first, then softly warned Jimmie and Mike about the hole in the threshold. Good of him to notice, Mike thought, because she and Jimmie might not have. One of them might have trapped a leg in it and been injured. A sour smell drifted up from the hole, the odor of rot.

Instinctively, Mike covered her mouth and nose with her hand, and stepped over the gaping wound. Jimmie followed, and before shutting the door, he produced several tapers from his pocket and soon had them both lit, casting their surroundings, and them, in a soft yellow-orange glow. He handed a taper to Mike. She smiled at him, at the thought that he was always prepared for adventure.

Once upon a time the Lynde Street house had been grand, Mike could tell. A wide hallway cut through the center of the residence, and a wide staircase with an elaborately carved railing curved once, then disappeared in its ascent. Mike stood with David beneath the remains of a huge chandelier that hung in the entryway, and she felt her mouth gather to issue a breathless "Ooh." David felt the same reaction—she saw it in his eyes—but he said nothing. Jimmie entered a room to their left, holding the taper at an angle so it wouldn't drip hot wax on his hand.

"We stay together," David said, and his words were an order, not a statement, a command Jimmie heeded. He waited for David and Mike just inside the door.

A parlor was still partially furnished with the remains of dusty, broken old chairs. An empty whatnot sat in a far corner. Old draperies, pulled open, drooped from the tops of several windows. Ash still gathered in the fireplace, and a few pieces of dusty wood still sat in an iron stand on the right side of the hearth. The marble mantelpiece, with its carvings of animal faces and scrolling at the ends, made Mike stand and stare. It had been magnificent years ago. It surely still could be, that was, if it and the room around it were cleaned and furnished properly. Mother would stare at it even longer, Mike thought, for she appreciated works of art.

Jimmie tried a chair that sat near the hearth, crossing his legs and pretending to smoke a cheroot. He feigned a dignified look, tilting his head and slitting his eyes at Mike, then telling "his man," David, to bring his slippers and stoke the fire. Mike laughed at him. David made a sound in the back of his throat, half laughter and half disbelief. One never knew what Jimmie might do next.

The other downstairs rooms were much the same as the parlor. Dark, a little frightening, shadows dancing here and there in the dim light of the two tapers.

"The old place has no life left in it," Jimmie complained. They had just entered what had been a study or a library, its walls of shelves bare and lonely now except for a few cracked and yellowed books. A carpet still partially covered the floor in this room. Imported. Turkish or Persian. Mike smiled to herself. And Mother thought her so "unrefined." She never worried about Mike's feelings when she talked about her so, and Mike, for the most part, had given up on pleasing the woman. She pleased herself, her father, David, Rebecca. To please Mother would have meant being someone else, someone totally unlike herself.

David went to inspect one of the books while Mike crossed the room and approached an old painting of a cathedral that hung on a far wall. "No, not as in people or ghosts, as you're wishing, but it is a grand old place," David murmured, aiming his remark at Jimmie.

"One could smoke a fine pipe in this room and surely be comfortable in the right chair," Jimmie said, folding his arms and leaning one shoulder against the fireplace. As usual, nothing took the humor from him.

"Beautiful," Mike said, breathing the words as she stared up at the painting.

The ceiling creaked suddenly, as if someone walked on the old flooring in a room directly above their heads. Mike's head shot up and her heart missed a beat. David stared at the ceiling, too, his eyes narrowed. Jimmie . . . well, Jimmie never even unfolded his arms. He stood in the same position, a grin now dancing across his face.

"It has life, after all," he said, and although his position hadn't changed, his voice had lowered.

"What was that sound?" Mike asked, of no one in particular.

"Old houses make sounds," David said, shrugging off the noise, going back to studying the book in his hands.

"Or *things* in old houses make noise," Jimmie amended.

"Stop now, before you frighten Mike," David ordered, shooting him a glare.

"I'm not frightened," Mike said. But that was a lie. Her

heart beat so fast now she wondered if it would beat right out of her chest.

"Let's go upstairs and see what's there," Jimmie suggested.

David read on, turning a page. "We'll go up in a minute."

Something scraped across the floor of the room above their heads, the screeching of chair legs across wood. Mike's mouth went dry. There *was* something up there. Something or someone.

Jimmie's grin widened. "Let's go up."

David had frozen in place. Now he glanced up, eyeing the ceiling. "No, I don't think so. I think we'll be leaving now."

He was scared, and his fear scared Mike. She had seen David nervous, apprehensive, but never *scared.* If he wanted to leave, she wanted to leave.

Jimmie scowled at both of them, and Mike swore he read her thoughts. Or perhaps he just knew her or found her predictable, knew that she followed David's lead. "Those noises are what we came for," Jimmie grumbled. "Now you're planning to turn tail and run before we've even discovered what's causing them?"

"I'm thinking of Mike," David said, glaring right back at Jimmie. Mike wished he wouldn't think about her so much, that he wouldn't protect her so often. It embarrassed her a little—and it made Jimmie think she was weak, that the smallest thing frightened her.

Someone—or something—groaned in the room above them. Another screech of chair legs across the floor. A weak cry for help. *"Help me, please!"*

"It's a spook," Jimmie said, straightening, "and I'm going to have a look at it."

"Maybe not," David remarked, looking curious and somewhat frightened all at once. "What ghost asks for help?"

Jimmie shrugged and started for the door. "Don't know. I've never met a spook. But I aim to tonight."

"Perhaps someone sneaked in, like us, and really is in need of help," Mike suggested, hoping that explained the noises.

David nodded, and they both followed Jimmie to the doorway just as the throaty voice issued another plea for help. Mike pulled her woolen shawl tightly around her shoulders and hurried off after David.

Jimmie was already halfway up the staircase by the time Mike took the first step. David had stopped to wait for her, and he took her hand and led her up, always her protector, always her companion and friend. They followed the curve of the stairs, hearing several low groans on the way up, and Mike heard David laugh under his breath when they spotted Jimmie stopped on the upstairs landing, waiting for them. For a few seconds, Mike saw the flicker of apprehension in Jimmie's eyes and knew that was why David had laughed—because Jimmie had been so brave and so excited about meeting the "spook," that is, until he reached the top of the stairs, drew closer, and heard the groans.

"Come on," David urged as he and Mike stepped past Jimmie.

A short distance down the hallway, they located the room that sat directly above what had been the study. And there, sprawled on the floor on the far side of the room lay a man in tattered clothing. A rickety chair sat nearby, and Mike wondered if the obviously ill man had been trying to pull himself up to it; that would explain the scraping of the chair legs across the floor. The room was large, but even from the doorway, Mike heard the rattle of his breath and knew his lungs were diseased.

"Well, he almost looks like a spook," Jimmie said over Mike's shoulder. She had half the notion to repeat to him Marjorie's favorite scoldings of her, to tell him he was being distasteful, inappropriate. Without medical attention, the man might very well become a spirit soon, and there was nothing funny about that. Jimmie should not jest about the fact.

"Very ill," David murmured under his breath, and he strode quickly over to the man and bent beside him.

The stranger's eyes were dull, his skin and mouth parched. David parted the remains of the man's shirt, turned his head, and put his ear to the man's chest to listen to the heart and lungs. Mike knew he had had many a medical conversation with her father and that he knew what he was doing. A moment later he lifted his head and gave her a doubtful look, one that said he did not believe the man would live. Mike moved closer, saw that the man's feet were shackled, and she fought a gasp.

Jimmie saw the shackle at the same time and said, "He escaped from the gaol," but Mike immediately knew that the shackle would make no difference in the care David gave the man. In David, she always sensed her father's compassion, his desire to help anyone or anything in distress. David often talked about the poor conditions in which the immigrants were forced to live, that they never had enough to eat and that he himself had often sneaked food from his own home and taken it to them. And it wasn't just the immigrants; it was all the poor of Boston, those who roamed the wharf areas and the dilapidated South End. He worried over the many who lived in filth with disease running rampant around them. Many times now, he had given to the poor the fish that he and Mike had caught during their afternoon excursions with Jimmie. Her father frequently said that medical care should be denied no one, and Mike knew that because he believed that, and was a fine example himself, frequently tending the indigent, no matter their living conditions, religious beliefs, or race, David also believed it.

The man was grasping David's arm and straining to say something more. David bent close to listen, then said, "We'll help you. Lie back now and rest." He glanced at Mike and Jimmie. "He needs water."

"There's an old well out back," Jimmie volunteered. "It could be dry."

"We have to find out. Mike, stay with him," David said, meaning she should stay with the ill man. "I'll go down to the well. Jimmie, go fetch Dr. Quinn."

Mike did not hesitate. She went to sit beside the rasping man. Jimmie balked, however, at fetching her father. "That will sure seal our fate," he said caustically.

"It can't be helped," David said. "It's more important that we help this man."

Jimmie hesitated, shaking his head. Then he turned and shuffled off, heading for the doorway.

"If you don't intend to move faster, I'll fetch the doctor myself," David told him.

"I'm going, I'm going," Jimmie muttered, and he wasn't happy at all about the fact. He would go, and he would fetch Dr. Quinn, and then when the whole thing was over, the three of them might end up shackled themselves—and not together—to his way of thinking. This was madness. Their exploration of the old Lynde Street House wasn't going as he'd planned in his mind.

Mike was scared of being discovered, too, but more frightened that the man might die if they didn't help him, or if they didn't fetch her father to help him. She didn't doubt that she would be punished in some way for sneaking out of the house, but that was truly the least of her concerns right now. She had never seen a person die, and she had no wish to see one die.

Fear leaped in the man's dull, glassy gray eyes, in his wild look. He tried to mouth words to her as David left the room and she heard his boots on the stairs as he thundered down in search of water. She didn't know who the man was, how he had come to be here, how long he had been here, and if he had been ill before he came. In truth, the answers to those questions mattered little to her—he was ill and in need of medical attention, and she, like David, meant to see that he was given it. But the questions swam in her head because she was curious by nature. She placed a soothing hand on the man's brow and brushed back his thin brown hair. She bent close and told him to hush, that he needn't expend his strength trying to talk when he needed it to heal.

"I won't heal," he managed, and she thought he had spent an awful amount of his strength summoning enough of a voice to cry for help when he heard them exploring downstairs.

"Yes, you will," she said, because she truly believed that

if he became her father's patient, he would recover, not die. She soothed him more, now kneeling beside him, and she felt his feverish brow heat her hand.

"No, I won't, I won't," he said. "The birds are coming. The walls . . . the walls are closing." She realized the fever was beginning to make him say strange things, make him "delirious," as Papa often said patients became when they grew feverish. Mike continued to stroke the man's brow, to reassure him, to urge him to preserve his strength.

David found her sitting just so when he returned from his search for water. He carried a wooden bucket by its rusted handle and he hurried over and knelt beside the man. "No dipper. I'll dip water in my hands," he told her. "Lift his head so he can drink."

Mike did as instructed, and at her urging the man sipped the water. David dipped more, and the man drank more, then his head rolled back and he rested. At first, Mike wondered if he had died, but the sound of his irregular, raspy breathing reassured her, although it was little comfort in whether or not he would recover.

When Dr. Quinn arrived a short time later he hesitated only a moment in the doorway. Mike and David were urging the man to drink again when Mike glanced up and there stood her father, watching them. She expected to see the flash of anger in his eyes, anger at her that she had sneaked from their home in the middle of the night. And although she caught a glimmer of concern and a small light of anger, mostly his eyes sparkled with pride.

"He's sick, Papa," she said, "very sick."

"I know, Mike," he responded, and he approached, Jimmie trailing him. He placed his medical bag on the floor near the ill man, opened it, and began pulling out the pieces of his stethoscope and fitting them together.

"I'm sorry, Dr. Quinn," David said, and Mike realized that he was apologizing because he was the oldest of the three, but mostly because her father always entrusted him, since the two of them had started venturing to the medical school, with watching over her. David feared losing her father's trust and respect because he hadn't discouraged their midnight exploration of the Lynde Street house.

"We'll discuss the matter another time," Mike's father said, and his voice was stern enough that she knew she, all three of them really, had caused him much worry, and still caused him much worry. She didn't know if Jimmy had told him how they had come to be here. She didn't even know if her father had asked, he always became so quiet and concentrated when summoned to the bedside of an ill person. But she knew he would ask the necessary questions later and accept nothing less than the truth. For all his kindness and his warm nature, her papa could be quite stern when a serious situation presented itself. For now, however, he concerned himself with the ill man.

"Any vomiting?" he asked. "Skin lesions? Loss of blood or other fluids through any orifice?"

"Not while we've observed him," David said, looking to Mike for agreement.

She nodded, then said, "That's right. But he became delirious while David was searching for water." Her father nodded at her several times, and she grew more nervous, if possible, because she sensed that he watched her closely. "Talking . . . about odd things. Things that made no sense," she stammered, and he nodded again, then put the bell of his stethoscope to the patient's chest and bent to listen.

He listened intently for several long moments, moving the bell from place to place. Then he lifted his head and exhaled heavily. "Pneumonia," he announced finally. "His lungs are heavy with fluid."

"Will he live?" David blurted, the very question that had been on the tip of Mike's tongue.

"It's unlikely," Dr. Quinn said, and Mike flinched.

She wanted the man to live. Perhaps because she, David, and Jimmie had discovered him. Perhaps because she and David had already nursed him some. If he did live, he would most likely be returned to the gaol when he recovered, and be guarded by some formidable constable while he recovered, and whatever length of time his recovery took would not be pleasant, surely, for those reasons. But she badly wanted him to live. Mike stared down at the man, and she fought tears.

"Now and then, you will lose a patient, my dear Michaela," her father said gently. "You must always be brave, but never indifferent."

She glanced up, suddenly wanting to throw herself into his arms. But there was always space between them whenever he took on the role of teacher and she took on the role of student. She almost hated the distance at times, and only her sense that it was a necessary thing, that it was a quiet respect, made her tolerate it.

"We must move him," Dr. Quinn said, dismantling his stethoscope. "He cannot stay here. We'll take him to Massachusetts General. But there are a few other important matters to tend first."

Mike wondered if he meant having a discussion with the three of them about their sneaking out of their homes in the middle of the night and then sneaking into this house. But he didn't mention the matter. Instead, he instructed Jimmie and David to stay right there with their patient while he took her and went after a blacksmith. Mike wondered why he needed a blacksmith, then she saw him eyeing the shackle and she knew suddenly. He meant to have it removed before he took the man to the hospital.

"Many people show no mercy to, or have no compassion for, an accused criminal," he explained. "Ill or not, he'll be taken away immediately and put back into deplorable conditions if that chain is sighted attached to him and he's reported to the authorities."

"Not to mention that he surely can't walk with that thing on," Jimmie piped in, shuffling around a little, as if he had a chain and shackles attached to *his* ankles. "How'd he get all the way upstairs, anyway? Say, when the blacksmith knocks them off, can I have them, Dr. Quinn? You know, just to play with."

Mike's father put away the last pieces of the stethoscope,

then snapped his bag shut and stood. "I believe you've done enough playing for one day, Jimmie Becker," he said with a severe look at the clowning boy, "during a poor hour and in a place where none of you should have ventured."

That said, he swept his woolen cape around him, told Mike to come along, and he left the room. She went without question, with slow steps at first, giving Jimmie a reprimanding look just before she walked through the doorway.

6

David and Jimmie were somehow returned to their respective homes without incident before Mike and her father delivered the patient to Massachusetts General. Michaela expected that they would all be punished, but little happened. In the days immediately following their Lynde Street house exploration and discovery, she anticipated hearing that David and Jimmie had been severely punished, and she expected some severe punishment herself. She shouldn't have sneaked out, and she was prepared to accept whatever discipline her parents brought down on her.

During those difficult days, the only thing she heard further about the incidents of that night, however, were from David and Jimmie themselves, who told her that Dr. Quinn had told them to sneak back into their homes as quietly as they had sneaked out. Jimmie thought that was wonderful, but baffling. He had surely thought the three of them wouldn't be allowed to leave their homes for a good year, or so he told David and Mike as they sat fishing again one afternoon the following week.

"Maybe Dr. Quinn suspected the same thing," David thought aloud.

"He hasn't said anything to me," Michaela said.

"How's Mr. Kearney?" Jimmie asked, referring to the ill man they had discovered in the Lynde Street house.

David had a bite on his line. He began pulling the line in slowly. "Improving. But Dr. Quinn says he's still very ill, that he could still die."

"He won't," Mike said.

While she usually never doubted her papa, this time she did. How could Mr. Kearney, who was now sitting up in bed, sometimes walking the hospital halls, and whose color and breathing were so much better, possibly be in danger of dying? She had watched the blacksmith work at removing his chain and shackles that night. She had covered her ears because the pounding of the anvil on the chains had been almost deafening, and she had been amazed that the resting Mr. Kearney was so ill he had not even flinched at the noise. There was such a difference in him, such an improvement, between that night and now, that he couldn't possibly be in danger of dying still.

That night Michaela had believed he might. Now she didn't, and she had passed the last several days believing in her heart that he wouldn't. She had taken books to the hospital the last two afternoons and read to him, something he had enjoyed immensely, and she had held conversations with him and found him to be a very pleasant man. She had seen him earlier today and he looked very well indeed, and now she believed that the reading and her conversations with him were helping him to recover.

"Mike, he still could," David said, as if warning her.

"He won't," she said, and she pulled her line in with a jerk, unhooked the worm she had baited some time ago, and tossed it out into the glimmering waters of the Charles River. "I'm finished for the day," she announced. "I haven't had even a bite, and I'm hungry."

"Here's one for you," David said, hauling in the largest fish Mike had ever seen. "All for you," he announced, and then the fish began flopping around on the riverbank, landing on Mike's lap for a time and flopping around there while she attempted to grab him and while Jimmie cackled.

She hadn't changed clothes today—she had run straight for the river, ready to fish—and she would surely have to change clothes straightaway when she reached her home. If Mother smelled her the woman would not be happy.

She finally wrestled the fish down and handed him to David, who sat laughing, too. She laughed slightly herself, imagining her expression while that fish flopped around on her lap.

"Take him to a family at the wharf," she told David, and he agreed, without much argument, to do that.

"Wait. I'll walk you home," he said, but Michaela, while she almost always enjoyed his companionship, lately wanted to be independent. With David, that was impossible, since he was her self-appointed guardian.

"Not necessary," she told him.

"Mike, I promised your father."

But she dashed off before he could sling the fish over his shoulder and get to his feet, and she knew he couldn't catch her while running with a large fish slung over his shoulder anyway, much less whenever she hiked her skirts up past her knees and ran as fast as she could.

She heard him call after her, and she ran even faster, laughing again when she heard Jimmie laugh. She ran past the numerous livery stables between the backs of Beacon, River, Mount Vernon streets and the river; past the boarding and baiting stables that also let out hacks and where the gentlemen who drove in from Charlestown or other areas behind fast trotters left their rigs while they went off on the business of their day. The horses lent the air a rich equine scent of leather and manure and perspiration. Flies swarmed the area, buzzing around Mike's head as she raced on.

She finally reached Massachusetts General, and there she read to Mr. Kearney again and walked with him down the hall. She even sat outside with him in chairs on an embankment that overlooked the river, and there she read more to him. He still had a mighty bad cough at times, a cough that left him gray and gasping for air, and she grew apprehensive whenever she spotted blood in his handkerchief.

He had several more bad spells while they sat together, and finally she raced off inside to fetch him another clean handkerchief. Whenever she visited, the doctors and nurses always smiled at her and called her cute and told her she would make a fine nurse one day. She always smiled back and thought to herself that she might not become a nurse, that she just might become a physician like her father.

Once back outside, she handed Mr. Kearney his handkerchief and asked if she could bring him a glass of water. He managed a smile through the last of his coughing as he pressed the handkerchief to one side of his mouth. "My little nurse . . . no. You know, Michaela . . ." More coughing, then his lungs seemed to settle a little, and he sat back in the chair and fought to catch his breath. "You know . . . you never asked . . . you never asked what I did . . . why I was there."

She was baffled. What he did? Why he was there? She wondered what he meant.

"Why, the contraption," he said, waving down toward his ankles.

Oh. Now she understood. The explanation was simple: "While you were very sick, Mr. Kearney, the important thing was that I help nurse you. Now that I've come to know you, I don't believe you could have done anything wrong. At least nothing that should have made them put those awful things on you."

He stared at her for a long moment. Then his face broke into a smile. He shook his head. "You're young, Michaela. Trusting. Wise for your age. Don't trust everyone as much."

"I'm like my father," she said, taking pride in the fact. "Trusting until I'm given reason not to trust."

"Your father is a good man."

She nodded, not needing to be told that. She knew. She tipped forward in her chair. *"You* never ask what *I* did, why *I* was there."

He laughed. "And I shan't. Not minding your parents, that is for certain."

She laughed with him. Seconds later, she sobered. "Where

will you go when you leave here, Mr. Kearney? What will you do? Have you family in the city?"

"Perished," he said, and he didn't blink an eye. "When I leave . . . I doubt I'll leave."

She studied him. "But you must leave one day. Patients don't remain here forever. They recover and then they leave."

"Oh, I'll leave, Michaela. It was wrong of me to say that. But I won't leave a healthy man. Read to me now. You've a gift, you know, the gift of healing a person inside. Such a thing surely cannot be taught. You've made me smile and laugh again, Michaela Quinn, and for that, I thank you."

He wouldn't leave a healthy man. She wondered what he meant by that. She didn't want to wonder. She sensed that his answer would not be what she wanted to hear. So she didn't question him. She went back to reading.

She walked to the hospital the next afternoon, meaning to read to him again. The nurses stared at her more than usual. The doctors smiled at her but they looked rather sad. Mike felt a sense of growing apprehension as she approached the ward in which Mr. Kearney occupied a bed.

She turned the corner and began walking through the two rows of beds. Her footsteps never slowed, even when she saw that the bed he had occupied was now empty and made up neatly in anticipation of the next patient. She didn't need to ask the nurses or the doctors about him; she now knew what he had meant. Mr. Kearney had somehow known that he wouldn't leave Massachusetts General alive. She didn't know how he had known, but he had known.

"It was only a short time ago, Miss Quinn," said one of the nurses behind Mike. "He simply fell asleep and never woke. He passed quietly."

Michaela touched the bed and blinked back tears. She couldn't breathe. She could scarcely even think suddenly. She had felt certain he would live. But he had known.

You must always be brave, but never indifferent.

Her father's words rang in her ears, making her square her shoulders, swallow hard, and inhale a deep breath. *Always brave . . .*

"Thank you," she said to the nurse.

Never indifferent . . .

She slowly and calmly left the ward and the hospital, and she fought tears the entire way home.

That night, she lay awake thinking about Mr. Kearney, the strangeness of how she, David, and Jimmie had found him, how she and David had made the quick decision to alert her father, how Mr. Kearney had seemed to be recovering so well, but how he had known about his upcoming death. She knew about death—she had known many people who had died during epidemics, many children, many adults, many friends of her family—but she had never had a hand in nursing someone who then went on to die. Something about that fact tore at her heart. She wondered if she might have done something different for him, if Mr. Kearney had received enough rest, if perhaps he had left his bed too soon. . . .

Her parents were arguing. She could hear them, the low, even sound of her father's calm voice, the higher sound of her mother's stern voice. They had not argued in some time, at least not that Mike knew, and she turned over in bed, not wanting to hear them argue now. The quarrel was about her; the quarrel was always about her.

A lengthy silence ensued, seeming longer than Mike knew it was. She didn't want to hear this, but their voices carried, and she knew they were arguing about the night she, David, and Jimmie had gone to the Lynde Street house.

"Joseph, you must draw the line somewhere. If Michaela is allowed to roam so at twelve or thirteen she'll be ruined. People will talk, and the talk will not be merciful. No decent man will ever look her way."

"She was with me."

"I don't believe that. I believe you are protecting her. And lately . . . why, lately she's been visiting some stranger at the hospital!"

"Not a stranger, Elizabeth, the patient we tended that night."

"A virtual stranger."

"I do not want her wandering anymore. I do not want her

83

fishing with those boys or going to the hospital to see that man. It's unseemly, Joseph."

"He expired this morning. She won't be calling at the hospital to see him anymore."

"Good."

Another silence followed. Michaela almost hated her mother during those moments. How insensitive! How cruel! A total lack of regard for human life if that life interfered with her plans or designs.

"You didn't go with Papa that night. He's lying for you," Marjorie said, her voice soft but fierce. Mike opened her eyes and saw Marjorie standing not far from her bed. Marjorie approached, and Michaela didn't move as her sister sat on the edge of the bed near her knees.

"I saw you. I heard you rise and leave the room. I heard you on the stairs, and then I watched out the window and saw you run across the paths with David and Jimmie. *And* I told Mama what I'd seen.

"He's lying for you," Marjorie said, glaring at Mike. Hate lit her eyes, absolute loathing that their father would do such a thing for Michaela. Neither had ever known him to lie for her, to tell a lie at all, and both were shocked. The lie had also deepened Marjorie's resentment of her, Mike could tell.

So Marjorie had seen her sneak away and had told their mother.

Mike made as if she were stretching, and with a quick snap of her knees, she shoved Marjorie off the bed. Marjorie landed on her bottom on the floor, and she came up seething, as Michaela knew she would.

"You! You'll not get away with anything else. I'll make certain of that! Mother has had enough of your roamings and your ill nature, and no matter what Father says, you'll not get away with anything else!"

Mike merely closed her eyes again. It was a wonder they hadn't disturbed Maureen, who hadn't moved a muscle during the exchange. But then, Maureen was hard to wake. She could often be found sleepwalking somewhere in the house, and it always took a good five minutes to rouse her from that, even longer from a dead sleep.

Michaela almost laughed aloud when she thought of Marjorie rubbing her backside on her way back to her bed. It surely smarted, and that did Mike's heart good. Their parents had stopped arguing. Usually, during or after such heated exchanges, Papa rose and went downstairs to his study for a time.

Mike still couldn't sleep. She finally left the room and went to sit with her father among his books and papers. They talked about Mr. Kearney, and how there was almost always a brief period in which the patient suffering from pneumonia seemed to be recovering. A relapse was almost always fatal, as in Mr. Kearney's case. He was proud of her, that she and David had had the good sense to send for him that night regardless of the consequences, and that she had helped nurse Mr. Kearney and had offered him her enjoyable company during his last days.

Michaela fell asleep on her father's lap, listening to him read about the nature of appendicitis.

"Mother said you were not to go fishing with those boys anymore. *Anymore,*" Marjorie stressed to Michaela several days later. Mike had seated herself on the kitchen floor of the house and was lacing up an old pair of boots.

True. Mama had said that. But Papa hadn't.

"I never said I was going fishing," Mike said, still lacing.

Marjorie clicked her tongue once and plopped her hands on her hips. "Where else would you be going in those old boots?"

"To the Common."

"To the Common." Marjorie tossed her head of chestnut ringlets and clicked her tongue again. At a huge oak table, -the cook, Mrs. Pitman, eyed them as she chopped vegetables. Nearby, trapped beneath an overturned wooden crate, a live chicken clucked and scratched the darkened bricks of the spacious hearth, oblivious to the fact that in a short time she would be simmering along with the vegetables, stewing among carrots, onions, and potatoes.

"The Common is certainly no place for a girl to wander alone," Marjorie remarked, sounding so much like their mother that Michaela almost cringed. Marjorie rarely entered the kitchen, feeling that to do so was beneath her. Only servants entered the kitchen. But she had been Mike's shadow since Mike had booted her off the bed the other night, and now here she was, glancing around as if she were in a foreign city, shifting her weight every few minutes, not looking altogether comfortable.

Mike preferred silence whenever Marjorie tried to provoke her into a conflict, one she would doubtless lose since Mother always took Marjorie's side. Now was no different. She continued with her boots, calmly untangling a lace.

"Those boys will come to no good," Marjorie said. *"You* will come to no good, if you have not already. Jimmie Becker causes trouble all up and down Charles and Pinckney streets, he is so terribly spoiled. Why, just yesterday I heard that he set the Emerson's prize horses loose. No one actually saw him do it, but he was seen running up the street moments later—and who else would do such a thing? He is known for his reckless ways. And you, keeping company with him and David Lewis, another—"

"Now, Miss Marjorie, you know talk like that angers Miss Mike," Mrs. Pitman cautioned.

Of course she knew, just as she knew that even now, Mike's temper was flaring. What right did Marjorie have to talk about Jimmie so? He didn't cause trouble, he just had fun. Well, fun from her point of view. She supposed other people, namely some adults, might think of him as a troublemaker. But she liked Jimmie, and Marjorie didn't even know him well, therefore she had no right to criticize him. Besides, she was just doing it to anger her, to try and provoke a reaction from her.

Mike gripped her laces a little tighter, the muscles around her eyes twitching, her neck tensing. She had better hurry with the laces or she might do something to Marjorie that she might later be made to regret. She couldn't lose her temper. She could not. Booting her off the bed the other night had earned her an entire morning in her room alone.

Marjorie spun toward the cook. "Do not *ever* attempt to correct me again," she said, her lips thin. Mrs. Pitman said nothing in return; she turned her attention back to her chopping. Michaela despised Marjorie's superior ways, which often made family members, friends, and servants alike feel as if they were no better than dirt beneath her boots. She spoke to too many people in such a way, to her sisters, to the group of girls with whom she often had tea parties in the parlor; to the maids, the butler, the gardener, the groom. No servant escaped Marjorie's caustic tongue.

Mike jerked at the laces now, which suddenly failed to cooperate.

"As I was saying," Marjorie continued, never, ever knowing when to stop, "David Lewis is an odd one, too, spending so much of his time at that medical school cutting up . . . and you, too!" She pulled a face. "His mind should be on becoming a marvelous attorney such as his father is. As for you, Michaela . . . Well, there may be no hope, if there ever was any, for you. You will have a reputation soon, too—and I know you know what I mean—if you continue to roam the city with those boys. I know you are going fishing with them today, so you might as well tell the truth and be done with it."

Mike got to her feet, her laces still dangling. She suddenly didn't care. She only wanted to get as far away from Marjorie as possible before she did something that would surely bring severe punishment down on her. She headed toward the open kitchen door, which led outside.

But Marjorie would have none of that. Not intending to let Michaela escape that easily, she blocked the doorway, placing her open hands high up on the frame, a saucy look slitting her eyes, her head tilted at a haughty angle.

"Move," Michaela ordered, glaring. She had had enough of her bothersome sister for one day. Quite enough. Quite enough of her being her shadow lately.

Marjorie gave her a maddening smile, sugary sweet and completely sickening. "Only after you tell me where you are going."

"I'll happily tell you where you're about to go," Mike retorted.

"Oh, come now. I—"

"Move," Mike ordered again. Marjorie shook her head slowly, back and forth, the smile still fixed on her face.

Michaela gave her sister a shove that sent her sprawling backward, tumbling down the three wooden steps and into the mud that had formed after this morning's rain, a continuation of the rain that had persisted for nearly three days straight. So much water had soaked the ground that worms had emerged, crawling on top of the wet soil and on the steps.

Splattered with mud, Marjorie screeched as Mike had never heard her screech, even during the time several months ago when Michaela had put a live frog beneath her counterpane.

Mike tore off from the house, knowing she didn't dare wait for Mama to come running. She would be sent up to her room and not permitted to come down for the rest of the day. Then she could not fish with Jimmie and David. She heard Marjorie screech again, this time for someone to leave her alone, to keep their filthy hands off of her, then Michaela rounded the corner of the house and soon reached Mount Vernon Street.

She shot up the passage, going as fast as her partially unlaced boots would take her. She tore through Louisburg Square and didn't slow down until she reached Pinckney Street. The nursemaid couldn't possibly catch her—Mama had sent the woman in pursuit before—and the other servants, all liking Mike's spirit, would make a weak effort if Mother sent any one of them.

She wouldn't, however. For a time her attention, and all of her attention, would be on Marjorie, on making certain Marjorie hadn't been harmed seriously and on finding out what had happened. Marjorie would leave out the part about taunting Mike by saying distasteful things about David, Jimmie, and her. But, of course, even if she didn't, Mother would agree with the things Marjorie had said.

The punishment was harsh, as Mike knew it would be. No dresses, no dancing, no teas, no parties, no *friends* for the entire next month. She was not permitted to leave the house, in fact. Michaela wondered if her father would intervene—

no afternoons at the medical school for a month?—but he was strangely silent. They knew each other well, and she knew he did not condone her pushing Marjorie into the mud. He hadn't condoned her sneaking out of the house that night, either, but she had helped save a life, albeit a temporary thing, by doing so, which was undoubtedly why he had intervened on her behalf in that matter. But this . . . this was a lesson in self-restraint, in learning to control her temper, which often flamed at Marjorie. No matter how much and how severely Marjorie provoked her, she should never react in a violent manner. Papa's unspoken words said everything.

The same week Mike's punishment was lifted, Maureen married. Marjorie was certainly old enough—seventeen now—that Mike wished it were her marrying and going away. While her other sisters lived in the Boston area, Mike missed them and never saw them often enough, to her way of thinking. And now . . . now only she and Marjorie remained at home. She and her least favorite sister, who had not, and might never, learn to control her jealousy of Mike and her spiteful, provoking behavior.

Grandmother Quinn died late that year. She passed quietly, with all the dignity she had displayed so well during the time Michaela had known her. She had once told Mike that she was the most unruly child she had ever known. "You have your grandfather's spirit, I am afraid," the woman had commented, turning away. But Michaela had not missed the slight smile on Grandmother Quinn's wrinkled old face, and she had thought then that at times her grandmother did not mind her unruliness so much.

Most of Boston turned out for Grandmother Quinn's funeral, or so it seemed to Mike. They filled every pew in the Tremont Street Church, stood in the aisles, and spilled out the doors. At the cemetery, they hovered around other graves although their attention was on Grandmother Quinn's coffin as it was lowered into the ground. The men wore somber faces. The women dabbed handkerchiefs at their eyes beneath black veils.

For the first time, Michaela saw her mother cry, and she

was so shocked she had to resist staring. She moved over, between Rebecca and Marjorie, thinking to squeeze in somewhere and hold her mother's hand. When Marjorie shoved her, instinct told her to shove back. But this was a dark day for her family and she wouldn't be the cause of trouble. So while her sisters gathered around to comfort Mother, Michaela went to Father, slipping her little hand down into his. He felt stiff and cold, and she could tell that he fought tears, too. Mother had Rebecca, Claudette, Maureen, and Marjorie to comfort her. But Father . . . well, he always had her. Always.

7

The Tremont Street Medical School wasn't such an unreasonable distance away, a mere jaunt down Charles Street, then over to Tremont. But wherever David was headed right now was more than a jaunt. Eleven-year-old Mike followed, running much of the time to keep up, keeping close to the edge of buildings and houses. She didn't know where David was going, but he surely didn't wish for her to follow him.

They had spent the morning at the medical school this time, David having a holiday from school and Mike's teacher not meaning to appear until this afternoon. They had returned to Beacon Hill from the school a short time ago and David had left her at her family's doorstep, where he mumbled something about going home. But he wasn't going home, Michaela had decided when she'd seen him go down Mount Vernon Street and head off in the opposite direction from his family's home. He wasn't going to Jimmie's house either, she felt certain, because Jimmy lived on Charles Street, and David was headed southeast of Charles. He was going somewhere else.

Mike had taken a quick look at her front door, knowing the teacher would be arriving at any moment—if she did not already wait inside—to take her off to the stuffy third-floor room where she studied their lessons. Michaela had made a swift decision: today she did not wish to sit up in that room with the other children, being scolded because she was fidgety and because she sometimes refused to answer the questions Mrs. Crane asked of her. Today she wished to follow David instead, because she sometimes had a wandering spirit and because he had piqued her curiosity.

So she had run off after him, hoping he wasn't such a huge distance ahead already that she couldn't spot him when she turned onto Joy Street. She saw the dome on the State House, and then a small child dashed in front of her and she and the boy tumbled on the cobblestone walkway. His nursemaid collected him, dusted him off, righted his clothing, and soothed him, all the while shooting Mike severe looks. Mike took only a few seconds to blink back tears of pain herself—she had scraped her arm on the cobblestones—and then she was off again, hearing the nursemaid shout behind her that she should take care lest she hurt someone. The boy wasn't hurt, Michaela felt certain. Any suspicion that he was hurt and she would have stayed, nursed him herself, and simply asked David later where he'd gone.

She spotted David nearly two blocks ahead of her and she had to forget completely the pain in her arm and race faster than before to close the gap between them. He wouldn't like her following him, she sensed that, otherwise he wouldn't have left her on the front steps. He hadn't left her there just so she would be home in time for her lessons; she had missed part of her lessons before because she and David had stayed for hours at the medical school. Mother wasn't always happy with her about that, but then Mama was rarely happy with her about anything.

Mike closed in on David as they neared Cranbridge Street, and thank goodness she did, too, because he then began making numerous twists and turns, going up one street and down another. The buildings and houses, some of stone, some of brick, some of wood, became older, worn, ramshackle, and suddenly Mike feared that if she lost him, she might never find her way home again. Her legs ached from walking so far, and she didn't know how much time had passed. But she suspected it was a good amount and that she would receive quite a scolding when she returned home. Where was David going? And with purpose, too, with strength and speed in his strides and a determined, concentrated look on his face, the same way he looked whenever he dissected one of their specimens.

She soon learned exactly where he was headed. She began smelling fish, the air became salty, and then warehouses began sprawling in front of her, their boards gray and cracked with age. People wandered in and out of the doors, mostly men who smelled of sweat and who carried crates and boxes. People spilled from ships docked at the wharves, strangers who gazed around in wonderment and confusion, doubtless feeling as dazed and maybe even as frightened as Mike felt now. Others bumped her, prodded her, grumbled at her as she pushed and shoved her way between them, feeling frantic that she had lost sight of David. Too many people roamed the dock area, and she, being so much smaller than most of them, couldn't see above a single head.

She finally scrambled up onto a stack of boxes and tried to glimpse David in the throng. She was terrified now, not knowing how to get home from here (she, David, and Jimmie always fished further upriver, away from the dock areas, where she had never ventured), trembling with the thought of having lost him. She had followed him and discovered where he was going. Now she simply wished to find him and go home. She glimpsed his dark head, bobbing some distance ahead, and she shouted his name over and over.

He turned back; he saw her, thank the Father, as Grandmother Quinn often said when a situation turned out fine. Or at least he heard her.

"Some fine threads ya've got there, little missy," some prunish old woman croaked, her skin marked with dark spots and weathered from the salt breeze. She pulled at the sleeve of Michaela's dress, hard enough that Mike went tumbling down, along with a number of crates, just as she thought she heard David shout her name. But maybe she was imagining. She wanted to go home so badly, she only thought she heard him.

She fought her way out from beneath the crates, then someone began tossing them aside. The old vagabond woman, mad as a hatter, still mumbling about Mike's fine threads. *She won't get her hands on me. She won't, she won't,* Mike told herself again and again. Another crate was pulled off her, then suddenly David's face was there, strong and drawn with concern.

"Mike! What are you doing here? You followed me . . . you had to have followed me! All this way, Mike! Leave her be," he ordered the old woman, who was pulling at Mike's dress again. The hag flinched away, still eyeing Michaela's dress. Then David hissed at her and she hobbled away grumbling.

David grabbed hold of Mike's arms and pulled her up off of the slime-covered planking. He now carried a cloth bag; on the way here, his hands had been empty.

"I was curious, that's all," Mike said, pushing away the tears she hadn't held back very well. They had started spilling when she realized the old woman, not David, was unburying her. "You said you were going home. But I saw you go the other way, and not to Jimmie's house, either."

He shook his head. "Come on."

"I'm sorry," she said, afraid he would be angry with her. His jaw was set, and he shook his head again.

"You shouldn't have followed me, Mike."

"I know. What do you have in the bag?"

"Never mind. Come on."

He had never been so gruff with her, and his impatience made Mike all the more curious. He started off, not letting go of her hand for even a second. His steps were larger than hers and Mike fought to keep up with him. Her legs still ached from the long walk here and she wondered aloud why he felt the need to go so fast.

"You shouldn't have followed me," he snapped. "Dr. Quinn would be furious if he knew."

"If he knew," Michaela echoed, eyeing him.

"He might find out. So might Mrs. Quinn. We're never gone to the medical school for so long. She might ask questions."

"What do you have in the bag?"

"Mike, never mind."

He was being stubborn, as "obstinate" as Mama frequently told her she was. They wove their way through the motley, unpleasant crowd, David leading the way but still holding tight to her hand until soon Mike spotted the wide mouth of the Charles River. A pleasant sight, for now Michaela knew that if anything happened, if she and David became separated again and she lost sight of him, all she need do was follow the water. She would soon come upon Charles Street, and from there, she could find her way home.

"I'm not a baby. Let loose of my hand now," she said, growing contrary with him.

"I didn't call you a baby."

"You're holding my hand like I'm one."

"You might have been hurt at the wharves!" he exploded, halting to glare at her.

She plopped her hands on her hips. "I *was* hurt, for your information. You were going so fast, I couldn't keep up. I ran into a boy, scraped my arm on the bricks, and bumped my head on those crates."

He stared at her. "Michaela, the wharves are no place for a girl of your . . . your . . . breeding."

That drew her up short. It was a strange remark, coming from him. And why had he called her Michaela instead of Mike? He always called her Mike. "You sound like my mother."

"Dr. Quinn would never forgive me if anything ever happened to you while you were with me."

"I wasn't with you. I was following," she argued, her temper flaring more by the second, more tears burning her eyes. Tears of frustration and irritation. He wouldn't tell her father, and he really was sounding like Mother right now. "You shouldn't have lied to me. You said you were going home. But you went the other direction. I didn't know you were going to the wharves. I never even knew how to get there!"

They had neared a square, where massive trees shaded brick paths and people of a calmer and more likable sort strolled peacefully and leisurely, men in dark suits with walking sticks and ladies in flowing light day dresses. Here and there sat wooden benches. Chickens pecked at the ground near some. A low brick wall surrounded a pretty fountain, and Mike plopped herself down on one edge of the wall and folded her arms in front of her, still unable to fight back her tears.

She had almost been lost at the docks, for heaven's sake, and now he was scolding her for it! Well, as she saw it, her wanderings were partly his fault. As she had explained to him, he had told her he was going home. But he hadn't gone home, and she had been curious—and hadn't known, for the life of her, where she was wandering to exactly until she had been in the thick of things.

He let her sit there for a few long moments by herself. Then he shuffled over and sat beside her. Michaela watched the graceful flow of people, mothers or nursemaids pushing perambulators, ladies with parasols, men looking dignified in their suits of clothing, as her papa often did, and she marveled at how different her world was than that of the ragtag people she had seen at the wharves. Despite being frightened, she had noticed the worn clothing and the dirty appearances of many, and the hollow, sad looks on some faces had told her that not all of them could help their appearance and manners.

"I'm sorry," David said. "I had something to do and I didn't want you to ask to go with me."

"I was just curious."

"I know," he said, and tipped forward to wipe a tear from her cheek. Mike flinched away, still angry with him.

A dog trotted toward them from the center green, sniffing the ground now and then, looking as if he followed a scent. He neared Mike and David and sniffed at David's bag, then began biting at it. David jerked the bag away and stomped his boot on the bricks, trying to scare the dog. The mongrel barked at David a number of times, then trotted off.

Mike slanted David a suspicious look, still wondering, now more than ever, what the bag contained. He sighed finally, said "Oh, all right," then leaned over to whisper in her ear.

Michaela's eyes widened at what she heard.

"Now, let's get you home so I can get this to the medical school."

They hadn't had the corpse of a larger animal, such as a dog, to study in quite some time, and it seemed David was desperate—and hungry to dissect and study. He had bought a corpse from someone at the dock.

"How do you know the man didn't kill the dog just to sell the body to you?" Mike asked, shocked.

"I must trust that he didn't," David answered simply. "Now, come on."

She went, but rather slowly at first. She couldn't rid her mind of the thought that perhaps the man had, and that if so, that broke the one rule her father had set for them when they began studying at the school—and it also violated a life, no matter that the remains were that of a dog.

"Say, did you hear Mr. Hawkins's explosions again last night?" he asked her as they walked along.

She couldn't help but laugh. "I did. The cats were going at it again in that vacant lot. Where does Mr. Hawkins get those things?"

She was talking about his mammoth torpedoes, of course, and David, laughing the entire time, explained that the man, who lived between their family's homes, always stocked the Independence Day fireworks to hurl at the cats when they commenced courting in the vacant lot at night, keeping the entire neighborhood awake. If someone did manage to doze off during the caterwaulings, they were blasted awake moments later during the explosions set off by Ezekiel Hawkins. The boys of Beacon Hill loved the blasts, but the adults were divided—which was worse, the cats or the torpedoes?

The conversation lightened the air between David and

Mike, and she soon found herself skipping along, laughing with him when he invoked images of the cats scrambling over the back fences, frightened nearly out of their skins.

One crisp fall morning that year, she woke early and wanted to surprise her papa by being the first to greet him when he started out on his calls for the day. She hid in his buggy beneath a blanket on the floor under the back seat of the small buggy, and there she fell asleep. When she woke, she felt the buggy bouncing along, and she poked her head up and rubbed her sleepy eyes. Father, wearing his woolen coat, sat tall and proud on the driver's seat, and the buggy had traveled a good mile down Charles Street, well past the Common!

"Papa?"

He twisted immediately. "Mike?"

"I meant only to say good morning to you."

"Ha! But here you are, along to keep me company!"

She had thought he would surely take her home. Instead he drove on, urging her to come up onto the seat with him, laughing and breathing a sigh of relief that she wore more than her night rail, that she was dressed.

"I never know what to expect from you next, my Michaela," he said jovially. "And that is the delight of it. I'm going to call on patients now, and sometimes you must wait in the buggy."

She felt happy but shocked that he meant to take her along, and she would do exactly as he instructed.

During his first call he performed a tooth extraction, and while she did not remain in the room for the procedure, she sat and read to the man's three small children. Mrs. Reid had died after the birth of the third child, who was now two years old and liked to be held on the lap. The tooth had been paining Mr. Reid for days, Dr. Quinn told Mike later, but he had been reluctant to have it pulled. This morning, however, it seemed the man had had enough of the bothersome thing. After the procedure, and after setting the buggy in motion, Dr. Quinn held the decayed tooth up for his, and Michaela's, inspection, showing her the rotted areas.

He next treated a Mrs. Duffin for carbuncle, a purulent inflammation of the skin, explaining later that the pus pockets must be lanced and drained and the patient bled in extreme cases, and Mrs. Duffin's was fast developing into an extreme case. He had provided ointment but even that seemed to be having no effect. They called upon a patient recovering from a hydrocele, and then another with bronchitis, and after each call, Dr. Quinn spoke to Michaela at times as if she were a colleague, as if he had long wanted someone to accompany him during his calls. She snuggled next to him on the driver's seat, enjoying his warmth and this precious time with him.

She knew the symptoms of many diseases because he had read to her so much from his medical journals, and yet he appeared greatly surprised and delighted, when he asked her opinion of the last patient they had seen, a Mrs. Telfer, and she answered correctly. The rash Mrs. Telfer complained of, and that was certainly present, contained circular blotches, as large as three inches in diameter and a bluish red in color. The blotches were elevated above the surrounding skin, presenting rounded papulae. All typical, Mike remembered from the readings and illustrations she had seen, of erythema nodosum.

"Exactly what I diagnosed," her father said with a look of wonder on his face.

They had dinner at the Tremont House, a prominent and lavish hotel, and they discussed their morning, the patients they had seen, the diagnoses, the treatments. She had surprised him with *her* diagnosis of their last patient, and he had looked at her since with respect and admiration. He had always displayed a great deal of both toward her, but they had increased now.

From the Tremont House, they went to the medical school, where Dr. Holmes seemed delighted with her reports of the various cases she and her father had seen that morning. He was still reeling from the medical society's shock over his recent paper, "The Contagiousness of Puerperal Fever," which he had read before the Society for Medical Improvement and which had recently been published in the *New England Quarterly Journal of Medicine*. It was wrong, many said, for anyone, particularly a man of their profession, to assume, to speak, to write and to publish, that every one of them had killed numerous new mothers by going straight from dissection or surgery rooms to delivery rooms. Dr. Holmes's reputation was suffering, Michaela had heard Father tell Mother. But if he was right—and what if he was?—the medical world would do well to listen.

While conversing with Mike, Dr. Holmes occasionally shot Papa looks of amazement—probably surprised that Dr. Quinn had taken her with him during his calls and that she was now discussing the diagnoses and treatments as if she herself were a medical student, or better, a physician. Her father merely smiled at the pleasant and often comical man and let her continue.

David appeared soon, bursting into the room, prepared to tell Dr. Quinn that Mike had been missing since morning.

"Absentminded me," Michaela's father said, "I forgot to send Elizabeth a message."

"I'll have one sent," Dr. Holmes said, then he engaged Mike in conversation again.

David sat nearby, soon looking amazed himself, his eyes filled with questions. Not until later, when she was alone with him peering over his shoulder while he dissected the leg of a cat, carefully slitting it open and examining each of the muscles and tendons, did she tell him about her morning. He sat strangely quiet, strangely serious.

Of course, he was always intense and serious during dissections, but this was different. His jaw was tense, his eyes flashed at her. She told him about making the diagnosis— the right one—because she wanted to share the excitement with him, and suddenly his scalpel slipped. He cursed, grabbed his hand just below his thumb, and growled at her, "You're destroying my concentration!"

She stared at him, stunned by his outburst, by his flash of anger at her. The events of this morning were incredible, utterly incredible—no experience could equal them—and yet he didn't care to hear any more? She had made a diagnosis, a right diagnosis, and yet instead of being happy for her and excited, he had shouted at her.

"Did you cut yourself?" she asked quietly.

"No," he answered. But she knew he had, and that he wouldn't share even that with her, let her nurse the cut. They shared *everything,* and yet today they didn't.

As she did with Marjorie during her outbursts, Mike fell silent. David went back to his dissection, and Michaela soon slipped off the stool on which she had been sitting for a good half hour and left the school, shuffling toward home, never once raising her head.

He didn't appear at the school for several weeks after that. Mike began dissecting, wanting to learn as much as possible, and she often thought of him. She considered calling at his home and trying to talk to him. But she didn't understand his outburst, didn't know what she had done to make him so angry. She blamed herself, then blamed him (he might have told her why he was angry with her), but mostly she cut and dissected and drew diagrams. She read medical textbooks, and once she even hid in the auditorium and listened to Dr. Holmes lecture on diseases of the heart. David didn't call at the town house. Neither did Jimmie. And Michaela began to wonder if she had lost her two best friends.

Nearly a month later, she saw David at a supper. She sat across from him at the Brimmers' large table, numerous dishes of food resting between them. She tried to catch his eye, but he would have none of that. He dined in silence, with conversation going on all around him. People were bubbling with excitement still that Samuel Morse had succeeded in sending a telegraph message from Washington, D.C. to Baltimore earlier this year. Possibilities were endless now. Communication across long distances would soon be extended beyond letters. Several guests discussed Emerson's *Essays;* others discussed the Foundation for Orphaned Children that a group of Beacon Hill women had lately formed. All of Boston was chuckling at Dr. Holmes's latest poem, which poked fun at his own profession: "If the poor victim needs must be percussed,/ Don't make an anvil

101

of his aching bust;/ Doctors exist within a hundred miles,/ Who thump a thorax as they'd hammer piles;/ So of your questions, don't in mercy try,/ To pump your patient absolutely dry;/ He's not a mollusk squirming on a dish,/ You're not Agassiz, and he's not a fish." Throughout the conversations and the numerous courses of food, conversation, and laughter, Mike remained as quiet as David.

She slipped outside later, despite the early November cold and first snowfall, into the garden area to breathe the fresh air. The fabric of her dress rustled in the crisp breeze, and although she shivered, the thought of returning inside so soon didn't occur to her.

"You'll freeze," a voice said, and she realized it was David's voice, that he was somewhere near. Overhead.

"I assumed your tongue had," she responded.

He jumped down off the tree branch on which he had been resting and landed on his feet in front of her. A few torches had been lit, and their flickering flames cast a coppery hue on his dark hair. He slanted a grin at her, then said, "*Your* tongue is sharp."

She smiled back. "It can be."

He watched her more as he sobered. "I've been jealous, you know. And not proud of it."

She tilted her head, wondering at him.

"Jealous of that morning you spent with him. Your father . . . He took you with him to see his patients, and he shared with you as he's never shared with me. I've been jealous."

She might have known, might have guessed. She had certainly seen enough jealousy from Marjorie. Funny, she could make a medical diagnosis but not diagnose something as simple as jealousy. She wondered if David was still jealous, if this would change their friendship forever.

"I apologize," he said. "And I apologize for my behavior that afternoon."

"David, if you ask, I'm certain he'll take you along," she remarked. "He longs for company. He seemed lonely that morning, glad for the conversation."

He nodded. "Michaela . . . apology accepted?"

She nodded, too. "Apology accepted."

He embraced her, and she held tight to him. For the first time, she listened to the beat of his heart, relished the warmth of his breath, the warmth of him; the solidity of him. She realized she loved him more deeply than she had known, that she had missed him more deeply than she had known.

They parted. He smiled down at her again, the smile of undying friendship. But there was something more between them, something that had not been present before. The thought occurred to Mike that he was handsome, and then her heart quickened as it had never quickened, and her palms grew damp.

She was nearly twelve, he was nearly sixteen—and there was something more.

8

Jimmie turned fourteen that December. He celebrated his birthday by playing pranks all up and down Beacon Street where the brownstones lined up for miles, where horseflesh was shown off by the well-to-do in summertime races, and where sleighs sported along in winter to the sound of hooves clopping and bells ringing. Among other things, Jimmie snatched the day's bread from beneath the McCloskeys' cook and settled beside a nearby pond to share it with his friends the ducks. Then he painted and feathered himself like a wild Indian and scared poor Mrs. Gough nearly out of her mind when she went out for an afternoon stroll and he jumped from behind the bushes and began whooping and waving a hatchet.

Of course only Mike and David knew who exactly caused the chaos on the fashionable street that day. And while David laughed only a little and shook his head, saying that Jimmie could thank his lucky stars he hadn't been caught, Michaela laughed until her sides ached and she was nearly doubled over with pain. The McCloskeys' cook always boasted of her fine bread and for a good long while Jimmie had wanted to sample it, and the Goughs thought they were Boston's most notable family, Mrs. Gough in particular.

Mrs. Gough might have had a heart attack, as Mike's mother said over supper that evening, and while that was true, Michaela still wished she could have seen the shock on the woman's face. She had certainly been snooty to her, David, and Jimmie countless times. Jimmie's eyes always lit so when he talked about his pranks . . . he'd had such fun, such a celebration . . . she couldn't help but laugh when she thought of his pranks. She'd never, ever tell anyone that she knew who had terrorized Beacon Street that day. To do so would be to violate Jimmie's trust and almost guarantee that she would never again be allowed outside her family's house. Oh, no . . . Mama, who already objected to Mike's "boyish" activities, would raise the roof if she ever learned that Michaela was protecting the culprit.

David turned sixteen in January on a day when the Charles froze almost solid and the ice cutters went out in force, eager to fill the warehouses with blocks. Mike turned twelve in February, and a few months later the spring of '45 arrived with heavy rains that flooded some streets and left others in a muddy mess and almost impassable. Rain fell so heavily during most of the season that by the time summer warmth blew in with June, most of the grass had died in the Common at the corner of Boyleston Street and Park Square. By July fifth, the grounds, and the squares around the city, were beginning to recover, and when the tents went up for Independence Day amusements, the Common wasn't such a terrible sight anymore.

Summertime brought more fishing and adventures with Jimmie and David, too. Jimmie usually took charge. One day, after he, Mike, and David had gathered in the Common, he announced that today's adventure would be an exploration of the river Charles. He loved the water, but he was bored with fishing, he told them. "I want to do something more."

Mike had always thought the river beautiful, had always loved watching the ships go in and out either on their way to other Massachusetts ports or to foreign harbors far across the ocean. The Charles was peaceful and serene, while the Atlantic could be tumultuous and violent in the midst of a storm, lashing ships and waterfront buildings. She saw no reason why they shouldn't spend the afternoon venturing upriver, exploring, wandering even a little beyond Boston.

Off they went to the deserted old boathouse where they stored their small boat. The water lapped and splashed as they rowed out into it. They passed numerous moored ships, listening to them groan and creak as the Charles stirred, swaying the vessels. They listened to people on the wharves—the hawkers, the painted, friendly women with whom Mike's mother had told her she should never speak, a group of ragged-looking children who laughed and joked as they threw stones out across the water; the gruff seamen who sometimes uttered words that shocked Mike. "Obscenities," David had once called the words as he'd taken Mike firmly by the elbow and led her away from a street corner on which a group of rowdies had formed.

The riverfront smelled of filth, of reeking fish, rotting wood, stale ale, and perspiring bodies. Beneath the heat of the summer sun, the odors were almost unbearable, although the Charles was certainly much cleaner and better to behold than South Bay, located on the other side of the city. In the distance, the State House dome crowned Beacon Hill and church steeples tapered nearly up to the sky, or so it seemed to Mike.

Once the boat passed more and more anchored ships, the unpleasant smells dissipated and Mike settled back in the tiny vessel. More space began appearing between buildings, and houses, uninterrupted by businesses, became more visible. Gulls swooped overhead, soaring beneath the clear blue sky, their cries carrying far.

"They'd come closer if I had bread," Jimmie remarked, settling back beside Michaela and clasping his hands behind his head.

"Especially bread from the McCloskeys' kitchen," she remarked, giggling. "I've never known anyone so daring as you, Jimmie."

"Or so mad," David teased, grinning. He jerked his head, shaking a lock of dark hair from his brow, and Mike silently marveled, as she frequently did of late, at his vivid blue eyes. Was it fair for a boy to have such beautiful eyes? Such long lashes and such shimmery hair? Of late, she often thought of David as handsome, frequently since that supper party last fall. But never, ever did she think of saying so aloud, to him, Jimmie, or to anyone in the world. That might embarrass David and her, make them both feel awkward, and ruin their friendship.

"My grandpappy worked in that shipyard when he first came over from England," Jimmie said, pointing to an area where beams and planks were piled high, where the skeleton of a ship in progress sat at this very moment.

"Looks like no one's about," David said, slowly rocking back and forth as he rowed.

"In the middle of summer, too," Mike marveled, squinting to have a better look around the shipyard. Not a body anywhere, by the looks of things.

"He didn't work there long," Jimmie remarked, glancing off, looking as distant as he always did whenever he got a wild idea. "Signed on with a crew and set out to sea soon after. He worked his way up and became a captain. Imagine that—mastering a vessel."

"An undertaking, to be sure," David said.

Michaela watched as Jimmie sat up, then stood, positioning himself dangerously close to the edge of the boat. But she knew he could swim—hardly a soul in Boston didn't know how to swim—and so she said nothing. A breeze flapped his shirtsleeves and lifted his hair, and he looked almost gallant, cocking his head and shielding his eyes from the sun as he stared off, then glanced about slowly, then up, then all around, as if checking something. As if they were aboard one of those monstrous sailing vessels, a schooner or a packet, and the crew, passengers, and cargo were his responsibility.

"Standing forward by the figurehead, hearing the wind fill the sails . . . imagine it!" he spouted, giving a flourish. His voice grew louder. "At the wheel is John, Cap'n Jimmie's faithful companion and First Mate. And there, in the deckhouse . . . why, 'tis David, lookin' over the maps 'n' charts. Near the binnacle stands Mike, awaitin' orders.

Passengers gather near the rails, still wavin' at kin on shore. The wind carries the ship out to sea while Jimmie stands tastin' the salty air. . . ."

David laughed at the tale. Mike couldn't help herself; she rose up and applauded, saying, "Bravo, bravo! I've never seen anyone use their imagination so. Surely you belong on a ship, Jimmie!"

"Surely!" he agreed, plopping down beside her. "That's where I plan to be one day—when I'm grown, you know."

"No, I didn't know. A ship, Jimmie? You plan to be a master?"

"For sure. Beacon Hill bores me silly. I can't stay here. One day, I'll own a fleet of ships, and I'll sail them back and forth from Boston harbor to Liverpool. I'll—"

"Why Liverpool?"

"Jimmie Becker, you're a dreamer," David remarked, laughing again. "Indeed, why Liverpool?"

"Why, 'tis where my grandpappy's from. He's told me so many stories about his life there, I've made up my mind to see it one day, even if I have to build and command my own ship to get there."

"So you'll be a captain. . . ." David said, grinning.

"I surely will, and just don't you make fun of me, David Lewis," Jimmie warned.

"I wouldn't dream of doing such a thing."

Jimmie scowled. "You're dreaming right now, right this minute. Put me aboard any ship in this river and I could take command of it today."

"I might do that."

"What do you plan to do with your life, young man?" Jimmie queried, imitating an elder. "After all, you'll be going off to university soon. It's time you decided."

Mike fastened her eyes on David. Off to university soon? Her heart quickened in panic. Why had she not thought of that—that he would be going to college soon? Well, no need for panic, she told herself. All fine Boston boys went to Harvard, just across the way in Cambridge. Not far at all.

They had never talked about this before, the three of

them—what they wanted to be when they grew up—and Michaela listened with interest.

"A medical doctor," David replied simply.

"I knew it," Jimmie said. "Why not an attorney like your father?"

"Because *that's* boring."

"*I've* thought of becoming a doctor," Mike said, excited by the conversation.

Jimmie's jaw dropped open. "Mike. You'll be a storekeeper, a seamstress, a teacher, a mother. Girls don't grow up and become doctors. Maybe you shouldn't be spending so much time at that medical school, being fooled."

She became indignant. "Why don't girls become doctors?"

"Because they don't."

Michaela sat up, feeling her temper flare at being told that she couldn't do something just because she was a girl. "They just don't? Why not?"

"Because they don't, that's all," Jimmie said, shrugging.

"They could," David said, smiling at Mike. He regarded her in an admiring sort of way, a way that warmed her and made her proud. He always regarded her that way of late.

Mike took time to return the smile, then she turned a glare on Jimmie. "Exactly. They could."

"Could, but don't. Besides, you'll have the whole of Boston in an uproar if you try to become a doctor. Girls don't become doctors."

"You play with me enough, Jimmie Becker. Did you all of a sudden remember that I'm a girl?"

"I remember it enough lately. We're all growing up, changing. Or hadn't you noticed?" he asked. "You've noticed. You've noticed David, that's what you've noticed, and he's noticed you, too."

Mike blushed furiously, wondering if she would ever be able to look David in the eye again. It was true; the evening of that supper party, the two of them had started looking at each other in a different way, a manner far different than they ever had. He had always tossed his head to get the hair out of his eyes, but lately when he did that, Mike found herself wishing he wouldn't. Something about the act made her breath catch in her throat.

"Stop, Jimmie. We're supposed to be having an adventure, not arguing," David reminded them, turning red himself.

Why had Jimmie had to go and do that? Mike wondered, irritated. Now he had made them both uncomfortable and surely they wouldn't have as good a time this afternoon as they would have had if Jimmie had kept his mouth shut.

"You can't become a doctor anyway, Mike," Jimmie continued. "Get the fool notion out of your head. Medical schools don't let girls in. Most colleges don't. Besides, even if one did, you're not getting enough education right now to make it through. Sure you know how to read and cipher, but while me'n David are learning Latin and geometry, you're learning music and dancing and how to make a good home—all so when you get old enough you can fetch a good husband."

"It's not true about medical schools! There must be one somewhere that girls can attend."

"It is too true."

"It is not, Jimmie. Some let girls in, surely."

"Ask David. Ask your father. Ask anyone!"

"I guess we won't be having an adventure today," David said, sighing.

Mike fastened a questioning gaze on him, and he continued rocking, rowing, hoping she wouldn't ask him to comment. "David?" he heard her say in her sweet, soft voice.

"What?"

"That's not true, is it? That no medical school lets girls in?"

David knew how she had always traipsed around behind her father, behind him—he'd seen it and experienced it firsthand. He had witnessed her playing with some of the contents of Dr. Quinn's medical bag the day she'd started crawling, and he knew how she liked to go into her father's library even now and study the many medical volumes there. She had gone with her father that day last year, accompanied him on his medical calls, and she had even come up with the right diagnosis when Dr. Quinn had asked her opinion about a patient's condition. David had witnessed Michaela's intelligence and her growing knowledge over the years, and while he knew that Jimmie, for some reason, was being intentionally cruel, he also knew that Jimmie was right; as far as he knew, no medical school accepted female students. David had begun to suspect more and more lately that she had it in her heart to become a doctor, but he had hoped he would not have to tell her what he was about to tell her now. He was about to break her heart and he didn't want to do that.

"Girls can't go to medical school, Michaela," he said softly, wishing he had it in him to lie to her.

She stared at him. "They can. . . . Yes, they can!"

"Jimmie's right besides—you probably don't have enough education in the right subjects to get through even if you managed to get in."

"Are you going to cry now?" Jimmie asked, taunting her. "Stop it. You don't cry when you get a fishing hook in your finger, Mike. Why cry over something stupid like not being able to go to medical school? You're definitely turning all girl."

"It's not true. It's not!"

"Jimmie," David scolded. "I wouldn't lie to you, Michaela."

"Well, bloody hell. Look at her—she has tears in her eyes!"

David stopped rowing. "Jimmie Becker, I mean it. Don't talk to her like that and don't curse in front of her."

Jimmie grew sullen, glaring at David suddenly. Then he said, "I guess you're right. After today, I won't forget anymore that she's a girl. Maybe she ought to be more of a girl, then she won't ever be fooled again and we won't either. People talk about her, how odd she is, that maybe she has one of those nervous disorders. You can't tell me you don't hear the talk, David. I've heard your own mother— "

"Stop, you hear?" David ordered, bolting from his position. He grabbed Jimmie by the shirtfront and jerked him close. "Stop. I mean it."

"Do you think people don't talk about *you*? I hate you, Jimmie," Mike said, swiping at the tears on her cheeks. But she knew in her heart that she didn't mean that, that she was just angry. In a way Jimmie was right—maybe she should be more of a girl. Michaela had never quite understood her sisters' excitement over such things as beautiful gowns, who was having what ball and when, who was having what supper and when, and whether every hair was in place and every wrinkle brushed away before one went out in public. Such fussings seemed like a waste of time.

"All right, David. All right," Jimmie said, looking pale and fearful. David was bigger and older, after all.

David loosened his hold on Jimmie's shirtfront, and Jimmie took up the oars again while David embraced Michaela, urging her head against his chest.

She fought more tears as she listened to his strong heartbeat, wondering what she would do. If David said no medical school would let her in because she was a girl, it must be true.

But it couldn't be true. It just couldn't be.

The trio didn't progress much farther up the Charles River. Jimmie turned the boat around soon after Mike let loose of David's shirt, turned her back on Jimmie, and quieted to an unusual degree. She always had quiet moments, being the thinker that she was, but she rarely grew sullen during them. Jimmie was thoroughly disgusted, rowing as fast as he could, and David glared at him now and then, wondering why he couldn't be more understanding about Michaela's desires. She had really never realized that she couldn't go to medical school. She admired her father and she wanted to be like him, and Jimmie had not only crushed that dream, he had ridiculed it.

Jimmie was right about girls not being allowed in medical school, sure, but he also was right about something else: he, Mike, and David were growing up and that was changing everything, the entire nature of their friendship. Up until a few months ago, they had been relaxed around each other. Then Michaela had appeared a little more grown up, having more shape about her and being grouped with the girls by her mother instead of being allowed to mingle with the boys during parties and social gatherings. Half of David still regarded her as a playmate. But the other half knew that their maturity, the mere difference in their sex, was beginning to separate them. They grew nervous around each other at times now, something that had never happened before, feeling at a loss for words and having clammy palms and other odd sensations.

The really embarrassing thing was that Jimmie had noticed it, tossing David odd looks from time to time when his tongue became twisted while he tried to talk to Mike. Jimmie had been mocking the uppity Garrisons one afternoon on the riverbank, pretending to hold a tea party, then humming and dancing around on the grass. Mike had started humming along with him, and David, thinking only to have fun, had caught her and begun dancing with her, twirling her around and around, both of them laughing, then quieting as the awareness crept in again and they stared at each other, him thinking how pretty she was becoming, how her hair shimmered and her skin glowed. Jimmie had broken them up finally with his usual antics. Only today did David realize how uncomfortable Jimmie must have felt that afternoon.

The boat bumped against the dock, and David wrapped the mooring rope around a stump there, securing the vessel. He meant to help Mike out, but she scrambled out by herself, paying him no mind when he called her name as she hiked up her skirts and raced off. He swore under his breath, wondering where she was going, hoping she would go straight home and not wander the streets by herself.

"Oh, let her go," Jimmie grumbled. "What does it matter anyway? You're strange about her lately, and I don't like it. I'm telling you—I don't like it."

David glared at him. "I don't care whether you like it. I like Michaela and you hurt her feelings. Why did you have to do that, Jimmie? You liked telling her she couldn't go to medical school because she's a girl!"

"You don't even call her Mike all the time anymore. Was I suppose to lie to her?"

"You didn't have to like it so much."

"She's too prissy lately, dancing around like that last week, wearing dresses all the time now. But she still fishes! Boy or girl? I ask myself lately, and I never know."

"You just said she's odd. You implied that she ought to be more of a girl. Now you're saying she's prissy. Don't call her names," David warned.

"Oh, what if I do?"

No response. David stood stock-still, feeling the anger slither beneath his skin. He didn't like Jimmie very much right now.

Jimmie slammed the oars down into the boat. "Prissy, sissy, missy . . . Baby girl!"

The taunting was too much. David rammed into Jimmie's middle, head first, tipping the boat and sending them both sprawling into the water. David surfaced first, sputtering as he grabbed the mooring post and hauled himself up onto the dock. Jimmie climbed up seconds later and David was on him almost as soon as his foot left the water.

The boys punched and tumbled, rolling off the dock into the dirt, grabbing and swinging as a small group of men from a nearby warehouse gathered round to laugh and place bets.

Mike raced all the way home, first up along the wide expanse of Charles Street to Mount Vernon. Mothers pushed their babies in perambulators and walked with their small children, heading in the direction of Louisburg Square. Michaela dodged her way between men in suits and hats, and between ladies sporting hats and colorful parasols. She blinked back tears, sniffed to keep her nose from running, and she held her head high as she raced along.

How many times had the taunting Marjorie told her she was headstrong and unfeminine because she was supposed to have been a boy, therefore she acted like a boy much of the time? Mike was the fifth child, and Dr. and Mrs. Quinn

114

had been expecting their long-awaited son. Then *she* had been born, surprising them.

Well, I should have been born a boy, Mike thought sourly, racing past stoop after stoop, railing after railing, pausing only once when her skirt became caught in an untrimmed rosebush that protruded from between the bars of an iron fence. She yanked it free, hearing it rip but giving only brief thought to the disapproving look Mother would give her when the maid pointed out the damage. Venting a little of her anger on the skirt felt good, and for a second or two, she actually thought about ripping the entire thing off her body and shredding it. Right here, right now, on the walkway. She even thought about wearing a pair of trousers around the city.

If I had been born a boy no one would tell me I couldn't attend medical school. I would have learned Latin and geometry by now—and other subjects commonly reserved for boys. No one would laugh at me when I said I wanted to be a medical doctor.

She hurried on.

She planned never to speak to Jimmie again. She didn't know about David yet. She just didn't know. He had defended her to Jimmie, but she wasn't really sure how he felt about her wanting to be a doctor—if he thought she should or shouldn't. He might still be jealous. And since she didn't know how he felt, she couldn't make a decision one way or another right now about whether to continue talking to him.

She had to go home and think; she had to lie quietly in her room, not feeling out of breath as she did now, and wait for the anger she felt to fade a little. It would—she knew it would. She had the worst temper of anyone she knew, and she had learned that allowing it to settle down before she made a decision enabled her to think more clearly.

She finally reached Louisburg Square, far ahead of the perambulators, mothers, and small children she had passed. She slowed down as she approached the iron railing and steps leading up to her family's home. She usually tried to enter quietly, not wanting to cause a stir or bring undue notice to herself from the staff or from her sisters or mother, and she usually entered through the kitchen door. But today she was in such a temper she didn't care who noticed her; she pushed open the door and walked in bold as brass.

Harrison, the butler, was playing watchdog, as usual. He hurried forth, dressed in his proper black and white, guardian of the Quinn's front entrance and of their respectability.

"*Mud* on the bottoms of your boots, Miss Michaela," he said, sniffing, stopping short in the entryway near the main staircase, which curved its way up to the second floor. The banister railing was dark with new polish.

"You're right, Harrison," Mike said smartly, lifting her chin. "I've been down at the riverfront again, as you already know, I'm certain."

He stiffened more, if possible. He didn't approve of her. Few people did. Her father did, and Rebecca also. But Rebecca had married and moved on long ago, and while Mike now saw her every week and sometimes twice a week, the visits were never enough and she missed having Rebecca here. Rebecca had two strong boys, Alexander and Nathaniel, who were always gay and giggled often when Mike called at the house. She and Rebecca sat on the floor and played with them, and Mike thought she had never seen Rebecca look happier than during those times. Papa was proud of his grandsons, too; he made a habit of calling at the Bradford house twice or more weekly, bouncing the boys on his knee and strolling up and down the walkways with them.

Claudette and Maureen visited often, though Claudette was expecting, and Maureen hoped to be with child soon. But of late they usually exhibited the same stiffness and disapproval with which Harrison greeted Mike now. Perhaps because they thought she should be settled by now, that she should act more ladylike. Michaela usually met their disapproval with quiet indifference, going about her business. But today, after that scene with Jimmie in the boat, she felt rebellious. Today she would meet no one's disapproval with quiet indifference.

"Sit and take them off," Harrison quietly ordered.

Mike raised her chin more. "I will not. They're my boots

and I'll wear them when and where I want, no matter their condition. Just as it's my life and I'll do with it what I want."

She did a horrible thing then, something for which she deserved the two days of confinement in her room that followed—a fact she freely admitted to David some five days later: Smiling wickedly, she took deliberate steps toward the staircase, grinding her boots, and the mud, into the entryway carpet. She would never, ever forget the look on Harrison's face, how his jaw dropped open, how his face paled, how his eyes widened so she thought they would pop right out of his head.

Then Mama appeared in the parlor doorway, just off the entryway, and stifled the rebellious moment. She ordered Michaela to remove the boots and take herself up to her room where she would stay put until otherwise notified. Mike knew better than to argue. Even Papa would not defend her in this.

"What are we to do with her, Joseph?" she heard her mother ask him on the third day, after Mike's sentence had been lifted and she had crept downstairs when she thought most of the staff had gone off to bed. She had thought her father was still calling on patients, or at his office, or perhaps still at Massachusetts General. She had hoped to read some from one of his many books. But the voices in the parlor had made her pause on her way to his study.

"She's high-spirited," he commented rather nonchalantly, and Michaela imagined him rubbing his bearded chin as he said it, as he always did when considering a matter.

"Oh, Joseph. Perhaps she has a nervous condition. Have you considered that? I've considered her birth lately, how harrowing it was, how she didn't breathe at first. Perhaps it damaged her in some way."

"Don't be foolish, Elizabeth. The girl is far above normal in intelligence. She was not damaged."

Another argument followed. More sharp words about her, about him needing to get her under control, about him not encouraging her rebellious ways and unconventional habits. Mother's voice rising in pitch, Father's staying the same, always the calm voice of reason.

117

Michaela realized that she was angry with him, too, as furious with him as she was with Jimmie. Why had he encouraged her medical interests all these years if no medical college would accept her because she was a girl? Why had he nurtured her, taught her, fed her need for knowledge? Doing so had only made her hungrier for more.

"Elizabeth," she heard her papa say, "Very well. I'll speak to Michaela in the morning."

The next morning, he called her into his study, where they had shared so many gentle times, and reprimanded her there. When she approached his desk where he sat, he told her to stop, and when she stopped, he breathed deeply, then began. She had expected gentle words, and instead she received harsh words. Harsh words from her father, who had never spoken harshly to her.

He hadn't scolded her for sneaking out that night and he hadn't scolded her the time she had pushed Marjorie into the mud. But for this, for completely defying Harrison and for *marking the carpet in front of him,* he would scold her.

She worried him of late, he said. She walked to the Tremont school by herself more and more often instead of waiting for the driver or for David, and he was aware that she neglected her lessons more and more. He was not proud of her right now, he said, and that alone made Michaela hang her head and want to cry.

"You never told me I couldn't go to medical school," she mumbled.

The remark seemed to baffle him. He was silent.

"Even if I could, if I had not been born a girl, I haven't enough education."

"Do you want to go to medical school, Mike?" he asked, finding his voice finally.

She looked up at him. "What else would I want to do, Papa? But I can't—girls are not allowed in medical school." Why had he not assumed she would want to attend a medical school? Had his thinking been affected, too, by the fact that she was a girl?

He rubbed his whiskered jaw and sat back in his chair. "My Mike wants to go to medical school. . . . I knew this might happen, and I've been unfair to you in never considering it seriously. But there is a possibility, you see . . . in Philadelphia. . . ." He went still, looked even more thoughtful, and his gaze fastened on her again. "Come here, Mike."

She approached him without balking, because when he said that, she always knew he meant to pull her onto his lap and that they would then have the quiet times together and the conversations she so loved. He did exactly that—pulled her onto his lap.

"What about your medical school?" she queried. Surely she could attend the Tremont Street school. Surely.

"I don't know," he mused. "It's not just my school, see. What about more schooling for now? What about an institution that teaches Latin, geometry, geography, history . . . other subjects?"

She stared at him. "For a girl?"

He nodded. "Many such schools are in existence for girls. But Mike . . . you haven't done your lessons of late. How can I be sure you will do your lessons in such a school?"

Latin, geometry, geography, history . . . She was hungry for more education, very hungry. She started to ask what was the sense if no medical school would take her as a student. But the possibility alone of learning more, of becoming well educated despite the fact that she had been born female, excited her.

"You can be assured," she said softly. "But in Philadelphia? Where is Philadelphia?"

"No, not in Philadelphia. Too far from here, and you are much too young for that. I was only thinking aloud about something there. I was thinking of medical school—but that will occur later. I have a number of colleagues in Philadelphia, physicians I know would take you under their wings. The city possesses a busy medical community, gifted doctors and educators, but more importantly, many of whom believe women should be given the opportunity to become physicians."

That excited Mike even more. She had older acquaintances who had gone off to various schools, the sons and daughters of family friends, some being her friends. She knew they often missed their families, as she would miss hers if she eventually went to study in Pennsylvania, even given the many conflicts she had had with her mother over the years. She didn't like to study ordinary subjects, and she didn't like to sit in a classroom. But if she had to study more and sit in a classroom for hours and days on end in order to become a medical doctor eventually, she would do exactly that.

During the following month, he wrote to several of his Philadelphia colleagues, and he also investigated the girls' schools in Boston. His decision was the Female Seminary, certainly not for the religion, but for its wide range of subjects and the thorough training of its teachers. It would be an intense schooling, and she would take a room there, returning home only on weekends.

He enrolled her for the following fall, but in the meantime he brought home Latin, history, and philosophy textbooks for her, and he took the liberty, to Mama's obvious agitation, of hiring an additional teacher, a Mr. Beecher, to come three times a week and school her in the subjects. Doubtless Mother was relieved that she no longer spent so much time with Jimmie and David—or so many afternoons at the Tremont school.

Mike thought her mother would surely object to the seminary, to her having more education. But then, perhaps she felt that the discipline and the lack of free time, which right now Michaela spent with Jimmie and David, would be good. She fell strangely quiet on the topic, and her only remark about the seminary to Mike was made while they were spending a rare quiet evening together in the sitting room with Martha, the personal maid. Elizabeth Quinn's brow creased slightly as she glanced up from her stitching and said, "Take care there, Michaela. While you assume I care little, I do hope you excel in everything, but particularly in music, drawing, painting, and embroidery. I hope you'll wish to keep a home one day. If so, you'll need the skills."

She was proper and even haughty, as always, but genuine concern burned in her eyes.

"I will, Mother," Mike responded, not adding that she actually had a desire to learn a few of those skills now, the ones her mother had mentioned. Recently Marjorie had gloated to her that David had attended several balls with his family last month and that he had danced with a number of girls. Mike had become painfully aware that he was older than she—she wasn't allowed to attend balls yet, and even if she were, she didn't dance well; she had never taken the time to learn to dance well. But suddenly, doing so was important to her.

"No doubt," Elizabeth said, still watching her. "You accomplish 'most anything you set your mind to."

Michaela thought she saw a flash of sadness in her mother's eyes, of love and regret. Then the flash was gone and Mama returned to her stitching, so proud, so stubborn, so closed—distant once again.

9

David did not go to Harvard; that fall he went off to Yale in Connecticut. Yale wasn't a tremendous distance away, but the decision troubled Michaela, and she wondered if her heart would break in two. She talked to Rebecca about her feelings, knowing she was young and that she was possibly only infatuated. Rebecca held her hand and told her that love was love, no matter if it began with infatuation. If it was an enduring sort of love then one day David would return from Yale and the relationship would continue and blossom.

David himself looked a little sad about his leaving, parting from family and friends . . . Mike, but he was also excited. He was going off to another world, outside the confines of Boston, and he was ready to see new things, learn new things, experience new things on his way into adulthood.

For the first time Mike felt the gap of their age difference; for the first time she thought about it, pondered it, wondered if it would make a difference in the overall scheme of things. She wondered if David would meet someone else before she had a chance to develop into a woman.

She threw herself into her own studies, eventually becoming too busy to dwell on his leaving. She was Michaela in the classroom and to all instructors, Mike to the new friends she made. She became fascinated by mythology and natural history, and she tolerated drawing and painting. Music she enjoyed—but then music had been an almost everyday occurrence in the Quinn household—and she found embroidery, when she applied herself, relaxing and satisfying. Mike was learning French and Greek, and improving rapidly in Latin, and Mother was stunned by her new devotion to her lessons. Papa was proud.

Michaela stitched some fine pieces and when she took them home one weekend and showed them to her mother, Elizabeth was surprised and seemed proud, too. She asked about Michaela's other studies and they talked about music for a time, new pieces she had learned to play and sing. One weekend they even sat together at the pianoforte and enjoyed the music together. All reservations on her mother's part about Father seeing to Michaela's extensive education seemed to dissipate, and Michaela's relationship with her mother improved.

In the back of Mike's mind almost constantly, however, was the fear that when the subject of medical school arose eventually, and it would, Elizabeth Quinn would revert back to the cold, reserved way she had always treated her youngest daughter.

David wrote from Yale, and when Mike received the letter and saw his name scribbled across the top of the envelope, she yelped with joy. She mutilated the envelope in tearing it open. Nearby, Sally Hampton, a classmate who had become a good friend, laughed from her bed in the room Michaela shared with three other girls. Then Sally demanded to know who the post was from.

"From *him,* of course," Catharine Huntley said, sauntering over, a grin skipping across her face, light dancing in her eyes. She was one who accomplished all the ladylike tasks with ease—music, needlework, drawing, painting, artificial flower work—and Mike was sometimes envious of her. But Catharine was a pleasant person, full of life and laughter, and Michaela enjoyed her company. "Mr. *Yale,*" Catharine teased, trying to snatch the letter from Mike's hands before Michaela had even unfolded it.

"No Yale student would look or think twice about a seminary girl," said Etha Crocker. Her bed sat next to Catharine's across the room, and she sat cross-legged on it, wearing nothing but her undergarments in the middle of a half dozen opened books. It was the third week of January, the room was drafty despite the hearth that heated it, and how Etha could wear so little clothing and not freeze was beyond Mike's understanding. Etha worked forever at her lessons, always studying, always jotting notes on her slate, seeming forever jealous and spiteful of those who did not work as hard. Mike received excellent marks, and while she worked hard to obtain them, she did not devote nearly the number of hours to studying that Etha did.

"There is one who apparently does," Sally responded, as Mike again turned away laughing from Catharine, who was still trying to snatch the missive. Sally had no patience with Etha. Michaela had grown up with Marjorie, however, and thought no person could be as terrible. She did not believe that Etha was jealous and spiteful in her heart. She felt instead that Etha was resentful of the free time the other girls had while she poured over her books, and Mike understood that. Sometimes she wished to be running the streets of Beacon Hill and Back Bay still instead of sitting in classrooms and studying.

"Oh, read it to us then," Catharine said, giving up her chase. Sally gave her a playful shove, which prompted a scowl from her classmate. Catharine scolded, "Miss Weathers would tell you that is unladylike," and with another sly smile she turned her attention back to Mike and the letter.

"Very well," Mike said, seeing that she might never get to read her letter if she didn't share it.

Catharine and Sally settled on the bed, now giving Mike a little space, and looked on eagerly as Michaela unfolded the papers. She clear her throat and began reading: " 'Dear Michaela . . .' "

" 'Dear . . .' he called her 'dear,' " Sally gasped. Catharine giggled and jabbed her with an elbow, and Mike tossed them a severe but playful look.

" 'Five months since I left Boston, and I am finally settled here at the college and in my studies,' " she read. " 'So much to learn! Mental algebra, botany, mineralogy, geology, moral science . . . While I once thought four years an extraordinary amount of time to spend at college before one went on to medical school, I now know my thinking was wrong. The extensive courses here and the more conservative milieu are what prompted my father to choose Yale over Harvard. But I must confess that the college and the seriousness of it surprise me. "No more dallying," Father said before I departed for Connecticut, and he meant it.

" 'The professors are something to behold. Some classmates have named them, appropriately I might add— Chevalier the Eloquent, Ticknor the Lively, Higginson the Volcano (and others). We have great fun with the names, and Higginson occasionally threatens us with the birch stick.

" 'We have little time aside from study, and we snatch what time we can to get up a game of football or cricket. Charles Eliot has become a fine friend, a master of elocution and rhetoric. His father is a medical doctor in New York City, and Charles intends to follow his path. Otis Parker has a fast pair of legs and a quick wit. Pity the classmates he teams off against in football! He has no need of botany, as he seems to have been born knowing every species of plant life.

" 'That is Yale. I have written to Dr. Quinn also and hope to keep up the correspondence. I find at times that I miss your flashing eyes, our dissections and discussions, our adventures on the river Charles and the streets of—' "

" 'Dissections'?" Catharine burst out.

"Adventures? What adventures?" Sally needed to know.

Both girls pressed in on Mike, craning to have a look at the letter themselves.

Fearing ridicule, Michaela had never said a word at the seminary school about her desire to attend medical school; nor had she said anything about the study of dissections and the drawings she had already done at the Tremont school. But why should she hide such things? she wondered now, tipping her head. She wished to become a medical doctor someday, and certainly she would have to face down any ridicule that came her way.

"David and I studied some together at the Tremont Street Medical School," she told Catharine. Well, it hadn't happened exactly that way. They hadn't been students exactly. "Under my father," she added.

"The rest, the rest!" Sally demanded, jumping up and down, wanting Mike to finish the letter.

"I see. . . ." said Catharine, and Michaela felt Etha's piercing gaze all of a sudden.

Sally snatched the letter from Mike's hands, but Michaela made no objection—it was nearly finished.

"'. . . adventures on the river Charles and the streets of Boston,'" Sally read. "'Write soon and tell of your studies at the seminary and your friends and classmates there. I do not know when I shall return home for a visit. Given the curriculum here, such a holiday may not be easy to come by. Yours truly, David A. Lewis.'"

Sally fell back on the bed with the letter still in hand and pressed the papers to her breast. "To receive such a thing!" she said, and sighed as she stared up at the ceiling. Catharine still stared at Mike with shock and uncertainty on her face.

Etha found her voice finally, just when her hard gaze threatened to unsettle Michaela. "You studied at the Tremont Medical School?" she queried softly. "How was such a thing possible? Oliver Holmes is a professor there. And Joseph . . . " Here she stalled and her eyes lit suddenly. ". . . *Quinn*. Michaela Quinn," she whispered. "Why did I not? . . . Dr. Quinn. He's—"

"My father," Mike said.

"But to while away your time at a medical school," Catharine remarked to Mike. "Whatever possessed you to do such a thing?"

"Her father's influence, of course," Etha said.

"You ninny," Catharine snapped. "This is not your conversation. Go back to your books."

Etha's face flushed, and she did exactly that—went back to her books. Catharine's remarks reminded Mike of the harshness of Marjorie's tongue and of her arrogant nature.

"Tell about the adventures," Sally suddenly demanded, bolting upright, a look of urgency marking her expression. She had to know, and she had to know *now*.

A smile crossed Michaela's lips. "Fishing, rowing, visiting the shops, playing pranks."

"Fishing?" Catharine blurted in disbelief.

Mike turned to her. "Fishing."

Catharine met her stare rather haughtily as the other two girls fell quiet. Finally, Catharine remarked, "What a positively nasty habit," and then she wandered off with a flip of her skirt and Michaela knew their short-lived friendship was over. Catharine was far too like Marjorie for Mike's peace of mind—and Michaela had just now discovered that!

"We were a team on Beacon Hill—David, Jimmie Becker, and myself," Mike said, turning her attention to Sally. "Friends forever."

"'I miss your flashing eyes. . . .'" Sally said dreamily, and then she squealed a little. "That sounds like more than friendship to me!"

"I think it was becoming so," Michaela mused aloud.

"Drat college and schooling!"

"Necessary things," Mike remarked, surprising herself. She had not always thought so. She almost hoped it would be some time before David returned home on holiday. She had much to accomplish yet. Her dancing still left much to be desired, she still wasn't old enough to attend balls, and she didn't want to hear about him dancing with other girls. Thirteen. She was *only thirteen*. Oh, to turn the hands of time! To be fifteen . . . sixteen now . . . To be ladylike and refined and . . . to be as she had never been! She would surprise him, she would dazzle him . . . she would win him.

Miss Steele appeared in the doorway, telling the girls it

was time they put away their belongings and settled into bed. She was gentle, Miss Steele, while Miss Coal was often gruff and harsh.

The girls hastened to do as the teacher said. Sally returned Mike's letter and went to her bed. Mike carefully folded the letter and placed it beneath her feather pillow. Catharine smoothed the skirts of the dresses she had tossed across the foot of her bed. Etha gathered her books one by one and stacked them on a small, nearby table.

To Michaela's surprise Etha smiled over at her just before she settled back on her pillows, snuggled beneath the coverlet, and Miss Steele began extinguishing the lamps.

Nearly a week later, Etha, who Michaela had caught staring at her now and then since the evening she had received the letter, leaned over toward Mike one afternoon while Miss Porter was demonstrating the art of velvet painting. "I want to become a medical doctor," Etha whispered, then withdrew quickly to stand prim and proper with her hands clasped before her.

She pretended to watch Miss Porter's demonstration, but Mike doubted whether she actually registered the teacher's fine strokes and the words she said; Etha's face had flushed. She flashed Michaela a shy smile.

No wonder the stares this past week, no wonder the stricken look on Etha's face when Mike mentioned to Sally and Catharine that she had studied some with David at the Tremont Medical School and that her father taught there with Dr. Holmes.

Michaela felt Etha's reluctance to mention her desires for fear of ridicule. She knew that reluctance herself—and she knew Etha's skittish nature dissuaded her also. Catharine could be cruel, as Mike had realized the evening they had read the letter, and she intimidated Etha, surely making it difficult for Etha to room with her, to express any of her feelings publicly.

"Let's talk later," Michaela whispered to Etha, and she straightened her face just as Miss Porter turned and fixed a stern look on the group of girls.

"Who is talking?" the woman demanded.

Long seconds of silence ensued, then Mike glimpsed Etha's hand flinch and start to raise.

Michaela stepped forward. "I was, Miss Porter."

The teacher stared at her, tilting her head, looking down her thin nose.

"I apologize," Mike said, but apparently it was too late.

"Come here."

Michaela approached the easel and the teacher, not knowing what to expect.

"Hold out your hand, palm up," Miss Porter said, collecting something from her desk. Mike saw that it was a long wooden ruler, and her eyes widened.

"Miss Porter, I—"

"Hold out your hand."

Michaela did as she was told.

When the first blow came, she gasped. With the second she squeezed her eyes shut. And with the third she felt her face flush and her eyes burn.

"Go up to your room now," Miss Porter said, "and there you'll stay until time for your next class. There will be no talking while I am talking." Her gaze covered the room as Michaela turned to walk away, fighting tears, her palm screaming with pain. The other girls shifted nervously. Mike was glad to leave the classroom.

But not glad at all when she heard that evening that she had failed the class. Failed painting because she had uttered a few words!

"You failed because of me," Etha fretted. "You shouldn't have told her you were talking. I talked first."

What will I tell Father? Michaela wondered to herself. *I promised him I would do well. Now I have a failing mark.* Mama would give her a haughty, disgusted look—Elizabeth Quinn was very good at delivering those. No matter that their relationship was much improved of late.

"Never mind," Mike said, grabbing a pelisse from the open trunk that sat at the foot of her bed. "Let's go walk the grounds and talk." They couldn't talk here, in their room. Catharine sat at the desk in the corner writing a letter, now and then dipping her pen in the inkpot. She kept glancing at them, and Mike knew she was listening to every word they said.

"Perhaps you should not have taken the blows for her," Catharine remarked smartly, glancing up again. She leveled a cool look on Michaela. "You *have* failed because of her."

"I took the blows because I was talking," Mike informed her. Then she took Etha by the elbow and urged her from the room.

"I have every intention of becoming a medical doctor myself," she told Etha moments later, as they strolled across the path several men had worked at clearing this morning. Snow had fallen heavily last night, a good two feet within a few short hours, and instead of the teachers taking the girls to hear a reading of poetry, they had made hot cocoa and gathered everyone in the spacious parlor to read themselves. The sun was setting, spreading gold, orange, red, and a mix of pastels across the western horizon, a backdrop for Massachusetts Avenue and Back Bay. A brief wind flapped the edges of Michaela's pelisse, cutting through her skin and chilling her to the bone. The smell of burning hickory and pine filled the air, and smoke clouded chimney tops.

"You do?" Etha asked, looking amazed. "But how? . . . I suppose your own father could teach you . . . has taught you. It must be easy for you."

Mike shook her head and laughed slightly. "No. My mother has always opposed my spending any amount of time at the Tremont school. My father fought her about the matter for years. And while more education for girls our age might be becoming the vogue, Mama opposes even that. The most important thing to a girl should be to develop delicate feminine skills so she might grow up and fetch a decent husband."

"Which we all plan to do one day anyway," Etha commented dryly.

Michaela smiled at that. "What I wanted to tell you was that my father says there's been talk for a few years now in Philadelphia of beginning a medical college for women. A Dr. Brian and several of his students at the Pennsylvania

130

Medical College have caused an uproar with the suggestion. Perhaps we have only to wait. Meanwhile I'll introduce you to my father the next time he visits, and perhaps he might arrange a visit from Dr. Holmes."

Etha brightened even more at that. She clapped her hands together quickly, excitedly. "A medical college for women! Imagine it. But suppose it's accomplished, Mike. Suppose it's accomplished and we become physicians. Will we be accepted by fellow doctors?"

Mike had not thought of that. The question was certainly something to ponder, something to explore, something that made an uneasy feeling crawl beneath her skin.

"I don't know, Etha," she murmured. "I honestly don't know."

During her father's next visit to the school, Michaela did exactly as she had said she would—she introduced him to Etha and told him that she, too, wished to become a medical doctor. He took them to a restaurant not far down Massachusetts Avenue, and there the three of them shared conversation over supper.

Etha's family was not socially prominent, her father being a Unitarian minister. But he felt that his daughter should be educated, particularly with topics such as women's rights being batted around. He also felt there was nothing worse than an intentionally uneducated human being. His exact words, Etha said, when she had suggested the seminary school. Then he had put together part of the family's savings and sent her packing.

They get along well, Michaela thought much later that evening, *my father and Etha.* Smiling to herself at the list of questions Etha had prepared for him and at his eagerness to answer every one thoroughly, Mike pulled the counterpane up around her shoulders and soon fell asleep.

Dr. Holmes visited within the month, just before the tulips began pushing their way up through the snow in the Public Garden. He brought his son Wendell, who was all of five years old, and they, Dr. Quinn, Mike, Sally, and Etha all boarded the Holmes's sleigh and soon shot up the wide expanse of Beacon Street. The bells jingled and the horses blew steam from their noses. Sally giggled at Wendell's attempt to do the same, and Mike tucked her hands deep beneath the fur lap robe as her father and Etha conversed. Etha happened to mention that she and Michaela had become close friends the day Miss Porter took the ruler to Mike's hand, and then Michaela's father was questioning her, pressing her for an account of what had happened.

He spent the following morning at the school, remonstrating with Miss Porter, and then taking issue with Mrs. Wright, the director, behind a heavy closed door. That evening, Miss Porter was dismissed from her duties, and Sally clapped her hands as they watched the teacher climb into a waiting carriage, her baggage in hand.

Maureen gave birth to her first child, a robust baby girl, exactly two weeks before the United States declared war on Mexico. She fell ill with the fever, frightening her family and friends nearly to death. Joseph Quinn said a prayer of thanks when she recovered—and Michaela had never heard her father pray. Marjorie had married and was now expecting, and Maureen's experience terrified her. Yet she spun away when Mike tried to reassure her.

The declaration of war stoked flames all over the country, and the issue became one that had become more and more common and heated since the turn of the century—*slavery*. The Whigs opposed the declaration; in fact, they had been opposed to absorbing Texas, formerly Mexican property, in the first place since it was certain to become a slave state. During the debate about whether to annex the Texas republic, William Garrison, who was still printing his *Liberator,* had flaunted the word *secession* on the front page of his publication, insisting that the New England states should not tolerate the admittance of another slave state. His sentiments prevailed in Boston, a city that was becoming more and more antislavery.

A number of reasons had led to the war. The annexation of California, Texas, and New Mexico had been talked about for years, as they all clung to the boundaries of the

United States, and in fact had drawn United States citizens onto their soil. Years before, Presidents Adams and Jackson had pressed Mexico to sell the territories to the United States, an offer the Mexican government had seen as an insult. Repeated offers had caused even more resentment, and then the Texans had declared their land a republic and had fought the Mexican forces to prove their independence. And almost as soon as they had won it they sent an envoy to Washington, D.C. requesting annexation by the United States. "Great Britain is lately on a mission to abolish slavery from the world," John Calhoun had expounded, "and she has her eye on all republics." Sufficient enough reason, the Secretary of State said, to absorb Texas.

Mexico had refused to recognize the Texans' victory and had considered the United States's annexation an outright declaration of war. An exploration of California had added wood to the fire; President Polk wanted the rich land for the United States, nothing would stop him from having it, or so the Boston newspapers claimed—and if he had to goad Mexico into war to obtain California, so be it. That proved to be true: another exploration party had gone to California, and the Secretary of War wrote a dispatch to the American consul at Monterey, strongly suggesting a union between the United States and California.

Shortly after the Texas annexation, President Polk had positioned General Zachary Taylor, "Old Rough and Ready," on the Nueces River, which represented the southwest border of Texas, and at nearly the same time yet a third exploration party was sent to California, prepared to encourage revolt. When a military faction, one that had been priming for war with the United States, revolted against their own Mexican government, Polk had ordered Taylor to cross the river—an outright act of war. Mexico owed the United States money for unpaid claims of American citizens, too, something Mexican representatives now refused to discuss, and while the refusal had outraged the majority of Americans, few wanted war. Then in late April Mexican forces had engaged Taylor in skirmishes along the Rio

Grande, placing Fort Texas under siege, and President Polk asked Congress for the declaration.

The conflict and opposition to it had a marked effect on Boston, and no citizen, regardless of his age or race, could ignore the war. In June, fifers marched the streets, drumming for military recruits. The city contributed few. James Russell Lowell had his say: "They just want this Californy, so's to lug new slave states in, to abuse ye and to scorn ye, an' to plunder ye like sin." If one was heard expressing support for the war one risked being clubbed by the ruffians who gathered on street corners and in public houses. But while Mike herself opposed the war, she also opposed the righteous violence, and she prayed for an end to it.

She spent several months at home that summer of 1846, and during that time she was given another opportunity to assist her father in caring for one of his patients, this time a woman in great distress during childbirth.

10

He didn't intend for her to attend the birth with him. It simply turned out that way.

She was awake late, sitting in the study reading when someone pounded on the Quinns' front door. Rather than wait for Harrison to rise and answer, Mike pulled open the door herself—and there stood a scruffy-looking man in rumpled homespun who twisted what was left of a hat in his hands.

"He's got to come quick, real quick," he gasped. "The doctor, Dr. Quinn. It's her time, and I know we haven't paid him nothing. But please, he's got to come. The women are trying to help her but she's screaming and I don't know what to do. He's got to—"

Mike laid a hand on the man's forearm, quickly taking in the situation. "I'll wake him," she said. "He'll come."

He nodded shakily, and she urged him into the entryway. Harrison appeared in his nightcap and gown right then and she told him to wake Dr. Quinn, that there was an urgent medical call. Harrison asked no questions. He shot off up the stairs, moving faster than Michaela had ever seen him move.

Mike ushered the man into the study and gave him a

snifter of brandy to calm his nerves. He pressed it to his lips and tossed it back seconds before her father appeared in the doorway.

"What is it, Mr. Avery?" Dr. Quinn asked, recognizing the man immediately.

"Dolly . . . it's her time," the man said, jumping up. "Something's not right. The women're scared. She's been screaming all day. Is she gonna die, Dr. Quinn?"

"I don't know," Mike's father said, gathering his bag. "We shall go see to her. Harrison is sending for the buggy and—"

"I have my wagon. She can't wait, Dr. Quinn. Please. Something's wrong. She's birthed before, and something ain't right this time."

Joseph nodded, and he and Mr. Avery started through the study doorway together.

Dr. Quinn glanced back. "Come, Mike," he ordered softly, and for a few seconds Michaela's feet did not move—she thought she had heard him wrong. He spoke louder: "Mike, come along."

She moved then, soon stepping out into the night with the two men, elated that her father was taking her out on another medical call, and what sounded like a rather serious one at that.

He handed her up onto the wagon seat, then he and Mr. Avery stepped up. Soon the frantic man took hold of the reins and they were bolting across town, the wagon rattling and bumping beneath them.

They reached the residence, an old gray shanty, some fifteen minutes later, and Mr. Avery jerked the two horses to a stop. In ordinary circumstances, Mike's father might have said something to him about his mistreatment of them— Joseph Quinn was gentle even with horses—but the urgency of the situation arrested his attention. Besides, Mr. Avery was off the wagon seat and bolting for the shanty before Joseph could open his mouth to say a word. Michaela heard the confined mother shrieking, a sound she had certainly heard during her sister's labors and deliveries; but the shouting and the shrieks of other women who attended this struggling mother unsettled Mike.

"The women in this family . . ." she heard her father mutter as he handed her down. "Calm them for me, Mike, or I shall be unable to manage a thing." She knew then that, no matter what, she must stay calm herself.

Inside the small house, three women skittered around the mother's bed in the back room. "Bleedin' like a stuck pig," one said over and over, wringing her hands, arranging the tattered coverlet. Another prayed again and again: "Sweet Jesus, deliver her safely to your house." The other, a heavy red-faced creature, shook like a wobbly drunk, tried to grab hold of the mother's thrashing legs, and screeched twice as loud as the confined woman every time the patient made a sound. Mrs. Avery was wild with pain, and Mike saw, even through her bloody shift, that her huge belly was taut.

So much blood . . . in pools on the sheets, splattered in places. . . . Michaela wondered briefly if there was as much during every delivery.

She put her attention on getting the frantic women out of the room so her father could work. Mr. Avery had gone white as a sheet. His wife strained with a pain, pulling her legs up and pushing with all her might. Another gush of blood marked the bedding, and he swooned dead away.

Dr. Quinn tore off his coat, shoved up his shirtsleeves, and sat on the bed near the mother's thighs, appearing mindless of the blood. He issued commands: "I need water . . . cloths . . . whiskey . . . a little milk." And when the women continued their fussings despite Michaela's attempts to quiet them and his attempts to secure the items from them, he barked Mike's name.

Her head snapped around.

"You want to be a medical doctor," he said, looking her straight in the eye. "It begins this night. Find the things I need and bring them. Placenta praevia . . ." he told her, and then she knew this was not a normal delivery. She knew what was happening because she had read about it, how when the placenta detached before the delivery of the child, the mother, in most cases, bled to death.

"Help us," she told the praying woman. She shook her, told her they might still save the mother if she helped, and then the attendant rocked her head slowly, trying to surface from her fear and shock.

Mike had to trust that the woman would go and bring back the things her father needed—he was calling to her again, telling her to fetch the bottle of ergotamine from his medical bag, which he had dropped near the bedside. His hands and arms were bloody clear up to his elbows now, and the mother was exposed from the top of her belly down. Knowing modesty had no place in this room at the moment, Michaela grabbed up the bag as the praying woman rushed from the room, hopefully going off to collect the things Dr. Quinn needed.

"Give her some," he told Mike when she pulled the bottle from the bag. "Make her drink it straight. I've no idea if we'll get the whiskey."

She uncorked the bottle, somehow held the mother's thrashing head, and poured a good amount of ergotamine into her mouth. "Drink," she urged. "It will help stay the flooding. Drink. Please drink."

Her own hands trembled, and she felt as if a cannonball of fear weighed heavily in the pit of her belly. The room was thick with the stench of blood, loud with the cries of the other two attendants, who, mercifully, now clung to each other near the door. Mike couldn't fathom how a person could live after the loss of so much blood. But the mother still had the strength to struggle, and she still had her mind about her somewhat—her eyes were wild with fear, but she swallowed the medication.

"Laudanum now," Dr. Quinn said. "It will ease the pain and calm her." Michaela hastened to recork the bottle of ergotamine and fetch the laudanum. The mother drank of that eagerly, then another pain seized her and she arched her back and strained.

"More ergot now," the doctor commanded, not looking up from his work between the mother's wide-spread legs. Mike exchanged bottles again.

The delivering woman gasped a deep breath and pushed

again. *"More,"* Dr. Quinn ordered her. *"Harder!"* She was losing her strength, Michaela could tell, her head falling back while the uterus was still tightly contracted.

"No," Mike told her hoarsely. "You must push. Deliver the child."

The praying woman returned with cloths and a basin of water. No milk and no whiskey. The weakening mother pushed again, and Michaela saw the infant's discolored head emerge and the grayish purple placenta along with it.

The child was dead . . . she just knew the child was dead. But she heard him make a strangling sound, then came a weak cry as his legs and feet slithered out. Mike grabbed several clean cloths from the praying woman's hands, placed them on the bed, then stared in wonderment and awe at the new life her father laid there. The boy was bloody and wrinkled and coated in places with a white substance. But he gathered his breath and let out a squall, and a second later, Michaela let out her own cry of joy.

"String in the bag," her father said, taking the basin of water from the praying woman and placing it on the bed. Mike quickly realized that he wasn't finished with the mother, that he was far from finished, that she was still hemorrhaging and that he had to concern himself with that; that he was handing care of the infant over to her. He would tell her how to tie off the cord and cut it, and she must follow his instruction.

She found the string, cut a good piece, tied it tight an inch from where it connected to the squalling baby. She was vaguely aware of her bloody hand searching through the medical bag for her father's scissors, then she came up with them. The cord was thick but the scissors were sharp, and she soon had the afterbirth wrapped in one of the cloths and pushed aside.

The infant was cool to touch, but his skin was flushing. The mother asked for him, and Dr. Quinn told Mike to put him to the mother's breast, that the suckling would help stay the bleeding also. "More ergot," he said as he reached into the medical bag and pulled out a large irrigating syringe.

As the baby began to suckle and the mother inspected

139

him weakly, the doctor filled the syringe with water and introduced it into the vagina, filling the uterus with coolness. Then he moved up, massaged the womb through the abdomen despite the gasps of pain from the mother, and compressed the area over the aorta. He repeated the process again and again, occasionally sending Mike off to fetch more water from the well to the left of the shanty and the now calmer attendants off for the whiskey and milk he had requested earlier.

The ergotamine was bitter, he would tell Michaela later, and she realized that he mixed it with a little whiskey and milk to flavor it for the mother. It seemed a small comfort to give the hemorrhaging Mrs. Avery, but a no less important one for the doctor to administer to his patient. Mr. Avery had come around, taken a quick look at his newborn son and weakening wife, paled again at the sight of the blood still oozing from Mrs. Avery, and hurried from the room.

Dr. Quinn worked diligently for several hours, douching, compressing, massaging, telling Mike to give more ergotamine and laudanum. He worked on even when Michaela thought Mrs. Avery had surely expired—when her head fell to one side, her eyelids slid shut, and she quieted. But she still breathed, Mike saw, and the physician still worked.

When he finally withdrew from the bed, the room reeked of the thick odor of old blood, and he appeared more weary than Mike had ever seen him. The attendants had long since gone off to the other room. One, being the unsuccessful midwife (the praying woman), had left the shanty altogether, muttering that even a doctor could not save Mrs. Avery. Now and then the infant woke at his mother's side and rooted, and Michaela put him to the breast.

"Will she live?" Mike could not help but ask her father.

"I do not know," he answered honestly.

The attendants—Mrs. Avery's sister and mother—came back and changed the bedding and the mother's shift. Intermittently, Dr. Quinn checked for more bleeding. Upon finding none, he and Mike settled in chairs beside the bed. She fell asleep there.

Near dawn, he woke her.

"Is she alive?" she asked, rubbing her eyes. She heard the infant cry, and she glanced over at the bed and saw him looking around.

"She's alive," her father said. "Though not entirely safe."

No need to ask what he meant—Michaela knew. Mrs. Avery was white as a sheet, and a bluish color stained the skin surrounding her lips.

Dr. Quinn gathered his bag. "Come along. For now, we've done all we can do. We shall sneak you in the kitchen door before Mother wakes. One look at you and she'll think you've been injured."

There was dried blood all over her dress, but she hadn't noticed before now. She hadn't cared. Her father smiled down at her, held out his hand, and Michaela took it.

"Come along, my little assistant," he said, and Mike beamed with pride.

Not two weeks later Mrs. Avery was doing splendidly, having regained much of her strength, embracing both Dr. Quinn and Michaela every time she saw them. The infant— they had named him Joseph after Mike's father—by fall was a bubbly baby with a hearty appetite, and his mother had recovered completely. Mike had told Etha all about the birth, and Etha listened with bright eyes, then wondered aloud at the miracle of it—and at Dr. Quinn's heroics.

But a sense of humility went hand in hand with the profession, Michaela had realized that evening, and her father had more a sense of mildness about him, both personally and professionally, than anyone she knew. He didn't think of himself as a hero, only a medical doctor. If she marveled aloud to him that he had saved the woman's life, he said nothing.

Soon the events of that night were discussed less and less, and she stopped calling him a hero because she sensed he disliked the word, the very thought. The events of that night, his swift treatments, and his humbleness about them were never far from Michaela's mind, however, and her recollections had a profound effect on her thinking and on her own conduct in future years.

An incredible development took place in medicine that autumn. A local dentist, Dr. Morton, had been conducting experiments with ether, a light, flammable liquid, for some time now. It had been known universally for years that ether had the same effect as "laughing gas," or nitrous oxide, reducing the person who breathed it into gales of laughter. "Ether parties" had become the rage among some outrageous people for a time, Mike had read only a few years ago in one of her father's journals. But by the 1840s, years after a Dr. Henry Hickman in Ludlow, England, experimented with giving animals carbon dioxide and nitrous oxide, a dentist in Hartford, Connecticut, had had a molar pulled while under the influence of the gas, and had then come to Massachusetts General only last year to demonstrate its effects.

The show had been a failure. Sadly so, Dr. Quinn had remarked, and Dr. Wells had been laughed out of Boston. "But was it?" Oliver Holmes speculated at the time. "A failure, that is?" And then he had become intrigued by Dr. Morton's experiments with the gas.

Morton, a dentist but also a medical student, had used ether on himself, on his pet spaniel, and then on a dental patient, finally deeming it more suitable for surgery, given its long-lasting power. Another demonstration was held at Massachusetts General, this time during surgery performed by John Warren.

Mike attended the spectacle with her father and Dr. Holmes, drawing curious and disapproving looks, and she held her breath for the longest time when Morton applied the ether and Dr. Warren removed a neck tumor without a peep from his patient.

The demonstration was a wild success, and Dr. Holmes wrote straightaway to Morton, suggesting humbly that the state produced by the gas be called anaesthesia, a word that signified insensibility to touch. Holmes was ecstatic over the discovery—no more screaming, suffering surgical patients—

and almost as joyous when his suggestion was applied by the medical community to the discovery.

Michaela wrote David a long letter about Dr. Morton, Dr. Warren, the anaesthesia, the surgery itself, and the way the patient woke and looked disoriented but undistressed (although the cutting of the tissue did cause him postoperative discomfort). She ended the letter by asking when he thought he might return home to visit—she missed him and their conversations.

He was caught up in his activities at Yale and in Connecticut, obviously. She received a brief note from him the following spring, that he hoped to get home the next year, that he was very busy with his studies. *So am I,* Mike thought, annoyed that she had not seen him in nearly two years now.

Several months later, after much thought, she became annoyed with *herself* for her impatience with him. Besides, she had to write him another letter and tell him the latest news: "A Dr. Gregory here has opened a school for women who wish to be trained as midwives. I do not find that particularly exciting and neither does my father. After all, women have attended laboring women for centuries. 'Why not a fully accredited medical school for women?' Father asked, and he sent Dr. Gregory a missive suggesting that.

"To which Dr. Gregory never responded," Michaela wrote after a moment's pause. "My father says Boston may never accept such a school, but that the idea is being considered in Philadelphia. Father approached the board of directors of the Tremont school about officially admitting me upon my graduation from the seminary. The answer was a quick negative one."

She paused again, glanced up and out the window over the little desk where she sat writing in the room she shared with Etha, Sally, and Catharine. David was much closer to New York State than she, but she had to pen her next thoughts anyway, give them solidity: "But . . . Elizabeth Blackwell has been admitted to Geneva Medical College," she wrote, and then she hesitated to get a fresh grip on her pen. "An enormous step, the acceptance of the first woman to study medicine."

Elizabeth Blackwell's story, dilemma, and acceptance into Geneva was being talked about and speculated about in medical communities. She had arrived in Philadelphia earlier this year with the intent of attending a medical college. She had been writing to colleges for some time now, having wanted to study medicine since the death of a close friend, who had suffered and died slowly of cancer. She had nursed her friend, spending endless days and nights at the bedside, and finally the patient had asked why she didn't study medicine—she would much rather have a woman care for her than a man. Elizabeth's family was poor, unable to put up the money needed for a medical education, and so Elizabeth had earned the money herself through becoming a governess and by teaching. When she had saved adequately, she had ridden into Philadelphia, bursting into the middle of the large medical community there and announcing her purpose. Then the letters . . . the requests for admittance to colleges . . . and finally her letter of acceptance from Geneva. But already she had begun her studies with a Dr. Warrington in Philadelphia, dissecting tendons, asking questions, preparing herself.

Mike relayed all the news to David. So much was happening! Exciting things! She had written him other letters, but this was her longest yet, and she laughed at herself when she sealed the envelope and raced off to take the letter to the post.

Indeed Elizabeth Blackwell's acceptance into Geneva College was an important step for women. Mike knew she herself was still young, that she had much to study and learn before she began applying to colleges. And she also realized, with her advanced maturity, that this Miss Blackwell was paving the way for her—and perhaps for a lot of other females who wished to study medicine.

Mike's father planned a trip to Pennsylvania for the two of them, stunning her with the news one evening at the seminary. In Philadelphia, she would meet his friends who had been discussing the possibility, in meetings among themselves and in correspondence with him, of founding a female medical college. Blackwell had made her impressions there, had recruited her admirers, had made the "medical center of the United States" sit up and take notice. A medical college for women was needed, announced Dr. Warrington, and he, and others, meant to work toward that goal.

Upon hearing the news that Father had planned the journey for them, Mama put up her icy barriers again. Until now, throughout the anaesthesia demonstration at Massachusetts General and throughout her father taking Michaela with him on more and more medical calls, she had been polite but quiet. Now she seemed forever hardened toward Mike.

Etha yelped with joy when Michaela told her the news, Rebecca hugged Mike tight, Sally helped her pack a trunk the day before her departure one early June day in 1848. And Dr. Holmes . . . That same afternoon, smiling his sly smile, he approached Michaela at the Tremont school and handed her a package wrapped in crisp brown paper.

Inside was a stethoscope, her very own.

PART THREE:

Michaela Quinn, M.D.

*Let opposition but quicken you to new enthusiasm for
the life work of your choice and strengthen
your spirit of consecration.*
— SARAH READ ADAMSON, DR DOLLEY

A new generation of women is upon the stage.
— LUCRETIA MOTT

11

Elizabeth Blackwell had returned to Philadelphia to work at Blockley, one of the poorhouses, between her sessions at Geneva College. She had been admitted to a medical school finally, but the directors at Blockley allowed her to study at that institution only as a nurse.

Mike had never expected this—that she might actually meet the remarkable woman while in Pennsylvania. Miss Blackwell had gone off to Geneva and would be there for some time, or so Michaela had thought. But the woman wasted not a moment, it seemed, and one evening Mike and her father happened upon Elizabeth when they attended a small supper at the home of Dr. William Elder, one of Joseph Quinn's close friends.

Upon Miss Blackwell's initial arrival in Philadelphia last year, she had presented Dr. Elder with a letter of introduction and he had excitedly taken her into his home, giving her lodging, and introducing her around to his medical acquaintances, then sending her to the various local colleges. But while many, mostly Quaker, physicians in the city had discussed the idea of women in medicine, no one had actually taken up the cause, and Elizabeth had been turned away from all medical schools in the city.

There was nothing pretentious about Elizabeth Blackwell. She was small, smiling, demure, pensive. She wore a navy blue gown, ruffled at the shoulders, and she appeared modest and dignified, her dark hair pulled back and secured in a chignon near the nape of her neck. No jewels, no haughty airs, no uplifted chin, no gloating about her recent accomplishment. In fact, she smiled almost shyly at the toasts that were made to her. When Mr. William Mullen, a successful, modern-thinking Philadelphia businessman, raised his wineglass yet again over the meal and asked Elizabeth if she knew Dr. Brian had written to him from Geneva, going on and on about what a wonderful student she made, Elizabeth's face reddened. She leaned over to Mike, who was in great awe, having been seated at the right hand of the woman, and said softly, "I simply speak my mind, albeit in a tactful fashion, and I refuse to be intimidated."

"And you study," Mike said, trembling a little. "You must study and study."

Elizabeth smiled. "I do. As you must."

Michaela became aware that she was staring at the woman, and she lowered her gaze to her plate. A second later, she flashed Elizabeth a smile. Elizabeth smiled back and placed her hand over Mike's. The six people gathered round the table, Dr. Elder's wife included, drank the toast.

There was no separation of male and female after this supper, although Mrs. Elder went off to help see to her children. After the evening meal, Michaela was accustomed to the men drifting away to smoke and the women getting up a game of cards or some other activity. But this party, minus Mrs. Elder, gathered in the drawing room, and soon a discussion of typhoid fever, or "ship fever" commenced. Mr. Mullen, while not a physician, had always been interested in medicine and had attended a number of lectures and even studied at the Pennsylvania Medical College, and he listened with interest now and took part in the discussion.

Philadelphia had its share of immigrants, and, as in Boston, they often spilled from incoming vessels with fever, diarrhea, prostration, headache, and intestinal inflammation.

Since returning to Philadelphia, Elizabeth Blackwell had made it her business to work among the wards of those suffering from the fever, the Irish and Germans whose only glimpse of the New World was very often the Philadelphia wharves and then the gray walls of Blockley. The alms-houses saw a steady flow of poor and sick, and Elizabeth made her rounds of them, apparently impressing Philadelphians with that work almost as much as she had impressed them last year with her efforts to gain admittance to a medical school.

Throughout the discussion and throughout her colleagues' and Mr. Mullen's praise, Elizabeth remained humble and open-minded. She considered suggestions, treatments, mulled over the unusual case of which Dr. Elder spoke. She then asked Mike's father about Dr. Holmes and the Tremont Street school. Then came a discussion of puerperal fever and Holmes's plea to the medical community that they heed his warnings and begin taking care with cleanliness between dissection rooms, laboratories, and laboring and delivering mothers.

William Mullen scoffed, but Dr. Elder wondered aloud, and in a tone of quiet distress, how many mothers he had murdered himself through ignorance.

"That seems extreme," Mr. Mullen said.

"But is it?" Elizabeth queried, and then the room fell silent for a few long moments. *Indeed,* Mike thought, *how many mothers have gone to their graves because of ignorance?*

"And if Holmes is right?" she asked rather timidly.

Mr. Mullen lifted his brow at her. An alarmed look flashed in Dr. Elder's eyes. Dr. Quinn drew deeply from his pipe and tipped his head, clearly considering the question (Michaela knew how he felt about this issue, she knew he thought Holmes had something), and Elizabeth, with a gentle smile and a knowing look, encouraged Mike, who then cleared her throat and spoke louder.

"If he's right . . . if the medical men who are berating him for his findings would dash away their exasperating pride and put the mothers' health first . . . Dr. Holmes is

151

not looking for criminal convictions," Mike said, concentrating on William Mullen. "He is looking to save lives."

The room fell silent again. Dr. Elder watched Mike in quiet, but seemingly pleased amazement. Mr. Mullen stared at Michaela as if wondering what right, at the tender age of fifteen, she had even to dare join in this discussion. A grin tickled her father's mouth around the stem of his pipe.

Elizabeth told Mr. Mullen, "Michaela . . . Mike . . . two years ago helped her father deliver a woman who exhibited placenta praevia. The outcome was a joyous one for both mother and child, I might add."

Michaela wondered who had told Elizabeth about the delivery and her involvement in it. But a quick look at her father, who sat calmly in an opposite chair, and she knew who had.

"Since then, Mike has occasionally accompanied Dr. Quinn on his medical calls at a prominent Boston hospital and throughout the city," Dr. Elder said.

"M-my father delivered the child and tended the mother," Mike told them all, her voice a near whisper.

"We worked together," Dr. Quinn said. "Mike administered ergotamine and laudanum throughout the hours—and cut the umbilical cord and tended the child."

"While you worked at staying the hemorrhaging," she mumbled.

"Midwifery," Mr. Mullen said, scoffing again.

"Several years before that she diagnosed a patient with a skin ailment," Elizabeth said, clearly becoming ruffled—she now sat forward and straight in her chair.

"And the pnuemonia victim in that old house?" Dr. Elder remarked to Michaela, whose embarrassment deepened.

Mike's father crossed one leg over the other. Clearly, he had introduced her to his friend long before this visit. "She has been a medical student since the day she was born," he told them all, "and lately we have both become increasingly interested in Geneva's acceptance of Miss Blackwell—and in the talk of starting a medical college for women here in Philadelphia. You initiated some of that talk, did you not, Mr. Mullen?"

William Mullen shifted near the mantelpiece. "Yes, but . . . forgive me. I've never encountered such a young . . ."

"Medical student?" Elizabeth asked, her eyes sparkling.

"Or such a level of intelligence in one so young?" Dr. Elder queried.

Michaela shifted on the settee.

"That explains her presence here," Mr. Mullen said. "Elder, you might have informed me."

His colleague grinned. "The interest is growing, my friend. Here sits yet another fine example of that."

Mr. Mullen drummed his fingertips on the mantelpiece, something he often did when contemplating, or so Mike would later learn. He swirled the water in his glass, too, and shot Michaela a wondering look from the corner of his eye. "So it is, Dr. Elder. So it is."

Both men were liberal Quakers, believers in the intelligence of women, and Dr. Elder was often a preceptor to medical students. That Mr. Mullen had trouble believing in her intelligence at so young an age did not surprise Mike; she often met people who, once engaged in conversation with her, were amazed. He was an advocate of medical education for women, her father had told her, and clearly that was the subject between him and Dr. Elder right now. There were others who were also advocates—a Dr. Longshore, a Dr. Moseley, a Dr. Gleason . . . all liberal Quakers, all leading men in this community.

"Ann Preston was recently turned away by the University of Pennsylvania," Elizabeth said. "And at Geneva . . . I hear they are refusing to accept any more women."

Again the room fell silent.

"Gentlemen . . ." Joseph Quinn said, rising from his chair. He approached Mr. Mullen at the hearth and stooped to tap his pipe bowl on the bricks. "Mr. Mullen, I hear you stand ready, financially, to help sponsor any endeavor. So do I. You'll need a building, and it will need to be fitted up."

Elizabeth's eyes brightened even more now. She glanced at each of the physicians, then at Mr. Mullen, then squeezed her hands together. Dr. Elder suggested a vacant house on

153

Arch Street, and Elizabeth commented that no one was better qualified to help fit up the medical school than Dr. Quinn, given the fact that he and Dr. Holmes, and a handful of other leading physicians in Boston, had started the successful Tremont Street Medical School.

"I must soon return to Boston," Joseph Quinn warned them. "But I will always make my advice and suggestions available."

The conversation went on. They would need a surgery theater, surgical instruments, microscopes. . . .

Michaela sat forth on the edge of the settee, intermittently catching her breath, watching, listening, absorbing. She was observing an important moment, she thought, the growth of a conception, perhaps a materialization. If this idea of Mullen's, the idea of a medical college for women, took hold, women everywhere would surely stand straight up and cheer.

A convention for women's rights was presently being held in Seneca Falls, New York, Elizabeth told Mike the next afternoon, as they settled in a carriage headed for Blockley. "I have been shunned by the women of Geneva," she said, "But, oh . . . what little they realize! As women, they do have rights . . . the right to their own clothes, their own money, *the right to vote*. Like slaves, we have minds. We can learn, we can be taught. We have the right to practice higher professions. *I will not settle for midwifery.*"

Mike went everywhere with Elizabeth Blackwell during the month she and her father stayed in Philadelphia. They tended patients in the Blockley wards, walked poplar-lined drives and the High Street Market, where they bought lemons and oranges and ate sweet buns. They attended a lecture given by John Greenleaf Whittier, and then one delivered by Dorothea Dix, who had taken up the cause of creating hospitals instead of prisons for the insane. Michaela watched Elizabeth dissect a human leg, under the direction of her father and Dr. Warrington, and she became completely absorbed in the process, finding it so much more gripping and interesting than David's and her dissections of small animals. Later, she drew diagrams from memory and her father corrected them for her.

She and Elizabeth attended the theater, sitting in a side box and watching the actors dance across the stage in the flickering gaslights. They encountered James Lowell in a coffeehouse on Walnut Street where he sat discussing his *Bigelow* poems with a gathering of friends and acquaintances, verses that humorously presented opposition to the Mexican War and the annexation of Texas. They accompanied Dr. Elder to the wharf one afternoon to send his wife off to visit her family in New York, and there they watched huge tubs of molasses, flour, and salt be loaded into a vessel for shipment abroad. Onions were sent off to Antigua, chocolate to Virginia, gunpowder to Jamaica. Corn, yarn, knives, furs, and pistols were shipped, to where, Mike never gathered. Rum and sugar were frequently imported from Barbados, Dr. Elder said—he did his share of shipping on the side. Linen arrived from Liverpool, rice from South Carolina, wine from Madeira, spirits from Jamaica.

Far from the classrooms of the Boston seminary, Mike filled her mind with things she had not always been permitted to observe. She took part in discussions, becoming bolder, with Elizabeth at her side, as the days wore on, having conversations with others about exciting subjects— with Elizabeth about Geneva, with Dr. Warrington about dissection, with Dr. Elder about the idea of the medical college, with her father about suturing wounds and dressing them with dry lint. One evening Dr. Elder spoke of a patient he had tended that morning, the result of a threshing-machine accident, and Michaela asked, most respectfully, why he had opted against amputation of the man's injured leg. Amputation was commonplace, after all, in the case of mutilations. Mr. Mullen stood at his side, watching her with interest, studying her, it seemed.

"There was a pulse in the foot," Dr. Elder answered simply, "and the limb was still warm, with good color."

It was quite a risk, given the possibility of infection and gangrene. But Dr. Elder was bold and innovative, and he would rather keep close watch on the leg, leaving it as long as he felt there was a chance to save it, taking it at the first sign of gangrene.

"You are as bright as three Elizabeth Blackwells," William Mullen finally told Mike the day before she and her father were scheduled to depart Philadelphia. When she smiled, he said, "Dr. Holmes may deserve some listening to, as you suggest. Indeed, he is not looking for criminal convictions."

Elizabeth and Dr. Elder accompanied her father and her to the wharf. There, Mike embraced her new friends, her champions. She wished Elizabeth much success during her next year at Geneva and told Dr. Elder to write her straightaway about the beginnings of the medical college. He laughed at her excitement, at her "crooked smile," and he marveled, as he had countless times now, that each of her eyes were a different shade of color. Then her father escorted her up the plank and a man followed with their trunks.

Mike knew how fortunate she was to have her own father believe in her so much—she had heard firsthand of Elizabeth's struggles to be noticed, had heard secondhand of Ann Preston's—and just before he extinguished the lamps in their cabin that night, she told her father exactly how she felt.

"Sleep now, Mike," he said, never one to take praise well.

But she couldn't. She was too filled with the happenings of the last few weeks, too elated by her experiences, the people she had met, the things she had done and seen. She couldn't wait to return home and talk to Etha—but she wished she could stay, also. She couldn't wait for the light of day so she might look over her drawings and notes.

And yet when daybreak began spilling into the porthole of the small cabin, she fell asleep. She woke much later, near noon, dressed quickly, and dashed off to find her father.

David had visited, her mother and Marjorie couldn't seem to wait to announce to her, Mother with a strange glow to her face, Marjorie with a sly smile, anticipating Michaela's disappointment that she had missed him. Mike tried, without success, to hide her despondency, to turn away before the hateful Marjorie could see her face fall.

She had missed David's visit. . . . They had not seen each other in *three years* and she had missed his visit. Why had he not written that he was coming home? Why had he not told her, his family, his friends, her, her family? Why had he planned a surprise visit, a summer holiday, when the last few summers he had worked so diligently at his studies and alongside a surgeon? He surely never suspected that she would be gone. Her entire life she had rarely journeyed outside of Boston.

He had come home to visit while she and Father were in Philadelphia.

Her heart ached. She almost could not catch her breath. She gripped the arm of a parlor side chair and almost toppled over with it.

"Perhaps this will teach you," Marjorie said. "Instead of pursuing medical nonsense in Philadelphia, you should have been home helping Mother plan your coming out. After all, you will turn sixteen soon."

She almost sounded like Mother. *Medical nonsense* . . . How many times had Mike heard their mother use exactly those words?

"Shut up, Marjorie," Mike snapped. She had to go upstairs . . . loosen her stays . . . lie on her bed. If only she had known David was coming. And yet if she had also known of her father's plans to take her to Philadelphia with him, she would have felt incredibly torn.

In a way, she was glad she had not known. What would she have done? Perhaps Father might have postponed their trip to Pennsylvania. But then she might have missed meeting and befriending Elizabeth Blackwell. And yet how could one miss what one never experienced? She felt light-headed, ill suddenly.

Mother was at her side in an instant, urging her to sit, telling Marjorie to fetch a wet cloth and a glass of water.

"She thinks to become a medical doctor one day," Marjorie said instead. "How can she think such a—"

"Marjorie, water and a wet cloth!" Mother's attention was on Mike and her near swooning, and she urged Michaela to sit back. She unfastened the buttons on the front of Mike's dress and then the laces of her corset, and when Marjorie finally brought the glass of water and the damp cloth, she snatched it from her hand. The room spun around Mike, and a thick feeling of nausea rose, souring her mouth. Three years . . . and she had missed David's visit.

Marjorie again: "It's really nothing so terrible. Not like—" Mother cut her off with a fierce look, then pressed the cloth to Michaela's face.

Michaela closed her eyes, relishing the comfort of the cool dampness on her skin. She had been so happy, so elated, so excited about returning home and telling Etha everything she had seen and done, about all the people she had met; how Philadelphia really was bulging, simply bulging, with medical happenings and people. And instead she had come home to this. Father had gone to his study after greeting Mother, and then Mike had found Marjorie in the parlor, apparently in the middle of a visit home. Marjorie had stood, greeted her in her cold way, and told her the news about David's visit just as Mother had stepped into the room.

When Michaela opened her eyes, Marjorie was gone, and there was only her mother.

"I believe he's become more than a childhood friend," Elizabeth Quinn remarked, studying her. Compassion lit her eyes, and she tipped her head and regarded Mike in a concerned way. In those moments, Mike felt close to her mother. She was only fifteen, but she was aware of her own maturity and so was Elizabeth.

"We've . . . we've written some," Michaela said breathlessly. "He's full of news of Yale and the medical community there. The physicians he's come to know and the ones with whom he's studying. He hardly notices me. He hardly cares. He's become far too busy to write but two letters a year. This past year, only one."

Elizabeth cocked a brow. "My . . . you are feeling sorry

for yourself. When has he had time to notice? And how? He's been in Connecticut."

Mike shifted in the chair, then looked away, to the open window where a lace curtain fluttered in the late summer breeze. They might have walked the Common together, gone rowing . . . talked about medicine and new developments. "Precisely," she mumbled. "When has he had time to notice?"

"Michaela, if you never listen to me again, listen to me now," her mother said, and Mike turned back to her, curious but also heavy-hearted.

"David is studying hard to become a surgeon and if you want his attentions, you must be patient. When he left Boston, you were twelve years old, an unkempt girl. He has no idea what you look like now," Elizabeth said softly, "what a lovely young woman you are growing into. How poised you've become. I didn't agree with your father sending you to that seminary, although I tried to see the benefit in it. I did try, Michaela, and now I have."

Mike's eyes filled with tears. *You must be patient*. . . . Three years . . . She *had* been patient. Now she was frightened. "How many more years until he returns?" she whispered. "Will he find someone there?"

Shaking her head, Elizabeth pressed a finger to Michaela's lips. Then she lifted the water glass and urged Michaela to drink.

He had left her a letter, penned the day before he departed Boston to journey back to Connecticut. She read it that evening while seated on her bed in the privacy of her room at the town house, the French lace of her tester softening the glow of the lamps even more. This room had become a comfort, a haven, the day Marjorie had married and moved out. To Michaela's surprise, Mother had redone the entire room, having the extra bed moved out, a small secretary and hearth chairs moved in. Mike herself had added a bookshelf, and, in recent years, more clothing and shoes in the armoire and perfume bottles on the vanity.

"I regret that I missed you," David began, and Michaela had to choke back more tears.

159

But Philadelphia! Your last letter was filled with exciting news of medical advancements for women in that city, and I know your father's surprise delighted you. How good of him to take you there. I trust the visit was a stimulating one.

I have spent the last year with a fine preceptor, a Dr. Bollingen, one of the best surgeons New England has to offer. I enter the medical school here next fall, and after the proper number of semesters, I may then travel to Paris to study with the masters there. Dr. Holmes did that, as you recall. Those who study there become the best physicians, or so Dr. Bollingen advises. Dr. Holmes agrees—I spoke to him while in Boston. The best medical doctors in the world, he said, are at la Pitié and the Hôtel de Dieu.

Michaela lay back on her feather pillows, turned the letter over, placed it on her breasts, and stared up at the canopy. *Paris . . . France.* So much farther away than Connecticut. A world away from Boston. When would David ever come home again? How long would he study abroad? "He is studying to become a surgeon," her mother had said. And then, "You must be patient."

She did not begrudge him his studies. She would never want, or ask, him to give them up for her. She was not sure he would anyway, if the selfish thought ever did occur to her. She simply missed him—and her heart ached to have him near.

"I have been neglectful of my correspondence with you," he wrote, "and for that, I apologize. I will endeavor to do better in that regard."

That sentence made her smile a little, rather sadly. Then she read on:

Did you hear of the women's convention that was held in Seneca Falls? It was quite an event, if the newspapers tell it right, and one in which I know you would be interested. The right of women to vote and own property was debated, and a woman named Susan

160

Anthony roused the troops with her orations regarding divorce. I champion the cause. For too long now women themselves have been regarded as property, have been excluded in political matters, and lose all rights when they speak marital vows. I could go on, and I usually do when the topic arises. I attended a gathering in May and witnessed a woman be cut off when she tried to express her opinion regarding the recent United States peace treaty with Mexico. She was quite intelligent and well read, as George Butler and I learned later when we engaged her in conversation on the political subject.

This letter was a lengthy one at least. Dr. Holmes had had much to say about her while David visited him. He had told David how she had helped her father deliver the woman suffering from placenta praevia and how she had asked a number of questions after the anaesthesia demonstration at the hospital. Dr. Holmes had told David that she was a fine example of why females should be allowed to study and practice medicine, and Mike glowed when she read that.

The renowned Boston physician and medical professor had also informed David that she was becoming quite a "lovely young lady," and David expressed his curiosity at that—something that made Michaela sit up in her bed and reread his entire last paragraph. Perhaps his curiosity will bring him back to Boston next year, she thought, and then she read on.

He himself was full of information and excitement: in nearby New York, an odd building was being constructed, a strange sight of cast iron instead of stone columns. The Broadway Theater now offered the comfort of cooler air during hot summer nights, put out by a steam-powered apparatus that provided ventilation of the entire building. "An amazing contraption," David wrote, "one that almost eliminates the bothersome flapping of fans during performances."

The letter ended with him telling her that he planned to make a return visit to Boston next summer, sooner if the opportunity arose. And again—he regreted that he had missed her.

Michaela reread his words over and over, hearing his voice in them. But somehow the voice was different. He sounded older, wiser, more pensive. More educated. She laughed at herself for thinking the last. Of course he was. He was a student at one of the finest institutions in the nation.

She fell asleep later with the papers still in hand and with a gentle breeze spilling in softly through the open bay windows.

Her despondency never really went away, the disappointment that she had missed him, that she had worked hard and long for the day when he would return and find her attractive. She *was* growing into a young woman, exactly as Mother said. Only last year she had begun having her monthly flow, and she had become accomplished in many areas over the last three years, areas in which attractive women of good social standing became accomplished. She had waited for him to visit . . . and she had missed him while she had been off pursuing her medical interests. He was nineteen years old now. *Nineteen.* She could not imagine that. She wondered how tall he was, if his face looked the same, if his eyes still had the same gentleness to them.

The following week she saw Jimmie Becker, home from studying in England, of all places (most good Boston boys went to Harvard or Yale, but then, when had Jimmie ever been a "good Boston boy?"), and she noted the change in his height and appearance and thought David must surely look different, too.

She was attending the theater with her parents when Jimmie approached their box during intermission. At first, she failed to recognize him, then she saw the mischievousness in his dark, dancing blue eyes and she knew him. She had seen him the last time two summers ago, when he had nearly taken a flogging from old Mr. Ellis after tossing the man's cat in Frog Pond and almost giving the animal a heart attack. Then, despite her anger with him still over the way he had treated her that day on the Charles River, when she, he, and David had been exploring the river, she had laughed when Mr. Ellis tore off after Jimmie with his cane, determined to "wallop that boy."

"Michaela Anne Quinn," Jimmie said, taking the seat beside her, the one her father had just vacated to go smoke. "Mike," Jimmie said, his voice lower now, and he took her hand and lifted it to his lips.

Jimmie Becker, the wild child, kissing her hand like a gentleman.

"My . . ." she said, fighting a grin, "If it isn't the terror of Beacon Hill. Jimmie Becker, I heard you bought a ship and went to Liverpool."

That made him toss his head and laugh. She was jesting, of course. She hadn't heard a thing about Jimmie, only that he had gone off to school in England.

"Delusions!" he said. "I'm studying law, if you can imagine that."

"How to break it, no doubt," she retorted.

He laughed again while Elizabeth Quinn stirred nearby.

"Mother, do you remember Jimmie Becker?" Michaela asked.

Mother smoothed one sleeve of her gown and gave him a haughty look. "All of Boston remembers Jimmie Becker. And will forever, I've no doubt."

He didn't bristle; he was accustomed to such disapproving airs, surely. "I made my mark," he said. "But Mike, you've developed a wit!" His eyes swept down over her in her lavender gown with its modest neckline—a look her mother missed, thank goodness—and Michaela tipped her head at him.

"I don't know why I expected you to blush," he told her the following afternoon, when he called at the house and they went strolling down Mount Vernon Street, her hand neatly placed on his forearm. Walking with Jimmie like this felt odd—Mike remembered the times they had run down the passage together with David, her hiking her skirts up, not giving a fig about propriety.

163

"Perhaps I'm still angry with you," she suggested, teasing him, "too angry to blush at anything you say."

He lifted a roguish brow, the fair-haired Jimmie with his flashing eyes. "Are you?"

"Well, you were terribly mean that day on the Charles River."

"Yes, I was, wasn't I? 'We're all growing up,' I believe I said. It was true, and I hated it. I knew we were changing, that life was changing, and I realized there was nothing I could do to stop that."

They strolled on, reflecting, passing two stately old men who sat conversing on a wrought-iron bench.

"David was here," she remarked, and her chest constricted with pain again. "I missed him. I was in Philadelphia with my father at the time."

"I was going to tell you he was here. He regretted not knowing you would be gone. But not half as much as he'll regret it when I write and inform him of how pretty you've grown," he said, his voice lowering with the last.

Now she did blush. It was such a nice, sweet compliment coming from Jimmie.

He reached over and tucked a stray tendril behind her neck, studied her, shook his head. "When have you and your family ever taken leave of Boston?"

"It wasn't—"

"Never," he said.

"There's talk in Philadelphia of starting a female medical college," she told him. "My father plans to help sponsor it."

After a long look, a smile began at one corner of Jimmie's mouth. "You may prove me wrong, then," he said. "You may get accepted to a medical college after all."

"'Girls don't go to medical school,'" she mocked. And then she straightened and tipped her head in that haughty Elizabeth Quinn way. "I may go *just* to prove you wrong."

He chuckled.

They walked on, all the way up to Charles Street, where she had watched him disappear around the corner many times.

"I wish I hadn't missed him," she said suddenly.

"He'll be back, Mike," he responded. "His family's here."

She drew a sharp breath. How she wished he had said, "You're here."

Days later she convinced her father to have their driver take her over to Charlestown, where Etha lived.

She grabbed Etha within seconds of spotting her tending a trellis of rambling roses, and she held tight to her. "There's so much to tell you," Michaela said, and then they began walking across the spacious lawn, chattering at each other.

Mike had missed Etha, and she hadn't realized how much until she had learned that David had been in Boston. Etha, like Rebecca, who was terribly busy with her household and rooms of children (five now!), understood her. She understood her tense relationship with her mother, she understood her feelings about David. And Etha, more than anyone in Boston besides her father, understood her desire to become a medical doctor.

They spread a blanket beneath a thick maple tree and soon had Michaela's notes and drawings from Philadelphia scattered about. Mike told about the dissections, about the discussions, about the many people she had met there, but most importantly, about Elizabeth Blackwell and her friendship with her. She told Etha about the Quaker doctors, how they truly believed that women were as intelligent as men and had every right to be educated at medical schools and to practice the profession.

She told Etha about Jimmie being in Boston, and then she told her that she had missed David. Etha looked as disappointed as Mike had felt and still felt, paling suddenly, bringing up the topic and her regret over and over again during the rest of the day. They lay back and read Longfellow's *Ballads and Other Poems,* and Mike told about meeting him, too.

"You're going along the next time I go to Philadelphia," she told Etha suddenly.

"I am?" Etha queried, clearly shocked—her eyes grew wide as saucers.

"Yes. I thought it unfair that you didn't go this time."

"I wasn't asked," Etha said, and she didn't mean the statement in a snobbish sort of way. She was just stating fact. "Oh, Michaela, my father hasn't the money to put me through the seminary *and* to send me to Philadelphia."

"We must think of something then," Mike said. "I'm sure we will."

Etha squeezed her hand. "You've become a very good friend."

Michaela embraced her again. "So have you."

Boston's aqueduct was opened that autumn to the sound of bells pealing, guns roaring, and people shouting. Philadelphia had had a water conduit for years, Mike knew. But the aqueduct was a new thing for Boston. For months trenches had been dug, and now water was being brought all the way from Lake Cochituate—from fifteen miles away!

The president of Harvard and all the professors rode in the parade that passed along Mount Vernon Street. Men in Oriental costumes entertained the crowds, a brass band marched by, and the Handel and Haydn Society paraded by on a float, ringing their bells. Mayor Josiah Quincy gave a fine speech about the improvement of Boston overall, the paving of some streets, and now this fine, modern thing— the aqueduct! And then the water was turned on and it shot eighty feet into the air.

Rebecca's young son, John, giggled when the water sprinkled him, and Claudette's little Mollie cried, saying it had soiled her gown. Marjorie was in the eighth month of her second pregnancy and she had elected to stay home. But the entire family called on her afterward to tell her of the excitement. Of course, she had seen much of it from her bedroom window, she informed them all. Maureen later remarked that she was the most contrary expectant woman she had ever met, and Mike thought to herself that crossness was nothing new for Marjorie.

John Quincy Adams, Massachusetts's fiery and durable politician, former president of the United States and Boston's oak, died at his post in Congress. Bostonians hadn't liked Adams much when he had gone off to Washington;

many had long ago grown tired of his and Henry Clay's relentless politics and his feud with Andrew Jackson that had lasted for years. And yet Adams's death cast a dark cloud over the city. People emerged to mourn him. Crowds attended the funeral. Harvard, and the lower schools, suspended classes for the day. "Fiery, yes," Michaela's father said of the man, but he also could convulse a roomful of people with his stories. "This is the last of earth," Adams had said, and then he had died with all the dignity he had exhibited in Boston and in Congress for years.

The funeral passed, Adams was interred forever in Massachusetts soil, and General Zachary Taylor, the tired military hero of the Mexican conflict, was instated as president. Autumn faded into the bleakness of winter, and news of the discovery of gold in California, which was now United States property, reached Boston in January of '49. David wrote from Yale:

The discovery is causing a disturbing unrest among men. I spoke to a shopkeeper today who is outfitting at least ten men a day for travel to California, and several of my classmen are among them. They have plans to travel to San Francisco by way of land, the Isthmus of Panama and also Cape Horn. . . .

That summer he returned home again, as promised, and this time Michaela was there to greet him.

167

12

Mike, her mother, Martha, and a seamstress hired specifically for the purpose spent two months constructing her debutante ball gown. Even Michaela admitted that it was a startling creation—a flounced underdress of evergreen silk that just touched the tops of her feet; a modestly low neckline, short, puffed sleeves, and an overskirt of point lace.

Mother spent hour upon hour working the fine lace that eventually made the broad collar, and when Martha stitched it in place, she did so with a glowing smile and tears in her eyes: Michaela was the last Quinn daughter who would have a coming out in this house.

A pink rosette was fastened in the center of the gown at Mike's waist, she wore one on her right wrist, and three more were pinned in her hair after Martha spent a good hour curling, brushing, and pinning, until tendrils tumbled softly about Michaela's forehead and large ringlets grazed her shoulders and spilled down her back. Father provided the pearl necklace that ended in a pink coral medallion, a sight that made Mike stare for the longest time before he took the liberty of lifting it from its velvet bed and fastening it around her neck.

Despite the weeks of preparation and the undeniable excitement in Mike's heart as Martha twirled the last ringlet, there was also disappointment. She had written to David months ago that her ball was being planned, and she had received his letter only two weeks ago in which he said he meant to attend. She had hoped for that, had asked Mother that the ball be held early in summer, though she hadn't expected it. And yet he hadn't arrived in Boston.

A debutante ball was a formal affair, one of the most important events in a New England girl's life, and Michaela had wanted David to be here. His family meant to be here, his mother and father and brothers. Even the mayor meant to attend. Meanwhile David was no doubt still in Connecticut, so busy working with his preceptor that he had forgotten all about his letter to her and his promise.

Mike fixed a smile in place, and Mother scolded her because her eyes were dull. "You cannot think of greeting people in such a state."

"Where is he?" Michaela said, spinning away, aware that she was acting childishly but unable to help herself.

"Do not ruin your evening," her mother said. "We have put months of planning into this, hours of work. You have looked forward to it. Your sisters will all be here, the Holmes family, the Beckers . . . practically everyone in Beacon Hill and other prominent people. Contain your disappointment, lift your chin. Prepare to charm them."

She did, somehow. She greeted, she danced, she smiled, she ate, she drank . . . And to make the evening enjoyable for Mother, she tried to avoid all talk of medical things; in fact, she avoided gatherings comprised only of men who seemed deep in discussion, the spark of debate lighting their eyes.

Mother had invited a number of would-be suitors, as she had done with each of her daughter's coming out balls, and Mike was polite, even charming, with all of them, too. She accepted refreshment from them, engaged them in conversation about Jenny Lind's upcoming appearance in Boston, the skill of the musicians Father had hired for tonight's event, the balloon race that was to be held next week. . . .

She smiled indulgently when they kissed the back of her hand, and she allowed them to sweep her away to dance. When Richard Davis appeared to ask for a turn, she went to him smiling, her curiosity making her look forward to conversation and dancing with him. He was a recent Harvard graduate, a rising attorney in the city, and Michaela had heard talk of his fiery debates. She expected confidence and composure from him, and instead he seemed nervous, almost stepping on her toes several times. She had to pull words out of him.

"Thank goodness you came along," she whispered to her father seconds later, after he had cut in on Richard. "He hardly speaks! How can that be?"

He laughed under his breath. Then he sobered. "I've never seen a lovelier debutante. Neither have they," he said, referring to her suitors. "You tongue-tie them all."

She smiled and tipped her head. "What about Mother?"

"Yes . . . well, since your mother."

"I thought so."

They swept around the room, around the other couples, before people who sat conversing in chairs that had been positioned against the walls.

"Late arrivals?" Father said, sweeping her around once more, glancing at the wide doorway that opened into the entryway. He was right, another small group had just arrived; Harrison was taking hats, and he had draped a light pelerine over his right forearm.

"Duty calls," Mike told her father, and he lifted her hand, kissed it, then turned toward the entryway. He had greeted many guests with her tonight, presenting her, truly introducing her formally into adult society.

She didn't know how many steps she took before she froze, her gaze fastened on one of the five people gathered around Harrison.

"Da . . . David," she whispered, her breath catching in her throat, her fingers clutching her father's arm.

He stood on the other side of the butler, somewhat taller than she remembered him, his dark hair combed neatly rather than in disarray as she had seen it so many times. He wore a bottle green broadcloth coat, a stock of the same color neatly tied over a high white collar; a white silk waistcoat and trousers.

He was twenty years old now, clearly grown, clearly different than she remembered him. He held himself erect and dignified, his shoulders squared, his chin tilted slightly; his eyes had more depth to them. But the gentleness was still evident, she saw, as his gaze locked with hers.

She never knew if the music really stopped as they stared at each other, as they absorbed the changes that had taken place in each of them during the last four years, if all conversation really ceased around her. It seemed so, and yet how was that possible? She had greeted many people during the course of the evening, and each time, the music and conversation, the ball and the celebration, continued. She held her breath, pressed her fingertips to her throat. Then she fought to regain her composure. She had to stop trembling so she could greet him and his family in a decent manner.

She watched him mouth her name, was vaguely aware that his family members stepped aside, that even Harrison had noticed the two of them staring, stricken, at each other, and that he, too, had stepped off. She felt her father's wondering gaze, relished the feel of David's eyes sweeping over her. Then he shook his head slightly and broke into an uncertain smile.

Mike gathered the poise and manners she had worked long and hard to obtain and forced her feet into motion again. Her father hesitated at the doorway (he would later tell her he had known then that he was giving her away), then he handed her off there.

She walked the rest of the way alone, finally stopping the distance of a mere two feet before David, her hands now grasping the sides of her full skirt. His smile was one of wonderment, of pleasant surprise.

"Hello, David," she said, and offered him her hand.

He took it, stared down at it for an everlasting moment, until Thomas, his oldest brother, who stood off to the right, cleared his throat. Then David planted a light kiss on the back of her hand, one she would forever cherish. "Michaela," he whispered. Then, a little louder: "*Michaela.*"

"Well," Sarah Lewis, David's mother, said. Mike heard the nervous flutter of her fan and then George Lewis saying he meant to dance with the young woman before any of his sons did. "All of them unmarried, too, Joseph," he remarked, as if suggesting that a proposal from at least one of them might well be on its way soon.

"They must stand in line tonight, George. No doubt blisters are already forming on Michaela's feet."

George meant what he said. He whisked Michaela away shortly after Sarah kissed her cheek, gave her a warm smile, and welcomed her into Boston society.

She danced a cotillion with him, then another with Thomas Lewis while David circulated in the gathering, greeting people and visiting with them. David danced the second cotillion, too, leading Lucy Hill out, bowing to her as the tune started, turning near her, dipping, then weaving his way through the dancers. Michaela stepped her way around him, smiling, then she moved on to the next dancer, finally working her way back to Thomas. Moments later she and Thomas started in to a waltz and Mike watched from the corner of her eye as David escorted Lucy back to her mother's side.

"Your father will have every available man in Boston rapping at his door beginning tomorrow," Thomas observed, shaking his head. He was taller than David, and his hair was even darker, appearing a glistening black tonight. He was handsome enough, educated enough, genteel enough . . . but Michaela was interested in only David.

"It may be a busy summer, after all," she remarked, not finding the thought of entertaining suitors a particularly thrilling one.

David appeared behind Thomas, tapping his shoulder, wanting to cut in.

"I knew you'd be along," Thomas teased, stepping aside. "Somehow I knew."

The first touch of David's hand on Michaela's seemed magical. Mike drew a deep breath as her eyes again met his, close this time, and his other hand slipped down to rest lightly on her waist. His fingers closed over hers and then they were twirling and dipping, and she realized that he had been waiting for a waltz, that he would not have been content to have her as his partner in a cotillion. He wanted to talk to her. He wanted to be close to her.

"My apologies," he said, "I arrived in Boston only a few hours ago. My ship stopped for repairs. Sprang a leak, it seems."

"I see," she told him. "Apologies accepted." She felt her face warm as she admitted, "I was so caught up, I hadn't noticed your family's absence. But there's really *no* need to pass that on. It surely won't be my last mistake this night." She laughed a little at herself, felt her face grow even warmer, and she self-consciously glanced away from him, then back. "It's such a formal affair. Mother has prepared for months and now I've taken the stage. All eyes are upon . . . Oh, David, I'm so glad to see you. You must think me a simpleminded, chattery girl," she said, glancing away again. She was ruining this. She just knew she was ruining their first time together in four years. She should close her mouth and not open it again.

He gave a low laugh. "Michaela . . . to the contrary. I have never thought you simpleminded. But you surprise me. I was prepared for an intelligent, educated girl—despite Jimmie's and my family's warnings—but not a devastating woman."

She thought she might miss a step. Then she thought she might float through the remainder of the waltz.

David laughed again, and the room seemed to brighten, a hundred glittering chandelier lights casting everything and everyone in a beautiful glow.

"How long will you be home?" she asked him, and he answered promptly—"For two months. Until the beginning of August."

Her heart danced. She couldn't remember when she had ever been happier, except in Philadelphia, walking the wards with Elizabeth Blackwell.

The dance soon ended and they wandered off for

refreshment, glasses of the flowing champagne that Michaela had not yet touched. She wondered if she had been waiting for him. But that was a silly thought—she had given up on him coming. More likely she had felt there was nothing to celebrate. If she couldn't have a debutante ball with David present, she would rather not have one at all. Certainly there had been no reason to sip champagne.

They drank, regarding each other over the rims of their glasses. They had trouble making conversation. The air between them felt awkward, charged. "You shall take leave of the seminary soon, I assume," he asked at the same time she inquired about his surgical studies under Dr. Bollingen.

They laughed, and Michaela felt certain she looked as embarrassed as he did, perhaps more. "You first," she said, and he shook his head no and insisted that she tell him what her plans were about school and after school.

"Perhaps one more year there," she told him.

"And then?"

She shrugged. "Then perhaps a school in Philadelphia. I've realized this one is lacking in some areas—botany and chemistry, among several other subjects. I would be close to the medical community there. Your turn now," Mike said.

"Paris," he answered simply.

She tensed, more so if possible, and sipped more champagne, trying to act nonchalantly. But her hand trembled. "So very far away, David," she remarked.

He studied her. She did not hide her misgivings well— she knew that. "But necessary. As is Philadelphia."

She nodded. He made his point. She would not quarrel with him over his wanting to study abroad; she would not stomp her foot and try to stand in his way. She couldn't anyway, she realized. For while she had loved him for years, she wasn't certain he loved her in the same way and would consider not going if she asked him to alter his plans—an act that would be horribly selfish of her.

Before he had stepped into this house a short time ago, spotted her and realized that Jimmie and his family had not been exaggerating about her having blossomed into a woman, he had regarded her as one of his childhood friends still. Their attraction to each other had begun shortly before he had gone off to Yale, but never had been given time to develop. She had culled too much from his letters; she had allowed her foolish imagination to stretch innocent statements into feelings that did not exist. Perhaps they had in his first writings, but the distance and the length of time that separated them had had its effect. And it was having another effect now—as they regarded each other as adults, not as children.

How handsome he is, Michaela thought. How strong the line of his jaw, how perfect the shape of his brow and nose. *Elegant* described him nicely. She felt proud, elated, excited, to be standing next to him, to have his attention fully on her.

They were seated next to each other at the banquet table, and Mike was reminded of a time they had been seated opposite each other at a meal, after her father had taken her with him on his medical rounds and David had grown jealous and sullen. David mentioned it, looking rather embarrassed over the event now, calling himself a "pouting boy." Then Mike turned her attention elsewhere, as was expected of her.

She pulled more words from Richard Davis, whom Mother had conveniently seated to her right, and she talked with others who were seated nearby, although she would much rather have shared discourse with only David. But she wouldn't be rude to her guests. They had come out tonight to honor her, after all, and she owed them an evening of the politeness, manners, and refinement she had spent these last years acquiring.

She nibbled nervously during the meal, just tasting the clams, the glazed pheasant, the lemon sauce that topped what looked like a delicious pudding, and she was constantly aware that although David delved into his own share of conversation with his neighbors, his gaze always strayed back to her.

The evening continued, filled with food, dancing, and conversation. Her father had hired a tiny monkey dressed in an oversized clown suit and its master to entertain her, and she was delighted by the monkey's antics, especially when he performed flips, strummed a tiny instrument, and pretended to sing. When he began pulling coins from her hair, Mike felt her head, wondering how. Then he pulled a fluffy baby chick from her sleeve and she thought she would topple off her chair with surprise. The crowd roared as she gathered the chick close, nuzzling the tiny creature against her cheek.

Hours later, when most everyone had departed and breakfast was being served to those who remained, Mike smiled over at David, who, conveniently, now sat to her right, and she thanked him for coming.

He dipped his head in acknowledgment. "*Charmante,* Michaela," he said softly. Then he made his intent known. "We're not finished. There are days and weeks ahead."

Indeed there were. He called the following afternoon, wondering if he might take her to the theater that evening to see *The Lady and the Devil.* Mother agreed—and she sent Martha along to chaperon. Mike at first grumbled about that, but hushed when Father said he thought that a fine idea. Then she raced off to riffle through her gowns, wondering what she would wear, for the first time fussing about her hair and slippers.

Mother shook her head and laughed, obviously pleased with the change—or the moments of madness, whatever the case might be. Martha stepped forth, made suggestions, then called for a bath to be prepared in the tub that had recently been installed in a small room on the second floor. And later, when David arrived with a carriage precisely at seven o'clock just as he had said he would, looking grand again, this time in black waistcoat and trousers, Martha squeezed Mike's elbow the slightest bit. She was excited for her, Michaela knew, and she stifled a cry of joy, flashing Martha a smile instead.

They sat in a side box and had a perfect view of the stage. The Lady was polished and cultivated and scornful of men; the Devil was handsome and refined and at first seemed evil. But as the acts wore on, the lady witnessed his compassion and the good deeds he so often hid, and she exposed him for what he really was, not a devil at all. David leaned over toward Mike and said, "So the next time you think you cannot abide a person . . ."

"Look deeper and find the good in them," she finished. He nodded, his eyes sparkling at her. He wore a sweet, spicy cologne that made Michaela want to draw closer to him. But she knew her limitations as a lady, and for once, she resisted the urge to do something rash.

She introduced him to Etha, and the three of them went numerous places during the next month. They experienced every type of respectable entertainment Boston had to offer and even created some of their own. They went to food fairs in Mechanics Hall, to a reception to celebrate the Charlestown Naval Yard's latest creation, a newly christened schooner; to a cat show where all species of the creature were displayed. They ate waffles sprinkled with sugar at the balloon races, and Mike and Etha laughed when David told them how, in New York, he and two classmates had snatched a man's balloon one morning and set off in it. They had taken it several miles before they worried about setting it down—and then it crashed into a line of trees and they were all cut and bruised. "But that wasn't the worst of it," he said. "The balloon was ruined. We spent months helping the man put together another one."

"You never wrote about that," Michaela teased him.

He grinned. "One of my Jimmie moments. I was temporarily mad."

During July, Mike and David sat with their families on the Common, where they enjoyed a parade and then, later, fireworks. They attended church together on two different Sundays, and on various days, they listened to lectures on astronomy and those given by the Free-Soilers, a group of abolitionists, in Faneuil Hall. They wouldn't mention the latter to Mrs. Quinn, said Martha, who always accompanied them, because the questions after the lecture had led to a heated debate, one in which Michaela had taken part, inspired by David.

He escorted her to medical lectures at the Athenaeum,

and she laughed with him one afternoon at Massachusetts General when Martha balked at the doors to the surgical gallery and said that as a chaperon, she would go only so far. She sat on a chair outside the doors, waiting patiently and primly with her hands in her lap until the demonstration ended and they reappeared.

Besides speaking out about freeing slaves, David and Mike attended meetings for the development of schools for the blind and homes for orphans, and they contributed time, energy, and resources toward creating food pantries for the poor and starving. One afternoon Etha accompanied them, and the three of them stood behind the counters, took up spoons and ladles, and dished out food to the lines of people.

This was the David Michaela had always sensed. This was the deeply compassionate person who, at the Lynde Street house that night so long ago, had gone upstairs when he suspected someone needed help. Anyone else might have run away had they been as frightened as she had known he was. She recalled him taking their fish to the poor and she knew he would have given even more at that time if he had had the resources. He would have done more, too, if he had had the voice needed to make things happen. Now he did. He prompted people into action with his insistence that this cause and that cause needed attention. And throughout every speech and every interaction, Michaela watched him with growing pride and love.

Martha became somewhat less attentive as the weeks wore on, intentionally so, Mike suspected. Martha liked David, she knew Mike fancied him a great deal, and she had hopes for them. She allowed them to walk off by themselves more and more while she busied herself with reading or with some other activity—feeding crumbs to the ducks that inhabited Boston's many ponds, or playing with the children who frequented the squares with their nursemaids or mothers.

She was truly neglectful only once, but the neglect would stay forever Michaela's and her secret, Mike knew.

David hired a hack to take them over to Charlestown

where they climbed the Bunker Hill Monument while Martha sat reading on a blanket she had spread on the green. She seemed absorbed in her book, merely smiling up at Mike and David moments later when they approached to tell her they wanted to walk off and explore. She waved them on and they strolled off with Michaela's hand resting lightly on David's arm.

They climbed rocks near the riverbank, then asked a man if they might take his small rowboat out for a time. He saw no harm in that, he said, grinning, as if he knew they were courting, and then he handed David the oars and off they went.

David rowed and smiled as Michaela softly sang a tune she had been taught in school. They went quietly along for a time, enjoying the serenity of the water, the lush riverbank in places and the busy wharves in other places. Then David turned the boat around and they returned it to its owner.

They didn't return immediately to the monument. They walked more instead, finding an area populated by trees. Tangled vines arched over a walkway here, providing a mixture of shadow and light. David talked excitedly about the schools and masters in Paris, and Michaela paused to have a closer look at the full red roses that grew to the right of the walkway. She bent to inhale the scent of one, then David reached around and plucked it from under her nose.

Michaela straightened, giving him an odd look, wondering what he was doing. He had grown quiet and introspective, and she wondered at the thoughts going through his head. He glanced up, giving her an uncertain look as he twirled the thorny stem of the rose between his thumb and forefinger.

"I shall miss you, Michaela," he said. "I shall truly miss you when I leave. I realized only this morning that in less than a week—"

"Hush," she said, putting her fingers to his lips. It was an unconscious act; she had lifted her hand without thinking. She didn't want him to finish that sentence. She didn't want to hear the words she knew he was about to say.

She saw a flash in his eyes, saw his intensity deepen, and

179

she started to withdraw her hand. He grabbed it, wrapping his fingers around hers and narrowing his eyes. She wasn't sure what he was doing, what he was thinking, why he was studying her hand. Why he held it. She knew only that the rhythm of her heart had increased, and that she was quite aware of the attraction between them in those moments. The most awkward time of her life . . . the most peculiar sensations going through her . . . the warmth of David's fingers wrapped around hers . . . the nearness of him.

His gaze shifted to her face, to her mouth. Michaela's throat went dry. He had designs . . . she now knew that he had designs.

"Would you be insulted if I kissed you?" he queried.

Mike closed her eyes, having no more breath, wondering if this was real, feeling his fingers move over hers and knowing it was. "No," she whispered. Then she opened her eyes and looked full upon his face. "No," she said again, and she swallowed hard.

Slowly he lowered his head, searching her eyes for any adverse reaction. She felt none and she showed none. His lips touched hers, lightly, sweetly, softly, tentatively. His mouth trembled—or was it hers? Michaela never knew.

He breathed deeply and smiled down at her. "What change years bring," he said. "What conflict. Medicine or Michaela . . . Paris or Boston."

She did not hesitate, for she knew what was in his heart. She knew his soul. "Medicine and Paris."

He pondered that for a moment. Nodding, he then withdrew, straightened his waistcoat, and offered her his arm.

Five days later she gathered a cape close over her shoulders to ward off the cool air that had blown in, and she saw him off at Boston harbor.

"Let's go home now, Michaela," Elizabeth Quinn said some time after the ship had slipped away, grown smaller and smaller, then blinked out altogether.

A light rain had started, and Mike searched the sky, wondering if it would calm. Everything seemed to be a shade of gray, the buildings, the water, her heart. Putting her mind back on her studies within a few weeks would be difficult.

She turned and went into her mother's open arms.

Thoreau published *Civil Disobedience* that year. Etha read part of his essay to Mike as they sat beneath a tree outside the school one afternoon: "There will never be a really free and enlightened State until the State comes to recognize the individual as a higher and independent power, from which all its own power and authority are derived. . . ." Thoreau recently had spent a night in jail for refusing to pay his poll tax, his private opposition to the late Mexican conflict. David would champion him, Michaela thought. Issues of great public concern must be addressed, he might say, and those that deserve more must be brought to light.

A chunk of California gold, rumored to weigh fifteen pounds, was displayed in a Washington Street window in August of '49. The "disturbing unrest among men" that David had spoken of in his letter to Michaela the year before took hold of the Boston population. It became common-place to see no less than thirty men a day in the Washington Street shops being outfitted for California, and the numbers increased as the weeks wore on. Mrs. Pitman, the cook in the Quinn household, shook her head and uttered impolite words when she learned that her son-in-law had set out. One morning the Beckers' upstairs maid found herself without a husband, with three tiny mouths to feed alone—and with only a brief note that said "Gone to Californy." "Why he bothered is beyond me," Mrs. Becker told Mike and Elizabeth during tea one Saturday afternoon.

The "fever" was not exclusive to the lower classes. Young Henry Abbott, not two months away from graduating at the top of his class at Harvard, took off, despite his father shouting to him from the dock. Mr. Ellis, scholar and respected schoolmaster, gave a night's notice to the parents of his students and at the boardinghouse where he had lived for as long as Michaela could remember. Dr. Langley never even notified his patients that he was leaving; Drs. Quinn

181

and Holmes and other Boston physicians simply began receiving calls from the abandoned. The Reverend Duffin of the Park Street Church deserted his flock one day in early May, causing Joseph to toss his hands in the air. "I have never seen anything the likes of this-this madness!" he said, clearly exasperated.

There never has been anything, Mike thought. Well, perhaps when Moses led the Israelites. But then, he had been leading them out of oppression, not toward promises of wealth and riches beyond their wildest imaginings.

"Folly," Dr. Holmes remarked as he peeked out a window at the Tremont Street School one afternoon, watching men fill their packs and wagons with supplies. "Away they go, in search of California gold."

"Will there be anyone left in Boston when it's done, Professor Holmes?" Michaela asked, trying to make light of the situation.

He laughed. "Well, we've plenty of bones in the grave-yards."

More meetings were held by the Free-Soilers in Faneuil Hall, and as the new decade began, tempers flared. Two by two the states had been coming into the Union for years, always one slave and one free. But lately the abolitionists were gaining ground. Last year slavery had been prohibited in the Minnesota Territory, established by Congress in March, and in September slavery had been disallowed in California. Henry Clay shouted objections on the senatorial floor when New Mexico Territory, also acquired after the recent war, formed its own state government and also banned slavery. This was becoming outrageous, or so proslavery advocates screamed. Then came the territory of Utah, also a free area, and demonstrations were held on the streets of Washington. A compromise was reached— Congress passed the Fugitive Slave Bill, which required the return of escaped slaves to their owners, no matter where they were caught. Fugitive slaves were not to be given jury trials—and they could not testify in their defense either.

"Placation," Joseph Quinn observed one evening as he and Michaela sat reading in the study. "We are building toward something terrible. Economics makes that inevitable. Bondage is a ghastly thing, but Southern plantations thrive on slavery; they cannot exist and continue to flourish without them. Northern states don't need slaves to survive, and the abolitionists intend to outlaw slavery state by state. There is no good solution."

He was right. Where would it end—or would it end? And *how* would it end? Both sides were becoming more and more vocal. He didn't say it, but Michaela wondered to herself when blood would be spilled. It was building to that.

The rush for gold and the rising conflict between the abolitionists and the pro-slavery advocates had turned most everyone's attention on California and Washington, D.C. But while the madness was going on around them, filling newspapers and being batted around city streets, something else was occurring states away from Massachusetts that arrested Michaela's and her father's attention: Mr. Mullen and Dr. Longshore had called a meeting at Philadelphia's Merchant's Hall for all those interested in forming a fully accredited medical college for women. Dr. Longshore had been elected secretary and sent to the Pennsylvania legislature to ask for a charter. His request had been granted in March, and the opening ceremonies of the Female Medical College of Pennsylvania were set for October.

13

Elizabeth Quinn at first sat in stunned silence when Mike's father announced that he planned to take Michaela and Etha to the opening ceremonies of the college.

She had been embroidering, and she stared down at her work for a time, one hand clenching the material as she fought hard for composure. Her hair had started graying long ago, and strands of it glimmered silver in the lamplight.

It was evening, a Saturday night. Etha, Michaela, and Martha had just returned from a theater outing with several young men, and they had come into the parlor where Father sat reading and Mother sat stitching. Etha would be staying the night, attending church with them in the morning. Father had glanced up from his reading and asked Michaela how would she and Etha like to visit Philadelphia soon. Mike had yelped with joy. Mother had tensed. Then Father had told them all that he had received news just today about the opening ceremonies of the college.

The news was hard for Mother, Mike realized. Word that a charter had been granted had startled her, but this announcement shook her visibly. Even when Maureen had lain near death, thrashing with childbed fever, Mother had

184

been calm, at least outwardly. Not so right now. Mike glanced from her mother to her father—who had lifted his brows—then back to Elizabeth.

Mother shook her head, inhaled, glanced up at Michaela. "David . . . What if David comes?"

"He's studying in France, Mother. He won't return until he's finished there. It's too long a journey. It could be years before he returns," Mike said, giving voice to the words she had not wanted to utter. She didn't like the fact, the truth of the words. But she had given him encouragement from her heart and she was determined to be patient. She went for outings with suitors occasionally, but she spoke often of David and led no one to believe that she had eyes for or thoughts of anyone but him.

"Did he mention marriage while he was here?" Mother asked.

Michaela shook her head.

"Well, why not, I wonder? He was certainly attentive enough. He came for you almost every day." She pulled her needle through the material. Jerked it, really. "He'll surely come for you again—it's quite obvious he's in love with you—and wouldn't you hate to be away when he comes? Off"—she thrust her needle into the material and glanced up at Mike—"in Philadelphia pursuing a medical diploma."

Michaela felt sorry for her mother in those moments. Elizabeth seemed angry, yes, but more on the verge of panic than anything. She had not believed the college would happen, that it would ever get a charter and then that it would ever be opened. She hadn't said anything, but Mike read everything in her eyes right now—the fallen hope, the fear that she would lose her youngest daughter to Philadelphia and its medical institution for women. After all the years of arguing, after all the sharp words and cutting looks between them, mother and daughter had finally developed a more civil relationship during the last three years. But Mike had known this was coming, that she and Mother would clash again one day over the subject of medical school. She had thought that, she had told Etha that. It was inevitable.

But she wasn't going off to attend medical school right

now. "I'm only going to the opening ceremonies of the college," she said. "I'm not going in pursuit of a medical diploma."

"Yet."

Michaela buried her hands deeper in the muff she had not relinquished to Harrison in the entryway. Her hands had been cold. They still were. "Yet," she said, echoing Mother.

"Elizabeth . . ." Joseph said, his brow wrinkling. He clearly meant to put an end to the conversation before it developed into a full-blown quarrel.

"You'll attend the college," Elizabeth told Michaela, her eyes glittering. She fought tears, Mike was sure of it. She rarely had seen her mother cry.

"And in the middle of things, David will arrive home and ask your father for your hand. And then what will you do? What choice will you make?" Mother pressed. "You will have to make one, you know. Marriage, children, a household . . . they occupy a woman, make her forget foolish notions."

"Stop," Mike said. Pleaded. "I have no foolish notions." Michaela saw her mother's goal clearly now; she realized Elizabeth had hoped that love and marriage would distract her and dash her desire to become a doctor.

"What choice, Michaela? David or medicine?"

Etha shifted uncomfortably on the settee to Mike's left. Joseph said he thought this had gone far enough, that it was as Michaela had said—they were only going to Philadelphia to attend the opening ceremonies.

"What will be your choice?" Mother demanded again, more forcefully this time. "What?"

"I'll manage both," Mike shot at her.

Elizabeth shook her head. "No. It's not possible. No man would want you to try, not even David. Oh, he might say yes at first. But then the children will start coming and the household will suffer. You *will* have to make a choice—David or medicine."

Michaela jumped up. She had had enough. She felt as if she had been backed into a corner and she was rattled herself now, seeing no way out. No good way. She had not quarreled with her mother like this in years, and she hated the angry words being flung back and forth.

"If I am ever forced to make a choice," she said tightly, "I will choose David without hesitation."

She couldn't stand the look of triumph on her mother's face. She spun away and fled the room just as Elizabeth turned on Joseph and said, "You sat here all evening with me and never said a word about the opening of that college. Yet Michaela comes in and you're full of news."

Mike tripped on her skirts going up the staircase, but Etha was there, gathering them up for her, and then they raced on together. Etha was there, too, to embrace Michaela moments later as she slammed onto her bed and shed a river of tears.

"That was horrid, just horrid," Etha said after a time.

Mike wiped at her eyes. *"She's* horrid."

"Well, she's your mother and I wasn't going to say so."

"You won't trouble me by saying it. She can be."

"Look," Etha said, withdrawing and sitting straight on the bed as she unfolded something. "We'll read this together. Dr. Quinn handed it to me. He meant for us to read it. I imagine he was reluctant to hand it to you after your mother began throwing such a tantrum. Then you went off and . . . Listen. Oh, Mike . . . listen! 'The object of this institution is to instruct respectable and intelligent females in the various branches of medical science; whose rights and privileges upon receiving the degree of the doctorate in this institution will not be inferior to those of the graduates of any other medical institution in this country or in Europe.'"

Michaela sniffed, sobering, suddenly listening intently and forgetting her mother's harsh words. "What is it?" she asked, squeezing close.

Etha closed the brochure and read from the front of it. "The First Annual Announcement of the Female Medical College of Pennsylvania." She squealed. "Imagine that. It's really happening!"

Mike pressed even closer. She reached to open the pamphlet. She read softly: "'Our object is not merely to qualify females as practitioners of medicine, but to teach a woman to know herself, to understand her organism. . . .'"

The announcement went on to describe the courses and list the physicians who would be teaching them. There would be a clinic and anatomical rooms, and many of the lectures would be delivered by renowned Philadelphia men of medicine. A list of textbooks was given, then a list of the fees.

Michaela glanced at Etha and they exchanged excited smiles. Reading this was exciting. Thinking about attending the opening ceremonies was exciting. Mike had heard Dr. Elder, Mr. Mullen, and her father discuss an idea that evening in Philadelphia, and now the idea was materializing. It was becoming real.

There would soon be a fully accredited medical college for women.

Claudette's son, Robert, fell ill the day before Michaela was supposed to leave for Philadelphia with her father and Etha. For months he had looked pale and as though he had been losing weight. Now he was seized by wracking coughs, and he was bringing up bloody phlegm. The signs were all there, the wasting away, the coughing, the blood. Michaela examined him with her father while the frightened Claudette stood across the room with Mother, clutching a handkerchief to her mouth.

"Will I die, Auntie Michaela?" the five-year-old child asked.

"No, Robert, of course not," she answered without thinking. She couldn't bear to tell him the truth, so she lied. Yes, he would die. Perhaps not tomorrow, perhaps not next week or next month. But sooner or later he would die. She had not heard of a single case of tuberculosis where the patient lived.

He knew she was lying. He studied her, then he closed his eyes and went to sleep. He had wanted the truth, and instead she had told him a lie.

Claudette became hysterical when she was taken downstairs and told the diagnosis. "How? *How?*" she demanded. "He hardly leaves this house!" Then she broke into sobs and wails. She took the snifter of brandy she was offered by Mother and she smashed it on the drawing room hearth.

Father tried to gather her in his arms, but she beat at him, telling him he was wrong, that Robby did not have tuberculosis and would not die. Then Charles, Claudette's husband, came rushing into the house and she flew to him, sobbing more, telling him that Robby was dying.

The trip to Philadelphia was canceled. Father tried to apologize to Mike and Etha, but Michaela shook her head no, cutting him off, and she embraced him. "There are more important things," Etha told him sincerely.

Claudette stayed so irrational for nearly two months, believing one moment that her son had some minor ailment and just needed a few day's rest, and convinced the next that he would be dead by morning. But by the end of October, with Robby wasting away more every week and struggling for breath much of the time, she became constantly despondent, and Mike knew she had realized that he would not live. There was no more wild swinging back and forth of Claudette's emotions.

Michaela attended Robert almost constantly throughout September and October, forgetting school, forgetting the medical college, forgetting everything but trying to make her nephew comfortable and praying silently for him. By December, the boy was a skeleton of the child he had once been. Claudette was now mad with grief and could not be consoled even by her other children. The nursemaid took complete charge of two-year-old William, and Elizabeth and Charles's mother took turns running their grieving children's household as well as their own. Father was at the bedside during his every spare moment, and he spent less and less time at the medical school and at the hospital. He had a number of grandchildren now and he adored them all. Even given his knowledge of disease, Mike wasn't sure he had convinced himself yet that Robby would die. He tried different medications. He made numerous notes. He remarked to Michaela at times that Robby seemed improved. But he fooled himself. He wanted so badly for Robby to live that he saw signs of improvement that were not there. And yet sometimes she found him sitting alone, leaned back in a chair rubbing his face, looking like the saddest man in the world.

Soon Mike and Dr. Quinn both realized where Robert had picked up the disease.

According to Claudette, Charles had made himself rather scarce this past year, spending longer and longer hours at his insurance office. In reality, he was running up debts and had turned to drink and to other women. "Washington Street whores," Claudette told Michaela softly one afternoon as the winter wind whistled by the eaves. Surely not, Mike said. It was true, Claudette assured her. And yet she still loved him, God help her.

Michaela kept the revelation to herself. But one night the grief and hopelessness felt by the entire family overcame Charles, and he spilled more than a few ugly secrets.

He stumbled into the house drunk. Michaela and her father were both there, having just come downstairs from tending Robby. Charles crashed into the table in the hallway, then began sobbing, spouting about his women, saying Robert was sick because of his sins, that he had known for the last year that *he* had the scourge. His eldest son had contracted the disease from him and now his punishment was Robby's death. He hasn't appeared sick, Michaela thought. But then, one victim might waste away more slowly than another. In Charles's case, much more slowly. Robert was young, besides, and he never had been a hearty boy.

"Hush, now, that's no way to talk," Mike told him.

"It's the truth, it's the truth," Charles wailed. "I have a woman . . . a woman! In a house on Hanover. The night Robby took sick I was with her. Didn't know he was sick till I came home."

Michaela felt light-headed. He had been keeping a woman? Not just visiting the Washington Street women, but keeping a mistress? Spending less and less time with his wife and his family—and *keeping another woman?*

Her father had withdrawn, leaving Mike to hold up Charles alone. He began coughing, and a small amount of blood splattered the nearby wall. He was wrong, she had thought until now. He didn't have the disease. But now she wondered if he did.

She urged him toward the parlor, the nearest room, and they were mere steps from it when her father caught Charles by the arm, jerked him around, and threw him against the entryway wall. Charles slid down to the floor, sobbing more, louder this time. Mike bit back a scream. He wasn't a violent man, her father. Charles's admission was simply too much for him.

Joseph hovered over him, a dark look on his face. "I handed you my daughter to love and honor," he seethed, and Michaela saw that he had balled his hand into a fist.

"Papa," she cried, using the name she had not called him in years as she tried to pull him away from Charles. "No. You can't do this!"

"You lying adulterer," Joseph accused. "You drunkard! You disgrace this household. Your son—*my grandson*—is upstairs dying and you come here spouting such things!"

Claudette had appeared on the stairs. Servants had come out of their rooms, their nightdresses rumpled, their eyes wide. Joseph grabbed Charles by the front of his shirt, despite Mike's attempt to pull her father's arm down. He raised his other arm, clearly meaning to hit his son-in-law.

"No," Claudette screeched. "Father, no!"

She tore down the stairs, almost stumbling over the hem of her shift, and she thrust herself between Charles and her father and pushed against Father. "Listen to me," she said. "Listen!"

The madness cleared from his eyes as he focused on her.

"Don't hurt him . . . please. Despite everything, I love him."

Long seconds ensued during which she and Father stared at each other. Finally her father stood, withdrew, and jerked at the hem of his waistcoat.

"Then summon another physician to care for him," he said gruffly. "I cannot abide the sight of the man."

Michaela had never in her life known her father to turn away from an ill person. But she watched it happen now, watched him go against all he believed—against the

191

Hippocratic oath, against even his private and professional convictions. He left the house in blind anger, forgetting his medical bag in the study—and she had never known him to forget his medical bag either. She would have it sent to him at the Mount Vernon Street house. Surely that was where he was headed.

"Help me with him, Michaela," Claudette pleaded, trying to get her arm under Charles's. He coughed. Blood stained his mouth. His face was ashen. He struggled for breath. "What did Father do to his mouth? He hit you, didn't he, Charles? You must help us now. Please, love . . . help us."

"He wasn't hit," Mike told her sister. She gripped Claudette's arm and looked her in the eye. "He, too, has the disease."

A moment passed. Claudette shook her head, denying what Michaela said. Mike wondered if she would rant again, the way she had after their father had told her about Robby, that he had the disease and would not live. Her heart was breaking for her sister, for the precious boy Claudette, and the entire family, was losing. And now this—she would eventually lose her husband, also. Mike wanted to weep for the shattered lives.

"God," Claudette whispered, and then she fainted dead away.

Charles disappeared two days after the confrontation with Father, and a rift developed between his family and Joseph, and between Father and Claudette. She blamed him for the fact that she didn't know where her husband was, or even whether he was dead or alive, and she forbade him to set foot in her home. She summoned Dr. Holmes to care for Robby, and he did so with a heavy heart, as he later told Michaela—and only because Robert was the grandson of his fine friend and colleague, Dr. Joseph Quinn.

Claudette had stopped smiling the day Robby's illness was diagnosed. Now she stopped interacting with her other children, even to kiss them good night. They often cried for Mommy and were told she was either indisposed or with Robby. Michaela spent a great deal of time with them, feeling they needed the attention of more than the nursemaid.

Robert finally passed quietly on a frigid March day when the snow piled in four-foot drifts against houses and buildings and was shoveled even higher on the sides of walkways and streets. He went off with his solemn mother holding his gray hand, her having no more tears to shed, and with his relatives lining the halls and filling the rooms of 416 Beacon Street. Only two relatives were absent—Robby's father and grandfather.

The nursemaid cried when she was told that Robert had expired, but six-year-old Mollie scowled and wondered aloud if Mommy would come out and play with her and William *now.* Her Aunt Maureen scolded her for the show of temper and her insensitivity, but Mike thought she understood Mollie. Mollie had feelings, too, and they had been set aside for a good eight months. She had known, as everyone had, that Robby was not going to live. His illness had upset the family and her relationship with her mother for a long time now, and finally, things might get back to normal.

"Will Papa come home now?" the girl asked Mike. "He went away because he couldn't stand Robby being sick, I know it."

"I don't know," Michaela answered truthfully.

Robert was buried the following morning. The sky was gray all day and snow fell throughout the brief service. Half of Boston turned out to see Robby off, and Michaela saw tears in even the tough Daniel Webster's eyes.

Still, no one had seen Charles. Although she knew they meant well, Mike hated the pitying looks people gave Claudette, the rest of the Quinns, and Charles's side of the family. Servants had tongues, and they had been wagging. People knew the details of what had happened the night Charles had come home drunk—and they knew the details of the things to which he had admitted. Behind closed doors and away from Charles's and Claudette's families they no doubt talked among themselves. Mike expected Mother and Marjorie at least to bristle with indignation over the scandal. Instead they politely accepted the sympathies offered for

Robert's death, and they lifted their heads and went about their business as usual during the ensuing weeks.

Nearly a month later, Claudette received a visit from an agent who claimed to have represented Charles in numerous investments that had gone sour . . . stock in another insurance company that had failed, money poured into the building of a ship that had sunk during its second ocean voyage . . . the purchase of a carriage company that had gone under quickly from mismanagement. . . . The papers went on and on, and Claudette became more pale with each one. When the agent mentioned that Mr. Atkins still owed him money, Claudette whispered, "Leave me, Mr. Reuther."

He did, and she locked herself in her room for two days, accepting only an occasional tray of food whenever Michaela stood at her door knocking, insisting that she at least eat.

Mike took the liberty of gathering the papers Mr. Reuther had left and taking them to Marcus, Rebecca's husband. He looked them over, even took them to George Lewis, David's father and a respected Boston attorney, who announced that they were legitimate. But the concern was Charles's accounts and the condition of his finances—whether or not his family could survive on what was left. With Charles missing, but not declared deceased, his will could not be opened. If there was a will. George had certainly not drawn one up for him.

Mr. Reuther provided the name of Charles's attorney, a Frank Hoover on Providence Street. And while Mr. Hoover would not reveal to Marcus the complete sum of Charles's accounts, he did say that Mr. Atkins had long ago authorized the release of funds for any household or personal expense of his wife's, and that Mrs. Atkins could expect to survive comfortably, in her present lifestyle, for possibly four years.

"Four years?" Claudette shrieked when Marcus told her. "And what happens after that?"

Mike managed to calm her with the medication Dr. Holmes had left with her in the event Claudette became hysterical.

The next day she learned that Claudette had dismissed the

upstairs maid, the scullery girl, the groom, and Mollie's private teacher. Within days she had sold the fine horses Charles had bought only last year, and the carriage and every saddle and article in the carriage house. Marcus tried to tell her the situation wasn't that desperate—that he had men out looking in every crack in the city for Charles and that he would be found. Meanwhile, Claudette continued with her madness, selling even much of her silver during the following month. She paid the agent, then told him to leave her home, that if he ever set foot in it again she would shoot him with the pistol Charles had left in a chest upstairs.

Throughout the madness, Michaela cared for the children, playing games with Mollie and taking over the role of teacher. Mike sat with little William many times, stacking blocks with him, pulling the wooden cart his aunt Rebecca had given him along the Beacon Street walkways, reading to him, coasting with him and Mollie all around Beacon Hill. She taught Mollie to ice-skate and William to fish, to Elizabeth Quinn's horror, and she sat with Mollie many times when the girl cried and wondered if her mother would ever feel better.

William was young, and although he knew he had a "mother" in the room down the hall and that now and again that woman made an appearance in the downstairs rooms, he had cried for her only in the beginning, when Robby's illness had fallen like a black cloud on the household. Little William now turned to his aunt Mike for all comforting and nurturing. And while Michaela wondered many times if her substituting for Claudette was right, she could not turn the boy away whenever he giggled and asked her to play with him, or whenever he rubbed his eyes sleepily and climbed up into her lap.

Mother remarked numerous times that she needed to marry and have children of her own, that it could not be healthy for her to take such an interest in Mollie and William. Michaela mentally waved Mother's words away— not only was she waiting for David, but right now these children needed someone to care for them, to nurture them, to sustain them. She would not turn her back on them.

• • •

The slavery crisis exploded in Boston that year. In February, a mob rescued the fugitive, Shadrach, from being returned to his master, irritating even the most conservative citizens. Then in April tempers flared again and blood was actually shed.

Michaela and Maureen were having afternoon tea in a Columbus Avenue shop when a boy no more than ten years old burst through the doors, shouting, "Johnny, Johnny, come quick! They've another one imprisoned in the courthouse! Caught him over near the harbor." The boy scrambled to a certain table where "Johnny" had frozen with a powdery confection halfway to his mouth.

Johnny's companion, a pretty girl in dark red velvet with ribbons in her hair, paled. "We can't let 'em do that. He hasn't a chance. Can't have a trial, can't testify. He'll be shipped off for sure! God help him."

"No, we'll help him," Johnny said. He stood, tossed a few coins on the table, then took the girl by the arm and away they went with the boy tailing them.

Mike and Maureen sat near a window, and they spotted a group of men and boys coming up the street with clubs in hand. Maureen gasped and clutched her hands together. "What do you think they mean to do?" she asked Michaela.

"Free the man," Mike stated. No matter how they had to do it. They had done so with Shadrack and they would do so now. It had come to this, to violence, the years of arguing back and forth, of appeasement, of admitting one free state for every slave state, of passing the compromise laws of 1850 that many Northerners hated. The group felt pressed into action. From their point of view, the Fugitive Slave Law, which would ship the man back to whomever he had escaped, left them no choice.

"They cannot do this," Michaela whispered, feeling torn. She didn't believe in enslavement. But violence was not the solution to the dilemma. "People will be killed this time," she said, and she jumped up, knowing she had to intervene somehow.

"You're not thinking of going out there?" Maureen demanded, aghast.

Mike never answered. Without grabbing her muff from the empty chair where she had placed it, she shot toward the door of the establishment.

Outside, she hiked up her skirts and raced down Columbus Avenue, trying to gain on the group, her cloak fluttering behind her. The moving crowd had grown more in the last few minutes, since it had passed the shop. It had multiplied, and there were more clubs. Men shouted and brandished their weapons. Some threw rocks at windows. Michaela realized the stones were hurled at the homes and shops of known proslavery citizens.

"No!" she shouted, grabbing the arm of a man who was preparing to throw another rock. "Don't do this! This is not the answer! We'll go before the—"

The man threw her off. She tumbled in the street, barely escaping a horse that tore by, his hooves pounding the pavement. She regained her footing and rushed after the crowd again.

Men came from both sides of the passage to join the mob, adding to its size and determination. Michaela shouted more, trying to be heard, trying to tell the people that violence would only breed violence. But that was what they wanted—they wanted a fight. Word of another Negro man imprisoned in the courthouse had pushed them beyond wanting to talk, beyond wanting to negotiate.

"Property is property!" someone shouted, and the mob growled and went after the person.

Mike tried to grab a club and she was thrown off again. This time she was not so lucky; she saw boots, then hooves. They crashed down on her head, her arms, her legs. . . . She heard herself scream, felt herself slip away.

Then mercifully the grayness blinked out and the pain ceased.

When she woke, days had passed. Moving hurt. Talking hurt. Being awake hurt.

She was in her bedroom at the town house—through her

swollen eyes she glimpsed the lace on the tester, and, when she forced her head to one side, her small secretary desk. Fierce pain gripped her head and she heard herself moan. Then she heard her father's voice, deep and comforting, and she saw him rise from the chair near the hearth.

"My God, you're conscious," he said at the bedside, and she heard the pain and heartache in his tone. "I wondered if you would wake. I wondered if—" His voice cracked. A groan tore from his chest. After Robby's death, Charles's disappearance, and his severed relationship with Claudette, he could not bear to lose her, too, he told Mike.

She summoned what little strength she had and reached over to touch his hand. She had seen her father torn apart these past months, ripped inside by the conflicts in his family.

"I won't leave you," she promised.

He dropped to his knees, bowed his head over her hand, and trembled with emotion. Tears slid down from the outside corners of Mike's eyes, and she whispered the promise again: *"I won't leave you, ever."*

Then she vowed something to herself, that she would see her family healed, even if doing so became her life's work. They could not continue like this. Her father could not continue like this.

Her right leg was fractured, she learned the next day. Joseph, remembering Dr. Elder's experience during his and Michaela's visit to Philadelphia, had felt a good pulse in the foot and elected to leave the limb. Her arms, face, and neck were bruised and cut, and her scalp had had to be stitched in two places. She had chest contusions, and breathing took effort at times because even it was painful. Her father dosed her with laudanum, and she was grateful. More days slipped by.

"What were you doing, running after that mob?" Elizabeth Quinn demanded on the sixth day, anxiety and relief showing on her face.

"Trying to stop them," Mike answered simply.

Mother shook her head. "Trying to stop them . . ."

"You made a gallant effort," Maureen commented, and

although she had already scolded Michaela severely for frightening her nearly to death, she also clearly admired Mike's courage in trying to intervene in the conflict.

"Heroics," Rebecca commented, smiling at Michaela. "But you might have been killed, you know."

"She wasn't the only one wounded," Marjorie reminded all of them. Then she spoke to Mike. "I thought you disagreed with slavery. Or did you attend those meetings at the hall to impress David?"

Michaela regarded her sister. Nothing about Marjorie's jealousy of her had improved with maturity and adulthood. "I would have led that group to speak to the judge had they been going about things peacefully."

"Well," Marjorie said, tossing her chin, "you would have been driven back along with the rest of the fanatics at the courthouse steps."

So the mob hadn't succeeded in freeing the fugitive slave. Mike didn't condone the violent way the men had been going about their mission, but she couldn't deny the disappointment she felt, and undoubtedly showed, upon hearing that the Negro man had not been rescued.

Thomas Simms, the fugitive, was still being held in chains, her father reported, and scattered bands of men still protested around the city, bashing in windows and terrorizing anyone who dared to utter a word in support of slavery; they clashed, too, with groups of men who upheld the safeguarding of property.

For nine days the two factions warred, and then the judge ruled in favor of Simms's owner. Funeral bells tolled— Mike heard them from her room—and Mr. Simms was led in shackles and under heavy escort, her father reported later, to a waiting brig at the wharf. Another effort was made to free him, and again the mob was driven back. Finally, the ship set out for Savannah.

Boston conservatives breathed sighs of relief. More meetings were held at Faneuil Hall, and they were broken up by proslavery crowds. More windows were smashed, more bodies battered. And then, just when Michaela began to wonder if the chaos would never end, the parties quieted.

People went back to their lives and the newspapers printed things other than reports of mob confrontations.

Western migration and settlement was becoming more and more popular, and in June, an article appeared in the *Boston Globe* that had originated in Terre Haute, Indiana and had already been reprinted in numerous eastern publications. "Go West, Young Man, Go West," urged the title. Then the article began telling about the rich, wide-open Western lands. The country was maturing and expanding, and the West was where it was happening.

More months went by. Father brought exciting news—an announcement of a course of medical lectures for women to be held in Boston next year and delivered by the faculty of the Female Medical College of Pennsylvania. Michaela had taken ample enough courses at the seminary that the staff there had elected to graduate her quietly, knowing the various situations in her family. She could start medical school at any time. Only she wouldn't go off to Pennsylvania knowing her father's and Claudette's state of mind. She wouldn't leave Mollie and William in the care of only their nursemaid. She wasn't sure she would even have time to attend the four months of lectures to be offered to women next year. She was excited by the news that the faculty of the Female Medical College was coming to offer women here ample opportunity to expand their minds and become educated in medical matters. But the news depressed her, too, because her attentions had to be focused elsewhere for now.

Mike healed and went back to spending much of her time at Claudette's home. Her sister was still morose, still secluded herself, still shut out family and friends for the most part. Michaela picked up with the children where she had left off, playing with them, caring for them, and trying desperately to draw Claudette out of her depression and reclusiveness.

Last fall Michaela had written to David, telling him about Robby's illness, and she had received a letter from him this past spring. She sat down to write back to him on a humid

August day, opening by expressing her happiness that his studies had gone so well—and that he had opted to travel in Europe before returning to the States. Then she went on to tell more about the conflicts that continued in her family:

Claudette still says daily that Father drove Charles away and is silent when I offer no opinion. Mother bothers Father to apologize to Claudette, saying this has gone on long enough, and she bothers Claudette to "gather her wits." Father has told me that while he is not proud of his behavior that night, Charles should be the one to apologize to his wife and family. Charles's family blames Father, too, and shunned him at Robert's funeral and at the gathering afterward, which gave people even more to gossip about, I am certain. Claudette forbade him ever again to set foot in her house, and she still holds to that. Father passed her on the street months ago, during one of the rare times she has gone outside her home, and she refused to acknowledge him. And so the circle continues. This family is torn apart.

Father grieves for Robby more deeply than anyone seems to realize. He loves his family. Excluding Robert, he now has twelve grandchildren and another one is expected from Marjorie soon. He would grieve the same for any of them. He is quiet, more introspective than I have ever seen him. I never thought I would describe my father as a solemn man, but that is what Robert's illness and death and the fracture in this family have made of him.

Etha and Claudette tell me I should apply to attend the Female Medical College in Philadelphia. But I cannot bear the thought of leaving Claudette in her present state, of leaving these motherless children, or of leaving my father when Rebecca and I are his only clear support in the family. Even Maureen wondered aloud recently if Charles was afraid of Father when he disappeared that evening. No one has suggested that perhaps Charles, feeling as though he had caused his wife and family enough grief, went off somewhere to waste away and die alone.

She cried throughout writing those initial paragraphs, realizing for the first time how deeply the division in her family had affected *her*. She soaked one handkerchief and started over with the writing numerous times because she smeared the ink. She reread the last paragraph, crying more, then she finished it with, "I will not leave this family, not even to attend medical school, until the conflicts are resolved."

She did not know when she had reached that conviction. Probably she had felt it all along. She had not known of her deep love for her family members, or of her unquestionable devotion to them, until Mother had remarked about it weeks ago, with love and pride—and impatience—showing on her face. That was the first time Michaela had stopped to consider it.

She continued the letter:

Dr. Elder wrote from Philadelphia that the opening of the college has been a success, more than he and Mr. Mullen and the others could have imagined. Forty women enrolled, many as matriculants. Classes are held Monday through Friday from ten A.M. to six P.M. and on Saturdays from ten to two. Clinics are held on Wednesdays and Saturdays. Eight women are preparing to graduate soon with medical degrees.

Michaela paused, studying her words, the pen in her hand, mixed feelings in her heart. "I had hoped to be among them," she wrote. "But I could not receive the college's degree for a time anyway, as graduates must be twenty-one years of age."

"Etha applied to the college and was accepted," she continued in yet another paragraph. "She worked as a teacher locally this past year to raise the tuition and boarding fees herself so they would not be a burden for her

202

family. She leaves for Philadelphia in November, and I am happy for her."

That was the truth—she was happy for Etha. But she also felt sad inside. She had not witnessed a surgery or a dissection in more than a year now, though the desire to become a medical doctor still burned in her soul. Etha was a year older than she, nineteen, and her plan was to attend sessions at the college and work under Dr. Elder's supervision for three years, since the college required that candidates for graduation serve three years with a preceptor. Michaela was only eighteen, and while she was certainly old enough to start the intensive work under a preceptor, the events of this past year had taught her where her priorities should lie.

"I went to see her," Claudette announced suddenly one evening as Michaela sat reading to her.

"Who?" Mike asked.

"That woman."

She studied Claudette. Then she realized what she was saying—that she had gone to see Charles's mistress.

"Oh, Claudette," was all Michaela could say.

"Last week, one afternoon when you went to see Rebecca," Claudette said. "She's very pretty. Her name is Janice. Even she doesn't know where he is. She hasn't seen him."

"Why do you do this to yourself and your children?" Michaela demanded softly, unable to help herself. The months of anguish had piled up. She had seen her father grow sad and solemn, a beaten man under his daughter's anger. She had cared for her niece and nephew, who always asked after their mother. She had tolerated Claudette's anger at Father and she had helped care for her sister because she loved her and would not take sides in this. But now, hearing of Claudette's visit to Charles's mistress and realizing that Claudette still dwelled on that woman and on her husband's return, giving scarcely a thought to her *children*, for the love of God . . . Michaela would not sit quietly through this.

"Charles is gone and he may never return," she said.

"And Father didn't chase him away. Charles's guilt chased him away."

Claudette tilted her chin and regarded Mike angrily. Suddenly Michaela didn't care. She had treated Claudette as if she were fragile, trying to help her through her grief, and now she had run out of patience. Instead of focusing on the children upstairs, Claudette had to know about Charles. She had had to see for herself what his mistress looked like, and if Charles was living with her.

"Mollie and William need you," Mike told her, and then she tossed aside the book she had been holding in her lap, left the room, and went up to them. She intended to take them to the Railroad Jubilee that was to begin tomorrow on the Common. William wanted to see the Light Guard parade the green, and Mollie wanted to see the brass band. Michaela couldn't wait to feast on a dish of ice cream while waiting to see what sort of poetry came out of Dr. Holmes for this occasion. Railroad lines were about to open that would connect Boston to Canada and to the West, and Holmes, who had verses for every event, would surely compose a pretty poem for this one.

14

The following March, a year and one month after Robby's death, Mike found Claudette reading to William in the nursery. She started past his room, thinking he was sleeping—it was a good hour beyond the childrens' bedtimes and she had already tucked them safely away for the night. Instead there was Claudette seated in a rocking chair with her youngest son, the book propped in front of them.

"Auntie Mike!" he called, squirming on his mother's lap.

Michaela was surprised to see them together, but she hesitated only a moment. She hurried on, heading for the guest room she had occupied for so long now, not wanting to disturb mother and son. But William was quick. He scampered up behind her and tugged on her skirt just as she placed her hand on the doorknob.

Mike turned and knelt before the boy, bringing herself down to his level. "Hello, Master William. What are you doing awake?"

"I couldn't seep. Mollie's seeping an' I couldn't find you."

"So you asked Mama to read you a story?"

He started to nod his head yes, then he stopped and shook it no. "I was cryin'. I wanted somebody."

"And Mama came?"

He nodded, his eyes wide. He looked so much like Robby during those moments, Michaela thought she would cry. The same blue eyes, the same curly brown hair, the same rumpled-looking appearance.

"That's wonderful," she said, smiling, although her heart constricted a little. She wanted to scoop him into her arms, but she didn't dare. The time wasn't right. She had become a mother to William in the absence of his own, and now the time may have come to hand him back to Claudette. At least for tonight. Seeing him on Claudette's lap had been such a surprise, a joyous one, and Mike had not wanted to interrupt the moment. For whatever reason, Claudette was finally paying attention to her youngest son, finally fulfilling one of his needs, and Michaela would never stand in the way of that, never interfere. She would encourage it. "Go back to her now and let her finish the story. Go ahead," she told William.

"You read to me, Auntie," he said. "You always read to me."

Michaela shook her head. She had not wanted this to happen. She had not wanted him to become so attached to her. But she had taken Claudette's place for so long now and the attachment was inevitable.

"Oh, William, let Mama read to you. Auntie Mike has a headache. I was going to put a cold cloth to my head and—"

"It's all right, Michaela," Claudette said from just outside his doorway.

Mike glanced at her, then back to William. No, Claudette should read to him, she felt certain of that. "My head hurts terribly," she told the boy. "I must lie down and close my eyes. Let Mama read to you. I'll read to you tomorrow."

He pressed his chubby hand to her forehead. "Don't get sick, Auntie. Pease don't get sick."

He was thinking of Robby—and of his mother—Michaela could tell. She knew him well, knew his expressions. She hugged him, then pulled away to smile down at him again. "I'm not sick, I promise, and I won't get sick. It's only a headache. It will be gone by morning. Run along now. Let Mama read you to sleep."

He turned around, not very happily—his lower lip protruded the slightest bit—and trudged off, his tiny nightdress just touching the floor. Hard to believe he would be put in breeches in a year and a half and be sent to a classroom to begin studies. He seemed so small in the large hall.

He stretched his arms up to his mother, and after a few seconds of hesitation in which Claudette stared at Michaela, choking back tears and silently thanking her, she scooped him up and carried him back into the room.

Claudette began spending time with her two living children again, working hard to reestablish her relationship with them. Mollie quickly learned that if she said anything about missing Papa, her mother's eyes would fill with tears and Claudette would be "indisposed" for the remainder of the day. Thereafter the girl avoided the subject when with her mother. Instead she told Michaela often that she missed her father and asked if he would ever come home. Mike's answer was sadly always the same: "I don't know."

Now and then Mollie mentioned Robby—Robby would do something this or that way, but she was always careful not to mention Robert's name, either, when with her mother. Even William, at his young age, seemed to realize that; he once told Jamie, one of Rebecca's boys, to hush when Jamie began talking about the time he and Robby had broken the ice on Frog Pond and scooped out a fish. The topic had come up because Rebecca's husband had begun talking about taking the boys fishing and Jamie wanted to let them all know that he had already fished—several years before with Robby. Claudette glanced away, and minutes later she excused herself and left the room where she, her children, Rebecca and her family, and Michaela had all gathered to visit. Claudette's grief over the loss of her oldest son cut deeply still, something that was evident to everyone, even the youngest family members.

It was too late for Mike to enroll in the lectures to be offered in Boston by the Female Medical College of Pennsylvania—the lectures had already begun. But she began precepting with her father, trying more aggressively to prepare herself for medical school in the event the rupture between Claudette and Father healed. She didn't know if it ever would—Claudette had not mentioned their father in months, which Michaela thought was a good sign since she had mentioned him only in anger since Charles's disappearance, and their father still seemed sad and pensive much of the time. Mike now wondered if he was afraid to approach Claudette—he once mentioned offhandedly that she would never forgive him anyway—but she did not broach the sensitive subject.

The precepting began with her accompanying him on medical calls, observing symptoms, pondering them, watching him, taking notes for her educational use, and sometimes helping him treat patients. Afterward, they always discussed his diagnoses and treatments, and he put before her textbooks and various journals so she could read about the sequelae, the aftereffects of ailments, and pathocoenosis—patterns of diseases.

That spring they called on patients with fever, fits, jaundice, diarrhea, dropsy, and ringworm, and they lanced the finger of a woman with a felon abscess. Mike watched Dr. Quinn dose patients carefully with tartar emetic, bromides, cinchona, opium, jalap, and other medications. He treated one patient with boiled milk, another with punch, another with tea and toast. . . . He applied leeches to inflamed eyes, and to treat a child with an extreme fever, he applied ice to the head and mustard plasters to the feet. Diarrhea could spread through a family and beyond with the same speed and deadliness of a plague, he told her, and it required immediate and diligent attention.

During the early summer months he taught her the sounds of a normal heart and normal lungs, and then one day he urged her to a bedside after he had applied his stethoscope to a male patient's chest and listened carefully for some time.

There was a splitting of the second heart sound, almost a grating, a rubbing, and other sounds Mike couldn't identify. "Pericarditis," he told her later. "Inflammation of the tissue encasing the heart." Pleurisy, or inflammation surrounding the lungs, could be detected by pleuritic friction sounds synchronous with systole, or the heart contracting and expelling blood. Dysfunctions of cardiac valves might be discovered by listening closely for swishing, or "whiffs." Whistling and wheezing breath sounds were always related to the condition of the airways, while any change in fremitus, or vibration, usually involved the lung tissue.

Some patients, upon being introduced to Michaela as Dr. Quinn's "medical student," expressed surprise that he was teaching a woman medicine. They stared at her, silently wondered at her, made a few comments to further express their astonishment. Most ultimately accepted her, seeing that Dr. Quinn was overseeing everything (as one man stated). But some were rude and declared right away that they didn't care to have a woman doctoring them. In those instances, Dr. Quinn was always polite, continuing his examination while Michaela quietly left the room.

At Massachusetts General, there was at first an uproar among the physicians on staff when she began attending early morning rounds. The first morning she attended the gathering of staff members and students, she and her father were greeted by silent, hostile stares. In the end, his reputation and the respect he always received as a knowledgeable physician broke the silence. He had his board with him, and he read aloud the notes made by students who had already examined certain patients. He asked questions, why the student thought this or that, what the symptoms led one to believe, what he would diagnose and how he would treat. And then, when rounds were finished, Dr. Abbot, Henry's father, said he wished to speak privately with Dr. Quinn.

But the conversation was hardly a private one. Other doctors trailed behind the two men and eventually joined them just before they exited the corridor.

"Pompous fools," was all Michaela's father would say about the meeting.

She attended rounds again the following morning, feeling certain that if the board of directors had forbidden her presence, Father would have told her. Somehow he had convinced them that she should be allowed a chance.

A different physician was in charge each morning. During the first few weeks of attending the rounds, Michaela quietly observed. Then she began to speak out if the student's diagnosis was wrong and the physician leading the rounds asked for other opinions. While some physicians bristled when she volunteered her thoughts, especially when she was right, others refused to hear her, a fact that exasperated her and further irritated Dr. Quinn. By May she seemed to have gained some respect, and by June, the doctors who had refused to listen to her now simply stiffened along with the others whenever she spoke.

Michaela didn't think for a moment that she was being accepted; rather, she knew the men were coming to grips with the fact that they could not turn her out of the institution without offending Dr. Joseph Quinn. She was being tolerated because of who her father was, that was all. Her being a medical student was far different from her being a young girl and roaming these halls, no matter that she had the intelligence and the knowledge, which exceeded that of the normal medical student, to become a fine physician.

She and her father had never spoken, and still did not, of the resistance she might face from some patients and even from colleagues in the medical profession. The resistance was silently understood; it didn't need to be discussed. Like Elizabeth Blackwell, she was a woman, and while Elizabeth had been accepted in medical school, had graduated from Geneva, and was now practicing in New York City—and having a difficult time of it according to her letters—women were still not accepted in the overall medical profession. As midwives, yes, but not in the classrooms of medical schools, not in hospitals, and certainly not at bedsides. Michaela was just now beginning to have a true sense of the prejudice Elizabeth still faced daily.

• • •

One unbelievably humid day in late June, Mike was with Claudette when a rapping began on the front door. When she pulled the door open, there stood a boy, nearly breathless from running, telling her that Mr. Atkins was at the home of Miss Janice Owens, too ill to climb out of the bed into which he had fallen, and that *he* had been sent to alert Mrs. Atkins.

Claudette emitted a noise behind Michaela, a sharp cry of alarm. Then she called orders to her remaining household staff, telling them to send for a buggy—and also for Dr. Quinn.

Mike had time to cast her an amazed look—there were hundreds of physicians in the city, after all—then she ran after the shawl she had draped over the arm of a parlor chair. She grabbed the shawl, turned around, and nearly ran into Mollie.

"I want to see Papa," the girl said.

"Perhaps later," Michaela told her. "Right now, we're not certain of how ill he is. It sounds as though he needs a doctor. Mommy and I are going, and you must stay here for now and tend the house. Will you do that for us, Mollie?"

After a few seconds of looking disappointed and sad, Mollie nodded. She felt as if she had an important duty to see to, and that satisfied her at the moment.

Mike dashed from the parlor and then from the front door with Claudette. Moments later, they scrambled up into the buggy before it came to a complete stop in front of the house. Soon it rattled off down the street while Claudette gripped Michaela's arm.

Before long the conveyance pulled to a stop in front of a small house with dark blue shutters. Claudette and Michaela were handed down by the driver while a blond woman of small stature pulled open the front door of the house and watched them approach. Her fine dress indicated she was not a servant, and it led Mike to believe she was Janice Owens.

Claudette never hesitated; she strode straight toward the woman and the house where Charles had undoubtedly committed adultery many times. The latter thought alone made Mike pause. She had watched her sister and her sister's children endure so much during the last year and a half, and she did not know if she could tolerate being near, and in the home of, the woman she felt was responsible for much of that grief.

"He is here?" Claudette asked the woman.

Miss Owens nodded, sadly, then took Claudette by the hand. "I had to send for you. I know how you love him."

Claudette squeezed the woman's hand, and Michaela watched her mouth the words "Thank you." Then she stepped over the threshold, indeed loving her husband so much that she would endure this humiliation, that she would see him in the home of his mistress.

Mike battled her own feelings, her own resentments. Then, because she adored Claudette, she, too, approached the house and stepped inside.

They were led straight to Charles, who lay prostrate in the middle of a large tester bed draped with green velvet. His respiration was fast and labored, and he began a coughing spell when he saw them, one that made him writhe with pain. Janice Owens pressed a bundle of cloths into Claudette's hand, and Claudette hurried over to nurse her husband.

"Oh, Charles. You didn't need to leave, love," she whispered as she sat on the bed and bent over him. "You didn't need to leave us."

She was crying; Michaela heard the emotion in her voice and she turned away and followed Miss Owens from the room, not wanting to infringe on the private moments between husband and wife.

"Would you like tea?" Miss Owens asked her when they reached the small parlor. She dropped down to a settee, then stood quickly, her nervousness obvious.

Michaela sat in a chair near a window and placed her hands in her lap. "No." Pray this was the beginning of the end of the ugliness and the pain. Charles was clearly dying, too wasted to last much longer. And Claudette—she had sent one of the servants after Father. Father! Had that been habit or had that been intentional? Mike could not guess. But she wondered. She hoped. She prayed for the healing of their relationship. "I've never known tea to mend broken hearts and shattered lives," she said softly, stiffly.

The room reverberated with awkward silence.

"I never knew there would be broken hearts and shattered lives," Janice Owens responded.

Mike looked up at her, and she felt certain all the resentment and anger she felt showed on her expression and in her eyes. "No, I don't imagine you did."

They stared at each other.

"You'll excuse me," the woman mumbled. Then she fled the room.

Michaela was not particularly proud that her sharp words made Miss Owens race off, but she welcomed the peace.

She wasn't sure how long she sat there staring out the window, watching people and conveyances pass back and forth out in the street. She closed her eyes rather than look around at the possessions of the woman with whom Charles had strayed. This house was more nicely furnished than her sister's since Claudette had started selling possessions, and Mike could not help but wonder if Charles had furnished the place.

Let him without sin cast the first stone. . . . That was in the Bible somewhere. Had Jesus said that? Michaela couldn't remember. She thought he had.

She didn't like the feelings roiling inside of her, the anger at Janice Owens, the blame she wanted to lay on the woman, her feeling that this house and its furnishings were filthy, her carefully controlled exasperation with Claudette that she was still so devoted to the husband who had committed adultery with another woman and squandered away much of their money in foolish investments.

She had never considered herself prudish or judgmental. She herself rarely had been one to uphold the rules of propriety. But this situation sickened her. The thought of her sister's husband keeping a mistress, and then of her trying to

213

make herself comfortable in the woman's parlor so Claudette might have some private time with Charles, unsettled her. She didn't want to judge Charles or Janice, but that was exactly what she was doing.

Presently Claudette entered the parlor, wringing her hands. "He's not coming, is he? He doesn't want to treat Charles. He doesn't want to get near him. Or perhaps it's because I told him to stay away."

She was talking about their father.

"I don't know," Michaela said, and the words tightened her stomach. She had said them so much this past year, to Mollie, to Claudette, even to William a time or two. She really didn't know why some horrible things had happened. She couldn't explain actions or the course of events or emotions. She wished she could.

"He's not coming," Claudette said again.

"He might be out with another patient."

Claudette wheeled around. "No patient is as important as my husband."

Mike sat back in her chair. She wouldn't tell her sister what she was thinking, that to their father every patient was equally important.

She had to learn that—her father's ability, for the most part, to set aside his differences and personal opinions so that he might simply treat the patient. The night Charles had told everyone his ugly secrets, she had felt pity for him and she had helped nurse him. But in the months since she had watched her sister's suffering, her resentment toward Charles had sprouted and grown. What if she had been called to Charles's bedside as a practicing physician today? Once she became a doctor—and since the family conflicts began she had wondered many times if she ever would— surely she would encounter patients whose morals conflicted with hers. Surely all physicians did.

Claudette had not mentioned Charles in months. She had been moving on finally, playing with her children, even laughing at times. Now Michaela had to wonder if her grieving would start all over again. She prayed not.

Feeling tired, Mike dropped her head against the back of the chair in which she sat.

"The best physician in all of Boston and he's not coming," Claudette whispered frantically.

"There is no saving him," Michaela told her sister brusquely, painfully and not without tears herself. Her voice sounded choked; her throat felt constricted. She would not have Claudette becoming near mad again, bouncing back and forth between reality and delusions. It couldn't start all over again. It simply couldn't. "The disease is too far advanced. I'm only a medical student, but even I can see that. A miracle, perhaps."

Claudette put her hands over her mouth.

"Don't expect Father to come and perform heroics," Mike went on. "Don't expect a miracle of *him*. Don't expect Charles to live and for life to be as it was. Do you understand? Robby is dead and Charles is dying."

Slowly Claudette nodded.

Michaela closed her eyes again. She wondered if she had the inner strength to endure another year or more, or possibly a lifetime, of chaos and sadness and grief if Charles's illness and inevitable death drove Claudette to insanity. She didn't. She couldn't. It was the first time she had ever doubted herself so deeply.

She must have drifted off; through the open window the sound of hoofbeats and the rattle of a buggy startled her, and when she glanced out, she saw her father climbing down from the driver's seat. Claudette had left the room.

Mike wondered how Claudette and Father would manage their first contact with each other in more than a year. Or had it been longer? She was too weary right now to figure the full amount of time.

Had the many months since Charles's indiscretion and Robby's death put more gray in his hair and beard? More lines on his face? Michaela thought so. She watched him face the house, and she almost gasped at the realization that he looked old to her. There was more gray and there were more lines, too. Why had she not noticed them before?

He studied the residence, as if wondering if he wanted to approach. Then he took a deep breath, fetched his bag from the buggy seat, straightened to his full height, and began walking toward the house.

That's how it's done, Michaela thought. *The physician gathers his courage, cloaks himself in resolve, and enters the sick one's house with his medical mind. With his own morals and standards safely tucked away.*

Mike rose to go meet him.

From the time he stepped into the house, he focused on Charles's care. Claudette met him at the door of the sickroom, pleading with him to help, and he said simply, "Take me to him." Doubtless he had considered many times his actions the last time he had seen Charles. Whether or not that had had any bearing on his decision to come here, or on his medical treatment of his son-in-law now, Michaela might never know. She certainly would never ask.

Charles was gasping at least thirty breaths a minute. He held the right side of his chest and groaned with pain. He shivered—goosebumps marked his skin, which varied in color from deathly pale to grayish blue. The skin of his neck hung in loose folds, stark evidence alone of the amount of weight he had lost. He had never been a heavy man. Now he was a skeleton.

"I'll need brandy and milk, rum and eggs," Dr. Quinn said as he approached the bed, pulling the pieces of his stethoscope out of his bag.

Michaela, who had assisted him many times now, went to work straightaway. If he could set his animosity aside, she could set hers aside. She had to. She asked Janice Owens for the items, and Miss Owens promptly went off to get them.

Charles was glancing frantically around the room, clearly frightened because he could scarcely catch his breath. And Mike knew from her studies and the knowledge she had absorbed from her father that Charles's terror made catching his breath even more difficult.

As she thought Dr. Quinn would, he administered chloral hydrate to sedate Charles, and then gave small doses of opium and hyoscine to ease his pain. Michaela managed to get Charles to drink the milk mixed with beaten raw egg, and Claudette bathed his face over and over with a cool cloth. Dr. Quinn treated Charles for fever, and he administered more opium nearly every hour, more than Mike had ever seen him give.

"I'll arrange to have him moved as soon as you say he's strong enough," Claudette told Father after Charles finally began resting more comfortably. She still expected him to live. Michaela rubbed the middle of her forehead, then crossed her arms and went to sit down in a chair across the room.

"I'm only making him comfortable," Father responded. "You must understand that."

Claudette stared at him. On the bed, Charles moaned. She hurried over to him, lifted his hand and pressed it to her cheek. She whispered things to him, Mike wasn't sure what. She and her father left the room.

In the parlor, Janice brought them soup and bread. They hadn't asked for anything and she hadn't offered. She had just appeared suddenly with a tray in hand some twenty minutes after they left the sickroom. Michaela wasn't sure what to think of the woman, why she was being so hospitable and kind after she—Mike—had made it clear that she didn't like her or approve of her.

Michaela said nothing when Janice sat the tray down on the table in front of them. Joseph, however, thanked the woman for her consideration, and while he didn't eat the soup and bread eagerly, as if he had a hearty appetite, he ate some slowly. Michaela wondered if he did so to avoid making Janice think he would take nothing from her hands.

"Eat," he told her when Miss Owens had gone. "You need the nourishment."

She couldn't. She shook her head. "How can you—"

He held up his hand, palm out, to stop her. "The judgment is not ours to make. We have all committed wrongdoings in one form or another. That does not mean the food she offers is poisoned."

She ate.

217

The hours dragged on. He continued the dosages of medication to make Charles comfortable.

Nightfall arrived, and through Janice's servant, Father sent a message to Mother to tell her where he was and what was happening, if she did not already know. He told Mike she should go home. But she didn't wish to leave Claudette. When Charles died, Claudette would need comfort, and she would want her to be close.

The end came near daybreak. Mike had settled in the parlor, curling her legs beneath her and resting her head against one wing of the chair. Her father rested in a similar chair near the hearth. Mike woke to a gentle shake, and there was Claudette kneeling beside the chair, looking up at her.

"He's gone," she said. No tears. No hysteria. Just wide glassy eyes and a pale face that reflected more sadness than anyone should have to bear in a lifetime. "What now, Michaela?"

Mike almost could not speak. When she did, her voice sounded cracked and far away: "Now you go home to Mollie and William, and we bury him."

Claudette nodded. She lay her head on Michaela's knee just as Father rose from the settee and left the room, probably to go see about Charles.

At the funeral, Claudette took the first step toward healing her relationship with Father.

She wore black silk, and a wisp of black gauze gently covered her face. When she sprinkled the first handful of dirt on top of Charles's coffin after it had been lowered into the grave, she did not shed a tear. She said a prayer over him, that his soul would be at peace. Then she lifted her veil, smoothed it back over her hat, and turned her face toward the sun.

She had lost much weight herself, and she was pale. But she absorbed the light in those long moments, as her family and friends stood watching her. Finally, she inhaled deeply and approached Father where he stood back some distance, clearly not knowing if he was even welcome.

The bell in the Park Street Church tolled noon as Claudette spoke to him. Then he offered her his arm, she took it, and they walked toward the waiting carriages, dignified, serene, rejoined.

Michaela cried, this time not in grief but in happiness.

15

Since the institution's opening it had been assumed by almost everyone that Michaela would attend the Female Medical College in Philadelphia. Then the conflicts and deaths had happened within the Quinn family and she had put off her schooling. Claudette, Mollie, and William were doing well, moving on with their lives, and Michaela was once again sleeping in her parents' home. Still, there were times when Claudette seemed far away, times when she secluded herself in her room and ate little, and for that reason, Michaela did not wish to leave Boston just yet. But, armed with a letter of recommendation from her father, she applied officially to the school that fall, to begin attending the following year.

"She should be recovered by now," Mother snapped to Mike when Claudette declined to attend a supper with them one day. It wasn't the first time she had canceled her attendance at an engagement, and Mother had long ago become impatient with her.

"Not everyone has your strength," Michaela said.

"You do."

It was their one common link, Mike realized. Their inner

strength. She had never known that before, had never thought about it.

"You would not have gone mad and dismissed half of your servants," Mother said. "Nor would you have sold most of your household furnishings."

Michaela was sitting at her dressing table brushing her hair. Her grip tightened on the brush. "Claudette did what she thought was best."

"Oh, Michaela, stop coddling her. Her situation was not so desperate. You would not have reacted so rashly."

Mike twisted around. "How do you know her situation was not so desperate, Mother? You stopped going to her house to help her shortly after Robby died. You didn't see the devastation that word of Charles's failed investments brought. You weren't present when Claudette was told she could live comfortably for perhaps four years. Only four years! What gives you the right to criticize her? She is not me. You're wrong—I might have sold everything in sight."

Elizabeth Quinn's eyes glittered with haughtiness and anger. "She is my daughter, that is what gives me the right. This family has endured enough embarrassment and disgrace."

With her skirts rustling, she turned and left the room, graceful and dignified. Like a queen leaving her court, Mike thought. That's what it was, then—Claudette's situation disturbed her not because she worried about her daughter's mental health, but because the circumstances and Claudette's reaction to them had heaped embarrassment after embarrassment on the family, from the confrontation between Charles and Father that night to word that Charles had left his family in dire financial straits.

Mother. Michaela had learned to tolerate her superior ways. But at times, they still irritated her to no end.

Mike went back to brushing her hair, trembling the entire time.

Her letter of acceptance from the medical school arrived just as winter began bearing down. She had not shared with her mother that she had applied to the school, nor did she share with her that she had been accepted. She would have to broach the subject sooner or later, she knew, but she didn't care to anytime soon. She had months ahead in which to make the announcement. For now, dealing with Mother's quiet disapproval over her preceptorial with Father and every time a letter arrived from Etha was enough.

In Philadelphia, Etha was having the time of her life, and it had been hard for a while—until Michaela's letter of acceptance came—to read her letters. She had written about Professor Moseley, how he would not tolerate tardiness, how he taught his anatomy and physiology classes through the use of models, drawings, and clinical instruction in the private dissection rooms. The corpses were preserved in whiskey barrels, and after much discussion among the governing body and the faculty, the students had been allowed to dissect a male. No one had made a big to-do about it inside the school. But outside the institution (somehow word of the dissection had slipped out) male medical students enrolled at other institutions had gathered to make trouble, and the police had had to be called out.

Etha had written that Professor Gleason was a fine surgeon, and he had a quick way with his scalpel during demonstrations. He became annoyed with any student who did not pay close attention. The professor of *materia medica* and therapeutics espoused ancient Greek medicine and the four humors—blood, phlegm, yellow bile, and black bile—and had a huge engraving of a bust of Hippocrates mounted in his lecture room. Professor Challoner taught chemistry with a flourish, combining this and that, waving away smoke, once singeing his eyebrows and beard in front of his class, then saying quite jovially, "That, my dear students, is what you mustn't do." Michaela laughed every time she thought of the episode. She had met Dr. Challoner while in Philadelphia and she remembered well the tone of his voice and the sparkle of his eye.

Etha was full of stories of gatherings that were held after hours, of meals taken in various homes while fascinating conversations went on around her. One old doctor, crippled now and too feeble to practice medicine anymore, recalled

Ben Franklin, who had owned a house just up the street. He had walked many a morning with the man and listened to him talk about improvements that could be made in his beloved Philadelphia. "Whether the subject is Benjamin Franklin or surgery methods or specific diseases and treatments, the discussions are always indepth and spellbinding. I can see you now, Michaela. You will thrive on attending the medical college and on being surrounded by the fine minds here. I only wish you were not arriving at the time I will be going home."

Michaela's—and Etha's—wish had been that they attend medical college together. They would obtain their medical education from the same institution and from the same physicians, but while Mike went off to Philadelphia to attend the college, Etha would return to Boston for preceptorial training under Dr. Quinn. Upon leaving for Philadelphia, Michaela still would have two years of preceptorship to serve, and she wasn't certain yet whether she would do that with her father or with another physician.

She reread all of Etha's letters that December, and felt her excitement rise again at the thought of returning to Philadelphia.

She took Mollie skating in January on the deep black ice of Back Bay, just beyond the Public Garden. Few people ever went very far up the bay when the ice froze; it became deceptive farther out. Tidal water rushed in and out of the Mill Dam gates and although the ice was just as dark, it thinned.

Michaela buried her hands deep in her muff and watched Mollie attempt her first figure eight. A resilient child—she fell, got up, tried again, fell, got up, tried again. Mike scratched the figures into the ice with ease. After all, skating had been a favorite pastime for Rebecca and her. Rarely did a child grow up in Boston, particularly in the Beacon Hill and Back Bay areas, without learning how to skate. She whizzed around the ice, showing Mollie how to turn her blades to slow and then to stop. She felt the wind chafe her cheeks. But her ears were warm at least, buried, like Mollie's, beneath a thick fur cap.

223

Someone grabbed her by the elbow, and she was quick enough on a pair of skates to whirl around and face the person. He went tumbling, cape, cap and all, and he shot across the ice on his bottom, upsetting at least six people. Bodies crashed and intermingled. People shouted objections. Mike thought maybe she should take Mollie and depart for home as quickly as possible. Since she had caused the upset, people might bear down on her at any moment.

She was looking around for Mollie when the sound of a voice speaking her name made her freeze: "Michaela Quinn, now that is a fine way to greet me! A fine way to welcome me home!"

It was David's voice.

David's voice.

Mike spun around and around on her skates, looking for him, wondering if she was dreaming, or if she was imagining his voice when it was really someone else speaking to her. She saw him crawling across the ice, now and then rubbing his left hip, and she cried out, thinking she had injured him. The people he had knocked down in his slide were regaining their footing. No one looked seriously injured. Except David.

"Oh, my God," Mike said. She skated over to him, and he snatched his hand away just as her blade came dangerously close. She stooped near him, grabbed hold of his arm, and tried to help him up. "You're not hurt . . . please tell me you're not hurt. Oh, David, I had no idea you were in Boston!"

"Aunt Michaela!" Mollie shouted.

Mike twisted around to try to catch sight of her niece. There was Mollie, safely doing figure eights, a little faster now and with more skill. Michaela twisted back toward David and then her right skate slipped out from under her and she went tumbling, too, down into his arms.

They both sat with their jaws open for a time. Then they laughed. David's eyes sparkled with mischievousness, and Mike felt his arms close around her. She wondered if he had caused her spill, if he had pulled the skate out from under her.

She wriggled free, knowing half of Beacon Hill was at the

bay on this fine day for skating. The sun glimmered down on the ice, giving it just enough of a sheen to make the surface slick. She certainly wouldn't give people anything more to gossip about. There had been quite enough talk about the Quinns in and around Boston these past few years.

"Are you hurt?" she asked David.

"And if I am?"

She studied him. His face had thinned a little. His lashes seemed to have thickened. The delicious scent of cinnamon drifted up from him. If he were hurt? . . . "Why, I would help you up and take you to my father."

He grinned. Then he lifted her hand and brought it to his lips. "Sweet Michaela, you are prettier than I remembered."

Three years since they had last seen each other. Distance and time had come between them again. And while they had written letters back and forth, as before, and Mike felt she knew him fairly well, the moment was still awkward. She remembered his kiss beneath the trees that day, the softness of his lips on hers. The temperature of the ice was stealing through her cape and her other clothes, and she felt uneasy, surrounded by so many people, and David still holding her hand.

She withdrew it, asking again, "Are you hurt?"

He shrugged. "Bruised."

"Can you stand?"

He smiled. "Not without assistance, surely."

That made her more uneasy—and impatient. While she was ecstatic to see him, he had not witnessed the terrible circumstances that had engulfed her family for so long. They were drawing stares.

"David, please," Michaela said softly, glancing away. She gathered her skirts, her resolve, and her wits, and she rose steadily until she again had her footing on the ice.

He tipped his head. "You're rather serious."

"I recently lived through a rather serious time."

"Laughter breathes life into the frailest of men," he said, deepening his voice and lifting his chin as if mocking someone.

225

"I'm hardly frail."

"Aunt Michaela!" Mollie called again. This time when Mike turned to catch sight of her, she watched her fall.

"I have to go," Michaela said, and then she raced off, now wondering if Mollie was hurt. Her heart pounded—*David had returned to Boston.*

Mollie had twisted her right wrist in trying to cushion her fall, and Mike was fussing over it when David neared them.

"You must be Mollie," he said, stooping to the girl's level. He moved well for a man with a bruised hip. Perhaps it was the laughter, Michaela thought caustically. Or perhaps there was no bruised hip.

"Could I look at your wrist, Mollie?" he asked. "I'm David Lewis, newly doctorized and fresh off a ship that came all the way from England. I was skating along, wondering how to acquire my first patient. Now here you are with a smarting joint."

Mike could not help the smile that touched her lips. He might not be charming Mollie—the girl turned her face into Michaela's skirt—but he was certainly charming her. Doctorized . . . Mike wondered whether that was even a recognized word.

Mollie peeked out at him, favoring her wrist. "My grandpapa is a doctor. He'll see to it." She sounded like Claudette had at a younger age. She even acted like her sometimes, a proper lady in a girl's body.

"I'm certain he will once we get you home," David said. "I studied with your grandfather when I was younger. I used to go to his Tremont Street School almost every day, along with your Aunt Michaela. He would show me his wrist if it were injured."

Mollie glanced up at Mike. Michaela nodded at her niece. "It's true."

Mollie had hidden her arm in the folds of Mike's skirt. She stretched her little arm out to David —*Dr. David Lewis.* Michaela thought with a burst of pride—and she placed her hand in his.

He was gentle in his examination. He closed his eyes as his fingertips probed and touched. He was seeing the tendons, the fragile bones, the muscles, the nerves, the network of tiny vessels that branched their way through the wrist. The concentration on his face despite skaters buzzing by and a million noises going on around him was amazing. Mollie gave a little cry at one probe and David's eyes popped open. "Ah," he said, and then she reclaimed her wrist.

"It's only twisted, right?" Mike queried. "It's not broken?"

He stood. "Thank you, Mollie. Now we'll take you to Grandfather and see what he thinks. For now, I suggest we remove our skates and walk you home.

"It's not twisted or broken," he told Michaela moments later. "I would say she tore something—a tendon or a ligament."

Mike closed her eyes. The last thing Claudette needed was an injured child.

"Easily fixed," David said presently, unlacing his skates.

Mike had already unlaced and removed Mollie's, put the child's boots back on her feet, and now Mollie was chasing a pair of ducks near the edge of the ice. "Be careful," Michaela called to her. "Stay back from the ice. What do you mean, 'easily fixed?'" she asked David.

"I can't tell you how many days I spent cutting and mending ligaments and tendons in the dissection laboratories at la Pitié. Easily fixed," he said again. He was not being arrogant. She saw that. He was stating fact. He knew what was wrong with Mollie's smarting wrist and he knew how to remedy the problem.

"Mollie, stay back," Mike called again. The girl would slip on the ice and injure something else, Michaela just knew.

"One would think you were her mother," David said, and he was not being impertinent; he was merely stating his observation.

Mike looked at him. "I was for more than a year."

He tipped his head and regarded her. Then he nodded, understanding.

• • •

Dr. Quinn agreed with the diagnosis. He was conservative where surgical measures were concerned, however, and he recommended giving Mollie's wrist a few weeks rest to see if it mended by itself.

Meanwhile, Michaela had a host of questions for David. She was curious about his studies in France, which he had not gone into detail about in his letters. She wanted to hear about the dissections he had done and the surgeries he had witnessed and participated in. She wondered about his travels—where he had gone, the things he had seen, the people he had met. And she wanted to know what he intended to do with his life now. Stay in Boston and start a practice? Travel to New York and work alongside a colleague there? She hoped the last was not so, but he had mentioned in one of his letters that he might do that. At the time, she had wondered if he had stopped to consider her feelings, that he had already been gone from home for years. And then she reminded herself, as she had many times, that he did not seem to care for her romantically as much as she cared for him. Assuming things where David was concerned would be a mistake, one that might bring her heartache.

He had supper at her parent's home the following evening, and he sat opposite Michaela at the table. Father wanted to hear about David's studies in France but Mother skillfully led him into talking about his travels, about the Colosseum in Rome and the pyramids in Egypt. He spoke of what scientists knew about the building of the pyramids, and that swayed his thoughts to the subject of slavery here in the United States. He had heard that the Free-Soilers had lately held a national convention, elected a president and vice president and had even supported a candidate for the highest office in America.

"The group has grown so much in Boston alone, there will never be another fugitive caught and condemned here," he said, his eyes glittering. "And what is this book, this *Uncle Tom's Cabin*?" he queried. "A depiction of the horrors of slavery."

"The Southern states will not set them free without a fight," Dr. Quinn predicted.

"I just purchased Miss Stowe's book," Mike said.

"We'll read it together," David told her. She agreed with a nod of her head.

Mother's eyelids fluttered, an indication that she was irritated. "Really, we could surely find a more pleasant subject to discuss over our meal. David, do you plan to stay in Boston, then?"

"Yes, Mrs. Quinn," he said quickly. Then he glanced at Michaela and added, "And see more of your daughter if she will allow me."

Mike lowered her gaze to her plate, feeling her face warm. He wanted to see more of her . . . and he planned to stay in Boston. She couldn't possibly be happier.

"That is a pleasant prospect," Mother remarked. "Michaela?"

Mike gathered her courage and glanced up at David. "I will," she said softly. "Allow you to see more of me, that is."

He smiled at her and seconds later, her father cleared his throat and asked David if he had been to the Boston Museum since returning home. There was a fine collection of Egyptian artifacts on display there right now, pieces he might be interested in seeing.

"I haven't been," David responded. "But . . . would you like to go there with me tomorrow afternoon, Michaela?"

Father tried to intervene, knowing she planned to accompany him on patient calls tomorrow afternoon. "She has a prior—"

"She would be delighted to visit the museum with you," Mother told him.

An awkward silence ensued.

"I don't want to take you away from anything," David told Mike.

"You aren't," Mother said.

Joseph cleared his throat. "Mrs. Quinn, Michaela should speak for herself." He had caught himself—if Mike wished to accompany David to the museum rather than attend patients with him, that was her prerogative.

Mike took a deep breath. "I would like that," she told David. "Going to the museum with you, that is."

"There we have it," Mother said, looking pleased. "It's settled. Michaela and David are going together to the museum tomorrow afternoon."

Mike wanted to crawl beneath the table, her mother embarrassed her so. Her attempts at matchmaking were far too obvious. The room felt stuffy suddenly, overheated—and in the middle of winter!

David became very attentive during the remaining winter months, calling often at the town house, escorting Michaela to various events around the city—to the pond for more skating, to the Athenaeum for an art show, to the theater to see *Julius Caesar* and the thriller *Ingomar the Barbarian*. Pentland's Circus arrived in Boston that spring, and they enjoyed it several times. They attended the show with Claudette, Mollie, and William, and were delighted at the equestrian stunts and the sparkle of the performers. Another time Martha accompanied them, conveniently losing sight of them after they purchased sweetmeats and went off to watch the bumbling clowns.

Michaela worried that she was neglecting her preceptorship, that David was a distraction from her studies and that she might not be prepared for school when the time came to leave for Philadelphia. But she had waited so long for him to return to Boston, to come home to her, and she would not discourage his attentiveness.

Spring blossomed into summer, and they became more comfortable with their relationship, feeling at ease around each other except during times when they both felt the awkward giddiness of the attraction between them. He ceased trying to be such an attentive gentleman and she ceased trying to impress him with continuous ladylike ways and conversation. She had always spoken her mind in her letters to him, and she recommended doing so now, particularly whenever medical topics arose. During outings and while dancing at balls, they discussed treatments of lunacy, melancholia, and dementia; how to set bones and bandage fractures; when to catheterize and when to cauterize. He was invited by her father to attend the student rounds at Massachusetts General, and he soon became Mike's instructor as well as her beau.

He also attended patients at the hospital, the poor and indigent of Boston—no respectable citizen ever became a patient at a hospital—and one afternoon Michaela watched him repair a vesico-vaginal fistula in a little girl who had suffered a fall the previous year. He catheterized first, introducing a bistoury—a metal instrument with a curved blade—along the closed path of the uretha, opening the bladder and draining the urine. Then, with more concentration than Michaela had ever seen in a surgeon, he set to work repairing the damage done by the child's fall. He cut, he tugged, he pulled, he stitched . . . then he pieced more tissue together and passed the needle and thread through again and again.

Michaela had often heard her father state that he himself had performed only one tracheotomy during the course of his medical practice thus far, and that his attempt had resulted in blood spurting from the arteries. Rather than continue with the procedure, he had pulled back, and the patient had expired soon afterward. Therefore when diphtheria struck several households in the South End, Dr. Quinn called on David, asking about his skill at performing tracheotomies. "I'm comfortable with them," David answered. And he accompanied Dr. Quinn to the households, performing the procedure with ease one day and again the next. He took a quick look at each afflicted child, listened to the decreasing breath sounds, then rolled up his sleeves and set to work. He opened each larynx above the cricoid and introduced a canula through the slit, giving the victims the precious air needed to sustain life.

Michaela assisted him in correcting clubfoot in another child by cutting the Achilles tendon a little to lengthen it.

Then he ordered a special wooden boot for the boy so he might walk instead of limp. He treated a strangulated hernia by dosing the patient with opium, grasping the skin around the tumor and applying gentle but steady pressure upward for nearly an hour. Hernias of such nature could be slowly lethal, sometimes even when called to the attention of a competent medical doctor. The treatment of this one, however, proved successful. The man left the hospital a week later after profusely thanking the physician who had "healed" him.

David took up his causes again, as Mike had known he would, treating the ill in the warehouse tenements, crusading to feed the poor, joining public endeavors to further the orphanages and the schools for the deaf and blind . . . to free every slave in the United States. Michaela took up the causes with him to the best of her ability, but even she shrank back when he told her he had been aiding the cause of all causes by harboring runaway slaves in a small cabin located near the western outskirts of Boston.

"My God, David, do you realize what could happen to your family if your activities are discovered?" she blurted.

His eyes glittered in the orange glow of the torches that lit the Lewis's formal gardens. Mike and David had eaten supper inside with his parents and brothers, then they had come outside to walk and talk. Hours before, he had been alerted to the presence of a fugitive in the cabin—and to the fact that the man had been beaten nearly to death before he had escaped—and the matter weighed heavily on his mind.

"I realize what could happen if that Negro is caught and shipped back," he said tightly. "I cannot overlook something I so strongly oppose."

She knew that. She knew he was a man of conviction. And she loved his resolve and his compassion. She truly did.

"I told Mother and Father I would go to the Berkshire Mountains with them," he said, changing the topic. "It's the first time in years all the family has been together."

Michaela's breath caught. The Berkshire Mountains— The Lewises had a summer home there, Pine Meadow. The family often had disappeared there for two months of the summer season when their sons were younger. But now was different. June had just breezed in . . . Mike counted months in her head. She would leave for Philadelphia in August, exactly two months from now. If David went on summer holiday with his family to the Berkshires, she wouldn't see him again until next summer, when she returned to visit between semesters of medical college.

"The usual two months?" she queried, trying not to sound alarmed. A mild wind whispered through the trees, stirring the nearby bushes. The fragrance of freshly bloomed flowers filled the air.

"Yes."

"I leave for college in August."

"I know."

He stopped suddenly on the path, turned toward her, grasped her hands in his and silently bid her to stop with him. They had not been left alone often these past months; for some reason, Martha had been especially attentive. "Come with us," he whispered.

"David, I can't possibly," Michaela said, shaking her head. "I must study with—"

"I want to go with the family, but I want to see you, too. You've become precious to me. Only a month then."

How could she say no to him? She would have had a difficult time saying no even if he hadn't said such a thing—that she had become precious to him. But saying no was even harder now, with him holding her hands and speaking so intimately.

He drew closer, lowered his head, pressed her against his chest. "Is it love I feel?" he queried, and she wasn't sure of whom he asked the question of—her or himself. "Is it love that makes me enjoy being with you so much? Is it love that makes me not want any more distance between us? Love that makes me not want to go to the Berkshires without you, and you to go off to Philadelphia? I've loved you since the day of our first waltz. Do you remember that, Michaela? Jimmie thought we were mad. So did I. But I've realized since that you're part of my soul. Go to Pine Meadow with me—and then marry me."

He would have kissed her then had she not pulled away in shock. He had never been what she would consider ardent with her, the exception being the kiss beneath the trees near the Bunker Hill Monument. And he had eased into that, speaking soft words and then asking if she would mind if he kissed her. But he was definitely ardent now, asking her to go with him and his family to their summer home and then to marry him. While she had certainly entertained the thought of receiving a proposal from him someday, she had never expected one so soon.

Mike turned away and approached the curving brick wall, thoughts going through her head. If she married him now, medical school would either be delayed or it would never happen. She had enrolled, she had been accepted, she was scheduled to begin this fall. She had already begun her preceptorship. "David or medical school?" she heard her mother demanding of her. And she had answered "David."

But she had waited and hoped for this day. She had dreamed of it, of the time when he would say he loved her and then propose to her.

Now she almost wished he had waited. Now she almost wished she were already at the medical college completing her education. But the fact remained that she was only nineteen and couldn't receive the college's diploma until she turned twenty-one.

Behind her, he cleared his throat. "If I've offended you with my touch and with my manner of proposal, I apologize." He sounded stiff and proper, obviously felt embarrassed and awkward.

She turned to face him, her hands clasped in front of her. "No . . . you haven't offended me. I . . ." She breathed deeply to gather her courage, and why she needed courage to express what she wanted to say was a mystery to her. "I have loved you my entire life." She tipped her head. "My

234

entire life. I cannot remember a day when I didn't love you. Except perhaps for that day on the Charles River when you and Jimmie told me girls couldn't go to medical school."

He smiled, remembering. The torchlight danced in his eyes and flickered shadows on his face. She wondered if he would mention the medical college in Philadelphia, if he would realize how torn she felt. She waited.

He said nothing.

She was about to change the course of her life. She knew that. She loved him too much not to. He had returned to Boston grown, an educated man. He was fast gaining respect at Massachusetts General and with patients in and around the city. He was an innovative surgeon, and he now wished to settle down to a wife. *Now.* And she could envision no other woman but herself in that role. Absolutely no other.

"I will," she whispered, watching him. She couldn't say no to him about this. She couldn't. For so long she had feared that he might never feel the same love for her that she felt for him. Now he did, and she couldn't say no to his proposal.

"You will? . . ."

"Go to the Berkshires with you and your family and marry you upon our return."

He seemed to stop breathing for a few precious seconds. Then he expelled a long breath and lifted her hand to his mouth. His lips remained there for what seemed an eternity. His eyes closed as he relished the touch and her acceptance.

She lifted her other hand to touch his jaw, the boldest move she had ever made, and at the first stroke he opened his eyes. She remembered the breeze over the river ruffling his hair the day he had been truthful with her and Jimmie had been cruel, and she remembered wanting to smooth it. She did so now, with tenderness and love. She would marry him. She would be his wife, have his children, share the joys of their life together.

He turned her hand over and kissed her palm. Then he offered her his arm and they returned to the house.

Inside, they made their announcements. Sarah Lewis immediately began fussing over Michaela, while George Lewis and his other two sons surrounded David, offering cheroots and congratulations.

16

"You've never done anything in a conventional fashion," Elizabeth Quinn remarked when Mike told her about the engagement. Mother was delighted, of course. How could she not be delighted to hear that Michaela planned to stay in Boston and marry David instead of going off to the Female Medical College of Pennsylvania? Michaela had finally told her about her acceptance there, and Mother had fallen into her usual sulking silence, as she often did when she disapproved of something. She even was delighted that Michaela planned to go to the Berkshire Mountains with the Lewis family. But she had to criticize something.

"David should have approached your father first," Mother added. "Joseph will not be happy with that."

"Father has allowed me to make my own decisions in recent years," Mike remarked.

Elizabeth nodded. "So he has."

In the end Father wasn't annoyed that David hadn't come to him first. He sat back in his chair near the study hearth and considered Michaela's announcement. He opened his mouth to say something, then snapped his jaw shut. "The Berkshires for a month?"

She nodded. "That is, if you approve." She meant that—she wouldn't go if he didn't approve. She would do nothing of which he didn't approve.

He rubbed his beard as he stared into the open mouth of the fireplace. "Yellow fever is sweeping New Orleans," he remarked. "A very bad thing, that disease. Chills, vomiting, fever, headache . . . hemorrhage from mucous membranes. A ghastly disease that leads to a ghastly death."

She sat in a chair across from him. "How did you hear?"

"At the wharf while seeing to Mrs. O'Donnell and her group. Some incoming sailors were turned away from the port there. Disease seems to run rampant down South, more so than here."

"Why is that?"

"The heat . . . the marshlands perhaps." He closed his eyes, looking weary, more tired than she had ever seen him. The lines on his face seemed more prominent; his beard was almost fully gray. How old was he now? Sixty-four? Sixty-five? Of late he did not move as quickly as he once had. She first had become fully aware of his advancing age back when Charles had shown up at Janice Owens's residence.

"I'll leave you to rest," she said, and she started to rise.

"No." He opened his eyes. "No need. Are you aware . . . we've never spent an entire month apart."

They hadn't, now that she considered it. She had always come home for weekends from the seminary, and he had even visited with her sometimes during the weekdays.

"I shall miss you," he told her simply.

She went to him, knelt beside the arm of his chair, took his wrinkled hand in hers, and smiled up at him. "I'll never be far from you, Father. It's only a month and it's only the Berkshires. Right here in Massachusetts."

He stroked her hair, and she laid her head on the arm of his chair.

"Robby used to talk of becoming a medical doctor," he said, staring off into the black fireplace again. "Two years now and I still think of him."

Robert's death had affected him profoundly—Michaela

had known that then and she knew it even more now. It had drawn some of the life from the grandfather who had worked desperately to save the boy. Mike listened to the scratch of a tree limb on one of the study windows.

"This is what you want, Mike? To go to Pine Meadow with the Lewises? To marry David when you return?"

She glanced up at him and nodded. "I love him . . . yes."

The tree limb scratched the window again. Thunder sounded in the distance. A horse whinnied out in the street. She meant that, that she wanted to go to Pine Meadow and that she wanted to marry David when they returned. The sadness she saw in her father's eyes made her sad, however, almost made her want to revoke her promises to David.

"I know," Joseph said, and then he closed his eyes again.

He fell asleep in the chair, and Mike sat across from him and did the same, not wanting to leave him.

She received another letter from Etha the next day. It arrived just as Martha was packing the last of her belongings. Michaela held the letter and stared at it for several long moments. Then she tossed it, unopened, into the trunk atop numerous gowns and accessories. Etha's letter would be filled with happenings at the college and with news of the Philadelphia medical community, and Mike did not have the stomach at the moment to read it. Not while she was trying to bar all thoughts of medical school from her mind. She took the letter with her, however, knowing she should read it sooner or later. She did miss Etha and their conversations, and she didn't want to ignore their friendship simply because she had made the choice her mother had predicated she would have to make.

The hills were beautiful—as they had been the one other time Mike had seen them, years before when her own family had visited them for a brief holiday. They were wild with scrub and pine, and the outcroppings of granite made marvelous steps for climbers. Besides riding all over the rolling estate, Michaela and David climbed the hills. The air seemed light. Blueberries grew here and there, and many an afternoon Mike plucked them from the bushes and ate them. The swift current in the river that cut between mountains drove the bubbling, frothing water over and around huge rocks. The sweet smell of clover filled the air in the south meadow, where one afternoon David caught Michaela in his arms and kissed her once again, lightly and sweetly.

She had never realized how confining Boston was, how different the air was there, how different the noise of the city was compared to the quiet of the country. She discovered in herself a love for the open land, for the serenity of it. She discovered that she loved to hear the trees whisper in the night breeze, that she loved to watch cows come through pasture gates at sunset. Riding a horse here was even more different, far more pleasant, than riding one in the city. Here, a horse did not have a million noises to spook it. It could enjoy the country air and openness, too.

"Dr. Burnhart is coming for supper this evening," David said. "He lives down the way, an old family friend. There will be laughing and dancing this evening. He's a jolly man."

David was right. Dr. Burnhart might be nearly seventy years old, but he brought his violin with him, and after supper of roasted lamb and numerous other dishes, no one was exempt from dancing, not even the maid. When George Lewis grabbed the Irish girl and began whirling her around, Mike expected to see Sarah Lewis reel with shock. Not so. Apparently Mrs. Lewis was accustomed to the antics that ensued whenever Dr. Burnhart arrived at Pine Meadow, and she merely sat back in her chair and smiled.

David and Dr. Burnhart had not seen each other in years, and the elderly man was delighted to hear that David had finally completed his studies and traveling and had already begun taking on patients in Boston. Mike settled opposite Sarah at a game table and they played cards while the men talked.

The disturbing effect the slavery issue was having in Boston was always a topic at social gatherings, and this event was no different. David, as always, became agitated over the topic, his voice rising in pitch and becoming tighter when he spoke of the fugitive slaves the Boston mobs had failed to rescue. He wondered aloud at the beatings they had taken upon being returned to their masters, and George quietly suggested that no one knew if they had received beatings upon being returned. David glared at his father, and Dr. Burnhart wisely chose to change the subject.

But as Mike feared might happened, he switched to a medical topic. He had several patients with recurring ovarian cysts. In fact, he had recently drained nine pints of fluid from one such cyst, thinking that would heal the problem. Only the cyst recently had presented itself again. The old doctor and David began discussing fevers of unknown origins because Dr. Burnhart right now had a patient who at first had exhibited no other symptom but fever. Michaela wanted to go sit with the men and listen more closely to their discussion; instead she tried to concentrate on her cards, tried to block out their words.

When Dr. Burnhart mentioned dosing the patient with tarter emetic and that the man then experienced vomiting, diarrhea, paleness, coolness to touch, and slowing of the pulse, Mike could bear it no longer. Dr. Burnhart assumed his patient's illness was some sort of intestinal ailment. But he was wrong. She had watched her father give tarter emetic many times and she knew its powerful effects. The vomiting and diarrhea were acceptable signs of purging, caused by the medication. But the paleness, coolness, and slowing of the patient's pulse . . . he might very well be in danger of cardiovascular collapse.

"Stop the medication," Michaela said.

The men fell quiet as they glanced her way. George Lewis rubbed his chin. Dr. Burnhart furrowed his brows and narrowed his eyes. Even David looked a little surprised.

Mike hardly cared. "The man is being purged to death."

"Michaela," Sarah whispered.

"Tarter emetic is a potent medication," Michaela continued, looking at the old doctor. "It should be stopped if the patient begins exhibiting symptoms such as you just described."

"Typical manifestations of purging, Michaela," David commented softly.

Dr. Burnhart sat a little straighter in his chair and gave her a disapproving, almost arrogant look, a look that had become all too familiar to Mike. "I believe I know how to treat my patient, young woman."

Mike waited to see if David would inform Dr. Burnhart that she had a considerable amount of medical knowledge. She waited to see if he would suggest that perhaps she knew what she was talking about. She could say so herself, but for some reason, she wanted, needed, to know if David would speak up for her, support her opinion.

He said nothing. He swirled the remaining brandy in the snifter he held. He glanced at the glass, then back to her. He shifted from one foot to the other, then slipped a hand into a trouser pocket in an attempt to look relaxed. But how well she knew him—he was anything but relaxed.

He would not speak for her. He expected her to go quietly back to her cards. Michaela's stomach tightened. Did he see her in a completely different light now that she was his fiancée? Did he expect her never again to involve herself in medical discussions? Did he expect her to forget the medical knowledge she had collected her entire life thus far? Did he expect her to settle into being nothing more than a dutiful wife?

She had the strong impression that she was embarrassing him, and that frustrated and angered her. As his fiancée, she could climb the granite rocks with him, ride between the pines and walk arm in arm with him along the banks of the Housatonic River. She could pluck blueberries with him in the scrub and search for four-leaf clovers in the meadows. But she could not sit in his family's parlor and discuss medicine with him and his colleagues. That was not proper behavior for his intended wife.

Mike looked Dr. Burnhart straight in the eye. "If the purging continues, your patient will expire within days."

"Michaela, it's your turn," Sarah said, trying to distract her, trying to salvage the evening.

But Mike's temper bubbled beneath her skin. If she had

been twelve years old again, without the advantage of schooling and the manners that had finally been instilled in her, she would not be in such careful control. As it was, she gathered her skirts, rose, and approached David as he stood near the hearth, her head tilted, her lips pursed.

He looked even more apprehensive now—and with good reason. She was about to throw a tantrum in an adult sort of way, one born of frustration and the shock she experienced upon realizing that he no longer meant to support her medical interests. No matter that she had given up on them herself, that she had committed herself to being his wife and eventually the mother of his children. Giving them up was *her* prerogative, certainly not his. He now meant to disregard her intelligence and expected her to behave like the wife of an upper-crust Bostonian? In an inane way when she was capable of so much more?

"You know me well, Dr. Lewis," she said. Then she repeated almost word for word what her mother had said to her when Elizabeth had learned of the engagement: "You know I've never done anything in a conventional fashion."

The room had fallen deathly quiet. David tossed back the remaining brandy in his snifter, not taking his eyes off her. She felt nearly as frustrated as she had felt the day he and Jimmie informed her that she couldn't go to medical school. Indeed David knew her well. He sensed her flaring temper and he was bracing for the explosion, waiting for her to embarrass him in front of his parents and their friend. Only she had grown up since that day on the Charles River. She had matured and become a poised woman.

She lifted her skirts and turned away from him with all the dignity she could muster, with all the haughtiness she had learned well in the Quinn household but that she rarely displayed. A show of temper, but a relatively small one.

She had just stepped into the hallway outside the room when she heard Dr. Burnhart tell David: "You mustn't tolerate such defiance once you're married." Michaela fought the urge to race back into the parlor and throw something at the man.

"You'll excuse me?" David asked, his voice strained.

She didn't want to talk to him right now. She was too angry with him. She took the stairs as fast as she possibly could. She heard him call her name, but she hurried into the guest room she had been occupying. She closed the door, turned the key in the lock, then planted her back against it and concentrated on catching her breath. A moment later, she heard him in the upstairs hallway, right outside her door.

"Michaela, we need to talk."

About tarter emetic and the dangers of overpurging? He certainly hadn't come to talk about that.

"Dr. Burnhart is a fine family friend."

And she shouldn't have challenged him? She hadn't meant to do that, she had merely stated what she knew to be true. Then all the frustration she hadn't known she had been suppressing these past weeks, a result of her fear that she might have to give up medicine entirely, had bubbled up and over. Aside from the many months she had devoted herself to Mollie and William and to helping Claudette through her grief, medicine had been her life. Involving herself in a discussion about a medical topic was a natural thing for her.

"Michaela."

She didn't answer. She pushed away from the door and began unfastening the front buttons of her bodice. She wanted to lie down. She wanted to sleep. She wanted to forget that David had disregarded her knowledge simply because she had agreed to marry him. He was the last person she had thought would do such a thing.

She slipped her gown off her shoulders, down her arms, and over the hoops she wore, finally stepping out of it and draping it across the foot of the bed. She unfastened the hoops at her waist, collapsed them, and set them against one side of the wardrobe.

David spoke her name several more times, then he gave up the battle and she heard his footsteps fade down the hallway. Her heart felt heavy and sad. She loved him, but she could not conduct herself in an unnatural way, no matter what his expectations.

The maid had unpacked her belongings days ago and placed them in both the chest of drawers and the wardrobe.

Mike approached the chest of drawers now, thinking to find a nightshift to slip on. They were in the top drawer.

So was Etha's still-unopened letter.

She removed it from the drawer and held it for a long time. Then she tossed herself back on the bed, opened the envelope, and began reading.

As usual, the letter was filled with happenings at the college and around Philadelphia, with detailed reports of her classes and the instructors. It was filled with life and happiness, and Mike could not help but smile, in a bitter-sweet way, over Etha's good fortune and cheerfulness. Etha had decided to stay on in Philadelphia for at least another year and do a preceptorial with a physician there. And to think Michaela would not have discovered that any time soon if she had not opened the letter. She felt bad about that now, not opening the letter as soon as she received it. The frustration of putting her medical career aside in favor of marriage had started building in her then. She had always read Etha's letters as soon as she received them.

She reread the letter, smiling again at times, feeling heavyhearted at other times. She missed Etha more than she had realized, more than she had let herself ponder—and she wanted to go to Philadelphia and share in the joy with her.

Breakfast was a quiet affair the next morning. When Michaela entered the dining room, David, seated at the table with his parents, rose to come around and pull back her chair. Mike felt somewhat meek this morning. Perhaps if she had been honest with herself from the time he had asked her to marry him, the air between them wouldn't be so tense now. His parents were gracious and warm, as always, although Michaela saw apprehension in Sarah's eyes.

"Would you care to go riding with me this morning?" David asked as he pushed the chair in for Mike and leaned slightly over her shoulder.

She smiled at him. She loved him. She always had and she always would. Her behavior last evening now embar-rassed her—she had reacted in her usual temperamental manner—and she could tell he wasn't sure of where he stood with her. She still felt irritated that he had expected her to been seen and not heard, and she meant to express that irritation to him at the appropriate time. But her frustration with him made her love him no less.

"Yes," she answered simply.

Relief passed over his face.

They rode along the hillsides, between the great pines, and along the riverbank. They raced through the meadows, laughing and shouting, catching crickets that jumped in the grasses. David put a number of them in a little pouch that he had tied to his saddle, then they rode back to the river, where Michaela knew he meant to fish. There he collected several long sticks, pulled twine from his pocket, and tied it securely to the ends of the sticks. They settled on the riverbank with their poles, tied crickets to the ends of their lines, and tossed the lines out into the glittering water.

"Jimmie finally did it—he purchased a merchant ship that will sail between the New England states and London," David said, lying back on the soft grass.

Mike had to laugh. "I teased him the last time I saw him. I told him I'd heard that he'd bought a ship. I hadn't really. But it doesn't surprise me that he has."

"I received a letter from him. He's coming home soon."

"Is he?" That was delightful news. Very delightful news.

"I plan to encourage his involvement in a few of Boston's deserving causes. My way of keeping him out of trouble." David chuckled. "Otherwise he might regress again to terrorizing the residents of Beacon Hill and Back Bay."

"He's harmless at this late date. Grown up. Given his size now it would be difficult for him to sneak into a kitchen unnoticed and snatch bread from under a cook's nose."

They watched the water ripple and shimmer in the midmorning sunshine. Birds chirped in the trees farther back on the riverbank.

"I was rather surprised that you agreed to leave Boston to come here with your family," Michaela remarked.

"Why?"

"So much happening in the city right now. So many 'deserving causes.' "

He grinned. "I do get caught up in them."

"Yes, you do," she said, smiling.

He had a bite on his line. The string tightened, the stick bowed slightly. He sat up and slowly began pulling the line in. He lost the fish, of course. They had no hooks. They were merely passing time. He tied another cricket on the line and tossed it back out.

"My silence last evening was unforgivable," he said. No excuses. No more reasoning that Dr. Burnhart was a family friend. No telling her she should have been more respectful and known her place.

Michaela glanced across the river, not really wanting to study the foliage on the other side but needing to look at anything but David at the moment. He was studying her, staring into her, it seemed, with an intensity she found unnerving. Looking into his eyes might melt her resolve, and she didn't want that to happen. It had already happened once. She didn't want to have the conversation with him that she knew was coming. But it had to be done. If they were to find true happiness together, she first had to be happy herself.

"Remember when I returned home the last time and we kissed beneath the trees in Charlestown?" he asked softly.

She felt her face flush, but she smiled. "How could I forget?"

"I was preparing to go off to Paris to study with the masters. I wanted to stay and marry you then. I said, 'Medicine or Michaela, Paris or Boston?' "

Mike shook her head. "I knew where your heart wanted to be. I knew where you needed to be to be happy. The time was wrong. We couldn't have—"

"The time is wrong now."

She looked at him finally. "Medicine has been my life, David. I have always discussed it, whether or not people approved. I cannot be expected to sit quietly playing cards in a drawing room while a medical topic is discussed nearby. I cannot play the part of the uneducated, senseless female. Not even for you. That you would expect me to

247

infuriates me. I want to marry you. I want to be your wife. But I also want to become a medical doctor."

"And when our children start arriving?"

Our children . . . The words had such a precious sound. They struck deep into her heart, deep into her womb. She wanted to have children. She wanted to have *his* children. But when they came, she wanted no regrets.

"Physicians work long hours, Michaela," he said. "They are called out in the middle of the night, early in the morning. . . . What if you have an infant and such a call comes? It will happen. It—"

"We," she said impatiently. "If *we* have an infant and such a call comes. We'll work together, that's what we'll do. We'll hire servants. We were both practically brought through infancy by our nursemaids."

He sat up, shook his head. Now he was the one who glanced off in the distance. "I want a wife."

She stared at him, at the aristocratic tilt to his jaw, nose, and brows. She had always admired those features. She had always thought him handsome. She still did. But she could not abide his thinking at the moment. "Not a wife exactly," she commented. "An ornament. I thought things were different between us." Different, that was, than between other couples.

His head whipped around. Shock flashed in his eyes. "Michaela," he admonished.

"David," she retorted, tossing aside her line. "I am not suited to play the roles our mothers played. I have always been independent in my thinking. I've always been unconventional. I cannot be put into a mold. What is the point of Elizabeth Blackwell, Susan Anthony . . . Amelia Bloomer . . . the Women's Convention? . . . Why circulate publications such as *Godey's Lady's Book* and *Lily*, if women like myself who truly believe that women can and should be so much more allow themselves to be cast in traditional roles? You once wrote to me about this. You thought it horrible that women were not always allowed to speak their opinions freely. I spoke mine last evening, but you did not support me in doing so."

She breathed deeply, trying to calm herself. Elizabeth Blackwell had had an effect on her. The woman's courage and resilience despite remarkable odds had earned her admiration, and given her courage to speak out, courage to march forward.

His gaze had come back to her. His jaw had tensed. She scrambled up from the grassy bank, walked off a distance of several feet, then swung back around.

"I cannot be what you expect me to be," she said, softening her voice. "You are one of the few who know medicine has been my life. Being a woman should not be a reason to prevent me from becoming a medical doctor. And wanting to become a wife and mother—those should not be reasons either."

He began pulling his line in again. He had turned his face and his attention away from her again. His expression had become closed. He looked resolved. "We have differing opinions, Michaela."

She felt hurt, more hurt than she could ever express to him in words. She swung away again, then swung back a second later. "I never . . . *never* thought I would hear such things from you! You have always known my mind. You knew my plans. Why the courtship, David, if this was how you felt?"

He gathered the line, set the sticks side by side on the grass, stood, and dusted his trousers.

"Months ago I applied to the Female Medical College of Pennsylvania," she said. "I was accepted. I'm enrolled in the fall session."

"You already told me," he responded dryly.

"Certainly not because you asked about my plans. And yet, you knew things . . . I told you things that I never confided to anyone else. I wrote to you about putting off medical school until Claudette recovered from her grief. You know I had plans to attend someday. You asked me to marry you. But you knew how I felt—and you knew how you felt. Why didn't you tell me what you expected from your wife before I accepted your proposal?"

He gave an exasperated sigh. He rubbed his jaw, glanced

249

away, then glanced back. "I knew your going to medical school wasn't compatible with marriage. I've been to medical school, remember?"

She fought tears. She fought for breath. She fought the knot in her throat. "I see," she managed finally. "I thought I could do this, David. I thought I could attend medical school and be married to you. Obviously, I can't."

Silence fell between them again. He stared off at the river.

"I love you, Michaela," he said presently. "I know you need to go to Philadelphia. I know you'll never be happy until you do."

She breathed deeply. "You don't know what it was like for me to know that those lectures for women were being held in Boston and that I couldn't attend them."

"You chose not to."

"Yes, I did. Another instance where the time was wrong. But now . . . If I don't go to medical college now, I may never have the opportunity to go."

He nodded slowly, his jaw tense, his mouth set in a hard line. "I know."

She reached out and eased her hand over his. A bold move, but one she felt compelled to make anyway. He forced himself to smile over at her, but the smile never quite reached his eyes. He was angry. He didn't understand, and she needed him to understand.

What lay ahead for them? she wondered as they sat contemplating each other. Would he meet someone else while she was away at college? What about when she returned? If he hadn't already married, would he reconsider what he wanted in a wife? She couldn't marry him if he wouldn't. A hard reality to accept, but one she had to face.

He put his arm around her and pulled her close. Michaela laid her head on his shoulder and released a long breath.

Theirs was probably the shortest engagement in the history of Boston.

In contrast, the month before her departure for Philadelphia was perhaps the longest of Michaela's life. She read over and over the Fourth Annual Announcement of the college.

The faculty had elected to increase the length of sessions to five months, following the example of the University of Pennsylvania. And even that amount of time, the announcement stated, was perhaps "too short for imparting adequate instruction in the many branches which are necessary to qualify students for taking charge of the health and lives of their fellow men." Mike's first session would begin October 1 and end on Saturday, February 25.

Dr. Quinn meant to accompany her to Philadelphia, and he scheduled their travel arrangements for early August. Martha helped Michaela pack several trunks of her belongings, including gowns, undergarments, and numerous books on different subjects, mostly medical and basic reference.

When the time came to leave for the train station, Mike found her mother seated in the parlor, quietly doing needlepoint. She had taken the news of the breakup of Michaela and David's engagement in silence but with a stern look on her face, and she hadn't flinched when Mike had told her that she planned to go to the college in Philadelphia this fall. "She's indifferent," Rebecca had commented to Michaela. But Elizabeth Quinn, beneath her icy exterior, was anything but indifferent about her daughter attending medical school. Mike had sampled her mother's disapproval enough times to know that.

Her hands folded in front of her hoop skirt, Michaela approached the settee where her mother sat, stopping a distance of several feet away. "We're leaving," she said.

Elizabeth glanced up. "I pray your journey is a safe one."

Indifference. Superficial indifference, that was. Inside, Mother was steaming. But during recent years, she had held her tongue more and more, knowing Mike would do what she wanted to do, not what was expected of her.

"I'll write," Michaela said.

Elizabeth had gone back to her needlepoint. "I don't especially care to hear about Philadelphia and the happenings there." The words were stated calmly, without sarcasm or bitterness. But they singed Mike no less.

"Very well, I won't write," she retorted, and she was sorry for the words the instant after she flung them. She was about to leave Boston and home for a good six months, and despite everything, she loved Mother and had wanted their good-bye to be a pleasant one. Oh, she had known how unrealistic that expectation was. But she had still prayed for it. She had employed indifference herself a number of times over the years in dealing with her mother, and yet, Elizabeth Quinn's acceptance and love meant so much to her. What she would give for Mother's encouragement . . . to know that the woman was proud of her.

"That is entirely your prerogative, Michaela."

Mike watched her mother work the needle and thread. What could she say, what could she ever do, to bridge the cool distance between them? *Nothing,* and that was the truly sad thing about the situation. Elizabeth Quinn disapproved in her heart of her daughter pursuing a medical diploma, and Michaela felt in her heart that the medical profession was her calling. They were both stubborn and both determined. There would be no bridging the distance. Perhaps not ever.

Mike left the parlor without speaking another word. Why even say good-bye? What was the sense in saying anything more? She would go off to medical school, and Mother would sit with her needlepoint, run the household, and maintain her proper place as a respectable wife and woman in Boston society.

Michaela went outside to the waiting carriage while Father entered the parlor to say good-bye to Mother. He arrived outside moments later, looking as somber as Mike felt, and she knew he had received the same reaction from her mother—indifference one moment, icy intolerance the next. She blamed him for Michaela's interest in medicine. She always had. He had misled her, to Mother's way of thinking. He had guided her into the most unconventional life for a woman, and ultimately even the promise of marriage to David had not been enough to tempt Mike away from the profession.

Neither Michaela nor Joseph saw Elizabeth rise from her seat and approach one of the two parlor windows when she heard the carriage pull away from in front of the town house. Her knuckles whitened as she clutched her lacy scarf, drawing it more securely about her shoulders. She felt a chill suddenly, so much of a cold bite she might have mistaken this mild August day for a late January one if she hadn't known better. She watched the carriage sway and bounce its way up Mount Vernon Street, disappearing moments later, and she knew she had lost Michaela finally.

Or had she ever really had Michaela, the spirited, strong-willed, passionate, devoted, loyal . . . *admirable* daughter she had struggled more than the usual amount to deliver into the world? She had had her for nine months, that was all, and that was the truth of the matter. Nine short months, growing inside of her. Enough time for a mother to develop an undeniable and unbreakable emotional bond with her child; Elizabeth would always love Michaela, no matter what. But Joseph had had Michaela since their daughter's birth, in spirit and mind, and now Joseph was taking her away for good, delivering Michaela into the hands of his colleagues in Philadelphia, into the hands of men who would fill her mind with more medical nonsense and then give her a diploma, a license to pursue medicine even further.

This day had been coming, threatening, for a long time. But oh, the aftermath it would surely bring! Michaela was being sheltered right now, being escorted to Philadelphia by her protective father. In that city she would be taught medicine by men who had, for whatever reason, decided to open a medical college for women, guarding them from the ridicule of those who did not agree with anyone doing such a thing. But what about afterward? What about when Michaela took her diploma and ventured out on her own? What about when she went out to try and acquire her own patients? They would shun her—*a female medical doctor?*

Perhaps then and only then Michaela would realize that she, her mother, had been right all these years. That women had no business pursuing such things. She and David would marry and she would settle down to the business of being a wife and mother. She would bring her children to visit, and Elizabeth would tug the little ones up onto her lap. Perhaps she would listen to Michaela play and sing for them—she played and sang sweeter than anyone Elizabeth had ever heard. She would teach them, the way she had taught Mollie, and she would tell them stories, the way she had with William. She would make a fine mother one day.

But for now she was gone. There would be none of her playing and singing for some time. Harrison would not greet her in the hall the way he always did, in a tone of great admiration. Martha would not brush, curl, and pin her hair the way she enjoyed doing almost every day. Elizabeth would not walk past the library, glance in, and see Michaela sitting there reading. Michaela would be gone for some time, and she, Elizabeth, had not even embraced her.

"Foolish woman," she scolded herself as she brushed away the tears that slid from her eyes. Such emotion was not a redeeming quality. It was a weakness. "None of this. She'll be gone for only six months. That is nothing to shed tears over."

She would instruct the maids to keep Michaela's room free of dust and dirt. It would not be closed off.

Michaela would be back, Elizabeth felt certain of that.

17

"How incredibly wonderful to see you!" Etha said, grabbing Mike and pulling her into an embrace almost as soon as Michaela stepped off the train. The platform was crowded with baggage, with people arriving and going, and with welcoming parties. "You look as though you've lost weight," Etha commented, pulling back to have a good look at Michaela. "Dr. Quinn, has she lost weight?"

"I believe she has," he answered, and Mike was glad he offered no explanation of why she might have. While the family conflicts had not been nearly as hard on her as they had been on him, they had drained Michaela. She had gone entire days without eating, concentrating so on caring for Mollie and William and on trying to pull Claudette through her grief that she sometimes had neglected herself. She had glanced at her face in the looking glass yesterday when Martha had prepared her hair and she had thought she appeared pale and thin.

"We shall feed you as soon as possible," Etha told her. Etha knew about the conflicts. She had been in Boston for some of them, and through letters, Michaela had updated her occasionally. But Mike did not wish to discuss her family problems at the train station.

"Don't fuss over me," Michaela said. "I'm well."

"Oh, really? That's why you have so much color in your cheeks."

"Etha."

"Mike." Etha snatched the bag from Michaela's left hand, took her by the elbow, and marched her along. "I can't wait to introduce you to some of the people I've met. I know you know a lot of people already, but you'll have classmates, some of whom I've met already. Then there are the women who are doing preceptorials with various physicians in the city. Some of the instructors have changed since I attended my last session. There are women professors now. Imagine that, Mike! Ann Preston joined the faculty. So did Martha Mowry! The college is not only happening, it's a success! It's expanded, and it's now the talk of Philadelphia."

"Also the talk of Boston," Dr. Quinn interjected.

"Blockley still won't admit female medical students to the wards. Neither will the other hospitals," Etha continued. "It's rumored that Ann Preston has been talking about opening a hospital for the college. We've had foreign students and . . . it still feels like a dream, Mike. It's the most exciting thing. The opening, the success, the expansion . . . Where will you be staying?"

Michaela couldn't help but laugh. Etha's excitement was . . . exciting. And infectious. "With Dr. Elder."

"Oh, I'm positively jealous." Etha hailed a hansom cab with quick waves of her arm. The driver came over to help gather the Quinns' trunks.

"I know a wonderful place to eat," Etha said. "A little café on Chestnut Street. I'm so happy I've planned to stay and do a preceptorial here. Meaning no offense to you, Dr. Quinn, but Michaela and I haven't seen each other in far too long. I'm giving up an opportunity to study with one of Boston's finest because I can't stand the thought of leaving your daughter just yet. I'm delighted she gave up her foolish notion of marrying and forgetting about medical school. Mike, I know you love him, but how could you?"

Mike flinched, an unconscious act on her part. Her breakup with David and the pain involved in realizing his

256

expectation of her as his fiancée and once they married were all too fresh in her mind and painful for her.

"I'm sorry," Etha said, squeezing Mike's arm. "That was insensitive of me."

"It's all right," Michaela told her. "It *was* a foolish notion." She smiled over at her father and he smiled back sadly. He knew well the heartache she had suffered upon realizing David's expectations. She had confided in him, as she confided to him almost everything in her life. He was much more than just her father—he was her teacher and her friend.

Soon the trunks were settled in the cab and so were Etha, Michaela, and Dr. Quinn. The conveyance rolled away from the wharves, past the High Street Market where Michaela had shopped with Elizabeth Blackwell. It turned up a street and began passing shops and homes.

"You'll love this café," Etha said, her eyes twinkling. "You'll love Philadelphia. You'll love the college. Did I mention I have a beau?"

Mike clapped her hands together. "No, you didn't. Do tell."

"He's . . ." Etha blushed as she glanced at Michaela's father. "Well, perhaps I should wait."

"Surely not on my account," he teased.

"Dr. Quinn!"

He laughed. So did Mike. She thought she had never seen Etha look so happy. She had certainly never seen her act so lively.

A popular bookstore, as Etha told Michaela and her father, sat above the café in a corner building. The café was fairly empty when they entered it and were seated, but several of Etha's acquaintances soon wandered in and she hailed them over and introduced them to the Quinns. One was Harriet Swain, a petite woman with a flame of curly red hair spilling over her shoulders and down her back, and the other was Phoebe Wright, who was taller than any woman Mike had ever seen. Both were former classmates of Etha's who also were doing preceptorials with physicians in the city. "Well, Phoebe has the good fortune to live here," Etha

257

said, smiling. "No missing her family. No boarding with strangers when she began medical school."

"I do believe Etha would become a Philadelphian if she had the opportunity," Phoebe said, her dark brown eyes sparkling with friendliness.

"Something she may soon be presented with," Harriet teased.

Etha blushed to her hairline, and Michaela guessed that Harriet was implying that the beau Etha had said nothing more about might very well propose to her soon. She wondered why Etha had not mentioned him in her letters.

"He's extraordinarily handsome," Harriet told Mike.

Phoebe clapped her hands together excitedly. "Another open-minded Quaker. If only the entire population were such!"

"Are congratulations in order?" Dr. Quinn asked.

"Oh, no," Etha gasped, blushing more, if possible. "I would never . . . without my parents meeting him first and . . . I respect their desire to have a hand in my choice. . . . What am I saying? What are *you* saying?" she asked Harriet. "It's nowhere near that! Dr. Quinn, I promise you, it's nowhere near that. Charles hasn't even broached the subject." Etha laughed in embarrassment. Harriet and Phoebe giggled. Etha gave a quick wave, playfully dismissing them. "The two of you had to walk in here right now."

"We would have been introduced sooner or later," Harriet said.

"You'll have a marvelous time with us," Phoebe assured Michaela with a slanted smile. "I promise you, we're not always so wicked."

Mike returned her smile. She had already looked forward to meeting Etha's friends and acquaintances, to beginning college and getting caught up in the branch of the medical community here that favored women. Now she looked forward to her time in Philadelphia even more. She looked forward to her studies, but she also looked forward to the camaraderie of the other women, both in and out of the college.

In Boston, Etha had been Michaela's only close female

friend; certainly most of the women in their home city were as close minded as the majority of the men when it came to females involving themselves in the medical profession. Here, things were different. Here, Mike could be more relaxed. She could surely talk medicine without having to fear disapproval.

She settled easily into Dr. Elder's home. His daughters, Jamie, Minna, and Alice, were young and close in age— ten, nine, and seven—and Mike took right up with them. They seemed bubbly and excited about having an "older girl" in the house, as Minna told her she was, particularly Jamie, who was developing an eye for fashion and who stayed in the room the entire time while Michaela unpacked her trunks. She had brought a number of plain day dresses, mostly dark in color, but she also had brought a number of bright, elaborately decorated day and evening gowns. She had packed a few hats, parasols, pelerines, and handkerchiefs, too, and she gave Jamie a smile of encouragement when the girl began eyeing the items. "Try them on," Michaela told her, and Jamie bounded up from the bed.

The family was a happy, pleasant one, and the Elder home brimmed with warmth. The cook sang robustly from the kitchen almost every evening, "except when we have guests," Mrs. Elder informed Michaela, and the maids hummed softly as they dusted, polished, and put things in order.

Etha called daily at the house. She always brought friends, or else she and Michaela went out to meet small groups of people in the coffeehouses, shops, and homes. Mike met Dr. Charles Pierce, Etha's beau and preceptor, who had a small office tucked back among rambling vines and foliage on Christian Street. He was stocky with brown hair and a slight beard and moustache, and when he looked at Etha, he beamed. There was a familiarity between them, a relaxed way. Etha adored him, that was clear, and Mike silently agreed with Phoebe and Harriet—it wouldn't be long before Charles proposed. When Etha later told Michaela that Charles had mentioned journeying to Boston to meet her parents next spring, Mike felt certain of it.

In no way did she find Charles a threat to her friendship with Etha. In fact, when he told her that Etha sometimes talked nonstop about her, there was not a hint of jealousy or annoyance in his eyes. The three of them rode out toward Germantown one afternoon, stopping to pick flowers in the meadows and walk among the trees, and that outing was the only time Michaela felt awkward when with the two of them. She had played the role of chaperon, Etha told her later, whether or not she knew it; Charles always insisted on having someone accompany them on their outings—he wouldn't tolerate unfavorable talk about her.

Mike met Miriam Tilson, who would be starting classes with her, in the bookstore above the café where she and her father had eaten with Etha that first day. Miriam had already eased her way into a small group of medical women, impressing them with her keenness and basic medical knowledge. Emma Judd also would be a classmate, as Mike learned when she met the tiny, rather serious-looking woman who arrived several days later to rent the room next to Etha's in Mrs. Bates's boardinghouse on Vine Street. Other classmates were arriving in the city, surely, or soon would be, Dr. Elder told Michaela and her father one afternoon. Nineteen were enrolled as students in the upcoming session, and a number more were enrolled as matriculants, wanting to increase their knowledge but not necessarily wanting a medical degree.

The middle of August arrived and Dr. Quinn prepared to return to Boston. He was pleased that Michaela had settled in Philadelphia with such ease, that she loved the people surrounding her, and that she was happy and excited about starting the upcoming session in the medical college.

"I worried about you," he said, kissing her forehead as they said good-bye at the station. She knew he was referring to the time immediately after she and David had broken their engagement. She had returned from Pine Meadow with a heavy heart, and she had kept her distance from everyone for weeks. Caught up in the activity here, she had hardly

260

thought of him these past weeks. The realization that he expected her to sacrifice her desire for a medical career to marry him still hurt her. She had waited for him for years. She had encouraged him to go to Paris and study there. And yet, because she was a woman, he had dropped his encouragement of *her* interests in medicine simply because he wanted a different sort of wife. Not a different sort, really. The same kind of wife most every other man had. As a doctor . . . *then* she would be a different wife.

"I'm fine, Father," Michaela said, embracing him. "I'll write often, I promise. Every few weeks. You'll have a thick collection of letters from me by the end of the session."

He chuckled at that. He touched her cheek, then he turned away to board the waiting train.

She stood on the platform, waving good-bye to him, until the train took the curves some distance down the rail and disappeared. Etha and Charles were waiting near the station, and Mike lifted her skirts and hurried over to them. The three of them planned to watch a surgery this afternoon at Blockley. Her attendance at the procedure would be Michaela's first at such an event since her arrival in Philadelphia, and she almost couldn't contain her excitement.

The college had been established in rented rooms in the back of a three-story brick building at 227 Arch Street. A small dispensary and clinic were an active part of the institution, and in those rooms, the students became familiar with various diseases and surgical procedures. Patients were examined before the class, and the symptoms of each and the diagnoses were discussed with the students listening and watching. The dispensary also provided instruction in pharmacology, familiarizing students with the preparation and dispension of medications, and with various ways of preserving the mixtures.

Every Monday, Tuesday, Thursday, and Friday, Professor Darlington demonstrated the art of surgery in the clinic from ten A.M. to eleven A.M. Lectures on the practice of medicine followed, except on Tuesdays and Thursdays, when the women studied obstetrics under Dr. Martha Mowry. Ann Preston taught physiology, lecturing in a most serious manner; Dr. Mark Kerr expounded about *materia medica* and therapeutics. Professor Johnson had replaced the colorful chemistry instructor Etha had spoken of in her letters so many times, although he seemed no less thorough. Clinic was held four times a week, and Mike spoke up, giving her opinions sometimes without being called upon. Her enthusiasm and the knowledge she had already acquired were impressive, she was told one afternoon by a smiling Dean Johnson, but she must give her classmates equal opportunity. After his comment, which Mike took good-naturedly, she forced herself not to speak up in clinic as often.

By far, Michaela's favorite class was anatomy. She listened to Dr. Fussell's lectures, relished Dr. Fowler's demonstrations, then she dissected to her heart's content, amazing the physicians without meaning to with her knowledge, her precise cuts, and with her quick sutures when the class began closing wounds and surgical incisions. She spent hours in the anatomy room, sometimes returning to study and dissect more after the classes ended for the day at six P.M. and the other students had left.

Dr. Fussell told her she was working far too hard, and Dr. Fowler commented that she didn't think Miss Quinn was "working." "You obviously thrive on your studies," she told Michaela, and thereafter, the doctor took Mike under her wing. She asked if Michaela would like to call on patients with her sometimes in the evenings and on the weekends, and Michaela responded eagerly, saying she certainly would like to.

Etha became busy with her preceptor, and while she and Mike still saw each other often, they had less time for outings and for social gatherings in the coffeehouses of Philadelphia. Michaela declined numerous invitations to parties and suppers in favor of studying in the chemistry laboratory and dissection rooms, and so she could accompany Almira Fowler on patient calls.

Dr. Fowler had only a handful of patients, a result of the numerous doctors swarming Philadelphia and of the stigma attached to women physicians, even in this seemingly open-minded city. Here, some doctors and many citizens were still up in arms about a medical college for women opening in their city. At least once a week male medical students gathered outside the house in which the female medical college held its classes and they shouted rude things and sometimes threw stones at the back of the house, where the classrooms, laboratories, and clinic were located. Occasionally several policemen turned up to run them off. Professor Harvey fired a shot at them one time when they would have invaded the house, and thereafter that kept the ruffians at bay during the daytime hours.

Two separate mornings the women students arrived at the school to find things smashed, and after the second incident, a meeting of the board of directors was held and the decision was made to hire a guard. It didn't take the male students long to learn that a man was on duty. He himself fired twice into the air one night to ward them off, and he gave them a firm warning—if they trespassed again the shot wouldn't go in the air.

Other incidents occurred away from the medical school. The women professors all experienced harassment on the city streets at different times, and yet they all refused protection when the other professors and physicians who supported female doctors offered to accompany them out and about. Ann Preston, Martha Mowry, and Almira Fowler all gained Michaela's and her classmates' admiration. Dr. Fowler hid a small pistol under the seat of her buggy. Ann Preston did the same, while Dr. Mowry once cracked her whip at some threatening male students. Mike was with Dr. Fowler only once when she saw the woman reach for her pistol. Some ruffians had plagued Mike and her all the way from a patient's home to the buggy, then grabbed the horse by the harness and refused to let him go despite his resistance and obvious fear. Almira's eyes had flashed, she produced the weapon, and the students fled. Before that, Michaela had doubted whether any of the women professors were capable of violence, even in the name of defense. Dr. Fowler might have been, had the young men not scattered.

By January, after seeing that they couldn't chase the women doctors out of the city, the male students' interest in threatening the three physicians died down. Dr. Preston commented that her ventures around the city had become peaceful, and Professor Mowry remarked that the students had stopped following her. Dr. Fowler did not seem as tense when Michaela accompanied her on medical calls to regular patients and to the indigent.

Michaela turned twenty-one on a snowy February day, and Etha and the Elders surprised her with a party, the only one Michaela attended during her years in medical school and in Philadelphia. Like Mike, Miriam Tilson also spent many after-class hours in the dissection room and chemistry laboratory, often smiling and saying she had to keep up with Mike somehow. The two women were in the laboratory when Etha, Harriet, and Phoebe showed up and dragged them away from their projects, taking them to the Elders' where a group of people waited.

There was a cake and music and dancing, and Mike had a wonderful time. Etha was responsible for it, Mike felt certain, and for Michaela's attendance. She gave Michaela a copy of *Walden* by Henry David Thoreau. "Although I don't know when you'll find time to read it," Etha remarked. "I will," Mike promised, and she did. She forced herself to stay away from the school for two entire evenings so she could read the essays, and when she told Etha that she had enjoyed Thoreau's accounts of the two years he spent at Walden Pond, she meant it.

Like Boston, Philadelphia was a hotbed of antislavery activity. Marches were held, opposing forces clashed, violence often erupted. Several national events added wood to the already popping fire: The Kansas-Nebraska Act, sponsored by Senator Stephen Douglas of Illinois, created two new territories and provided "popular sovereignty," or so the senator said. People who settled in the territories would have the right to decide whether the territories, when they were admitted into the Union, would be slave or free. "No slavery north of the southern boundary of Missouri?" one man shouted incredulously in a coffeehouse one evening, where Etha and Michaela sat talking. He was referring to one of the terms set forth in the Compromise of 1850, a promise that would now be broken. "Douglas's law will not happen," the man vowed, slamming his fist down on the table.

In June, word reached Philadelphia that yet another fugitive had been apprehended in Boston. Anthony Burns had escaped bondage in Virginia, and while abolitionists and women's suffrage groups were holding conventions in Michaela's home city, a judge there had ordered Burns shipped back to his owner. "He was heavily guarded," Dr. Quinn wrote to Mike. "Buildings were draped in black and church bells tolled." Months later, Burns was sold to a master who then sold him to some Bostonians, who subsequently set him free.

When word trickled out that holding Burns, bringing him into court, guarding him, and shipping him back to Virginia had cost the United States government an estimated one hundred thousand dollars, abolitionists were outraged. The demonstrations increased, and not just in Philadelphia. They were held in New York, Chicago, Baltimore, Washington, D.C., in Cleveland, and Cincinnati.

The national conflicts were heating up more and more, it seemed. Southerners feared the antislavery forces because cotton had become a huge commodity and virtually the entire economic welfare of the numerous Southern cotton plantations depended on slavery. But more and more Northern forces were backing the abolitionists. In Michigan, the Republican Party rose from a motley group of Whigs, Free-Soilers, Northern Democrats, and disaffecting individuals from various other groups. The formation of the new party was a direct result of antislavery forces and of opposition to the Kansas-Nebraska Act.

Dr. Fowler had long since become Michaela's self-appointed preceptor, and so while Etha returned to Boston that spring to be with her family and to do a preceptorial for a year under Dr. Quinn, Mike chose to stay in Philadelphia. Charles soon visited Etha in Boston. He met her family, most importantly her father, and he reported that all had gone well. On his return, he blurted the news of his and Etha's engagement. Mike gave a cry of joy and threw herself at him, catching him in an embrace.

"Studying under your father is wonderful," Etha soon wrote to Michaela. *"I must admit, however, that while the opposition to women doctors and medical students was sometimes daunting in Philadelphia, it is, at times, almost discouraging here. I miss Charles, too."*

She wrote that David had gone off to New York to practice medicine with a friend there. *"I didn't know if you knew,"* Etha said.

> I know he's not your fiancé anymore, but I know you still care. (I simply know *you*.) I'm certain he'll return. New York may have him for now, but his family is here, as you will be in a short time. I cannot believe he has stopped caring about you or that he will ever be content without you. David has never struck me as a man who would settle for a woman without opinions or for one who did not follow her heart. He might try to settle for such a creature, but he will soon discover his unhappiness in such an arrangement.

So Etha thought he still cared about her. Michaela sat staring at the letter in her room at the Elders' home. If he really cared, he wouldn't have treated her dreams and ambitions so callously. He would have waited for her. He wouldn't have gone off to New York to practice medicine with his friend. He would have written to her here by now, asked how she was, how college was progressing, and he would have shared his plans.

She moved across the room, opened the French doors, stepped out onto the balcony, and breathed the cool evening air. It was September, and classes would start again soon. She wouldn't think too much about David; she wouldn't dwell on thoughts of him and on how heartbroken she had been at this time last year, on how disappointed she felt now. The pain caused by the dissolvement of their engagement seemed less, a distant twinge, unless she turned the events of the last eight years or so over in her head.

She wouldn't. Not very much anyway. Given David's opinion that she couldn't be his wife *and* be a practicing medical doctor, and given his lack of contact with her this past year and his recent move to New York, he was the last person she would allow to preoccupy her. Right now, medical school and her preceptorship required her full attention.

College continued. The months went by entirely too fast. But wasn't that always the case when one was having fun? And during the passing months, Mike and Miriam forged a friendship in the dissection room of the college, although it was nothing like the close one shared by Michaela and Etha. Mike enjoyed Miriam's companionship, but they soon became friendly rivals. For Michaela, the rivalry was not a conscious thing; she simply realized one day that Miriam was competing with her. Miriam let her know her marks on every paper and project. If Mike raised her hand in class to speak out, Miriam did also. If Michaela took notes during lectures, Miriam took notes, and likewise, if Mike did not feel the need to take notes, Miriam did not either.

The rivalry annoyed Michaela only when she learned that Miriam had asked if she could do a preceptorial with Dr. Fowler. Would she never have time away from this classmate? she wondered in exasperation. Then she told Almira, "She has an unquenchable desire to compete with me."

"She's deserving of an equal opportunity," Dr. Fowler commented after a scrutinizing look.

Thereafter, rather than irritate her instructor by having Almira think she wanted Miriam turned away because of the rivalry, Mike tolerated Miriam's presence during patient calls.

Winter stole the color from another fall, another new year arrived, and Michaela's and Miriam's second and final session at the Female Medical College of Pennsylvania ended. They continued their preceptorships, and Michaela turned her thoughts toward the subject of her thesis, *The*

Influence of the Nervous System on the Functions of Respiration and Digestion. Miriam asked numerous times about the subject of Mike's dissertation, but Michaela kept her thoughts on the matter to herself. Miriam seemed exasperated with her at times. "I thought we were friends," she said once. "Friends share things."

Mike snapped at her, saying that if she told her, then Miriam might straightaway decide to write her thesis on the same subject—never mind that she had two years of preceptorship to serve still before she could graduate.

Miriam winced with hurt, and Michaela was instantly sorry that she had grumbled. She told Miriam the subject of her dissertation. After that, Miriam became quiet and somewhat distant, and she didn't warm to Mike again until they attended a supper in the home of a supporting Philadelphia physician. Even then, Miriam was careful to keep clear of medical topics when speaking with Michaela. However, when a medical discussion arose and Mike expressed her opinion on the method of treatment, Miriam was quick to express hers, too.

The college's fourth commencement was held in the Musical Fund Hall. William Mullen, the president, all faculty members, the board of corporators, and friends of the institution occupied seats on the platform. At the first commencement, a band of fifty policemen had been positioned at the hall to ward off a group of five hundred male medical students. But since that threat was considerably less now, only a handful of officers were stationed in various places outside and inside the hall for this year's ceremony. Dr. Elder had been invited to give the opening address, and he beamed out at the graduates just before he began to speak: "Another class . . . another group of doctresses to be sent out into the world . . ."

Michaela had never been more proud in her life. Rebecca, Claudette, Father, and Etha had all come from Boston, and she couldn't help but glance back at them, a smile fixed on her face, tears threatening to burn her eyes.

Dr. Elder continued. He spoke of the duties of the

physician, no matter whether the physician was a male or female. He spoke of supporting the patient spiritually as well as physically. He spoke of knowing no limitations in medicine, of always keeping the mind open to new theories and practices, and when he finished, every student looked inspired.

Mr. Mullen took the podium and began calling out names and presenting diplomas. When he called Mike's name—Michaela Anne Quinn—and she approached the platform and accepted her degree, the events seemed almost unreal. What a struggle to get to the platform—the worry that she might not be able to attend medical school because she was female; Robby's illness and death, Charles's ugly secrets and disappearance, Claudette's grief, the pain and scandal that pervaded those events; the fear that she might have to give up her aspirations to become a medical doctor in favor of becoming a wife; David's opinion that she should, something that had lanced her heart so deeply it still hurt if she allowed herself to think of their last day together at Pine Meadow.

Once back in her chair, she couldn't resist the temptation to untie the ribbon that bound the diploma. She unrolled the degree. She read the printing—"Female Medical College of Pennsylvania . . . Doctor of Medicine . . . Michaela Anne Quinn." The diploma was signed by William Mullen, it was official.

She was now Michaela Quinn, *M.D.*

18

She had thought to acquire her own patients once she returned to Boston. Unfortunately, she encountered the same sort of resistance to that idea that Elizabeth Blackwell once had written to her about from New York: no respectable citizen would consent to become the patient of an independently practicing female doctor. If Michaela accompanied her father on his patient calls, that was a different matter altogether. People allowed her to examine them with him looking on. They allowed her to express her *opinion* about their symptoms. Then they looked to the "real" doctor for diagnosis and treatment.

Mike felt humiliated and exasperated at times; she felt she was still a medical student, that she was still in preceptorship under the careful supervision of an attending physician. No matter that she was a fully licensed doctor now herself, that she had worked diligently off and on for five years, intensely for the last three of those, to earn her degree. The fact that she held a medical diploma from an accredited college was not taken into consideration. How many times did she tell patients she was a medical doctor? How many times did she explain her thorough training? How many times did she call on patients alone, only to be turned away at doorsteps? To consider the numbers that would answer each of those questions would be daunting.

She finally found release for her desire to be what she was—a trained medical doctor—with the Boston Dispensary, the charitable organization that sent physicians out among the indigent.

"I can send you to District Eight," Dr. Adams told her. "It's the only district in which we currently need another physician."

He was lying—Michaela saw the lie in his eyes, in the arrogant tilt to his chin. He wanted to make this as difficult as possible for her. She was one of the first female doctors in Boston, after all, and the majority of male physicians were feeling threatened. They hadn't thought she would accomplish her goal of obtaining a medical diploma. But she had proven them wrong. Of course, male pride dictated that they must make establishing a patient load difficult for her. If they allowed it at all.

"Of course those Irish . . . they're filthy, Miss Quinn. You'll need a strong stomach," Dr. Adams remarked.

Mike snatched the tickets, requests for treatment, from his hand. "It's *Dr.* Quinn, and I happen to be Irish myself. My father worked District Eight for years without difficulty. I shall follow his fine example in doing the same."

Dr. Abbott, who, some four years ago, had tried without success to convince her father to drop her from student rounds at Massachusetts General, entered the dispensary office just as Michaela was about to storm out. He ignored her every time she accompanied her father on patient calls at the hospital, and he turned his nose up at her now. Then his beady eyes landed on the tickets in her hand.

"Rest assured, even they won't have you," he said.

He and Dr. Adams, and perhaps many other physicians, would say anything to her without her father around, it seemed.

"They'll be happy to see another doctor who doesn't regard them as riffraff," she retorted. Then she swept by him and left the office.

They were indeed happy to see her. Patients with stomach

illnesses, a woman with an enlarged liver, a young man who had suffered a fall at the docks and who Mike quickly determined had broken several ribs . . . She treated a young girl with asthma by giving her stramonium seeds, to be rolled and smoked like tobacco, a treatment Michaela had learned from Dr. Fowler. The girl's mother at first looked at Michaela as if she were mad. But when her daughter smoked the seeds and obtained relief from her attack, the mother couldn't thank Mike enough.

Michaela shared her experiences with Etha, who also was having a difficult time gaining the trust of patients and respect from fellow physicians. Finally, Etha, too, began attending the Irish in the warehouse area. Her mother had fallen ill with a cancer, one that would surely take her life sooner or later, and Etha sat with her and treated her, too. For that reason, she and Charles put off their wedding date. Etha would not go off to Philadelphia and marry while her mother lay dying.

The two young doctors served District Eight diligently throughout the ensuing winter, diagnosing, treating, and many times, making friends. From the poor, they expected no payment, although grateful people sometimes offered them bowls of stew or slices of bread. Mike and Etha supplied medications themselves, purchasing them from a local apothecary, and both doctors' purses soon began to empty.

For years, Michaela's father had given her a certain amount of money every month. He still did. Since her graduation from medical college, he had also given her half of the moneys paid him when she accompanied him on patient calls. The latter was fine, perfectly acceptable. But the allowance . . . She was almost twenty-four years old, and she couldn't expect her father always to provide for her. She and Etha continued visiting and treating the Irish in the warehouse district. But Etha tutored children again on the side to earn extra income, and Mike again called on patients with her father, swallowing her pride, knowing that at least he, whenever they withdrew from each sickroom after he examined the patient, respected her opinions and diagnoses.

She was not a medical student to him any longer; in his eyes she was a licensed medical doctor, one fully capable of treating patients, no matter that she was a woman.

As usual, Mother was cold and distant. Mike shared meals with her parents. She spoke with her mother often, or tried. But Elizabeth Quinn was aloof and haughty. If her husband and youngest daughter began discussing a medical topic, she rose and left the room. If they were preparing to go out on medical calls, she turned away from them. She was inhospitable to Etha whenever she called at the house, and when several medical journals disappeared from Michaela's room one day, Mike, after carefully questioning Martha, felt certain that Mother had taken them.

The nation turned the corner and entered another year. The stands and pushcarts that always lined the Tremont Street Mall during the months before a presidential election appeared once again. Mike and Etha bought doughnuts on the mall one afternoon and little mugs of cider. They listened to the political men spout about the evils of Buchanan—he supported the Fugitive Slave Law, after all. For that reason alone, how could anyone even consider voting for him? The men were there every day. They spread their forces out all over the city, and while the outcries and protests generated results in Boston, Bostonians didn't represent the country. Buchanan was elected that fall, a few weeks before Etha's mother finally succumbed to her cancer.

In January, Massachusetts's abolitionist forces held a disunion meeting in Worcester to discuss a peaceful separation of the North and the South. William Lloyd Garrison insisted that there be "no union with slaveholders," and for the first time, Michaela heard people talk about the possibility of war. Months later a financial panic hit the nation, a result of overspeculation in railway securities and real estate. The Eliots, who had sported the first bathtub in a Boston home, had to put up their Beacon Street house for sale. Mr. Eliot's entire library was put up for sale, too, and Mr. Eliot himself disappeared for a time, a ruined and shamed man. Meanwhile, Henry Longfellow, James Lowell, and Dr. Holmes decided to start a new magazine.

"We plan to call it the *Atlantic Monthly*," Professor Holmes told Michaela when she called on him one afternoon at the Tremont Medical School. "Underwood . . . the gall of the man," he said with an irritated wave of his arm. "He went to England to get British writers. *British* writers. What kind of thinking is that? We've enough American writers to make a go of it. Can't we have a publication without England?"

Dr. Holmes's son, Wendell, was preparing to go off to Harvard. Michaela, her father, and Etha had supper with the Holmes family one evening, and Mike was enthralled by how much Wendell had grown, both in mind and body. He was a strapping boy, and when he made his entrance into the room by bursting in with his mouth full of seedcake and with his hand clutching a small loaf of brown bread, she was reminded of Jimmie Becker. Who, by the way, she'd not heard anything about in ages. But then, neither had she heard anything about David, except that the Lewis's, too, had suffered some from the financial panic.

Buchanan was inaugurated right before the Supreme Court handed down its decision in another fugitive case that no one had ever expected would get so far in the American judicial system. Dred Scott's owner had taken him from Missouri to Illinois, a free state, in 1837. And later, in the mid-1840s, Scott had sued for his freedom on the grounds that his stay in the free state ended his slavery. Not so, said the Supreme Court. Besides, slaves were not United States citizens, therefore how could a slave sue?

So young Wendell went off to Harvard that year, following in his father's footsteps, and the Dred Scott decision prompted more than mere discussions of war—people threatened it.

In September, Etha went to Philadelphia to marry Charles. Her father, Joseph, and Michaela accompanied her, and when Mike pulled from a trunk the wedding gown she and Etha had spent so many hours stitching, she burst into tears. Everything came down on Mike at once, it seemed. She was beginning to long for marital companionship herself and for children, and the fact of the matter was, she was now twenty-five years old, unmarried, and time had a way of going forward, not backward. She might have been married by now. And it had just occurred to her that Etha would no longer be a mere carriage ride away.

Etha sat with her on the floor and they cried, then laughed together. They talked about Etha starting her new life. They talked about a few things that had happened in the seminary—in Boston, they had run into Catharine one day, who had become a dutiful, proper wife, just as they had known she would be, and who was pregnant with her second child. They talked about the years they had spent in medical school, about the new students they had recently met when they visited the college, how bright eyed and eager they were. They talked about visiting each other at least twice a year. After all, only a railway journey separated them, Etha said. Mike laughed at that remark. Yes, she said, and a few hundred miles.

She cried more during the wedding, this time because Etha looked so beautiful and Charles looked so adoring of his wife-to-be. She cried because she knew they would be incredibly happy, that they would have a houseful of children and practice medicine together, and because Etha's dreams were coming true.

Fortunately, she was drained of tears by the time she, her father, and Mr. Crocker boarded the train to journey back to Boston. Etha and Charles would be going to England for their honeymoon, but they didn't plan to leave until tomorrow. Michaela had told Etha that she expected a full account of their adventures in that country when she returned, and Etha had promised exactly that. They had slept only four hours the night before the wedding because they had stayed awake talking, and now Mike felt exhausted.

Once settled in her seat on the train, she looped her arm through her father's, laid her head on his shoulder, and promptly fell asleep.

• • •

275

Back in Boston, Michaela was again faced with the fact that she couldn't practice medicine independently of her father except with the dispensary, and that was work for which she saw no financial compensation. The financial aspect would hardly matter if she didn't feel the need to be totally independent. She loved living with her father. She loved everything about being with him. But her mother's haughtiness and superior ways were often intolerable. Mike would have liked to have supper without feeling the disapproving air and the sense of tension that filled every room Mother occupied. She would have liked to come and go without feeling that Elizabeth Quinn knew her every move, particularly since Mother didn't like her every move. She would have liked to live under her own roof and not still feel like a child at times, having no say over her meals and sometimes still finding her clothes laid out for her.

Where medicine was concerned, she learned the virtues of patience and discretion during the ensuing months. She learned to stay quiet and keep her distance while her father examined patients, even if that distance was the length of a room. She learned to hold her tongue. She learned to offer no opinion about symptoms and diagnoses until she and her father were out of earshot or unless she was asked. When they called on patients together, she disciplined herself once again to be his assistant rather than a fellow doctor.

"You must be incredibly frustrated," Rebecca commented one evening.

Mike forced a twisted smile.

"Well, you know that where my family is concerned, I would never want you to stand in the background," Rebecca told her.

"I know," Michaela said, touching her arm. Rebecca was the same sweet, adoring sister she had always been. The same sensitive, encouraging person. Mike sighed. "How do I gain their trust? Can I?" That was the really terrible thing. She didn't know if it was possible to gain the trust of the paying patients in Boston, the ones who could afford to snub her and whose business she needed.

Nationally and politically, alarming things were happen-

276

ing. Months before, word had begun trickling from Illinois of a backwoods, rail-splitting political man who was full of wit, facts, and dates, and who had a droll way of speaking. He was Abraham Lincoln, the Republican candidate for the Illinois Senate, and when he took on his opponent, Stephen Douglas, in a series of debates in Illinois towns, suddenly the nation was more aware than ever of the increasing gap between the Northern and Southern states. The outspoken Lincoln stated that Americans would have to make a decision regarding slavery, that either the whole country should accept it or eliminate it. While Senator Douglas did not uphold slavery, he respected the right of people in a given territory to decide the issue for themselves. Douglas was reelected, but Lincoln's views made him a much-discussed man.

Another rush west began when gold was discovered at Pike's Peak in Colorado. As with the California gold rush, people packed and headed that way in search of the nuggets that would hopefully bring them fortune. To Michaela, Colorado seemed as distant as California. There were Indians along the way, and wilderness; so many people had died during the trek to California that Mike almost couldn't believe anyone else would try to cross the vast Midwest. But, miners aside, settlers had long since been pouring that way daily, in search of inexpensive land and a fresh start. Stagecoaches could take a person across the country in a relatively short time. But for those who had to find their own way across the land, the journey was a lengthy and exhausting one.

In December of that year, three-year-old Kevin Palfrey from District Eight fell so ill with fever one night that, after they failed to locate Michaela, his parents took him to Massachusetts General. When Mike called at the warehouse the next day and learned where he was, she went directly there. Unfortunately Dr. Abbott was in the ward when she called. He spotted her assessing Kevin's heart and lungs, and he hurried over.

"May I speak with you, Miss Quinn?"

Despite his lack of professional deference, Michaela

responded to him, only because she did not wish to cause a scene in the ward. Patients occupied every bed, save two. "Certainly," Mike said, and she walked off, leading the way out into the hall.

"You are not a practicing physician in this institution," Dr. Abbott said, hardly giving her a chance to turn and face him.

Michaela clasped her hands before her skirt. "You and I differ on that, Doctor. I am a practicing physician wherever I go."

His face tightened. "You are not on staff here."

"I'm certain that can be remedied," she said, although she was instantly sorry for the retort—she wasn't certain at all. "Excuse me now. I must return to my patient."

The glare he gave her as she walked away from him seared her back. She had a fight on her hands now. The matter of getting an appointment to the staff of this institution was now one of pride. And lately, she found that she often could not back down from situations where her pride was involved. Perhaps because she felt so stifled, having to play the role, at least in public, of being her father's assistant rather than his colleague. That would be like being the docent at a medical school when one was educated enough to be the instructor. Sooner or later, frustration and outrage would set in.

She wrote to the board and requested to speak with the members as a group, intending to ask for an appointment to the staff. She received a letter in return from Dr. Channing, the director, an apology that the members had full slates for several months; not even one member would have the time to grant her an interview.

She investigated, pried, found out the majority of members' schedules, what times they normally came and went from Massachusetts General. She caught Drs. Paine and Jordan in a corridor one morning and rattled off her request as quickly as possible while they continued walking, ignoring her. Dr. Cooke approached, chastising her for even thinking about requesting an appointment to the staff of the "upstanding" institution, then he and the two other board members hurried off together.

She encountered Dr. Stone on Washington Avenue one afternoon and when he refused to listen to her, she followed him into a barber shop, all the while trying to impress him with her knowledge of diseases and their treatments— trying to prove to him that she was a good physician. Inside the shop, with four other men looking on, he finally spoke to her. "Your level of knowledge has nothing to do with my withholding my opinion," he said with a sniff. "It has to do with your being a woman."

She learned that Dr. Channing and his wife always attended the theater on Tuesday evenings and she positioned herself near the doors of the hall the following Tuesday and waited for him. He saw her—he looked straight at her— although he pretended that he didn't. She stepped in front of the door just as he would have entered, and he growled at her to get out of his path or he would shout for a policeman. What did she think she was doing, trying to bully her way onto the staff? That wouldn't work in normal circumstances, and it certainly wasn't ladylike behavior.

He was right. Her pursuit of physicians who had made clear that they did not wish to speak with her was ridiculous as well as foolish. Besides, she wasn't a bully by nature and such behavior went against her every belief. But then, so did their intentional disregard of the fact that she was a fully qualified medical doctor. However, she pursued none of the other four board members.

A simple request, and her father would crusade for her and probably get her the appointment. But she wanted, *needed,* to do this on her own. She wouldn't have him always leading the way for her, clearing the path of brush and thorns. She had to clear it herself. She had to stand on her own as a doctor somehow.

To her surprise, Dr. Peter Aldrich called on her at home one evening. When she spotted him in the entryway, she thought he was there to see her father. But no, Harrison announced him to *her,* and Dr. Aldrich, upon greeting her, said, "Dr. Quinn, if I might have a moment of your time . . ."

He supported her, and he wanted to let her know that. Unfortunately, his voice was only one of ten, and none of the other nine board physicians supported her. Her father could exert a great amount of influence, however. He was well respected by his colleagues, well liked by citizens and by the community in general—and a threat to withdraw his financial and professional support of Massachusetts General would have an impact. In other words, Dr. Aldrich also felt that Joseph Quinn could get her the appointment. All he had to do was indicate his desire.

Mike thanked Dr. Aldrich for his support. She also thanked him for taking the time to call and tell her how to go about getting appointed to the staff. However, she explained, she didn't want her father to get her the appointment. Dr. Aldrich studied her, finally breaking into a smile.

She offered him refreshment. He accepted, and then he asked if she would do him the honor of accompanying him to the upcoming lecture to be given before the Boston Medical Society.

She had forgotten that he was a bachelor. She would like to attend the meeting alone, not walking in anyone's shadow, not leaning on anyone for support or protection. But that was unrealistic. If she tried to attend the meeting alone, she would receive hostile stares and maybe even have to endure cutting remarks. She could attend with her father, or she could attend with Dr. Aldrich, and none of that would happen. Provided she kept her mouth shut. That was the other condition. She could not voice her opinions in the discussions that always sprang up after lectures.

So she attended the lecture with Dr. Aldrich *and* her father, and she requested that they leave just as the discussion was getting started.

Not two weeks later, Mike received a letter from the board of directors of Massachusetts General which addressed her as *Dr. Michaela Quinn,* congratulated her on her appointment as a staff member, and welcomed her to the institution.

She was stunned, but also oddly disappointed. The appointment was certainly not her doing, and she had wanted no one's help or influence in getting it. Dr. Aldrich had had nothing to do with her getting it, or so he told her when she called on him. That left only two other physicians in the city of Boston who would go out of their way to assist her in her endeavors—her father and Dr. Holmes.

"I've brandished no influence," Professor Holmes told her at the Tremont Street Medical School. He was peering into a microscope. "But that does not mean that I did not relate the grumblings I heard about your desire for the appointment to your father." He glanced up, flashing her a crooked smile.

"Oh, Dr. Holmes," she said, feeling defeated. How could she walk the halls of Massachusetts General with pride and dignity, knowing her father had secured the appointment for her? Knowing that everyone knew? She had the appointment now, but it would earn her no respect. Rather, it might make fellow physicians resent her all the more.

"What? You're disappointed?" Holmes blurted, his face falling. "We thought you would be delighted, and you're disappointed?"

"Please don't misunderstand," Michaela rushed to explain. "It's not that I don't appreciate what you and my father have done. It's not that I don't want the appointment. I had hoped to get it myself, you see, through persistence and respect."

The distinguished man raised and lowered his gray brows, peered into his microscope once more, then glanced back at her. He wrinkled his face, and finally, he kicked himself in the shin. "Lolly, lolly, lolly, Oliver's big folly."

"Oh, Dr. Holmes," Mike said, this time unable to help a smile. She loved him nearly as much as she loved her father. She respected him as much, too, and she looked to him for guidance as much. He was forever witty, possessing an unflagging sense of humor even during the most unhumorous times.

"Well, even if you aren't delighted with the appointment, your father is," he told her. "Therefore"—he paused to give her a meaningful look—"I would choose my words carefully when speaking with him."

She nodded slowly, immediately digesting his sage advice. "I'll thank him."

"Ah," he said, giving a quick nod. "Now, come here and tell me what you think of this. Muscle tissue from a thirty-eight-year-old man who experienced frequent cramping and aches. I'm in the habit of consulting colleagues, and since you're here, occupying a chair in my laboratory, Dr. Quinn, I would appreciate hearing your thoughts on the matter."

Smiling wider, Michaela deserted her chair in favor of him and his microscope.

She had already written to Etha about her struggle to get an appointment to the staff. Now she wrote about her frustration in having the appointment dropped in her lap by Professor Holmes and her father. "They mean well, my champions. But I worry. When will our "new breed of woman" successfully stand alone?"

She knew Etha would know what she meant, that female doctors must find a way to function independently of male doctors. Otherwise the opening of the college in Philadelphia and the awarding of diplomas to the graduates meant little.

19

David returned from New York. Mike and her father had just finished examining a patient in the hospital, and when she pulled open the bedside curtain, there David stood, tall, dark eyed, his hair neatly combed. He wore striped trousers and a black waistcoat over a white shirt and gray stock, and for a moment, as Mike stared at him, she almost could not breathe. She was glad to see him. Despite everything, she was still so glad to see him.

He dipped his head in greeting, first to her father, then to her. "Dr. Quinn . . . Michaela."

Joseph Quinn grinned, obviously happy to see David, too. "New York could never hold a Bostonian for long. Welcome home."

"Thank you, sir. Home it certainly is."

David's gaze fell on Mike again, soft, tender, imploring. "How are you?" he asked.

She managed a smile. "I'm well."

"I'll wait for you at the nurse's desk," her father said. Michaela nodded, and he walked off.

"I hear you've taken Boston by storm," David remarked presently.

As happy as she was to see him, his grin and his sudden appearance here also annoyed Mike. She hadn't seen him or heard from him in how long now . . . more than five years? He might at least have written.

"My *father* has taken Boston by storm," she responded, brushing by him. "If not for him I would have no patients—and no appointment at Massachusetts General."

David laughed under his breath. "Don't be absurd, Michaela. Your name is all over the medical community."

She spun on him. "*Absurd?* Absurd is not contacting someone you say you care about for five years."

The grin faded. "You might have contacted me, also," he said after a moment.

"I didn't know how."

"Didn't know how, or didn't want to? Michaela, my family lives here. Finding out how would have been easy."

That was true. She could have asked Sarah or George Lewis, or either of David's brothers, for his New York address. Maybe he was right, she hadn't wanted to contact him. Maybe she was still resentful of his feeling that she couldn't be his wife and be a doctor at the same time. He hadn't given her a chance.

"You look official," he said. "Congratulations."

"For? . . ."

"Your degree. Your success here."

"Thank you." Michaela hesitated, clutching her medical bag. Being near him after so long, especially given the fact that they were no longer romantically involved, made her feel awkward. "I—I have to go. Father is waiting to discuss this case with me, and I have patients at the warehouses. I promised—"

"You go there alone?" David queried, looking surprised.

"Yes, I . . . No one has ever tried to harm me. Besides, no one who lives there would allow anyone a chance to harm me."

He smiled slightly. "You've won their loyalty."

She gathered one side of her skirts, preparing to walk off. "It would seem so. I really must go."

"All right," David said, nodding slowly. "Have supper with me, Michaela?"

Oh, certainly. Have supper with him and lose her heart all over again. She held only a fragile grasp on it now. She still cared too much. She might never be able to regard their relationship as a mere friendship. She certainly couldn't have a casual meal with him.

"I'm very busy for the next few weeks," she responded.

"Well, I'm home to stay," he said. "We'll arrange something when your schedule clears."

Being direct with him was obviously the only good course of action.

"I'd rather not," Mike told him, and without giving him a chance to speak further, she walked away, possibly the most difficult thing she had ever done in her life.

He turned up two weeks later in the surgery gallery while she and her father were preparing to perform a mastectomy on a patient who had developed a tumor in her left breast weeks ago. The tumor had grown rapidly since, and Mike felt that the only course of action was surgical removal of the breast. Her father had concurred, and she had brought the patient to Massachusetts General, where conditions were more favorable than in the Irish tenements.

A nurse administered chloroform, and just as Michaela picked up her scalpel, preparing to perform the surgery, she spotted David standing in the gallery beside Dr. Aldrich.

Mike concentrated on the task ahead. She stood to the right of the patient, drew the tumor up, placed the knife beneath it, and began cutting through the skin and fatty tissue, an inch to half an inch deep. The cancer extended somewhat into the armpit, and she was forced to cut away part of the pectoralis major muscle to ensure that the tumor was adequately removed.

After she had freed the last of the tissue and muscle, she dropped it into a waiting basin. Then she began tying off the small arteries while her father watched. Finally, he placed a linen bandage over the wound, and Michaela withdrew to wash her hands over a basin on the opposite side of the room.

David came down from the gallery. "Fine, quick work,"

he said, as she returned to the patient to check bleeding. Mrs. Bell was rousing, groaning low and moving around a little.

"Give her laudanum when she wakes fully, please," Michaela instructed the nurse. The woman nodded as she removed bloody cloths and washed the blood from Mrs. Bell's skin. Michaela thanked David for his favorable observation, and she began to unroll her sleeves.

"I would be honored if you would have supper with me," he said.

He didn't give up easily, it seemed.

Joseph Quinn pulled off his surgical apron as the nurse glanced up from her work and met Mike's gaze, her brows uplifted.

"I believe I declined such an invitation from you several weeks ago," Michaela responded, her voice low as she stepped aside. She walked over to a small desk, picked up a pen, dipped it in ink, and began making notes about the procedure.

David followed her there. "Michaela. Must I beg? I've seen you only once since returning to Boston, and I might not have seen you today if Peter hadn't told me you'd scheduled a surgery here. I've been hesitant to call at your home for fear you would close the door in my face. My heart has been twisted since you declined that first invitation. It will surely break in two if you decline this one."

The nurse snickered. Wonderful. David planned to make a spectacle of himself. The nurse would carry news of the scene beyond this room, and soon the entire institution would be aflame with talk of the display she had witnessed. Even Father now wore a grin. But he respected her privacy, and he exited the surgical room, probably planning to wait for her in the hall.

"I shall be miserable, Michaela," David warned playfully. "Utterly miserable."

"Stop," she ordered under her breath, low enough that surely the nurse could not hear her, but loud enough for David to hear. "Do you think this is comical? You . . . turning up and showing me attention again after you made clear to me that I could never be your wife and a doctor at the same time? What are you doing? I *am* a doctor. Since I know what you don't want, what *do* you want, David? For us to resume our friendship? I question whether such a thing is even possible."

That sobered him. The nurse glanced over once more. She was dosing Mrs. Bell with laudanum. Michaela should go speak with her patient, tell her she would like for her to stay in the hospital for several days so the nurses could observe her for hemorrhage, a very real possibility given the many small arteries Mike had had to tie off.

"Perhaps I'd like an opportunity to apologize for my conduct at Pine Meadow," David said. "For expecting you to give up a medical career for marriage and motherhood. I should never have expected that, knowing how you love medicine. I wouldn't now."

Michaela couldn't help herself; her head whipped around and her eyes met his. There was sincerity in his gaze, regret. But what did the things he'd said mean? Was he leading up to something? She asked herself the question again— *why is he here?* Surely not to pick up the pieces of their romantic relationship. Surely not to court her again. Surely not to propose again.

And yet, he seemed interested, very interested.

Should she take a chance? It was so like him to leave, come back some time later, and expect her to be available for him. She always opened to him, welcomed his attention, fell in love more deeply. And then each time, something else took her from him.

"I thought you would have married by now," she said, giving voice to the long-suppressed belief.

"I thought the same of you." David reached up and pushed a stray tendril behind her ear.

Michaela, ever conscious of the nurse's curious glances, flinched away. "Come for me at seven this evening," she whispered to David, and then she hurried over to the surgical table where her patient was now twisting with pain. "The procedure is finished, Mrs. Bell," she told the woman.

"The laudanum will ease the pain soon. Try to lie still. You must avoid jarring the wound."

Mike was aware of David walking out of the room. She heard every click of his shoes on the floor, heard him open the door, and then heard him shut it softly.

"You must feel flattered, Dr. Quinn," the nurse commented, smiling.

Michaela shot a worried look at the door. If it were the first time she had received such attention from David, she would be. But it wasn't the first time, and nothing was ever certain where she and David were concerned. She had learned that a long time ago.

He loved her too much, he said, to think about marriage to someone else. He had tried. No one brought him as much joy. No one made him feel the things she did. He had been wrong, very wrong, to assume that she could be a whole and happy person without practicing medicine. He accepted that part of her simply because it *was* a part of her; it had been wrong of him to try to excise it.

He spoke well, and against her better judgment—wasn't he always here today and gone tomorrow? —Michaela began seeing him again.

They attended medical lectures together, the theater, a meeting of the Free-Soilers at which it was discussed whether the Kansas constitutional convention would be ratified to include slavery or not. They called on patients together, assisted each other with surgeries, and sought each other's medical consultation. Together they read in scientific journals about the first producing oil well, located in Pennsylvania, and about Professor Farmer's demonstration of electrical home lighting in the parlor of his home at Salem.

Mike became caught up again in his whirlwind and it felt wonderful. Although, if she stopped to consider her reservations about their courtship, she became fearful and insecure. The thought that nothing was certain where David was concerned stayed with her, no matter how much she chided herself.

Rebecca told her how much happier she looked. Maureen remarked that she actually smiled again, genuine smiles. Etha wrote from Philadelphia, expressing her happiness for Mike—and to relate that she was expecting a child. Michaela read the news and cried out with joy, then raced off to tell Father, Rebecca, Dr. Holmes, everyone. Mother became livelier, planning more teas and suppers, and having numerous dresses made for Michaela with the hope that she would become interested in social events once again now that David had returned and they had resumed their relationship.

She did become interested in social events again. They attended suppers and balls. They danced, ate, and drank to their hearts' content. They were never far from each other, or if they had to be, they weren't for long. They attended a few Emerson readings during late spring, and they marveled together over the *Globe*'s account of a tightrope walker crossing a cable above the seething waters of Niagara Falls. "The man is mad!" David commented, and Michaela agreed.

That summer, he took her to Lake Quinsigamond in Worcester to watch the regatta between the Harvard and Yale students. Half of Massachusetts turned out for the event, it seemed, roaring with approval when the Harvard men in their six-oared shells outrowed the Yale students. Afterward, they joined the picnic celebration and shared little cups of ice cream.

In late October, as was the case with most of the nation, they focused their attention on the abolitionist John Brown in Virginia. Wanting to establish a nonslavery republic in the Appalachians and fight slavery with fugitive slaves and Caucasian abolitionists, Brown and his forces had seized the federal arsenal at Harper's Ferry. Proslavery Virginia wasted no time in trying Brown. In December he was hanged in Charlestown for murder, conspiracy, and treason, and David became riveted on the event and what Brown had stood for.

Antislavery forces in Boston held a mock funeral for the rebel leader, and eulogy after eulogy was given. David delivered one that quickly developed into much more, almost a cry for war. "Virginia has hung a savior. Has she no more respect for mankind? Has she no shame, no guilt? Two days ago, she murdered a man who despised oppression, who fought the bondage of his fellow men! When he saw that words would not reach beyond the miles of cotton and tobacco and penetrate the Southern masters, John Brown became desperate. Only arms will work, he decided, and so he sought them. Let us remember Brown as a liberator of men. Let the day of his hanging be written forever in the annals of history as the day of a new revolution! Let us remember his example and not hesitate to follow it."

During his heated speech, Mike began to wonder if David would fight slavery with his very life if called upon. She had always known his feelings, that he strongly opposed slavery. But she had never before suspected that he might be willing to sacrifice his own life for the cause. The words he spoke—"Let us remember his example and not hesitate to follow it"—were spoken for the gathering. But they were meant for himself also.

Michaela wrote to Etha: "If the Northern and Southern states ever clash in war—God forbid—over the issue of slavery, will David be first in line to enlist in the necessary forces?"

The thought frightened Mike so, she sometimes couldn't breathe well.

"Do you know what Longfellow wrote about Brown's hanging?" David asked her days later.

"I've no idea," she said, still gripped with ominous dread.

"That his execution will 'sow the wind to reap the whirlwind—which will soon come.' There is an election next year, and it will surely be the deciding factor."

The deciding factor in what? Whether or not there would be a war? That's what he was saying. More and more lately he talked about war. He seemed to want it.

"Can't you fight slavery another way?" she asked him. There had been a day when she had enjoyed attending the Free-Soiler meetings with him, when she had enjoyed hearing him speak his views. But now his views leaned toward violence, and they frightened her so much, she often didn't care to hear them. And that sentiment, in turn, shamed her. She cared about gaining the freedom of oppressed people. But she obviously put her personal happiness first. She couldn't seem to help doing that, even as much as she silently scolded herself for it. If a war developed, David would join in the conflict, and they would be separated again.

Michaela couldn't stand the thought.

Shortly after the start of the New Year, Mike noticed that her father was limping. Whenever he sat, he did so slowly and his face always tightened. When she asked him about the limp he said he had a touch of gout—he was getting old, after all. Then she asked him if he had been examined by a fellow physician or if he was treating himself. Of course she knew he was getting old, that he had been old for some time now.

"Treating myself," he said, and pride refused to allow him to discuss the matter further. His health was a private matter to him.

"A man like your father must be allowed his dignity," Professor Holmes remarked when Michaela asked him if he had noticed her father's limp, that Dr. Quinn was slow getting up and down, and that he seemed to be in pain at times. "Of course, I've noticed," Holmes then went on, peering at her over his reading glasses. "But the physician rarely makes a good patient. If he doesn't take his medicine well, it's better to leave him alone."

Mike nodded.

"Why must Dr. Holmes always be so wise?" she asked David later, rather irritably. Together they were perusing the books in the relatively new Boston Public Library.

"Because he's Dr. Holmes," David responded.

Michaela tossed her head. "For lack of a better explanation . . ."

"You're frustrated because you know he's right, that leaving your father alone, not asking about his health, is the best course of action."

"But I want to ask about his health. I want to know how

he's treating himself, if something more than gout plagues him."

"If he decides he wants you to know, he'll tell you," David said. Then he slanted her a curious look. "I don't imagine you would make a very good patient either, Dr. Quinn."

His point was well taken, although Mike scowled at him. "Well, I might."

An attendant stuck her head around the corner and warned them, "Quiet, now." Then she disappeared as quickly as she had appeared.

Mike put her hand over her mouth to stifle a giggle. She planted her back against a row of books.

David grinned. "You'll get us thrown out with your argumentative nature."

He eased closer to her, so close she could feel the warmth of his breath. He sobered as his eyes searched hers, and suddenly she knew his intent, that he meant to kiss her, right here and now, between the rows of shelved books.

"David . . ." she said, glancing around to see if anyone was watching.

"Sh," he urged, placing his finger on her lips. "Seems as though it has taken me forever to get us back to this point. I felt . . . I still feel . . . you deserve so much from me after I disappointed you so badly."

He paused, swallowing as if nervous. "So I'm back to this point . . . and for days I've wanted to ask if you would again consider marrying me, Michaela Quinn. That is, if you will consider becoming my wife and not giving up your practice of medicine in the process."

His lips took the place of his finger, and Mike surely would have been lost in their softness and in his musky scent if the kiss had lasted longer than a few seconds. He broke it off, and he withdrew to study her. Then he grinned and reminded her of where they were.

The attendant appeared again, passing their aisle, and Michaela and David jerked away from each other. She turned around and pretended to be studying several books.

He pulled a book from the shelf, opened it, and turned the pages.

"Yes," she said suddenly, flashing him a grin.

He lifted a brow. "Yes? To becoming my wife and not giving up your practice of medicine in the process?"

"Yes," she said again, and she pulled a book from the shelf and quickly exited the aisle.

"Did you find what you were looking for?" the attendant asked from nearby.

Mike nodded. Yes, oh, yes, she certainly had.

In the months ahead, Michaela began stitching on her wedding gown, a creation of white lace, silk, and pearls, and David became more and more caught up in freeing the slaves. In February he took a brief trip to New York to hear Abraham Lincoln deliver a speech at Cooper Union. Lincoln made clear his no-compromise position on slavery, and David returned to Boston a crusader for the man.

Jimmie Becker returned home and his parents held a ball in his honor. He was an attorney now, a barrister as the English called their lawyers. And while he was educated and could act refined when the notion struck him, he was still as outrageous and adventurous as ever. He grabbed Mike nearly as soon as she and David were announced in the ballroom and he waltzed her away. Later, David teased Jimmie about stealing her from him, and Jimmie grinned, saying, "I very well might, my friend, if you don't keep your eyes peeled."

Some time later, when she was taking in a breath a fresh air near a pair of French doors, Michaela heard a group of men talking about David. Boston was divided on the issue of whether slaves were property or citizens, and while some forces were violently opposed, others felt certain that slaves were property and that slave owners should be left alone. For the first time, Mike heard David referred to as an abolitionist, and not in a favorable sense of the word. David was right now speaking to a group of men on the other side of the ballroom. His expression was tight and his eyes were fiery, aglow, as they always were, with the passion he felt for his cause.

"He's becoming a zealot," Henry James said.

Andrew Cori agreed, and Edward Reuther commented that David was indeed fanatical of late. "To attack the issue of slavery is to attack the Southern economy," Edward remarked. "Slaves are property, and the plantation owners are merely property owners."

A zealot . . . fanatical . . . Michaela wished the issues would die down. She wished David would calm down. But he was being understanding and accepting of her desire to marry, have a family, and still practice medicine, therefore she meant to be as supportive of his desires as possible.

While her wedding gown came together, David kept his eyes on the presidential election campaigns that were gathering force, and he spoke of little else. In May, the Republican National Convention nominated Lincoln for the office. At the Democratic Convention, Southern delegates walked out over platform disputes, finally deciding to form a rebel group of Democrats. In June, the Northern Democratics nominated Douglas, who supported congressional noninterference in the slavery issue, while the Southern Democrats spoke out for John Breckinridge, the only nominee who upheld slavery. Many people speculated that Lincoln took big chances with his political career by opposing slavery publicly, and although David had become a staunch supporter of Lincoln, even he had to agree with the sentiment.

Almost every Harvard faculty member favored "the right to own property." So did a considerable amount of the student body. After spending most of the spring and summer trying to dissuade the faculty and students, David finally became frustrated. "I can't believe some people fail to see the immorality of bondage!" he told Mike one afternoon. Usually, where his political views were concerned, she listened but only rarely offered her opinion. Now was no different.

A small group of undergraduates held a meeting in Tremont Temple on the college grounds, and David later told Michaela how some of the men had stuffed their hats with handkerchiefs to soften the blows they feared might be dealt by the proslavery forces that gathered there, too. Mike closed her eyes and shook her head. She feared for his safety more and more lately.

Mike went to Philadelphia for a few weeks that year to visit Etha, Charles, their new baby boy, and all the friends and acquaintances in the city. The college was doing well, graduating fresh students every year. The same political issues that gripped Boston, that gripped the entire country, also raged in Philadelphia. Proslavery and antislavery forces clashed here, too. There was no escaping the conflict, it seemed.

Michaela returned home, where more violent outbreaks occurred. South Carolina threatened outright secession from the Union if Abraham Lincoln was elected, and the abolitionists encouraged Northern secession. People who had friends and relatives in the South tried to be supportive of their loved ones or tried to be neutral, almost an impossible thing to do. And as election day neared, the entire city, indeed the entire country, braced for the outcome. Most of Boston's trees were bare of leaves, although the brittle leaves of the chrysanthemums remained. Mud froze in ruts on the unpaved roadways, and by November, the city had already received a good amount of early snow.

Lincoln won the election by popular vote, and citizens gasped. Many had thought Douglas would slide in and the issue of slavery would die down, but even Mike knew that the debates and the hostility and blows had driven the subject too far. There really was no turning back now.

In the weeks immediately following the election, the normally fiery South Carolina was strangely quiet. Ominously quiet. Then she struck, seceding from the Union just days before Christmas.

Most of Boston reeled with shock. In New England, the normal citizen had not wanted separation, however much the majority of abolitionists did. The radicals had encouraged secession of the New England states, and now they snubbed South Carolina, saying good riddance. But many

Bostonians cried for union—a sentiment that also was reflected by much of the North, as the *Globe* reported.

Mr. Lincoln would not tolerate this, John Andrew, the governor-elect of Massachusetts, reportedly predicted. And while the man was ushered into the highest state office during a howling January snowstorm, Dr. Holmes wrote a poem welcoming South Carolina back:

Oh Caroline, Caroline, child of the sun,
We can never forget that our hearts have been one,
Our foreheads both sprinkled in Liberty's name,
From the fountain of blood with the finger of flame . . .
Go, then, our rash sister! afar and aloof,
Run wild in the sunshine away from our roof;
But when your heart aches and your feet have grown
sore,
Remember the pathway that leads to our door!

The clever professor predicted peace. This separation could not continue, South Carolina would come crawling back. Lincoln was still in the West, celebrating his victory, but he soon would be in Washington, D.C., where he would be inaugurated into the presidency.

During January and February, the Southern states slipped away one by one, fearing an abolitionist president, so many that at times Michaela had trouble remembering them all: Mississippi, Florida, Alabama, Georgia, Louisiana, Texas . . . Their actions seemed unbelievable. New England was dazed.

"Charleston, South Carolina is a hotbed of rebels," Jimmie remarked when he called on Mike one day and they sat playing cards. "If troubles begins, it will begin there."

His prediction proved right. In January, a federal ship was sent by President Buchanan to supply and reinforce the federal garrison at Fort Sumter, which lay in Charleston harbor. Prompted by orders from their governor, the South Carolina state battery fired on the unarmed vessel.

David was one of the few opposers of slavery who shook his head and said secession was not the answer, that the bondage would still continue if the Union simply let the states go. Joseph Quinn, when he spoke of the secessions, looked grave and leaned toward Governor Andrew's prediction—that Lincoln, who valued the Union as a whole, would not tolerate such acts of rebellion.

But a lot of people still scoffed at the idea of war, that there would even be one. South Carolina's state battery had been playing, they said, firing a few harmless shots. Things would calm down. Life would go on, continue as it had been.

And yet, in February, Jefferson Davis was elected president of the Confederate States of America, and the Southerners formed a provisional Congress. The White House was quiet. Was Buchanan now ignoring the growing conflict? Preparing to hand what had rapidly become a full rebellion over to the president-elect as soon as Lincoln took office? It was Lincoln's fight, after all, this slavery thing.

People laughed at Massachusetts governor Andrew when he began gathering the state militia and calling for overcoats and rifles for the recruits. When Michaela heard the news, she felt cold the entire day. David would soon enlist, in her heart, she knew he would. What was the sense in continuing with her wedding gown, with the many pearls she was so carefully and so lovingly stitching on to it?

Yet she did continue. If David enlisted surely nothing would happen to him. He would stay safe. If there was a war, it would be a short one, or so many people predicted; after all, how could the Southern states, with only King Cotton to sustain them, support a lengthy military conflict?

Unlike many who ridiculed the governor, David responded to his cry, and he, like Andrew and others, became known as an "overcoat," the new political slang for warmonger.

"They'll laugh and ridicule until the day Lincoln arrives in Washington and announces a state of war," David told Mike bitterly one morning when he returned from a warehouse where he and other supporters of Governor Andrew had spent hours packing rifles for shipment.

On Cambridge Street, a company of militia drilled.

Jimmie was among them, having remained in the States, worried that if war broke out harbors might be blockaded. Then, getting back to see his family might be virtually impossible for a time. Volunteers were needed in the Home Guard. The Fourth Battalion called for recruits—it would go to Fort Independence and guard Boston harbor if necessary, if and when it obtained enough men. The Massachusetts legislature finally gave Governor Andrew money for more overcoats, and the wool mills began bidding for contracts.

People still scoffed, but the war had, in reality, arrived in Boston, and Lincoln, as yet, had not even been inaugurated. Michaela was relieved that David had not been out drilling with the Home Guard or preparing to guard the harbor with the Fourth Battalion. But then, she knew it was only a matter of time before he joined the militia.

March arrived, unseasonably warm and muggy. The sky over Boston was a clear blue, a strange sight for this time of year, Mike thought as she and David strolled the Common and watched the bare branches of the huge elms sway in the light breeze. The air was still nippy at times, and Michaela pulled her cloak more snugly around her.

"The Fort Sumter provisions are running low again," David remarked.

Michaela drew a deep breath. "I'd like to spend one afternoon with you discussing something besides the 'inevitable war.'" Sarcasm laced her voice. She couldn't seem to help herself. She was sick of the conflicts, sick of their lives revolving around them, sick of fearing whether she would have him tomorrow.

"I hardly think of anything else," he said, and he continued walking.

Did he not realize how his words stung her? That she took them to mean he was so caught up in thoughts of the conflicts between the Northern and Southern states that he rarely even thought of her? He was with her, but lately he was never really with her; she might be resting her arm on his, but his mind was in Charleston harbor, on the militia drilling on Cambridge Street, on what Lincoln's first move would be once he was inaugurated.

"Sometimes I wonder if we'll ever have a life together, David," Mike remarked.

He studied her. She had his attention. She was amazed. Since January, his full concentration had been on the impending war.

"We'll be married in June," he said. "In three months."

She laughed bitterly. "If a war doesn't explode in our faces first."

"Michaela, you sound angry."

"I am. Why is it all happening now? You haven't said anything, but I know you plan to enlist, David. There's no need to say anything. I can't imagine you not enlisting."

"You're wrong," he said, flinching.

She spotted Dr. Holmes with Neddy, his son. The two of them were strolling along, dropping bread crumbs for the birds.

"No, I'm not," Mike told David. She sighed. "At any rate, I plan to put the matter aside for the day. I plan to have a day without talk of Charleston and Lincoln and the Confederacy. If you would like to spend it with me, that would be wonderful. Neddy!" she called, starting off, waving to her friends. "Dr. Holmes . . . good afternoon!"

The professor and his son glanced around. "Ah, look!" he said, nudging Neddy gently on the shoulder. "There she is . . . Dr. Quinn. Yes, it is a good afternoon, Michaela. Would you like to help us here?"

"I would!"

Dropping crumbs and listening to Neddy giggle as the birds pecked them up was the most fun Mike had had in more than a month.

David wandered their way, hands in his trouser pockets, and soon even he was smiling at Neddy's excitement. Michaela handed him a chunk of bread. He smiled at her as he took it, and he apologized for being such a bore.

So they fed the birds, and while she was sure they were never far from David's mind, Michaela ignored the national conflicts for one afternoon.

But one could never escape them for long. While President Buchanan was busy signing a congressional act to establish the territories of Nevada and Dakota, the rebels were making an official Confederate flag. "Stars and Bars," they called it. Then, on the same day they presented their flag to the divided nation, Abraham Lincoln was sworn in as president.

As had been predicted, he wasted no time in reacting to the Charleston threat. On March ninth, he sent provisions to Fort Sumter, and that Friday, the twelfth, a day Michaela would never forget, Confederate forces bombarded the fort.

Lincoln sent out a call for state militias. Boston's newspapers carried the headline "Civil War Is upon Us!"

And David joined the Fourth Battalion.

20

Sentiments changed almost overnight in Boston. Those who had scoffed sobered. Those who had said there would never be a war cursed the Southern states that had seceded and the states that were threatening to secede. Those who had laughed and turned *overcoat* into a derogatory word used to describe war zealots were now thankful for Governor Andrew's foresight. If South Carolina, if the entire South, wanted a fight, she would get it.

Many still thought the fight would be a short one, that the South couldn't support a war for long—and Mike prayed they were right.

For months afterward, events happened in a whirlwind: Virginia pulled out of the Union, President Lincoln issued an order to blockade all Confederate ports; in Norfolk, the Union forces destroyed and evacuated the naval yard. . . . A surge of cold air gripped Boston the third week of April, just as Mike stitched the last of the pearls onto her wedding gown. Militia men from around the state marched into the city in driving sleet, preparing for transfer south.

Michaela helped hand out overcoats one afternoon. Along with a number of other volunteers, she stood beneath an awning amid crates, and that's exactly where she was when she spotted David staring at her from the street corner. She knew by the look of dread on his face and by the way he hung back reluctantly that the Fourth Battalion, to which Jimmie also belonged, would be moving out soon. He was dressed in Zouave trousers, baggy, light blue, tucked into gaiters. He wore a dark blue tunic, and a red cap rested on his head.

Thank goodness he wouldn't be in the middle of any fighting. At least Mike assumed that since he would be a military doctor he wouldn't be in the fighting lines. He didn't want to go, she could tell. He didn't want to leave her. But his convictions dictated that he must.

She approached him, and she took his hand in hers and pressed it to her cheek.

"Your mother said you finished the gown," he remarked.

Mike smiled. "I did."

"We're off to Fort Independence within the week. Marry me before then, Michaela."

She shook her head. She wouldn't begin their life together in a mad rush, with him going off to war within a few days of their wedding. "Young Wendell joined, too, you know. Dr. Holmes predicts only a three-month war, and I've never known him to be wrong about anything."

He embraced her. "Pray that he's right." He trembled, the feverish orator, the man who had pressed for confrontation.

"I will, David," she said. "I'll pray every day."

Most of Boston turned out to watch the Fourth board the ship that would take them out to the armory. Michaela waved David off, and an hour later, she threw herself into her work more than ever, surfacing only to eat and sleep during the next few weeks.

One Sunday she joined a large group of women in filling baskets with cakes, wines, tobacco, and other items. They rowed out to the fort and visited with their husbands, friends, and acquaintances. The militia needed officers, David told Mike as they visited, and officials had spread the word that garrison duty would qualify a man for a commission. The war would be short, he now said, too, and Michaela read the unspoken words in his eyes: *The war will be short, and the postponement of our wedding won't be for long.*

She was used to his vacillating. It came as no surprise to her that weeks ago he had held her and asked her to marry him within days, yet now he seemed relieved that they had postponed the wedding.

He had to fight his war, and if she wanted him, she had to let him. Michaela knew that. She had known that long ago, when he had first enlisted his aid in freeing the slaves. She would never truly have him anyway until the conflict between the North and the South was over.

"It's madness, putting off the wedding until the war is over," her mother objected.

"I would rather postpone it than be married in the middle of chaos," Michaela responded.

Chaos was precisely the right word for the state of things, for the rapid pace of events. Arkansas seceded, then North Carolina, and the very next day, the Confederates chose Richmond as their capital. Near the middle of June, the Fourth Battalion returned from duty at the fort, traveling on the steamship *Nelly Baker.* The Germania Band played *Yankee Doodle,* and then the battalion marched in all its glory to the Common. There, Michael embraced David, held him tight, then withdrew to have a look at him.

"I still have all my fingers and toes," he said, grinning.

She shot him a playful scowl. "How you jest!"

They celebrated Independence Day together, feasting on lobster salad, wine, and then later, ice cream as they watched the brass band march in the parade that sauntered up Mount Vernon Street and turned the corner at Tremont.

On July ninth, the day after Tennessee joined the Confederacy, David was appointed captain in the Twentieth Massachusetts Infantry. Wendell Holmes, who had just graduated from Harvard despite serving in the battalion at Fort Independence, was appointed lieutenant. In late July, just after news reached Boston of a Union disaster at Bull

Run in Virginia, David, Wendell, Jimmie, and a host of other young men boarded the railroad cars that would take them away.

"I don't know how you stand the thought of him leaving . . . what he's going into," Claudette told Michaela. "But then, you have such inner strength. I've always admired you for that."

Mike walked away from the train station without looking back once. She again threw herself into her work, calling on patients in District Eight, working long hours at the hospital, calling on patients with her father. He was the only person who ever saw her shed a tear of fear over the possibility that David could be injured or killed if the Twentieth were engaged in battle.

Dr. Holmes helped keep her spirits up. He was always jovial and upbeat despite the fact that Wendell also had gone off with the militia. Mrs. Holmes headed a group of women who worked tirelessly at stitching shirts and knitting socks for "our soldiers." She was such a courageous woman, but now and then Michaela would see her looking distant and would know her mind was on Wendell, on wondering whether he was safe. Rebecca joined the group. So did Claudette. And while stitching and knitting were not her favorite things to do, Mike herself finally began helping with the cause.

For a time, her worries seemed almost silly. David's infantry unit was currently located only eight miles south of the city, near Readville Station; no danger lurked in the bushes there. "Governor Andrew was here to review the troops," David wrote to Michaela. "He made a speech which barely could be heard because the wind blew so hard, and then he left and the regiment has since sat and waited, wondering if it will ever receive marching orders."

Marching orders finally came in early September. The infantry division went to Connecticut, then took a steamer to New York, where it marched up Broadway. David wrote letters, thank goodness, because without them Mike might have gone mad. In Washington, D.C., General Scott reviewed the regiment from a balcony, and then the troops went on to a camp located in a wheat field some two miles from Edward's Ferry on the Potomac River.

"All is quiet here," David wrote. "We set up our medical tents. We treat a case of dysentery now and then, but never fear—there have been no bullet wounds or otherwise to keep the doctors busy."

A rather distasteful joke on his part, Michaela thought sourly. While she sat in Boston and worried, he wrote from his camp near Virginia and jested about a lack of bullet wounds to keep the army doctors busy!

In October, he wrote that the rebels were now camped not a mile away, across the river, and that they moved so softly and with such care and skill among the trees, they often could not be heard or detected. Sometimes shots were fired and a man failed to return from guard duty. The news chilled Mike.

Dr. Holmes told her that Wendell had written, that a friend of his had actually talked to a rebel. "When're you fellas goin' to Richmond?" the rebel had shouted across the water, and the Yankee had called back, "The day before you boys go to Washington!"

Confederate forces were too close to the Massachusetts infantry for any Bostonian's peace of mind. The city became quiet. Dr. Holmes did not seem as jovial. Michaela lost sleep. People waited, never knowing what news the next telegraphed message might bring. The sons and lovers and husbands of this city, of Massachusetts, were in the middle of the war now, and there were no more parades or picnics.

The next news about the Twentieth arrived in late October, and it was not good. The *Globe* and *Post* both reported that there had been an engagement between Union and Confederate forces somewhere by Leesburg in Virginia. Two days later the newspapers listed the regiments involved in the battle—and the Twentieth appeared on the list.

All of Boston waited in cold fear. People massed outside the telegraph and newspaper offices. They had to know.

Mike sat with Mrs. Holmes, who seemed calm for the most part but who intermittently wrung a handkerchief in her hands. Michaela pulled young Neddy up onto her lap and read to him, trying to put their minds on something else. Doing so seemed impossible. Neddy asked if his brother was hurt, and Mike told him they didn't yet know.

More news trickled in. Wendell was in the field hospital. He had been hit in the chest, but he was doing well. The *Post* carried a full account of the battle, telling how it had begun on Ball's Bluff, high above the river. The enemy had hidden in the tall grass of a nearby field and in the thick trees some distance off. The rebels had charged from the woods yelping like Indians, overtaking the Union forces. The battle was a disaster for the North. The men had fought all day. They had been driven down the bluff to the water's edge and the river had run with blood. They had never expected to lose the battle . . . there had been no provisions for escape, no waiting boats or rafts.

Michaela felt nauseated.

The list of injured was lengthy, and it continued to run for days, growing longer every time she read it. David's name never appeared. He must be fine then, she thought, safe in the medical camps, too busy treating the many wounded to think about writing.

Dr. Holmes traveled to the field hospital to collect his wounded son, and the twenty-year-old Wendell who returned to Boston was not the same bright-eyed, cheery, energetic youth he had been. He had seen blood and death; he had seen limbs blown away, had heard the cries of mortally wounded comrades; many of his friends had died on that bluff and in that river. He was pale, barely able to walk, thin as a twig.

Mrs. Holmes tended him herself, changing the bread poultices on his wound, carrying trays of food to him. Dr. Holmes could not bring himself to perform surgery on his own son, so Joseph Quinn etherized Wendell while Michaela probed his wound for the ball. It had missed his heart and lungs by inches.

He seemed to feel better the next morning, although he was in pain still and required laudanum. Mike sat with him while her father went off on rounds and while Professor Holmes caught up on sleep. Mrs. Holmes brought another tray of food, tea, toast, and softly poached eggs.

"I'm sorry," Wendell whispered, and Michaela realized that he was talking to her.

She smiled at him. "For being wounded? Well, you did cause everyone a terrible amount of worry."

"He had more courage than anyone that day," he said, and now Mike wasn't sure what he was talking about. Was he delirious? Perhaps she should cut back on his dosage of medication.

"He brought the wagon down," Wendell said. "Men were still firing. He told me he meant to collect me straightaway and take me back to the medical tents. He went to get a litter. That was the last anyone saw of him."

Michaela stared at Wendell. Realization set in.

No. She didn't breathe. She couldn't. Her lungs were on fire. Her throat was on fire. Her eyes were on fire.

"What is it? What's the matter?" Mrs. Holmes pressed.

"Wendell, who are you talking about?" Mike managed to ask. Her voice sounded shrill, far away. "You're not talking about David. Tell me you're not."

He swallowed. "I'm sorry. You hadn't heard . . . That must mean his family hasn't either. You'll tell them, Michaela? Tell them . . ." He swallowed again, and blinked slowly and weakly. "Tell them David is missing. I would wager my life that the rebs took him."

Mike turned away from the bed, walked across the room, leaned her head against the doorframe. David . . . missing in action . . .

Her mind went wild with assumptions. He was either lying mortally wounded or dead in those trees near Leesburg. Or he was chained in some Confederate prison.

Michaela began volunteering time with an auxiliary group of the Army Medical Corps. The commission organized hospital units and taught officers how to care for their sick and wounded men if necessary; it fitted up hospital ships, equipping them with bandages, medicines, and supplies and it sent men and women into the field to nurse the wounded.

Eight hundred rebel prisoners were received at the fort in the harbor, and people stared that way with hatred in their eyes. Bostonians had thrown themselves into the war effort. No more balking, no more ridiculing, no more arguing that slaves were property. Their boys and men had been killed and wounded in Virginia, and citizens were now indignant, angry, and determined to win the war. Mr. and Mrs. Lewis wrote letter after letter, hoping to enlist some official's aid in finding David. Every day Sarah checked at the post, and every day she walked out empty-handed.

November, December, and January passed, and all was quiet on the Virginia front. People grumbled that the Union general McClellan was giving new grass time to grow on the Leesburg battlefield. At the White House, Lincoln wondered aloud if he could borrow the army if McClellan did not wish to use it.

Then the battles came, on land and in water, and they became so numerous that Mike could not remember them all. In North Carolina, in Virginia, in Tennessee . . . Union general Ulysses S. Grant captured an important fort on the Cumberland River and demanded of the Confederate generals, "No terms but unconditional and immediate surrender." The next month he beat more rebel forces on the Tennessee River, while McClellan continued to battle them in Virginia. Many Northern people had friends and relatives in the South, and they were torn with worry.

"A necessary war, but a tragic one," Michaela's father remarked one quiet evening as the two of them sat reading in the study. "I saw a patient today whose sister married a Southerner several years ago and moved to Georgia. She's not heard a word since last November."

In March, Wendell Holmes, fully recovered now, was promoted to captain and recalled. This time he would find his regiment in Hampton, Virginia. The rebels had retreated, and McClellan had ordered the entire army to advance.

The war raged, and yet life continued. Claudette planned to remarry, and Michaela was joyous over the news. An older gentleman Claudette had met at the Park Street Church had been courting her. Mollie and William loved Mr. Nolan, and they helped their mother plan the small wedding. When Mollie asked why they weren't having a grand to-do, Claudette said, "One mustn't think of being frivolous during such difficult times."

Mike worried more over her father's health. After he climbed stairs he often had terrible trouble catching his breath. His legs pained him more; he was slower getting up after sitting for lengthy periods, and he did not hide so well anymore the painful expression on his face. But he still would not discuss his medical problems. Older gentlemen carried walking sticks for fashion more than anything, but he began to rely on his, and he rarely went out without it.

Wendell wrote about the war in Virginia. Guns had to be mounted, earthworks dug, it rained forever there. His comrades slept in the water at night and stood their posts in it during daylight. They put their beds up on poles, put their shelters on stilts, and still they were wet. Medical problems abounded. Scurvy erupted. Dysentery broke out. There was little food. The men stole watermelons from fields and chickens from hen houses; they searched long and hard for berries and sometimes ate them green. Not all of the rebels wore gray; some came straight from the frontier and they were the really dangerous ones, the ones who knew how to live in the wilderness. They often wore homespun dyed with butternut, and if you came upon a nice looking fellow dressed just so, it was best to shoot first and ask questions later.

It was a horrible war and it no longer excited Wendell. It no longer excited any soldier, judging by the letters that poured into Boston. But then, what war was anything but horrible?

Casualty numbers filtered into the city. As a result of the Peninsular Campaign in Virginia alone, sixteen thousand Union troops were killed, wounded, or missing. And that didn't include the casualties of Bull Run and Shiloh. Men returned to Boston minus limbs, and they told of things the mind could not imagine.

Outside the post office one afternoon, Michaela watched a woman tear open a letter, read briefly, then sink to the ground weeping. Mike caught the woman in her arms and snatched up the letter before it became soaked in a puddle. An acquaintance of the woman's son was writing to tell of his friend's last words—and of his wish that he write to her and tell her how brave he had been in battle.

"I don't care, I don't care how brave he was," the woman moaned.

Michaela held her for a long time, rocking, tears burning her eyes. She always felt the same way when she considered Wendell's words about David's bravery on the Leesburg battlefield.

And then came word that the rebel general Lee was threatening a Northern invasion, that he was knocking on the door of western Maryland. An engagement took place there, the battle of Antietam Creek. McClellan repelled Lee, but the North alone lost some two thousand men, and another nine thousand were wounded. The numbers . . . every time numbers trickled into Boston, Mike was horrified. She could not imagine so many people dead or wounded.

Wendell had been shot through the neck. The Holmeses received a telegraph, and Dr. Holmes, now a sober man, prepared for travel to Philadelphia and from there, south. He meant to find his son. If Wendell died, he wouldn't have him buried in some foreign place.

Lincoln issued the Emancipation Proclamation, freeing all slaves as of January 1, 1863. If there was a soft spot left in the South's heart for the North, it disappeared that day. The proclamation was an outrage, they said. Who was this Illinois politician anyway that he felt it his right to interfere so in their lives? In Boston, the possibility of assassination was whispered about, and while some people shuddered at Lincoln's boldness, others posted banners around the city, hailing the president.

Professor Holmes returned to Boston with Wendell, who was not mortally wounded. He had been taken in at a farmhouse, and after searching in strange cities and places for him, even on the battlefield, Dr. Holmes had finally found him and promptly walked them both directly to the train station. Wendell was quiet and distant. When he spoke of the war, he spoke of hating it. At home, he healed, and then he was called up again.

More battles took place . . . more men were killed, wounded, disfigured. All this chaos, all this death and destruction, all this ugliness, from a war many had predicted would last only three months.

As more months dragged by and then turned into years, Michaela began to give up hope that David would ever be found. Sarah never did, and she nearly drove George mad with her insistence that David was alive somewhere. Mr. Lewis told her to give it up, and Sarah shouted at him, in front of Mike, that she would never "give it up." Prisoners of war were sometimes exchanged by opposing sides, and if David was a prisoner, she meant to get him back. "We're not even sure he's alive," George said, trying to talk sense into her. "You talk to her, Michaela."

But Mike didn't know what to say. If David was a prisoner of war somewhere, she wanted him found. But she could see Mr. Lewis's side of the dilemma, too. Finding David was consuming Sarah Lewis. Rather than comment at all, Michaela merely left the room.

While the United States was fighting to hold on to its states, more territories were formed in the West—Arizona and Idaho. More museums opened in Boston, and skating on wheels became popular. If one could skate on thin blades on ice, one could surely skate on wheels on dry land, Dr. Holmes said, and he went off with Neddy to try it himself.

When General Grant announced in April of '64 that he was discontinuing the practice of exchanging prisoners because the exchange was prolonging the war, Sarah wept for an entire week. The Yankee officials had given up on getting back their own men, she cried. "How can they do this? George, how can they do this?"

She wrote more letters to Washington, D.C., pleading with senators, congressmen, the president himself. The response was always the same: They sympathized, but with the many prisoners sitting in Confederate jails, finding one among them all would be impossible until the war was over.

"He'll be dead by then!" Sarah wailed.

"How do you know he's not already dead?" her husband asked.

Consumed by fear and grief, Sarah threw the stack of letters at him and stomped from the parlor.

Michaela gathered the papers, knowing David's mother would want them later.

"If only he had had the sense to marry you years ago," George said, staring into a crackling fire.

Mike paused in her task and smiled gently and sadly up at him.

He smiled back, and his eyes were glassy and red. "You know, as I know, that he's not coming home this time, don't you, Michaela? He's dead. Wherever he is, he's dead."

She choked back tears. "Yes, I think I've known for some time, Mr. Lewis." She hadn't dared a look at her wedding dress in months because she'd known.

He nodded, pinching the bridge of his nose and tilting his face down. Mike gathered the rest of the letters and prepared to leave him. No man liked to show his tears; dignity was a fragile thing.

"You're a wonderful woman," George managed. "I'm proud that David chose you. But go on with your life, Michaela. Find someone else and go on. It's finally, truly over. He's not coming home."

She could hardly see the papers now, her eyes were so filled with tears. She certainly couldn't speak. He was right,

312

and she really had known for some time that David was not coming home.

She placed the letters on a nearby table, then left the room and walked straight home.

There, she found her father in his study, and she went right to him, dropped down beside his chair, and laid her head on his knee. She told him about her brief conversation with George Lewis, and then she cried as she had never cried. David was dead, had been probably since Leesburg, and although she had known in her heart, she had not dealt with the realization. Now she did.

Confederate general Robert E. Lee won a huge victory over Union forces at Chancellorsville that May. Wendell was wounded again, this time in the foot. At first he'd thought his leg had been blown off, and then he had awakened in a hospital and realized that it was still there. But ligaments and tendons had been torn away, and this wound put Wendell at home for a good nine months, to the Holmes's relief. He was fortunate, he told Michaela. Unlike Jimmie Becker and others who had succumbed at Chancellorsville, he still had his life.

When Mike heard about Jimmie, she secluded herself away for days, cried, ate little, threw a porcelain vase and smashed it against a wall. Was there to be no end to this? To the death and destruction, to the ruination of peoples' lives? The Beckers were crushed. The Lewises were crushed. So were hundreds of other Boston families who had lost men. The war was horrible, and Michaela hated it at least as much as Wendell did.

She wrote long letters to Etha about all the tragedies and about the common sight on the city streets of women in mourning garb. Etha wrote back telling much the same about conditions among the population of Philadelphia. "The war has devastated people," she said, "and the sooner it is ended, the better."

Chancellorsville had been a feather in General Lee's cap, but the tide turned when he lost some thirty thousand men at the Potomac River in July. Another twenty-nine thousand surrendered at Vicksburg the day before Independence Day, and Union control of the Mississippi River after that battle split the Confederacy in two. It also doomed it, Joseph Quinn said. Lee had now lost a third of his army, and Confederate forces could no longer use the mighty and advantageous Mississippi to transport troops and supplies. The war would surely be over soon.

And yet it continued.

While Northern and Southern forces battled, presidential campaigns began again. The Republicans nominated Lincoln and the Democrats nominated General McClellan. The issue this time was the war, or rather, Lincoln's "mishandling" of it, or so the Democrats claimed.

In September, Atlanta, Georgia, a strategic Southern point, fell to a Union general whose name for years afterward would make Southerners shudder: William Tecumseh Sherman. Few people in Boston knew anything about him, had ever even heard of him. But celebrations were held all over Beacon Hill when word arrived that he had taken Atlanta. Nevada was admitted into the Union, another star in the Union flag, and Abraham Lincoln was reelected president.

In November, General Sherman began his march to the sea, sweeping sixty miles through Georgia, burning Atlanta and then everything in his path that he deemed useful to the Confederates. He ravaged the countryside, meaning to starve the rebels out, and his actions disemboweled the Confederacy. Grant had already vowed to take Richmond, and together the two Union generals became the military might of the war, the heroes who would bring the nightmare to a close. Sherman continued burning and ravaging into '65, Grant closed in on the rebel general Lee, Lincoln was inaugurated into a second term, and Richmond finally fell into Union hands on April second.

The evening of April ninth, Mike's father entered the study where she sat reading. He carried a bottle of champagne, and a grin danced on his face. "They've surrendered," he said, breathless with excitement, his eyes sparkling. "It's over. God . . . thank God. It's over!"

"Lee surrendered?" Michaela blurted, jumping up.

Her father nodded. "To General Grant. Today! In Virginia!"

She had never heard him sound so excited about anything. They drank several glasses of champagne. They laughed and talked. They expressed disbelief and joy. *Lee had surrendered!*

The next day, they joined in the parades that marched through Boston, and in the following days, they attended dances and suppers. The city celebrated, and it seemed the celebrations might go on forever. The war was virtually ended. The Confederate forces were decimated. Now to gather the surrenders of rebel generals Johnston and Davis. What did they have left to fight with?

On April fourteenth, a tragic event put a brake on Northern celebrations. Late that evening, Mike was waltzing with Dr. Holmes in the Beckers' gallery with a dozen other couples when the violinist suddenly stopped playing.

"Here, now," Professor Holmes objected. "What is—"

Mrs. Becker, tears filling her eyes, held up a hand to stop him. In her other hand she held a small piece of paper.

"Whatever is it, Amelia?" he asked, startled by the stricken look on her face.

"Message . . . the um . . . just arrived," she mumbled, glancing down at the paper. "It's . . . at the theater . . ." She shook her head, too choked up to say more.

Dr. Holmes urged her to sit, and after she sank down onto a nearby chair, he took the paper from her hand.

He read the words on it, paled at least as much as Mrs. Becker had, then glanced up at the many curious pairs of eyes. "President Lincoln was shot while attending the theater earlier this evening," he said finally. "His injury is thought to be mortal."

Gasps and cries of outrage and disbelief filled the gallery. Their champion, Lincoln, who had promised to free the slaves and who had; the man who had not faltered in the face of early Union defeats; the man who had boldly delivered an inspiring speech on the Gettysburg field where so many men had died. . . . Their Lincoln could not possibly lie near death, the result of an assassin's bullet.

But he did, and when he died the following morning, there was hardly a dry eye in Boston.

In his inaugural address that year, the great man had urged all citizens to work toward putting the country back together. "With malice toward none, with charity for all, with firmness in the right . . . let us strive on to finish the work we are in, to bind up the nation's wounds. . . ." The address was reread at a memorial service in the Park Street Church, just as the train that carried the deceased president's body began its long journey to Illinois. There, Mr. Lincoln would be interred in the soil from which he had arisen and fired a nation.

Life began to settle down. But when would it ever really return to normal? At least there were no more reports of battles. Men came home from the war looking hollow and half-starved, and more and more people wore mourning black as the lists of deceased grew.

Michaela felt hollow and sad, numb with shock. It seemed almost unbelievable that David and Jimmie would never again walk the length of Mount Vernon Street on their way to see her; it seemed unbelievable that her childhood playmates were gone, that she would never speak with them again.

Alongside her father, she treated patients with numerous ragged stumps, the results of rapidly amputated limbs in the army medical hospitals. She worked with Dr. Peter Aldrich, too, who asked her time and again if she would have supper with him. She always declined politely, and he always said that he understood. Her heart was still with David, and Peter seemed to realize that.

The patients in District Eight were still the only patients who would allow Mike to treat them without her father or another physician looking on; trying to practice medicine as a female doctor continued to be frustrating.

Etha wrote of her relief that the war was over. She was practicing medicine alongside her husband, and she was content with that. Thank goodness, she said, because she doubted, as a woman physician, whether she could maintain a medical practice on her own. "But there is exciting news elsewhere. Remember Miriam Tilson from medical college? I received a letter from her. She has been in California practicing medicine independently. She reports that Alice is in Denver doing the same. People are more accepting of women doctors in the West, or so it seems. There, the journey between settlements might be days or weeks, and a doctor is a doctor, no matter the sex."

No matter the sex? That seemed almost unbelievable.

Michaela shared the news with her father, who expressed his amazement and excitement. "But you're not thinking of going West, are you?" he asked suspiciously.

"Oh, no," Mike teased. "Not as long as you remain in Boston. Besides, the West seems so distant and wild."

"It is that," he remarked.

Etha had included Miriam's address in her letter, and that evening Michaela sat and wrote her rival classmate a note. She was curious about the status of women doctors there, she said. She had heard from Etha that patients were more receptive.

At Massachusetts General the next day, after they finished lancing a boil on a woman's left leg, Peter Aldrich leaned Mike's way over a washbasin, and said, "All right, you won't have supper with me. Granted, my manners are not always what they should be. But I promise you, they are much better at things like poetry readings. Mr. Whittier will be at the Athenaeum next week. Please do me the honor of attending the reading with me," he said, and then he waited.

Michaela balked. "Dr. Aldrich, I—"

"I know, I know," he interrupted. "You're still very much in love with the memory of David Lewis. Attend as my friend then."

She agreed to do that.

Her mother saw her preparing to go out for the evening and became curious. "Someone new?" Elizabeth queried.

Michaela glanced up at her in the looking glass over the dressing table. Mother still, always, had hopes that she would marry and settle down to a family, stop her ridiculous practice of medicine. "A friend," Mike said.

"Oh? Who?" Elizabeth Quinn was dying of curiosity.

"Peter Aldrich."

"Oh . . . " Mother was pleased. Michaela could tell from her tone of voice and the brightness of her eyes. "A very nice man. I'll tell Martha she should go along."

Mike shook her head. "I'm thirty-three years old, Mother. I don't need a chaperon." A veritable spinster. Thirty-three years old and unmarried . . . Michaela hated that word—*spinster*—but that's what she was.

"Martha should go along," Elizabeth insisted.

"No," Michaela said firmly, glancing again at her mother in the looking glass.

Elizabeth sighed heavily. "You are entirely stubborn," she said as she walked away. "Will there ever come a day when we no longer quarrel?"

Their quarrels were less, actually. Mother, over the years, had quietly accustomed herself to the fact that Mike was bent on practicing medicine. Their relationship was better, less stormy. Even so, Michaela knew her mother would inquire about Dr. Aldrich every day, and that she would encourage the relationship in any way possible.

The poetry reading was pleasant. Whittier read from several selections, then he read "Snowbound," which described a blazing hearth, family members, sparkling snowbanks, a schoolmaster . . . a New England homestead buried in snow.

After the reading Peter and Michaela drank cider in a little shop on Washington Avenue. He had a mild manner about him that she found refreshing. He was at least ten years older than she, fair-haired with light blue eyes and a rather thin build. He had attended medical school in Connecticut and had then come to Boston with a friend and

318

elected to stay and practice medicine. Here he had be-friended her father, Dr. Holmes, and a host of other physicians. He had watched Michaela grow from a young girl into a woman. He had followed her progress over the years. He supported female physicians; in fact, in '51 he had helped sponsor the lectures that were held in Boston by the faculty of the Female Medical College.

Michaela enjoyed the time she spent with Peter Aldrich that evening. She liked talking to him. She felt relaxed with him. And although she had no interest in pursuing a romantic relationship at the moment—her heart really was still in pain over David's memory—she agreed to have supper with him the following week.

David was never far from Mike's mind when she read certain things in the local newspapers. That spring—the year was '66—a federal civil rights act was passed that granted citizenship to all persons born in the United States except Indians. If David were here, he would have another cause to fight, Michaela knew. He would take it up without blinking an eye, without hesitating. "Why shouldn't Indians be granted citizenship?" he would demand with fire in his eyes. And he would probably consider going to Washington, D.C. to speak to congressmen, senators, and President Johnson himself.

The following February, Michaela planned a surprise birth-day celebration for her father. He would soon turn sixty-four, and yet he still went off to the medical school every day. He also still called on patients with her at Massachusetts General and around the city. Her family, indeed everyone in Boston, had been so riveted on the war during those terrible years that birthdays and holidays had been neglected. Mike was determined that would not happen this year.

She had the cook make a huge cake, and despite the frigid temperature outside and the wintry conditions, she ordered ice cream from a shop on Tremont Street. She hired musi-cians, and then hired temporary servants for the evening to help the cook. She chose food and drinks, and the more she planned, the more excited she became.

She sent missives to her sisters, telling of the surprise party, then she visited each one to make certain they planned to attend with their husbands and children. She invited Peter, the Holmes family, the Lewises, the Beckers, and a number of other close friends. Mother shook her head but smiled when Mike had the halls and staircases strung with ribbon the afternoon of the party while Father was out.

Everyone began arriving, and Mike positioned them in the various rooms, then executed the next part of her plan: She sent a letter to the medical school, where she knew Dr. Holmes was delaying her father, and she asked her father to come home—and to bring Professor Holmes with him. The message might frighten Father nearly out of his skin, but Michaela could think of no other way to get him home. Sometimes he spent entire evenings at the school or at the hospital, and she didn't intend for that to happen this evening.

It wasn't long before the two men appeared. Mike watched them from a parlor window, both men with their top hats and what she knew was gray, almost silvery hair, beneath. Both men carried their walking sticks and medical bags. They wore dark woolen coats, and snow sprinkled their shoulders. Marjorie clamped a hand over Baby Owen's mouth, and Claudette told William to hush, that grandfather was coming and wouldn't be surprised if he suspected they were all here. Mother held one of Maureen's daughters and Rebecca rocked the other one, the sleeping infant, in her arms. That baby had been the surprise of all surprises—Maureen had thought herself too old and her body too changed to bear any more children. But then she had become pregnant.

Footsteps sounded in the hall. Dr. Holmes remarked that the house certainly was quiet—he wondered why they had been called here—and Michaela chose that moment to open the parlor door.

Everyone shouted *"Surprise!"* and after his wide eyes settled, Joseph Quinn's entire face lit with joy. Mike read his thoughts because she knew the meaningfulness of such a gathering to him . . . his family all under one roof again on his birthday. Nothing could be better. Nothing could make him happier.

The food was brought out. The musicians played. Father held almost every one of his grandchildren on his lap at different times during the course of the evening. He danced with his daughters and his granddaughters, slower than he once had, but he still danced. He danced with Claudette three different times—he had had a special fondness for her since their reunion—and then he urged Michaela into a slow waltz.

"This is *your* doing," he accused, his eyes sparkling as he glanced around the room, then back to her.

Mike smiled. "Ah, it is, is it? And who told you that?"

"No one. I know."

"Happy birthday, Papa," she said, using the name she had always called him as a girl.

"Tomorrow is *your* birthday, and what will we do?"

"Seeing you so happy is plenty enough," Michaela responded.

He danced with Mother next. Then he somehow got down on the floor to play with his grandsons. Holmes laughed at him, called him a doting grandfather.

"You're right, of course," Father said, then he warned Oliver that he had better not see a poem written in the *Atlantic Monthly* about an old man rollicking on the floor with his grandchildren.

If the children had not tired, the party might have gone on much longer than it did. But they were a variety of ages, and when many of them began yawning and rubbing sleepy eyes, their mothers decided to take them home.

"The party is at an end. It's past your bedtime, Joseph," Dr. Holmes teased.

"And when is yours, Oliver?" Father teased right back. "Sometimes I wonder if your mouth and brain ever sleep."

Professor Holmes shot him a playful scowl, then he went on his way.

People trickled out. The servants began cleaning, Mother went up to bed, and Michaela sat with her father in his study. Recently he had received the newest edition of the *New England Quarterly Journal of Medicine,* and they read several articles in it together—"To Tie or to Cauterize" and "Treating the Psychotic Patient."

The hour was late when he began nodding off. He often slept in his chair these days. It was comfortable, he said, whereas lying down was not always. Michaela kissed his cheek and told him she was going up to bed. He said he meant to smoke a little, then see about sleeping himself.

"Mike," he said, just as she started through the doorway.

She turned back.

He grinned at her. "That was quite an affair."

She laughed. "Happy birthday," she said again, then she left the room.

Later, someone's wailing woke her. Martha, she thought, scrambling out of bed. *What's the matter? What's happened? Why would anyone be crying so?* Michaela had no idea what time it was, whether it was still night or now morning.

She shot out of the room, not bothering to grab her wrap, and she took the stairs so fast she worried that she might fall. She reached the first floor and turned frantically, looking all around for the maid.

"It's your father!" Martha cried when she saw Michaela. The maid had just rushed out of the study. "Dr. Quinn . . . it's Dr. Quinn . . . Dr. Quinn . . . Mrs. Quinn sent for Dr. Holmes. Oh . . . it's your father!"

Mike asked no questions. She sped into the study, her hair streaming around her face, her breath caught in her throat. Mother stood near the fireplace, looking lost and pale. Father still sat in his chair. But his skin was gray, and Mike knew . . . Oh, dear God, she knew. . . .

"How does one die sitting in a chair?" Mother asked softly, in a state of total disbelief, and then she turned away.

Michaela approached her father. His pipe sat on the

nearby table. His journal sat, overturned, in his lap. He had passed quietly in his sleep, a smile still fixed on his mouth.

"Oh, no. Oh, Papa," she whispered, and she sank to her knees beside him.

21

It seemed impossible that the next day Michaela stood beside her father's coffin, looking down at the man who had been her friend, her confidant, her teacher, her colleague. . . . It seemed unreal that he didn't rise, open his eyes, embrace her, smile at her, that he didn't take up his medical bag and tell her to come along, that they had calls to make.

So many times as a little girl she had sat on his lap and read with him. She remembered him saving her box of specimens when Mother would have burned it. She remembered talking to him about Marjorie's severe dislike of her; he had listened, then told her she must love even those who disliked her and mistreated her, that everyone had redeeming qualities. She recalled coming downstairs to sit with him in the study some nights when she would have snuggled up to Rebecca and tried to fall asleep, only Rebecca had married and gone off.

She remembered him holding her hand, walking all around Beacon Hill with her . . . coming to the aid of the sick man in the Lynde Street house that night . . . not punishing her for sneaking out . . . telling her to be brave but never indifferent. He had promptly sent her off to school when she indicated to him that she wanted more education and that she wanted to go to medical school someday. She had worked for every good mark with him in mind, and she had been overjoyed when he had told her outright how proud he was of her.

She recalled walking the streets of Philadelphia with him, sitting in Dr. Elder's house with him when he volunteered to sponsor the Female Medical College—and knowing he did it mostly for her, so that his daughter who entertained medical aspirations could get a thorough education. He had encouraged her so, nourished her interest in medicine, never once ridiculed her, never once told her that she should forget the foolish nonsense going through her head and marry and settle down.

He had supported her no matter what, risking his professional reputation. And when she had returned from Philadelphia a degreed and licensed medical doctor and he had quietly realized that she couldn't survive as a physician without the aid of a male doctor, well, he had been there for that, too, just as quietly and proudly showing his support of her by taking her around with him, and always introducing her as his daughter, Dr. Quinn. *Dr. Mike,* he had sometimes called her, and they had shared many smiles over that.

The love between father and daughter had been unconditional, the respect between physicians profound. Only Michaela now realized that she had made a horrible mistake in one regard: She had never contemplated what life might be like without him.

"Papa," she whispered, touching the back of her hand to his cheek. She would miss him more than she could possibly miss anything or anyone else in her life. She already did.

"Michaela, you should be with the rest of us, accepting condolences from people who've come to see your father for the last time," her mother scolded from behind her. She was worried about appearances. What did they matter right now? Here Father lay, unmoving, *dead,* his eyes closed, his hands neatly folded. Soon he would be lowered into the ground, never to be seen again, and Mother was fretting over proprieties.

325

Until now Michaela scarcely had been aware of the people who trickled into the parlor, who spoke in low tones and occasionally flashed concerned looks her way. Now she saw people glance her way, whisper, and smile sadly at her.

Rebecca had been with her most of the day, of course. So had Claudette. Marjorie had commented that everyone died sooner or later, but even she had been fighting tears when she made the remark. Maureen had sobbed uncontrollably most of the morning. Mike felt stunned inside, in a state of total shock and disbelief.

"Michaela, our guests," Mother reprimanded again, stepping up beside the casket.

"I don't care," Mike said. "I've so little time left with him. There are things . . . matters I had hoped to discuss with him."

Elizabeth Quinn gasped, then a second passed in which she tried to compose herself. "Have you gone mad? He's dead, Michaela. Dead."

Fighting tears and a horrible ache in her breast, Mike nodded slowly. "I know."

Another second passed. Michaela imagined a light touch on her shoulder, perhaps a gesture of affection and understanding. But no . . . From Elizabeth Quinn? Such things had been rare between Mike and her. Sometimes Michaela was still convinced that her mother despised her, or at least disapproved of her. She was the daughter who always insisted on being unconventional. The daughter who always ignored her mother's advice to marry, settle, and have children, as every respectable woman did. Michaela did not want to be respected in that sense; she wanted to be understood. While she never had been against marrying and having a family, in her heart she did believe she should do so simply because her mother thought it was time. Rather, past time.

"Michae—"

"You greet them," Mike said, and she slipped her hand beneath her father's.

• • •

Days later, Michaela carried on, as she knew her father would have wanted her to do. She had patients in District Eight who were no doubt wondering where she was. She and her father had called regularly on certain patients around the city. And then there were those at Massachusetts General, many who came in off the streets and were assigned to doctors, and the ones she and her father had placed in the wards for various reasons.

She wore mourning garb, and as she strode down a dimly lit hospital corridor, Mike received stares from the nurses and other employees. Doubtless they were surprised to see her out so soon, especially back to work, following her father's death. But many knew her dedication to her patients and the profession, and so their obvious shock surprised her.

"Good morning, Mrs. Bauer," she greeted, approaching the nurses' desk and the woman who presently sat behind it. "Might I see my list of new patients? Also my father's. I'll be taking his patients, considering . . . considering the circumstances."

She placed her medical bag on one corner of the cluttered desk and reached for the clasp at her neck, preparing to remove her cloak. She shivered. "I believe the cold has gotten worse. There'll surely be more snow today. As if we've not had enough. Winter is beautiful, but by the time February arrives, I'm . . . Is something the matter, Mrs. Bauer?"

The older, plumpish woman still sat staring at Michaela. Color had risen in Mrs. Bauer's cheeks and her respiratory rate had increased. No doubt her heart was pounding.

The nurse placed her open hand on her chest. "Dr.—Miss Quinn. I'm so surprised. . . . So soon after Dr. Quinn's passing and yet here you are, come to see patients and I . . . How sorry I was to hear about Dr. Quinn! Such a fine physician and so loved by one and all . . . his patients."

The woman was acting positively odd. Instinct told Michaela that the shock of seeing her so soon after her father's death was not the only reason. And no nurse here at the hospital referred to her as "Miss Quinn" since she had earned her medical degree and received her appointment to the staff of this institution. "I'll pass your condolences on to my family. Thank you, Mrs. Bauer. The lists, please. I've a busy day ahead of me."

"There are no lists," Mrs. Bauer said in a rush, as if having to spit the words out before her flash of courage fled.

Michaela stared at the woman, apprehension clenching her stomach. She lowered her hand from the cloak clasp and curled her fingers around the handle of her medical bag. "I see. They've been misplaced?" There were always lists. The indigent and others poured into Massachusetts General, especially during the cold season.

Mrs. Bauer shook her head.

"Then where are they?"

"Dr. Quinn is deceased, and Dr. Channing . . ." Mrs. Bauer blinked, now avoiding Michaela's hard gaze. She twisted her lips, and finally wrung her hands over the desk. "Well, you're no longer on staff here, Miss Quinn. Dr. Channing and the board, they—"

"*Dr.* Quinn," Michaela corrected. No longer on staff? "*Why* am I no longer on staff?"

"Dr. Channing offered me no explanation. He simply came to me yesterday morning and said he and the board had voted . . . voted to replace you. Now that your father's gone, that is."

Outrage flooded Michaela. "I see. Well, I believe I'm due an explanation."

How dare the man! How dare the board! Like her mother, did the members assume that her father's death meant she would no longer practice medicine? Peter Aldrich was on that board. But then he had only one vote. Mike breathed deeply, attempting to calm herself inside. Her hands trembled.

"Dr. Quinn," Mrs. Bauer mumbled.

"Where is Dr. Channing?"

"Wha—? Oh." The woman swallowed. "He left a half hour ago, saying he was going to breakfast with Dr. Aldrich at the Tremont Hotel."

"Thank you."

Michaela snatched her bag from the desk and spun

around, heading back down the corridor, planning to pay Dr. Channing a visit, and not this afternoon or tomorrow either. *Now.*

"Dr. Quinn," Mrs. Bauer called, racing after her. "Don't go there. Give it up. Save yourself embarrassment and more pain. You'll gain nothing by confronting Dr. Channing." The woman planted herself in front of Michaela and shook her head. "Don't do this. Please, Dr. Quinn."

By now, Michaela was breathing harder, too. Absolute fury and disbelief raced through her veins and pounded in her head. No one would keep her from paying Dr. Channing a visit. No one and nothing. If a winter blizzard blasted Boston at this moment, she would fight her way through the storm to get at him.

"Remove yourself from my path, Mrs. Bauer," Mike said, her voice low. She held the woman's gaze, her chin tilted, her shoulders erect. She might be slight in stature, but even that hardly mattered at present.

Mrs. Bauer finally stepped aside, crossing herself, mumbling what sounded like a prayer under her breath.

Michaela had brought her father's buggy, and as she and her father always did, she had left it out in front of the hospital. She wasted no time tossing her bag on the seat, climbing up, and settling beside it, flicking the reins and setting off on the crooked cobblestone street.

People were out in force, despite the overall grayness of the day and the extreme chill in the air, wandering in and out of shops, carrying packages, riding in carriages. Reins jingled, icicles clung to awnings, horses whickered and snorted frosty breath. Michaela's gaze settled on the street ahead, and only when someone shouted did she realize that she had almost run a man down. She called an apology, watching the man to make certain he was only shaken up, not hurt, then she hurried on.

Presently she reined the buggy in front of the hotel and scrambled down from the seat, out of habit lifting her skirts to save the hems from dirt. Someone opened the hotel door for her; she was so intent on getting inside and finding Dr. Channing that she didn't stop even to thank the person.

She had been inside the Tremont Street Hotel a number of times, so she knew exactly where the dining room was. From the elegantly appointed lobby she turned left and strode down the hall. Another left into a large room and she was surrounded by tables and chairs and people.

She glanced around, spotting Dr. Channing within seconds. With determined strides she approached the table where he sat opposite Peter.

She greeted Peter, who nodded his acknowledgment and did her the courtesy of standing and offering her his chair if she wished to join them. She had no quarrel with him, and she declined the offer, thanking him politely. But Dr. Channing sat, appearing composed as he stirred a small lump of sugar into a cup of coffee.

"Dr. Channing," Michaela bit out. "I demand to know why I've been removed from the staff of Massachusetts General."

Seconds passed, though they seemed like long moments. Peter inhaled deeply. "Michaela, I tried—"

"Please," she told him. "I understand. I know you have only one vote."

"Miss Quinn, I advise setting aside a time when you and I might discuss this in private," Dr. Channing said, glancing up at her with one eye slightly squinted.

She squared her shoulders even more, tilted her head, and set her jaw. "I am Michaela Quinn, M.D., graduate of the Female Medical College of Pennsylvania. For years I worked alongside my father in his practice and at the medical institution where you are director. To my knowledge, there have been no complaints against me and—"

"Correction. There have been many."

"Impossible," she argued. "My patients hold me in high regard. They trust my medical knowledge and judgment."

"The people in District Eight who have no alternative?" he scoffed.

Mike drew a deep breath, for patience more than anything. "Again, Dr. Channing, I demand to know why I've been removed from the staff of Massachusetts General."

He studied her, his green eyes narrowing as he lifted his

cup and sipped coffee. Michaela swore he fought a grin. The insolence, the arrogance . . . If she had been raised any differently she might have considered knocking the cup from his hand. She was so furious, she trembled even worse now than when Mrs. Bauer had told her that the board had voted to remove her.

"Very well," he finally responded, lowering the cup. "If you insist on having an explanation here, in the middle of a busy hotel dining room."

"I do."

"Your father came to me when you graduated from that women's college and against my better judgment and that of numerous other board members, we added you to the staff. But mind you, only because your father was a physician of such excellent repute. A number of us felt you would be a hindrance and even a distraction. What woman enters the medical field? I asked. What woman has the mind to? The occasion of your father's death is a sad one, but the opportunity was there to fill both his and your positions with two excellent physicians who recently arrived in Boston. Yesterday the board voted to do exactly that."

Michaela stood speechless, and Dr. Channing sat looking smug and self-satisfied, enjoying her shock, perhaps waiting for her—a woman—to burst into tears. And if she stood here too long beside him, a man who obviously thought women existed only to wipe his boots and fetch his slippers, she very well might burst into tears.

"How dare you," she finally managed. "I'm as good, if not better, a physician than any male doctor. The nurses, my patients, and other physicians trust my judgment and knowledge."

"Do they really? We shall see. In the coming days, we shall see."

"How dare you question my abilities based on the fact that I'm a woman?"

"Nurses, my dear Michaela, are taught to do doctors' bidding without question. Patients trusted you only because your father was always there looking on when you treated them. As for physicians' faith in you . . . If you glanced

331

into a mirror even once you would realize that the physicians were there only to be in the presence of a handsome woman, not because you have remarkable medical judgment and knowledge."

"That is enough," Peter said, standing as he stared in obvious horror at Dr. Channing.

"I treated patients many times when my father was not about," Mike argued.

"Only because they knew he was close at hand if complications arose."

"Michaela," Peter said gently. "We'll leave. We'll—"

"Dr. Quinn," Michaela virtually shouted.

People were beginning to stare. Mike breathed deeply. She shouldn't be taking her frustrations out on Peter. She wondered for the first time at what, exactly, she had hoped to gain by coming here. She had sensed Dr. Channing's dislike a long time ago. Her instincts had been right, and since that was how things stood there was no point in having this confrontation; he was not about to change his mind and try to convince the board to appoint her to the staff again.

She could argue more, asking how he could do this to her father, attempt to ruin the medical career of the daughter Joseph Quinn had treasured. But Michaela had long ago stopped using her father and his upstanding reputation as a crutch. She had to stand on her own. Somehow, some way.

"Dr. Aldrich," she said in a much lower tone, "my apologies for interrupting your meal." Michaela turned away from the table, preparing to leave the dining room and the hotel.

"No, wait," he said. "I'm going with you."

"If you are counting on your father's patients to become yours, think again," Dr. Channing warned Mike. "They've already started drifting to other physicians."

Michaela fought tears. He might be right, at least about the patients who had never allowed her to examine or treat them without her father looking on.

First David, then her father . . . On top of those two losses, Mike couldn't bear the thought of losing her standing as a doctor in the community. Why did Dr. Channing hate her so? Simply because she was a woman? Because he felt threatened by her? There was no need for that. She'd not entered the medical field to prove she could do what any man could do. She'd entered it because she loved medicine and because she loved helping people.

She didn't look back. Her head held high, she walked alongside Peter from the dining room and the hotel. He handed her up into the buggy, then he climbed up beside her, took the reins, and clicked the horse into motion. Soon they turned the corner, then another, and another.

At the town house, Peter handed her down. "Should I stay for a while?" he queried.

"Thank you, but no," she said, forcing a smile. "I plan to lie down. I'll have someone take you home."

Harrison took care of doing that, thank goodness, because Michaela suddenly felt so tired, she wondered if she could climb the staircase to the second floor.

She brushed past her mother on the stairs, who had just spotted Peter and pasted a smile on her face on her way down to greet him. If the household weren't still in mourning, Mother would be inviting him to supper. She always did. Only this time, she had to settle for fawning over him, commenting on how wonderful he looked and that it was so nice of him to bring Michaela home—she should never have gone out, after all, considering her emotional state right now.

Mike continued up the staircase, finally reaching the second floor and closing herself in her room. Relative quiet. Thank God. She leaned back against the bedroom door and dropped her face into her hands. Then the tears spilled.

She had been removed from the staff.

It was a blow, a huge blow she felt in her stomach and her chest. Professionally it might mean disaster. Doctors either resigned if they planned to move on, or they left one hospital for another if dissatisfied with the institution. Only those whose ethics, techniques, and dedication were in question were *removed*. Or so Michaela had read. She had never heard personally of any physician being removed from staff by a board vote. When other medical institutions in Boston heard of this, Michaela Quinn, M.D. would be turned away from doorsteps.

She angrily brushed the tears from her cheeks. Surely Dr. Channing was wrong about the patients. She had treated them with her father so many times that by now they surely trusted her. She would call on every one over the next week and make certain the fact was established that although her father had passed away, she planned to continue treating the patients they had always seen together. She would start this afternoon, as soon as Peter left and Mother put her attention on something else. She would dry up her tears, march back downstairs, and climb right back into that buggy.

Which is exactly what she did.

"Mrs. Lindsay, I only want to make certain the stubs are healing properly," Mike assured as the woman peered out at her through a partially opened front door. Snow swirled around Michaela's head and the icy wind bit her cheeks. She gripped the front of her cloak, pulling the garment more snugly around her. Father had amputated the first two fingers of Anna Lindsay's left hand only two days before his death, after the fingers had been crushed beneath a trunk and infection had set in.

"Dr. Seidel's been tending them for me," Mrs. Lindsay responded. "I didn't know what to think, with Dr. Quinn gone now."

"I'll be tending our patients on my own," Michaela assured. "I've decided to—"

"On your own?"

Michaela nodded. The woman might at least let her come in and warm herself by the fire.

"Dr. Seidel's tending me," Mrs. Lindsay said again, only this time Michaela knew Anna was talking about her overall care. In the future, Dr. Seidel would be taking care of any medical problems she might have.

"I see," Mike said. "Very well, then. Should you need my services in the future, Mrs. Lindsay, please do not hesitate to—"

"I won't be needing them."

Michaela let that go. She turned and walked down the steps. Anna Lindsay was only one patient—and only the first she had called on. There were others, many others.

The rest of the day went the same. Patients were reluctant to speak with her, reluctant to open their doors to her, reluctant to let her examine them. If they let her examine them at all—most refused. Adam Stewart would not let her anywhere near his wife, who was now in her eighth month of pregnancy. Lee Gregory allowed her to inspect the thigh wound her father had stitched a little more than a week before, but when she took a pair of surgical scissors from her bag and told him it was time to remove the stitches, he stopped her there, saying he'd prefer to get a second opinion. She and her father together had repaired Rebecca Woods's rectal fistula, but now, like Anna Simms, Rebecca had sought the services of another physician.

"I didn't know if you'd keep going," Rebecca said apologetically. "You know, at the doctoring."

"Why wouldn't I?" Mike queried.

Shrugging, Rebecca drew her knitted shawl more closely about her shoulders, as if to ward off a chill Michaela had brought. "It doesn't seem normal, that's all."

"I'll always be a doctor, Mrs. Woods. Make no mistake about that. I attended medical college, one that is more thorough than most, and I have a medical license."

Rebecca nodded. Michaela took her bag, climbed back into her buggy, and went on to the next patient. Two weeks ago she and her father had removed a large bladder stone from Glenda York, and Mike hoped that Mrs. York would be strong enough now, following the surgery, that she could remove the remaining stone.

Mrs. York would have none of that, and neither would her husband—at least not from Michaela. Mike examined Glenda, but the minute she said that the other stone should be removed as soon as possible, Glenda paled and asked if Michaela knew a physician who would be willing to do the surgery.

"Myself," Mike said, trying not to sound insulted.

"Are—are you sure?"

"Don't fret now, Glenda, we'll find one, a good one," Mr. York said, squeezing his wife's shoulders from behind.

"Mr. York, I'm a competent surgeon," Michaela insisted.

"I didn't say you weren't. But isn't it a patient's right to choose his own doctor?"

"The patient is your wife."

"That's right, and I think she'd feel more comfortable with a different doctor."

"Mrs. York, what are your thoughts?" Mike asked.

The woman hesitated, studying her hands for a time. Then she lifted her gaze to Michaela's. "I'd like to see someone else just to be sure."

Mike nodded slowly, feeling her heart sink. She should not feel insulted. Indeed, getting a second opinion was a patient's right.

The days and the visits continued much the same, and by the end of the second week, Michaela had only a handful of paying patients left. Four, to be exact. One with improving pneumonia, one with severe gout, one who had recently discovered that she was pregnant, and one with a heart condition, an arrhythmia that seemed to be responding nicely to digitalis. District Eight was always open to her. But if she ever wanted complete independence, and that included financial independence, she couldn't practice medicine in only District Eight.

"What do I do?" she asked of no one in particular one afternoon as she stood at a parlor window. Peter was here. They had shared tea and little sweet cakes Mother had eagerly brought from the kitchen. Restless, Mike had walked to the window to stare out at the activity on Mount Vernon Street.

"Join my practice," he suggested without hesitation. He knew of her frustrations. He knew that many of her patients had turned away from her. "What Dr. Channing and the other board members did to you was unfair. Despicable. Yes, you're a woman, but you are also a physician, a fine one. Join my practice, Michaela. We'll share patients. I've so many of late, the work is exhausting me. And many . . . many of the newer ones were yours and your father's."

Mike closed her eyes, took a deep breath, then watched the activity in the street again. But blankly, without any thought of anything that was happening beyond this room. It would be so easy, joining his practice, not fighting for patients as she had been doing for nearly two weeks now, sharing in medicine with someone who respected her opinions as much as Father had. Oh, for the ease of it all again. And yet she didn't want to hide behind another cloak. She didn't want to trail in anyone's path. She was a medical doctor, and she shouldn't have to be anyone's shadow.

Michaela stared at the snowflakes on the panes, at the powder piled on the steps, beside stoops, and around lamp posts on the opposite side of the street. Another Boston winter, so cold yet so serene . . . Father had loved winter, and he was missing the last few months of this one. Whenever Michaela allowed thoughts like that to creep into her head, she experienced moments of great sadness.

She felt sad all the time lately. She saw her father everywhere—at the medical school, in the carriage house, strolling through the Common. She saw David and Jimmie, too; David in the library, where he had proposed the second time, Jimmie skidding along Mount Vernon Street on his way up to Charles. She had found herself traveling along Lynde Street one day, and the sight of the house where the three of them had found the ill man had made her burst into tears. It had been purchased by someone and refurbished, but when she looked at it she saw the same house that she, Jimmie, and David had sneaked into that night. Whenever she went to the Irish tenements in the warehouse district and saw the Charles River she wanted to cry. How many times had she, Jimmie, and David fished in that river? Jimmie and David had left Boston a number of times during the past years, but now they were really gone, never to return again. Etha was gone, too. *Change* . . . Why did life have to change so?

She watched several passersby dip their heads and bury their chins in their wraps. So alive, moving along. A young man skidded playfully on a patch of ice and managed to stop within inches of an approaching carriage. But what if he hadn't been able to stop? Some things were within one's control; others were not. She hadn't been able to stop David from enlisting in the Union army and from applying for a commission. Jimmie's and her father's death certainly had been beyond her control. And now, here she was, floundering.

"What if you died tomorrow, Peter?" she asked suddenly, watching the carriage driver jump down, shake a finger at the boy and give him a tongue-lashing.

"What?" Peter responded. "I rarely wonder about that."

Smiling sadly, Michaela glanced at him over her shoulder. "Not many of us do. Even as wonderful a man as my father was, he didn't. Well, I suppose he did at times, long enough to write a will and to instruct Mother in the event something ever did happen to him. Perhaps he even anticipated where my medical career was concerned. Certainly no one expects to live forever, although most of us hope we'll live to a ripe age. My father respected me as a physician, but I know he had another thought in mind when he asked me to join his practice. With his backing, other physicians and their patients would surely come to respect me as a doctor, despite the fact that I'm a woman. But he was wrong. They respected him, not me." She turned back to the window. "While I'm flattered by your offer, I must decline it."

She sensed him move from the settee where he sat, felt his warmth when he joined her where she stood.

"You're a woman of profound character and judgment, Michaela Quinn," he remarked gently.

She gave a short laugh. "What a spectacle I made of myself in that hotel dining room."

"No, no." He shook his head. "I admired you more than ever during those moments."

The carriage driver had moved on. The young man continued frolicking on the ice and soon a boy joined him. Michaela smiled at their muffled shouts of glee.

"I received a letter from my classmate yesterday," she said. "Miriam Tilson . . . the one who went off to California and found patients there in a small town where she

338

happens to be the only physician. I told you about her, didn't I?"

Peter nodded.

"No ill or injured person turns her away because she's a woman," Mike said. "Of course, she's the only doctor for miles. But that's another thing. Boston is overflowing with physicians, Peter. Have you ever considered that? Have you ever considered going somewhere else to practice?"

He didn't answer; he stared at her instead.

She gave a small laugh. "Well, of course not. You haven't a need to. But I, Peter . . . I've thought about that of late. I've considered it almost since the day Etha wrote and told me about Miriam and one of my other classmates. Dr. Reynolds from right here in Boston went west last year because western settlers are in dire need of doctors."

Peter tipped his head and narrowed his eyes. "Michaela, what are you thinking?"

She laughed. "Nothing, really. Well, I was considering. But I'm not sure. . . . I've been beyond Boston so rarely."

"Exactly."

"That doesn't mean I couldn't venture off," she said.

"I wasn't challenging you," he teased.

Mike watched the boy spin around and around. She glanced at Peter again. "Your offer is flattering, but I really must decline. I must stand on my own as a physician."

He smiled. "I understand. Will I see you at the Athenaeum this evening?"

She'd forgotten all about the weekly lecture. She had missed the last one, understandably, but going this evening might lift her spirits.

"Of course," she said, walking with him to the parlor door and then beyond.

In the entryway, he gave her one last smile just before slipping back out into the cold as inconspicuously as he had arrived.

Mother joined Mike in the parlor moments later, pouring tea and wanting to know about her visit with Dr. Aldrich.

"A colleague, nothing more," Mike told her, as she had

339

many times. Then she added, "He asked me to join his practice."

Elizabeth Quinn froze with the silver pitcher in hand. "And your response was?"

"No, of course." Michaela dipped her head. "I couldn't possibly."

That delighted Mother, no doubt. She continued pouring the tea, composed once again. "You've no idea how relieved I am to hear that. I hear your father's patients are going to other physicians."

"They were my patients, too," Mike said, more sharply than she intended. She wouldn't tolerate her mother reveling in her failure.

Elizabeth dared not respond to that. "Mr. Bowen is coming to supper this evening, but only in the capacity of legal counsel, mind you. Entertaining him as a guest in any other capacity so soon after your father's death would be unseemly. Although he would be perfect for you. I know Dr. Aldrich has been calling, but perhaps seeing someone other than a physician might do you some good."

Michaela rose from the wing chair in which she had sat upon returning to the parlor and began pacing before the hearth. The fire popped and glowed behind a brass screen. She stopped suddenly and turned on her mother. "Do you miss Father?" She asked the question without compassion, with haughtiness, in challenge.

Mother's eyes widened. "What a horrible thing to ask me."

"I don't think so. You've hardly missed a step. We put him in his grave and you immediately began working on marrying me off again. Your delight at the fact that most of our patients have drifted off is far too evident. Do you feel, Mother? Have you ever shed a tear for anyone? Do you miss him at all? Do you care about *me* and what *I* want for my life?"

Elizabeth's hand trembled as she lowered the pitcher to the service tray and stood. Her eyes glittered with anger. "How dare you, Michaela Quinn? Marjorie seems to be the only daughter of mine who is not clenched by grief right

340

now. Even you, whether or not you realize it. The grand-children ask for Joseph every day, I'm told, and no one seems capable of talking to them with dry eyes. Every member of this family needs strength right now, and I am that strength."

That quieted Mike, made her thoughtful. She felt so discomposed inside, losing David, losing Father, losing her staff position at Massachusetts General—a fact she had not yet revealed to Mother—losing many of her patients to other physicians because they did not trust a woman doctor. Her mother was right, she held this family together right now during this horrible time of grief. Mike had had no right to attack her verbally.

"I apologize. I'm so frightened, Mother," Michaela admitted, her voice almost a whisper. "I wish I had a portion of your strength." She fought tears again; she seemed forever to fight tears lately.

To her surprise, her mother reached out, squeezed her hand, and smiled at her. "I've seen the same strength in you many times, Michaela."

Mike managed to smile back. Then she glanced at the fire. "Mr. Bowen coming for supper . . . I plan to attend the weekly lecture at the Athenaeum this evening."

"But you'll surely need to eat something beforehand."

Michaela shook her head. "I've had no appetite."

"You will soon," Mother said, and she sat back on the settee and sipped from a teacup.

22

Two opulent mansions had been joined to form the Athenaeum, and the amphitheater where the medical lecture was always held was located on the second floor of one of the mansions. It was swarming with physicians this evening, men clad in dark cloaks and hats, suits of broadcloth beneath. Clusters of doctors formed here and there, and many a brow lifted at the sight of Michaela, at her appearance alone at the lecture. She had always attended with her father. Dr. Channing and his staff might be able to exclude her from treating patients at Massachusetts General, but she was an upstanding member of the Boston Medical Society and no one could keep her from attending a lecture. No one.

She was in the process of unfastening her cloak to hand it over to an attendant when the nearby conversation of a group of doctors snared her interest.

". . . imagine advertising for a doctor?"

"Uncouth!"

"What is surprising about that, gentlemen? If Colorado Springs needs a physician, how else are the townspeople going to find one? They are in the middle of a group of mountains, from what I've heard."

"True. But when one considers the fact that there is surely no hospital or medical institution within hundreds of miles of Colorado Springs, and that the territory, like most of the western territories, is filled with criminals and Indians . . . Well, any doctor who ventures that way will surely spend every hour of the day removing bullets. When he's not ducking them!"

Laughter rose from the group.

"What was the editor of the *Globe* thinking when he decided to print the advertisement? That a Boston physician might get it in his head to answer such a plea? Why, even to pay for such an advertisement, the paupers of Colorado Springs must have had to save for a year!"

More laughter.

Michaela saw no humor in the statements. A pauper or a rich man, a patient was a patient.

"Michaela," Peter greeted, stepping up beside her. "I was beginning to think I wouldn't find you this evening. May I?" he asked, reaching for her cloak.

Smiling, Mike nodded her consent. He lifted the cloak from her shoulders and handed it to the attendant.

"Have you heard about the advertisement in the *Globe*?" Michaela couldn't help but ask Peter.

He lifted a brow. "I have. You're not considering it?"

"Why shouldn't I?" she queried as they moved through the crowd. "You know I'm interested in what I've been hearing about the opportunities for physicians in the West. I've been made to feel very unwelcome in Boston by my colleagues since Father's death. Not to mention the fact that I now have only four patients. A certain level of frustration—"

"Three," Peter said. "Three patients."

Mike stopped midstep and spun to face him. "What do you mean?"

"I was called to the home of Robert Doyle shortly after I left you this afternoon. You apparently had been treating him for pneumonia."

"Yes. He was doing well when I left him yesterday evening. He was much improved."

"He expired two hours ago."

Michaela wasn't sure how long she stood staring at Peter. Physicians filed past them into the amphitheater to take seats.

"He was—" Mike swallowed. "He was in no respiratory distress when I left him yesterday. No fever. I swear to you, Peter, he was better."

"I believe you. He had a sudden turn for the worse this afternoon."

"And the family wanted a second opinion?"

Peter nodded.

"To lose a patient is horrible enough," Michaela said under her breath. "To lose one now, when my reputation, my medical judgment . . . everything is in question, is unspeakable. When word of this makes the rounds, I'll have no patients at all."

"Would you like to skip the lecture and go have a cup of hot cider instead?" he asked.

"No, I . . . I came to hear the lecture."

Nodding, he motioned her toward the amphitheater doors. Feeling almost numb with shock, Michaela walked that way.

Once inside the theater, she did not miss the numerous disapproving gazes that fastened on her, nor did she miss the fact that every seat was already occupied and that not one man moved to give his up for her. Very well, she didn't want differential treatment. But clearly her colleagues were not just being rude to a lady; they were being rude to a woman physician whom they found threatening. They did not want her here, or anywhere in Boston, perhaps not even in the entire state of Massachusetts. Clearly if she wanted to continue being a doctor, she would have to do something drastic.

Then and there she made up her mind: She meant at least to have a look at the Colorado Springs advertisement for a physician.

"Not one gentleman in the house," Peter commented through gritted teeth.

Michaela tossed him a gentle smile. "I beg to differ. There is one."

He smiled back.

Her fear about losing the three patients she had left was not unfounded. When she called on Mr. Parker, the man with gout, he refused to open his door. Mrs. Richards sent a missive to inform Michaela that she had retained the services of another doctor. And Mr. Frazier, her patient with the arrhythmia, patted her hand and smiled kindly while telling her that Dr. Aldrich had agreed to call on him twice a week—although Aldrich had spoken highly of her and told the patient that he was releasing a fine medical doctor.

That afternoon, after calling on Mr. Frazier, Michaela walked into her family's house and went directly to her father's study, a room she had not entered since his death. She searched around the top of his desk. Not finding what she was looking for, she hurried back out into the hall, calling for Harrison. A moment passed before the butler appeared.

"Miss Michaela, what is it?" he asked. "You sound frantic."

"I very well might be in a moment. The *Globe*, Harrison. Father always subscribed. Does it still come? What about this week's? You used to place them on his desk. I don't see one."

Harrison looked surprised, both brows lifted. "There's hardly been time to cancel it. Mrs. Quinn instructed me to get rid of it."

"Oh." Michaela gripped the sides of her skirt and grimaced. "Oh, no. Where did you put it, Harrison?"

"I gave it to Fiona. By now, she's probably already burned it in the kitchen fire." Fiona was the scullery maid.

"Tell me you didn't!"

"But I did, Miss Michaela."

Mike lifted the hem of her skirts and tore past Harrison and down the hall.

Fiona was seated before the hearth when Mike raced into

the kitchen, and she was feeding the fire with the end of a twirled paper—undoubtedly this week's issue of the *Globe*.

"Stop!" Michaela fairly screeched. She shot across the room, bumping into the side of the huge oak cutting table, knocking over utensils and dishes and scaring the kitchen tabby cat. The animal hissed at her, then bounded up from the hearth onto the top of a nearby cupboard.

Mike snatched the paper from a baffled-looking Fiona and stomped on the fiery end of it until she had killed the flames. Fiona's eyes were twin saucers in her face.

"Never fear. I haven't gone mad. I really haven't," Michaela assured the girl breathlessly as she plopped herself on the hearth bricks beside Fiona and commenced to untwirl the paper. She lowered her voice. "There's an advertisement somewhere in here for a doctor in Colorado Springs."

"Colorado Springs?" Fiona blurted. "Why, Miss Michaela, that's way out West. You're not thinking of—"

"I most certainly am. Lower your voice," Michaela scolded. "I can't practice medicine at Massachusetts General anymore, and as of an hour ago, I no longer have a single paying patient in Boston. How am I supposed to survive? I hear doctors are needed in the West, sorely needed, and I plan to go where I'm needed. My father would agree. I know he would. He would be outraged that people are standing in the way of my practicing what's in my heart, and what I'm degreed and licensed to do."

Mike blew ashes from the paper and began scanning the type. "I don't imagine *they'll* mind that I'm a woman. I didn't attend medical school to entertain afternoon guests in the parlor with tea and sweet cakes. I didn't work for years alongside my father to sit and knit and gossip and attend social events. I gave up parties so I could learn about medicine, so I could learn to preserve human life, and if there is a place where— Here it is! Look, Fiona. I found it!"

Michaela placed the paper on the hearth and smoothed it with her fingers. Then she began reading. "Wanted. Doctor for the town of Colorado Springs, Colorado Territory. Urgent response requested by telegram!"

"Oh . . . my . . . lord," Fiona whispered, clapping a hand to her cheek. "Miss Michaela, you are serious."

Mike laughed. "Quite serious. I now feel better than I have in weeks, too."

"Whatever will Mrs. Quinn say?" Harrison asked from the doorway.

Michaela crumpled the paper and tossed it into the fire herself. Then she approached Harrison and the doorway, smiling, actually smiling. "She'll not have anything to say until I tell her what I intend to do. Then, rest assured, she'll have plenty to say." She laughed. "Well, at least I haven't ground mud into any carpet this time."

Harrison broke into a smile at that, and as Michaela strode up the hall, she heard Fiona's girlish laughter.

When she woke the next morning, she wasn't quite as sure anymore of what she wanted to do. She called on Dr. Holmes at the medical school, and found him making notes in his small office.

"You are awfully troubled lately, Dr. Mike," he said fondly, making her smile. He waved his pen at her. "Do not think to fool me. Wendell tries when something at school is troubling him, and he never succeeds." When the war ended, Wendell had made up his mind to attend law school, and he currently was working diligently toward becoming the country's finest attorney.

Michaela took the empty chair opposite the professor's desk. "I miss my father," she said, suddenly fighting tears.

Holmes was quiet for a moment as he studied her. "I know. How can one not miss such a great man?" No cleverness, no humor. Just a simple but elegant statement.

Mike wiped her eyes with a handkerchief. "There was an advertisement in the *Globe* for a doctor in the—"

"Town of Colorado Springs," he said. "Boston physicians think they are too good for the frontier."

Michaela took a deep breath. "What would you say, Dr. Holmes, if I told you I've considered responding to the advertisement?"

347

He studied her more. "Physicians should go where they are needed—David went to the battlefield."

Mike considered that. The statement prompted a sad smile. "Yes, he did, didn't he?"

Holmes continued. "I would say, as I have always said about you, that you are courageous. If I did not think you were one of the best physicians in this nation, I would not have allowed you to perform surgery on my son. Colorado Springs will be a fortunate little town if you go there."

How he flattered her! The charming Dr. Holmes. Michaela's face warmed as she glanced down at her hands.

"I'm not indulging you, Dr. Quinn. I speak the truth."

She glanced up at him. "I'll miss you if I go."

He grinned. "I *will* expect letters from time to time."

"Of course," she said, laughing a little.

"Filled with details of frontier medicine. Medical conditions there will be far different than here, Michaela. You can order medicines, but they may take weeks and months to reach you. And you will surely encounter other difficulties."

She nodded. She had already considered those things. She shook her head at herself. "I remember when gold was discovered in California and then in the Colorado Territory. I thought people were mad the way they were dashing off by wagon and train, going to some foreign place in search of—"

"Riches. But not everyone who has gone West has gone for gold," Holmes said. "Many have gone for opportunity."

He was right, of course. It seemed he was forever right.

He leaned forward, looking at her intently. "If conditions are intolerable or the situation simply does not work, you can always come home."

Going to Colorado Springs and practicing medicine there was the biggest thing Mike had ever considered doing, and the thought of it frightened her more than she cared to admit. She knew she could come home if the conditions there were intolerable. But she had a certain amount of pride, and when she decided to do something she did so with an inordinate amount of resolve. If she went to Colorado Springs she would not return to Boston a failure. She would

348

return to Boston to visit her family and to discuss her success.

She stood, holding her bag in front of her. "I'm going to the telegraph office," she announced, although she felt stiff and unsure of herself.

"Should I accompany you?"

Mike jumped at that. "Yes, I would—" She caught herself. She had sought Dr. Holmes's advice as a colleague and a friend. But actually sending the telegraph . . . She adored the professor, but sending the telegraph was something she needed to do by herself. "Thank you, but no. I have to learn to stand alone."

He grinned again as he stood to walk her out.

The trip to the telegraph office was a short one. Mike allowed herself no more doubt. She climbed down from her buggy, marched into the office, and wrote out a simple message: "I am interested in your position of town doctor." She signed the note "Michaela Quinn, M.D.," then she handed it to the telegraph operator. If the townspeople had any trouble digesting the thought of a woman physician, surely they would respond soon and say so.

"How long before it's sent?" she asked the operator.

"Right away," he said.

After paying the telegram fee, Mike walked back outside. The March air was frigid, and she pulled her cloak closer about her body, then lifted her skirts and climbed up into the buggy.

She went home from there and spent the day waiting. She walked into her father's study for the first time since his death. She ran her hand over his journals, over the leather binding on his medical books. In his will he had left them all to her. Everything in this room. "To my daughter Michaela, I leave any and all possessions pertaining to the science of medicine—all books, journals, medicines, supplies, and instruments." He had left her other things—his financial interest in the Tremont Street Medical School and several properties he owned in other areas of Boston. But having his medical books and journals was more meaningful than anything.

She sat in the very chair where he had died that terrible morning, and she spoke to him. She told him that she was considering the position of town doctor in the settlement of Colorado Springs, that all of their patients had slowly drifted away from her and that she couldn't be happy unless she was practicing medicine. She knew he understood that. She related Dr. Holmes's advice to her, and then she laughed through her tears and told her father how frightened she'd been marching into the telegraph office and sending the message.

She settled back in his chair and read again the last few medical articles they had read together, and as she did, a sense of peace settled over her. She glanced around at his study. She felt his presence here, but as with the books and other things in this room, she also felt it could be moved; no matter where she went, he would be with her. All the things he had said to her over the years, all of his gentle guidance, his mannerisms, his professionalism . . . all those things were in her head and no one and nothing could ever take them away. With that realization, a sense of peace began to settle over her.

His medical bag sat on his desk, and she approached it with a sense of reverence. The leather was creased and cracked in places. The handle was worn. She stared at the bag, realized that she was the new Dr. Quinn, and then she picked it up and carried it back with her to the chair.

She held the bag in her lap, leaned her head against one wing of the chair, and there she drifted off to sleep.

The following day she told Peter she had sent the telegram. He looked a little sad for a moment, then he smiled brightly. He had entertained hopes for the two of them, Mike thought. But she thought of him as only a friend and she doubted that she could ever think of him as more. That evening she dashed off a letter to Etha, telling her that she had sent the telegram, and then the following morning she rushed off to see Rebecca.

"Mike, *Colorado Territory?*" Rebecca blurted.

350

"Think of her as a doctor right now, not as your sister," Marcus, her husband, suggested gently.

"As a physician, there is nothing left for me here," Michaela said.

Her sister had paled. "What about New York or Philadelphia?"

Mike shook her head. "Both cities are swarming with physicians. Besides, as a female doctor, I would face the same opposition there."

"When you told me about Miriam's letter I never dreamed you were thinking of traveling west!"

"Physicians go where they're needed," Mike said, repeating Dr. Holmes's words.

Rebecca grabbed her and embraced her. "I'll worry about you."

"I must be what I was trained to be."

"I know," Rebecca said, and then she pulled away and shook her head at her sister. "From the day you were born, I knew you were a different sort of girl."

"And you were right." They laughed together and embraced again, then Rebecca poured tea and wondered aloud how their mother would take this news.

A response to Mike's telegram arrived some three days later. She was in the study again when someone knocked on the door. It was Harrison, and he held a piece of paper. The normally austere man grinned as Michaela snatched the paper from him and opened it. She turned away to read it. Seconds later, she turned back to him.

"Well, Miss Michaela?"

"They—they want me as soon as possible," she said. Then she laughed. "Harrison, *they want me as soon as possible.*"

His smile widened. "Of course they do, Miss Michaela."

"Who wants you as soon as possible?" Mother asked from the doorway.

Mike couldn't imagine how she, Rebecca, Harrison, and Fiona had managed to keep their secret from Mother for this long. Michaela glanced at Harrison, who was suddenly austere again, at least outwardly. Then she turned her full attention on her mother.

"I answered an advertisement for a doctor," Mike explained, her heart beating faster. "The townspeople want me to come as soon as possible."

Mother stared at her. "You're leaving Boston?"

Michaela nodded.

"Where are you going?"

Mike swallowed. "To . . . to the Colorado Territory."

Mother's mouth fell open slightly. She stared at Michaela for the longest time, saying nothing, obviously trying to determine if Michaela was serious.

"They need a doctor, and I—"

Mother spun around and exited the study. Her heels clicked all the way up the hall, then quieted.

Mike wasn't sure why she had even tried to explain; her mother had never been interested in explanations where she and medicine were concerned. Perhaps she had hoped to ease the stricken look on Mother's face.

"When will you be leaving, Miss Michaela?" Harrison queried.

"I'm not sure yet," Michaela answered softly. "After the spring thaw begins."

He nodded, then started off.

"Please send Martha up to look in on Mother after a while," Mike suggested.

"I will," Harrison said, and then he was gone.

When Claudette heard the news, she, as always, thought Mike was amazing. Maureen was startled, like Rebecca, but she slowly accustomed herself to the thought of Michaela going away. Although she and Rebecca both remained skeptical, they respected Mike's desire to practice medicine and they realized that she couldn't do that here in Boston. She would be back to visit, she told them. They were her sisters, her family, after all, and she didn't plan to leave and forget them. She loved them so much she couldn't do that even if she wanted to.

Marjorie told Michaela outright that she had always known

she was a little mad, but certainly now she had gone completely mad. How could she even think of doing such a thing to Mother so soon after Father's death? Leaving her when she knew it would devastate her.

"Mother expects to run my life," Michaela finally snapped at Marjorie. "I won't allow anyone to do that."

Marjorie informed her that she was ungrateful, that she had always been ungrateful, and then she stomped away, her perfect curls bouncing on her shoulders.

Mother barely spoke to Michaela during the following weeks. Mike began packing what medical books she wanted to have shipped. She also packed medicines, bottles, other supplies, and equipment. Martha helped her pack clothes and other personal belongings.

Michaela planned to go through Philadelphia and see Etha, and she had written Etha weeks ago about her plans. She couldn't wait to see Etha and talk to her in person; she couldn't wait to get to Colorado Springs and actually feel no animosity simply because she was a female doctor.

She left Boston in April. The air was warm enough that the rain did not turn to ice as it fell. Rebecca, Claudette, Maureen, Peter, and Dr. Holmes accompanied her to the train station. Rebecca and Claudette both cried. Maureen hugged Michaela so tightly Mike thought she might break in two. Peter held her hand for an inordinate amount of time and said he knew no other woman like her. Dr. Holmes simply grinned and said, "Remember your promise to write, Dr. Quinn." She told him she certainly would, and then she boarded the train.

Mike sat in a window seat, and minutes later the train puffed, lurched, and pulled away from the platform. She lifted her hand and waved at her sisters and friends. They became smaller and smaller as the train belched and gained speed, and then they disappeared altogether.

She settled back against the seat, clutching her father's medical bag, *her* medical bag. She wondered at the sadness in her breast, and then the next minute, at the excitement and anticipation crawling beneath her skin. Behind her loomed the city in which she had been born and raised, in which she had spent so many years loving, respecting, admiring, and being tutored by her father; the city in which she had almost married. Ahead lay Colorado Springs and new patients, people in need of medical attention who undoubtedly would not question the fact that she was a woman.

Ahead lay her future as a doctor, her entire life.